**Two brand-new stories in every volume...
twice a month!**

Duets Vol. #75

Isabel Sharpe kicks off the month with a very special
Double Duets on the theme of "manhunting."
Enjoy the chase as these heroines track down the
men of their dreams! This writer "pens a fresh tale
with solid characterization and snappy dialogue..."
says *Romantic Times Magazine*.

Duets Vol. #76

Two talented new writers join the Duets lineup
this month! Please welcome Sandra Kelly and
Wendy Etherington, who have crafted two funny
related tales about heroines fixing up "money pits"—
and the romantic chaos that ensues with
the heroes in their lives! Enjoy.

Be sure to pick up both Duets volumes today!

Suiteheart of a Deal

"It's my parents!" Beck exclaimed.

"They can't find out we're not a real couple—
it'll ruin everything!" Rainey added.

His eyes traveled up the stairs. "The bedrooms!
The separate bedrooms! Quick, we have to move
your things into my room!"

"But why?" Rainey huffed.

"They've driven a huge distance. They'll want to
stay overnight."

In a flash they charged into her room. While
she hastily pulled together the unmade bed,
he yanked her clothes from the closet.

"Hurry!" Beck ran into his room with a truckload
of Rainey's things and rushed back to her room.
She frantically emptied drawers and stuffed his
outstretched arms. He shot next door and
returned again.

The doorbell sounded.

"Okay, you get ready and I'll get the door."
Before leaving, he asked, "Are we still fighting?"

"No!" Rainey wheezed. "We can't. It's show time."

For more, turn to page 9

Termites?

Rebecca screamed.

Alex charged into the room. "What's wrong?" He grabbed her shoulders. "What happened?"

She swallowed hard. "I—uh…no, nothing."

How could this be happening? First a broken dishwasher, then a leaky roof and electrical problems. And now termites, for heaven's sake. Alex would surely back out of the deal, she'd never find another buyer for this expensive, tacky, handyman's delight, she'd go bankrupt *and* lose the house….

Alex shook her slightly. "Rebecca, what is it?"

She swallowed again. "Nothing. It's silly. A spot on my china." Snatching the top plate from the table, she licked her thumb and rubbed the imaginary speck.

"You screamed over a spot?" he asked, his tone revealing his incredulity.

She smiled brightly. "Silly, I know. I'm a little neurotic about my grandmother's china."

He raised one black eyebrow, as if neurotic was an extreme understatement. "Well, if you're sure you're all right…" He turned to go, leaving Rebecca to contemplate the broken dreams, heartache and plastic buckets that all lay in her immediate future.

For more, turn to page 197

HARLEQUIN DUETS

ISBN 0-373-44142-8

Copyright in the collection:
Copyright © 2002 by Harlequin Books S.A.

The publisher acknowledges the copyright holders
of the individual works as follows:

SUITEHEART OF A DEAL
Copyright © 2002 by Sandra Kelly

MY PLACE OR YOURS?
Copyright © 2002 by Wendy Etherington

This edition published by arrangement with Harlequin Books S.A.

® and TM are trademarks of the publisher. Trademarks indicated with ® are registered in the United States Patent and Trademark Office, the Canadian Trade Marks Office and in other countries.

Visit us at www.eHarlequin.com

Printed in U.S.A.

Suiteheart
of a Deal

Sandra
Kelly

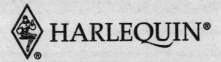

HARLEQUIN®

TORONTO • NEW YORK • LONDON
AMSTERDAM • PARIS • SYDNEY • HAMBURG
STOCKHOLM • ATHENS • TOKYO • MILAN • MADRID
PRAGUE • WARSAW • BUDAPEST • AUCKLAND

Dear Reader,

Love is funny, don't you think?

My favorite love stories are always those in which there's more going on than meets the reader's eye. So it's fitting that my first published novel should be about two people who are so taken with one another that they just can't see what's happening around them. That's definitely the case with Rainey and Beck, two fools for love who were easily fooled. We should all be as gullible!

Special thanks to Duets editor Kathryn Lye for seeing the humor in Rainey and Beck's situation, and to the people of Bragg Creek, Alberta, for lending me their town. The folks who live in my Bragg Creek are nutty and sneaky, but the real residents of that breathtakingly beautiful place are, I assure you, the nicest folks you'll ever meet.

Enjoy!

Sandra Kelly

For my husband, Bob. Thanks for waiting.

1

"OKAY, SO YOU'RE, ah, married, huh? Ah, let me see now... Oh, man! Would you *look* at the time? I have an important meeting in, ah, in less than, ah, I'm *sure* it's in less than an hour...."

Rainey Miller laughed aloud. She couldn't hold it in any longer. Never had she seen a man blush so deeply—or backpeddle so swiftly. The guy was too funny. He obviously wasn't too bright, though.

Why would he assume that just because a woman was seated alone that she must be single? Everybody from around here knew that, aside from a few young chambermaids and reservations clerks, there were no single, available women at the Honeymoon Haven. Only couples in love, celebrating their honeymoon, or a major anniversary. This guy had to be a tourist.

When her spontaneous eruption drew curious stares from the other guests in the Haven's quaint dining room, Rainey quickly withdrew into the shadow of the huge potted fern beside her table. The last thing she wanted was to attract the attention of the brain-damaged Lothario who had made her laugh in the first place.

For twenty minutes she had eavesdropped—unintentionally, of course—while the guy did his darndest to entice the stunning blonde seated at the next table. The plant enabled Rainey to watch the show, undetected.

And what a show it was! Hovering over the woman's table, oozing testosterone, he had tried every dumb line in the book, right down to, "You remind me of somebody I used to know." He had tried flattery, complimenting her on her beautiful blue eyes and sweet smile. He had offered her a "free" massage, whatever that meant. After telling him twice to get lost, the poor woman had finally been reduced to muttering, "Look, buster, I'm married. I'm on my honeymoon, and my husband will be here any minute!"

Romeo's immediate and lightning-fast retreat was just about the funniest thing Rainey had ever seen. He might not be a Rhodes Scholar, but she would give him points for cheesy charm.

When he backed away from the table, she got a better look at the guy. My, but he was gorgeous. Tall and athletically built, with a mop of shoulder-length dark-blond hair fingered back from a classically handsome face. He had high cheekbones and full, sensuous lips that promised unspeakable pleasures. Rainey found herself staring at those lips and wondering how the blonde could resist them— married or not.

On second glance, Romeo didn't look like a tourist. Rainey had spent all her childhood summers in this sleepy little town just west of Calgary. She could easily distinguish the locals from the imports. Everything about Romeo screamed local. The faded jeans, the unbuttoned flannel shirt over a dark-blue T-shirt, the scuffed hiking boots. Plus he had the wind-whipped complexion of an outdoorsman. The tourists usually had delicate city skin and were turned out in stiff new duds straight from the L.L. Bean catalogue.

Rainey sighed. Ever since her breakup with Trevor last month, she had hardly glanced at a man, much less noticed a finely sculptured mouth. One thing was for sure, if she ever got involved with another man, it definitely wouldn't be someone like superstud here. She could tell just by looking at him that he was a flake. No sooner would you fall head over heels for the guy than he'd start mumbling that he just couldn't make a commitment "at this time." Meaning, of course, that he just couldn't make one with *you.*

Or worse, he'd win your heart, then make a play for your best friend, the way Trevor had for Rainey's friend, Dana.

Besides, Rainey wasn't here to get caught up in another messy romance. She was here to take her rightful place as owner and general manager of the Honeymoon Haven, Canada's most famous getaway for lovers, in the beautiful town of Bragg Creek, Alberta. She had worked hard for it and she was ready. Well, almost ready.

Learn everything there is to know about running a hotel, and when I pass on I'll leave the Haven to you. That's what Rainey's childless great-aunt Lilly had told her when she was just a kid. Rainey took the offer seriously. She grew weary just thinking about the ten long years she toiled nights and weekends at the Royal York Hotel in Toronto while dozing through business courses during the day. It was a grueling life. No fun whatsoever. But she had done it. Lilly had passed away peacefully last week, and Rainey's time had come. Now if only she could get over her terror.

She was wrestling with that emotion when Romeo finally spotted her. Oh, no. He was coming her way, mischief plastered all over his stubbled mug.

"Well, well, what do we have here?" he murmured, placing his hands flat on Rainey's table and locking eyes with her. "A beautiful woman, all alone." He gave her what he undoubtedly thought was an irresistible smile.

How charming. And what a waste. He had about as much chance of scoring with Rainey as he had of being abducted by aliens. Less, actually.

She glanced at her watch. It was nearly one o'clock. After a sleepless night followed by a turbulent, early-morning flight from Toronto to Calgary, she was exhausted. She had just enough time to catch a nap and freshen up before her three o'clock meeting with Lilly's attorney. On the telephone this morning he had advised her of last-minute changes to Lilly's will, changes he couldn't discuss over the phone. She would shake Romeo off quickly. In the meantime, why not have a little fun?

She ventured a coy smile and nodded in the direction of the blonde. "Surely you must be exhausted from trying to pick up beautiful women."

Romeo's grin quickly dissolved into a pout. "Ouch! That wasn't very nice, was it?" Recovering quickly, he added, "Besides, I never get tired of picking up beautiful women, especially women as gorgeous as you."

While Rainey laughed, his amber eyes took in her dark, shoulder-length hair, her heart-shaped face, her slender neck and the cleavage showing just above the top of her scooped-neck blouse. Rainey knew she should have thrown the blouse away. She was a little too well endowed for it.

She shook her head. "You're some piece of work, aren't you?" It was a lame retort, but it was the best she could do. Rainey wasn't intimidated by them, but neither was she used to guys like Romeo here. Sexual predators on the prowl. Trevor may have been a wolf, but he came across as a lamb.

Superstud cocked his head sideways and gave her a playful look. "I could be the man of your dreams, if you'd just give me the chance."

A crazy thought popped into Rainey's head: *Honey, you are the man of my dreams; you just aren't the man of my reality.*

"Really, how so?" Feigning deep interest, she let her green eyes slide over him just as seductively as his had slid over her. What was the harm? He was about to strike out anyway.

He sighed wearily. "Well, first of all, let's get one thing out of the way. Are you on your honeymoon?"

"Nope."

His dark-blond eyebrows shot up. "Married?"

"Nope."

He took a deep breath and made a big show of expelling it. "Whew, it must be my lucky day. Okay, then, here's what would happen…" Before Rainey could object, he dropped into the chair next to hers. "We'd start the evening with a nice meal at the Bragg Creek Steak Pit. Ever heard of it?"

Rainey nodded. She and her parents had dined there at least once a week, all those summers ago. The food was fabulous.

"Terrific. Then we'd take a stroll through town, just so the locals could see what a good score you made." He actually kept a straight face while awaiting her reaction.

Good score? Good grief! If this guy wasn't the most arrogant, conceited jerk who had ever lived, Rainey sure would like to meet his competition. "Of course," she purred. "That's a given. Then what would we do?"

"Then we'd retire to my cottage out on Bear Road. Did I tell you that I own a beautiful cottage?"

"Nope. We hadn't got that far. We were still in town, showing off my good score."

He nodded earnestly. "Well, I do. Then we'd strip you down to your undoubtedly gorgeous birthday suit and I'd give you a long, slow massage. On the house, of course."

At the mention of the words *long* and *slow,* Rainey felt a serious blush coming on. But hey, there was no way she was going to fall under the spell of this frivolous creature. No, sir. And what exactly did he mean by "on the house?"

She peeked at her watch again. It was almost time for the fun to end. "Need I ask what we would do after that?"

In a voice more seductive, more nakedly intimate than any voice she had ever heard, he leaned forward and murmured, "That's easy. I'd make you forget every man you've ever known."

Rainey blinked. For one fleeting moment, Mr. Insincerity had sounded almost, well, sincere. As if he couldn't think of anything in the world he would rather do, or anyone he would rather do it with.

Whoa! Wait a minute. There you had it. There was the power of the hunter to entice his prey just before snaring, and then devouring, it. That she had been enticed, even for a millisecond, left Rainey feeling foolish. She wasn't about to be devoured—not again. She grabbed her purse and stood to leave. There was no check to pay, of course. The owner of the Honeymoon Haven dined for free.

"Look," she said curtly, "I have to run. It's been fun chatting with you. Best of luck on the hunt."

Jumping to his feet, Romeo seemed genuinely disappointed. "Hey, not so fast! I didn't get your name. Let's get to know one another."

Rainey laughed derisively. "If you don't mind, I'd rather not exchange names. I'm going to file this little encounter away under the heading 'Anonymous.' Or maybe 'Meaningless.'"

He feigned devastation. "Meaningless? Now there you go again, hurting my feelings. I thought we had something here. I thought we really, you know, *connected.*"

Right, thought Rainey, I know what kind of connection you're looking for! Shaking her head, she tried to ease past the flake without brushing up against him, but it proved impossible. The tables were placed too close together, and the huge potted plants between them didn't help. She made a mental note to lose the greenery and reconfigure the room.

Romeo stood fast and she had no choice but to clutch one of his muscular arms, to steady herself as she made her way around him. It was either that or fall into the plant. "Well, you thought wrong," she snapped.

He finally stepped aside and let her pass, but not before taking one last shot. "Hey, look, I meant what I said about wanting to get to know you. You give as good as you get. I like that in a woman."

There it was again, that well-rehearsed sincerity. Rainey wasn't buying it, but she was charmed nonetheless. She offered him a small, conciliatory smile. "Uh-huh, and I suppose you're going to tell me now that I have beautiful eyes, and that I remind you of somebody you used to know."

Thrilled to have captivated her a few seconds longer, he leaned forward and gushed, "You *do* have beautiful eyes. What are they? Green? Hazel?"

"Green," Rainey called over her shoulder as she marched out of the dining room and into the wide corridor leading to the lobby. Why was she still talking to this jerk? And why was he following her? He'd given up on the blonde pretty quickly. Of course, she hadn't cut him one inch of slack. Rainey should have known better than to flirt with a flirt.

Close on her heels, he declared, "And, for your information, you don't remind me of anyone. You're an original."

Rainey abruptly stopped and turned around, and Romeo crashed into her. "Whoa there!" He grasped her forearms. When she didn't fall, he released her, but not before lightly caressing the bare skin below her short sleeves. His touch felt strangely soothing.

"Look, buster," Rainey muttered, sounding to herself like the exasperated blonde, "I'm tired and I have a very important meeting in less than two hours. It's time for you to run along now."

He lit up like a neon sign. "Hey, what an interesting coincidence! I, too, have an important meeting this afternoon. See, we already have something in common."

As she turned smartly on her heel and headed for the lobby, Rainey muttered, "Oh, I doubt very much that we have anything in common." When she reached the wide staircase leading to Lilly's private apartment and the second-floor suites, Romeo was still on her tail, trying to persuade her that dinner at the Steak Pit, say, around seven, was definitely her best bet for tonight.

At her wit's end, she confronted him one last time. "Surely you're not going to follow me upstairs!"

"Aha! So you're staying here at the inn. I may not know your name, but at least I know where to find you." He grinned as if that were a major coup.

"Get lost!"

"Okay, okay!" Backing away, he raised both hands to signal defeat. "I know when I'm not wanted." He tilted his leonine head sideways and wagged a finger at her. "But sooner or later you'll be seeing me again. And I promise you won't be able to resist me next time."

"Oh, yes, I will," Rainey said to herself as she climbed the creaky stairs. "You can count on it."

STILL SHAKING HER HEAD, Rainey let herself into Lilly's apartment—her apartment now—and locked the door behind her. She wouldn't put it past Romeo to have followed her up the stairs. For all she knew, he might be the town nutcase. Then again, he might just be a harmless hustler. That was more likely.

Whew, but he was a hunk! *Delicious* was actually the word that came to mind. Too bad he was such a pest. She made a silent vow to avoid him at all costs. It probably wouldn't be easy in a town of only five hundred people.

Strolling through the stuffy, eerily silent apartment toward the bedroom, she took her first good look at the place. The decor was floral and fussy, with an abundance of overstuffed colonial furniture crammed together, and knickknacks crowding every dusty ledge and tabletop. There were dozens of family photos in gilt frames, and worn cushions in every shade of pastel, and doilies and candles and incense and... Rainey did a double take. Candles? Incense? Seconds later, she spotted a Ouija board resting on a TV tray. Why on earth would Lilly have had a Ouija board?

Realizing she would have to redecorate, Rainey felt a sharp stab of guilt. How could she do that? This had been her beloved aunt Lilly's home for nearly fifty years. Moving even a single picture would be sacrilegious. But what choice did she have? This just wasn't her taste.

She went into the bedroom and kicked off her shoes. Lord, she was tired. There was so much to think about, so much to do. After her meeting this afternoon she would take a leisurely tour of the Haven. Frankly, the place seemed rundown. The paint in the lobby was scuffed and worn, and the carpet was threadbare in spots. She had already scheduled a meeting for first thing tomorrow with Hollis Harriman, the bookkeeper. In a brief exchange this morning, he had seemed anxious to show her the books as soon as possible.

Rainey suddenly realized just how demanding her new job was going to be. Everyone would be looking to her to make decisions and solve problems and provide inspiration. Her last position at the Royal York Hotel had been that of reservations supervisor. The job had required tact and patience, but it couldn't compare with being general manager. With only thirty-two suites, the Haven was small stuff when compared to the Royal York, but, even so, the prospect of managing the entire operation, all by herself, was more daunting than she cared to admit.

A new feeling crept up on her now—loneliness. She was in a new town and she had no friends here, no family to provide support. Nobody to joke with, play with, confide in. She was truly alone.

She was also too tired to think about much of anything right now. After puzzling over it for a few minutes, she set Lilly's old manual alarm clock for two-fifteen and fell across the bed, fully clothed.

She dreamed about a giant set of lips over dazzling white teeth, bearing down on her from above, ready to devour her one bite at a time.

2

"SURELY THERE MUST be some mistake! Could you...could you check again?"

Heart pounding, palms sweating, Rainey leaned forward in her chair and looked frantically at the file lying open on the polished rosewood desk. Several documents lay atop the open folder, stapled together with little blue paper corners. They looked awfully official.

Nate Frome of the firm of Wilson, Hutchinson, Frome sat on the other side of the desk. He was a tall, slender man with dark hair, the bland good looks of a television news anchor, and the brisk manner of a busy lawyer. Rainey guessed he was a few years older than she.

He nodded sympathetically. "I'm afraid there's no mistake, Rainey. Your great aunt amended her will just six weeks ago. She was physically ill, but she wasn't mentally incapacitated. The will is valid."

Rainey slumped back in her chair, stunned beyond words. Half the Haven? How could Lilly have done that? How could she have left only half the inn to Rainey and the other half to some guy named Beckett Mahoney? Why, she hadn't even left Rainey a controlling interest in the place. Instead she had doomed her to equal partnership with a total stranger. It wasn't fair! Rainey had kept her part of their deal, but Lilly had reneged on hers. Why?

Fighting tears, she asked, "Who, pray tell, is Beckett Mahoney?"

From the look of mild disdain on his face, Rainey instantly got the impression that Nate knew this—this *Mahoney* person, and that he didn't much care for him. And, furthermore, that there was a pretty good chance Rainey wasn't going to care for him, either. A feeling of doom descended on her.

"Actually, he's an old friend of mine, Rainey. We grew up together. Ah, well, maybe *friend* is too strong a word for…'' Nate paused and cleared his throat. "He was a close friend of Lilly's. He helped out around the Haven quite a bit, with repairs and that sort of thing. I think they played poker together once in a while. She was very fond of him.''

Rainey furrowed her brows. "Repairs? Is he some sort of handyman?'' She envisioned an aging Mr. Fix-It, a stooped and arthritic grandfatherly type, shuffling around after Lilly with a tool kit in his hand. Terrific. Just what she needed.

"Ah, well, you might say that.'' Nate chuckled. "Beck is certainly known to be, ah, quite handy.'' Seeing the bewildered look on Rainey's face, he adopted a more serious tone. "To be fair, Beck is actually a very accomplished man, Rainey. He's licensed to fly small aircraft and gives lessons at the Springbank Airport near Calgary. He also gives ski lessons and volunteers for the Banff ski patrol. He's a trained mountain guide and a pretty fair climber, too.''

A climber? "How old is Mr. Mahoney?''

"I believe Beck is thirty-two.''

Thirty-two. Well, that wasn't so bad, really. At least he was only four years older than Rainey. Even so. An equal partner. She just plain didn't want one. Arghhh! If sweet, funny, eccentric, Great-Aunt Lilly were alive, Rainey would kill her.

Nate gave her a warning look. "Rainey, you probably should know that Beck has a bit of a reputation with the ladies.''

Terrific, thought Rainey. We've swung all the way from handyman to ladies' man. "What sort of reputation?"

"Ah, well, some of it is exaggerated, I'm sure, but let's just say that Beck is well-known in these parts."

Rainey leaned forward on her seat. "Define 'parts.'"

"Calgary, Bragg Creek, Canmore, Banff, Lake Louise, some parts of British Columbia, maybe even Washington State…"

She slumped back again. "Okay, I get the picture."

While Rainey battled wildly mixed emotions—on the one hand she felt cheated; on the other hand she felt relieved—Nate casually added, "Oh, I forgot to mention, he's also a licensed masseuse. Actually, he has a salon at the Haven."

A masseuse? Wait a minute. Hadn't the hustler in the dining room offered to give Rainey a massage? *On the house?* Surely…oh, no…surely Romeo wasn't Beck Mahoney. Then again, he must be. He was about the right age. And how many masseuses could there be in a town the size of Bragg Creek?

"Nate," Rainey asked with mounting dread, "is Beck Mahoney tall and blond?"

"He sure is. I take it you've met Beck?" His expression suggested that if Rainey had met the man, she would definitely remember him.

"I may have. I'm not sure."

"Well, you'll be meeting him shortly." Nate glanced at his watch. "I asked him to join us at three-thirty. Your aunt said you would probably be a little upset, and that I should speak with you first."

A *little* upset? While an astonished Nate looked on, Rainey threw back her head and laughed hysterically. Romeo as a business partner! It was too rich. She had just managed to get one hustler out of her life, and now she was going into business with another. Could things get any worse?

"MAN, OH MAN, what's with this traffic," Beck grumbled to himself as he cruised well below the speed limit along the Trans-Canada Highway between Bragg Creek and Banff. "Don't these people know I'm late for an important date?"

Every summer, it was the same. Tourists and more tourists, clogging up the roadways of the Bow Valley Corridor, the steadily rising stretch of land that paralleled the Bow River west from Calgary, past Bragg Creek and Canmore, to the Rockies. But it was mid-September and most of them should have packed up and gone home by now. Obviously these road hogs didn't know when to clear out.

Beck always looked forward to the lull between the summer tourists—the hikers and climbers and fishermen—and the droves of skiers who showed up in November when the region's numerous ski hills opened for business. It gave him a welcome break from being nice to strangers from Winnipeg and Montreal and Denver and Dallas.

Normally he used the time to do a little fishing of his own, or to help Lilly with one of her pet projects. Last year he had lovingly restored the aqua-blue 1967 Ford Fairlane she had been smart enough to keep. He chuckled, recalling how his only reward for doing the work had been the privilege of chauffeuring her and her cackling, whiskey-addled cronies from one crazy appointment to another. Facials, makeovers, color charting sessions—they couldn't get enough. Once, he had even taken them to see a psychic in Calgary. Imagine a bunch of eighty-year-olds consulting with a psychic. Now *that* was optimism.

With Lilly gone—gee, he was going to miss the darn girl!—he had no particular project in mind for this autumn break. Unless, of course... Speeding up to pass a sluggish camper van with Montana plates, his mind drifted to a pair of mesmerizing green eyes framed by a pert, pretty face and a crown of dark, silky hair. The mystery woman in the restaurant. What a babe.

Beck couldn't remember the last time he'd seen a woman worth taking a second look at. Sure he could have his pick of women anywhere in the corridor. But he'd never met one who looked quite like her, or sounded like her—ooh, that throaty, sexy voice—or who could dish it out *and* take it. She was in his head now, and he sensed it was going to be hard to get her out.

Who was she? There weren't many single women hanging around the Haven. Maybe she was somebody's mistress. Lots of secret lovers, some quite famous, appreciated Lilly's legendary discretion.

Nah, somehow he didn't think so. Not in this case. She was too fine to settle for second spot.

Maybe she was a new resident in town. Nah, that was even less likely. Tourist attractions aside, Bragg Creek was mostly a bedroom community for the families who preferred its Nordic beauty and small-town friendliness to the concrete hustle and bustle of Calgary. It didn't attract too many singles—especially gorgeous single women.

And hey, what did it matter anyway? After that scene in the restaurant, he'd be lucky if Gorgeous Green Eyes didn't cross the road to avoid him. Talk about making a bad first impression! Maybe he should do a little damage control—go back to the Haven later today and track her down. It was crazy, and probably pointless, but he was itching to tell her: Look, don't take me too seriously, okay? It's just that I need something to do until…

Yeah well, why bother? Once she found out about the money, she'd be no different than the others—salivating all over him every chance she got. He'd manage to keep it under wraps for a while, but sooner or later somebody would clue her in.

Dammit, he needed to fall in love with somebody for

real and get married as soon as possible. The sooner he got married, the sooner he'd be able to get his hands on the second half of his trust fund. Then he could get a law degree and give his aching knees a rest. A man couldn't give skiing lessons forever.

Three more years before they would cut the check. It seemed like an eternity.

Too bad about the babe with the shining eyes and the voluptuous curves. He had no trouble picturing himself married to her. He'd come home every night from his thriving practice in environmental law to find her wrapped in a white silk kimono, stoking the fire in his cottage, a snifter of brandy already poured for him. It made a nice picture.

What the hell, she probably knew about the money already. After all, she'd been in town for more than ten minutes.

As the corridor's rolling foothills gradually gave way to the steely peaks of the Rockies, Beck marveled once again at the fact that Lilly had named him in her will. Man, what a shock. It hadn't occurred to him for one second that she would leave him something. Oh, sure, he'd done some minor repair work around the Haven, and he'd given her more than a few foot massages over the years. But that didn't amount to much. She had treated him like a son, and he'd been happy to help out an old lady with no kids of her own.

He'd also given her a lot of his hard-earned cash. What a poker player old Lilly had been! He had called her Poker Face Miller and she had nicknamed him Beck and Call.

What could she possibly have left him? He sure hoped it was the Fairlane.

"ANGELA, you sweet thing, you're looking mighty fine today. Mighty fine indeed."

Calmer now but still shaky, Rainey groaned and turned

halfway around in her chair. The buttery voice behind her was unmistakable. Beck Mahoney, alias Romeo, alias Superstud, alias Mr. Insincerity, had burst into the reception area adjacent to Nate's office and managed to get all of three steps into the room before finding a woman to charm.

Through the frosted glass between the two rooms, Rainey saw the blurred image of the flustered, middle-aged receptionist waving a hand in Beck's direction. "Oh, get away with you, Beck Mahoney!" she admonished him with a girlish giggle. Beck grasped her hand in midair and planted a kiss on the back of it. "Angela, if I were twenty years older…"

Suddenly a group of boisterous young clerks appeared out of nowhere and began to *ooh* and *ah* over a preening Beck. "All hands on Beck!" a girlish voice shrieked, and they gathered around him like a pack of starstruck groupies.

"Beck, honey," one cried with petulance, "you said you would call me and you didn't!"

"You told me the same thing!" someone else whined.

"Girls, girls," Beck drawled. "Patience. There's plenty of me to go around. Speaking of which, who wants to climb the Galatea Trail and have a picnic at Mirror Lake on Sunday?"

"I do!" they all cried.

Gently pulling free from their clutches, he said, "Okay, well, I'll definitely be taking one of you. I don't want to hurt anybody's feelings, so I won't say who it's going to be right now. If it's you, you'll know soon enough."

Groaning good-naturedly, the young women dispersed. Beck burst into Nate's office. "Nate, old boy," he bellowed, "I see you've still got a license to practise. How can that—" spotting Rainey, he stopped dead in his tracks "—possibly be?" His gorgeous mouth fell open and his face turned beet red.

Rising to her feet, Rainey managed a tight smile. "Hello, Romeo. How's the hunt going?"

"I…" His blush actually deepened another shade.

Dripping sarcasm, she quipped, "Ooh, he blushes all the time. I *like* that in a man."

"What are you doing here?" he asked with wide-eyed astonishment. "For that matter, who are you?"

Nate gestured between them. "Beck Mahoney, meet Rainey Miller. Though it seems you've already had the pleasure."

The look of total bewilderment on Beck's scarlet face gradually gave way to a sheepish grin. "Well, I'll be. Gorgeous Green Eyes is Lilly Miller's favorite niece. I was right. This *is* my lucky day."

"In more ways than one," Rainey said dryly. "As it turns out, you're my new business partner."

"Your new what?" His amber eyes darted from Rainey to Nate and back again. He waved a hand in the air. "Okay, you've lost me now."

Nate motioned for them to sit down and then told a bug-eyed Beck what he had just told Rainey—that he was half owner of the Honeymoon Haven, effective immediately. Beck looked like he didn't know whether to jump for joy or jump out the second-floor window onto busy Banff Avenue.

Breaking a thick silence, he murmured to himself, "Half the Haven? Man, I would have been thrilled if she'd just left me her car."

Nate rifled through the papers on his desk. "I believe she did leave you the Fairlane."

Beck's eyebrows shot up. "Half of it or all of it?"

Even the humorless lawyer had to laugh at that. "Every inch of it, Beck. I assure you."

"Cool!" Shaking his head, Beck turned to Rainey. "But

I don't get it. Weren't you supposed to inherit the inn? That's what she told everybody."

"Apparently she had second thoughts," Rainey muttered.

"No kidding!"

For the next twenty minutes, Rainey stubbornly ignored Beck's furtive glances while Nate went over the fine details of the will, coming finally to the section on special instructions.

"As you know," he said to Rainey, "your aunt waived a memorial service. She stipulated instead that a party be held to commemorate her life, not her death. The party is to take place at the inn, as soon as you feel ready."

Rainey nodded. It was a wonderful idea. Lilly had been a real live wire. Nothing short of a lively send-off would do. Beck nodded, too, and Rainey felt a stab of resentment. How *dare* he presume to… Ah, wait a minute. He was a full partner here, whether she liked it or not.

No sooner had that thought knocked her over than Nate threw her another curve. "Rainey," he began cautiously, "Lilly made one additional request." He paused and she tensed. Surely there wasn't more bad news? "She asked that her apartment at the Haven be converted to a wedding chapel. Apparently it was always a dream of hers, but she never got around to it."

"That's right," Beck said. "She talked about it often."

Rainey gasped. "A wedding chapel! But where will I live?"

"Hey, did I mention that I own a beautiful cottage?" Beck joked.

Eyes blazing, she turned toward him. "Beck Mahoney, if I hear one more word about that cottage, I'll scream!"

He held up both hands. "Gotcha. Not one word. I promise."

"One more thing," Nate added. "She asked that the

party be held in the chapel. I'm not sure why. Perhaps it was because she never married.''

While Beck and Nate discussed the transfer of ownership, Rainey struggled to get her thoughts in order. Her mind was spinning. No, she didn't want a partner. Yes, she was grateful for a partner. No, she didn't want Beck Mahoney as a partner. Yes, she... Good grief, what did he know about running an inn? He was a ski bum, for heaven's sake. A pilot. A masseuse. A playboy!

With a not-too-discreet glance at his watch, Nate indicated that the meeting was over. Rainey thanked him, grabbed her purse and hurried out. She was halfway to her rental car when Beck caught up to her.

''Hey, lady, wait just one minute!'' He grabbed her arm and spun her around. ''Don't you think we should sit down and talk about this? I know you don't think much of me, but the fact is that we're partners now.''

''I didn't ask for a partner!''

''I didn't ask for one, either!''

''Yes, but...'' Oh, darn. It was true. When you got right down to it, Beck was no more responsible for their predicament than she was. He was stunned, too. Obviously, Lilly hadn't seen fit to tell him about this.

And, darn it all, as much as Rainey wanted to hate the guy, she just couldn't. Underneath that phony charm, there was something faintly likable about him.

''Look,'' she said softly. ''I'm in shock, Beck. I need a little time to digest this. I expect you do, too.''

''You've got that right. Listen, why don't we grab that dinner at the Steak Pit tonight? Talk things over. I don't know about you, but I'll be famished by seven o'clock.''

Rainey bit her lower lip. It was tempting. All she had eaten today was a salad at lunchtime, and she'd mostly picked at it. A juicy steak and a baked potato would really hit the spot. ''Sure,'' she muttered.

Romeo backed away, grinning. "Terrific! I'll meet you there."

Just then, an attractive, fire-breathing redhead burst through the throng of tourists across the street and shouted, "Beck Mahoney, you snake. You said you'd call!"

3

THE STEAK PIT was exactly as Rainey remembered it. Rustic and cozy, with dark, rough-hewn wood paneling, an assortment of copper bric-a-brac and antique-stained glass lamps that cast a soft glow over each of the small, intimate booths.

She had arrived early and been pleasantly surprised to learn that Beck had called ahead and reserved the best booth in the restaurant, near a bank of windows overlooking the dense forest and the rippling, pale-green waters of the glacier-fed Elbow River. Seated alone at their table, she gazed out the window into the woods. Shafts of twilight fell between the trees, giving the entire scene a golden glow. It took her breath away.

She was calmer now, better able to think. In the past two hours she had more or less become resigned to her fate. After all, what options did she have? One: Buy Beck out. Hah! With what? Two: Kill Beck. Sure! Go to jail. Three: Convince him to act as a silent partner and leave the running of the inn to her. Right! She couldn't imagine the guy being silent for ten seconds.

Nope, for all intents and purposes it looked like she and Romeo would just have to get along—according to a few ground rules, of course.

Her thoughts drifted to Trevor. After the meeting with Nate Frome, she had gone back to the Haven to find two telephone messages: one from him, the other from Dana. She had called Dana back right away but got only her machine. There were no hard feelings between them. After all, it wasn't Dana's fault if Trevor was a jerk. His message she tossed straight into the garbage. What could he possibly have to say that she would want to hear?

Then she had wandered around the inn, poking her head into the big kitchen with its long wooden chopping table and antiquated ovens, the cluttered housekeeping quarters and each of the unoccupied suites. There were a lot of those—far too many for this time of year. It seemed to Rainey that when she was a child the inn was full all the time. She had clear memories of Lilly turning disappointed travelers away at the front desk.

Oh, well, at least the place was spotless. Rainey smiled, recalling her impromptu encounter with Freda Norman, the head housekeeper.

"I see you're here!" someone had barked over Rainey's shoulder as she peered into one of the empty suites. Startled, she turned around and came face-to-face with a barrel-shaped woman of perhaps sixty, with thick gray hair held back, oddly enough, with a series of purple plastic butterfly clips. Childishly cute, they seemed out of place atop the menacing scowl on her masculine face. The woman thrust out a huge hand and introduced herself as Mrs. Norman. Rainey got the message: there'll be no first names here.

"It's a pleasure to meet you, Mrs. Norman."

The women shook hands. Freda Norman had a handshake that would intimidate a grizzly bear.

"What do you think of my inn?" she shouted, even though Rainey was just inches away.

Rainey blinked. *Her* inn? "Well, frankly, Mrs. Norman, it looks a little tired."

"Humph, don't we all!" Looking Rainey up and down with mild contempt, she added, "Came out here from Tronna, huh?"

Suppressing a smile, Rainey replied, "Yes, just this

morning.'' Why did she think Mrs. Norman would be thrilled if she hopped on a plane and headed straight back to ''Tronna?''

''Hope you had a nice trip!'' Mrs. Norman growled as if Rainey were just another guest at the Haven. With that, she abruptly excused herself to carry out a final inspection of the rooms. Rainey stood there for a moment, shaking her head. There had been no welcoming remarks, no best wishes for a good working relationship, none of the professional etiquette she was accustomed to.

As for the wear and tear she had spotted this morning, that had turned out to be just the tip of the iceberg. On the outside the Haven still presented itself as a stunning example of Laurentian architecture. Its cedar roof shingles, dark wood siding and stone pillars were in relatively good shape. But inside the place was a wreck. The white plaster walls were crumbling and the oak floors creaked terribly. All the windows needed replacing and the furnishings were tired and dated. How could Lilly have let the place get so rundown?

''Good evening.''

Startled, Rainey jumped a little as Beck slid into the booth. He was clean shaven, his unruly hair neatly combed back. He smelled like sandalwood. A soft black sweater accentuated his tan and turned his amber eyes a deeper shade of gold. Up close, Rainey noticed little flecks of dark brown in those eyes.

''E-e-evening,'' she stammered, annoyed with herself for suddenly being nervous. Two seconds alone with this guy and her mouth was dry, her knees trembling slightly under the table. What *was* it about Beck? What special power did he have with women? He was gorgeous, no question about it, but lots of men were attractive without being so darned compelling. No, Beck had something else, something special.

"You look absolutely beautiful," he murmured. Eyes glowing, he frankly appraised every inch of her that was visible above the table. Rainey felt her skin grow warm. After changing her clothes exactly seven times, she had settled on a short-sleeved, loose-fitting paisley dress that was neutral enough for a business meeting but dressy enough for dinner. Beck's penetrating gaze made it feel like the most daring lingerie imaginable.

That was it. That was his unique gift, she realized—Beck had the rare and oh-so-useful ability to make a woman feel beautiful and sexy and cherished and safe just by paying her special attention. No wonder he was irresistible.

Well, that was fine for Beck, but she just had to resist him. They were business partners, and if there was one thing Rainey had learned at the Royal York, it was not to get involved with a colleague. Trevor had taught her that one.

She decided to hit him with ground rule number one. "You know, Beck, if we're going to work together, I think you should stop flirting with me."

His eyes widened. "Who's flirting? I mean it."

"You're flirting. You're *always* flirting."

He shook his head. "You're right, you're right. I'll try to stop. But I have to warn you—a tiger can't easily change its stripes." He grinned.

A pouty waitress sidled up to their table and fixed her adoring baby blues on Beck. Before Rainey could open her mouth, he took the liberty of ordering for both of them. Rainey should have been offended, but somehow she wasn't. It was good that he had a take-charge attitude and a commanding presence. He was going to need them.

"Very good, Beck," the waitress intoned with more meaning, strictly speaking, than a steak deserved. Then she sashayed off to the kitchen without so much as a backward glance at Rainey.

Beck turned his full attention to Rainey again. "*I* think if we're going to work together we should get to know one another. I already know a little about you."

"Oh, really? What do you know?"

"I know you were born and raised in Toronto. I know you vacationed here every summer until about five years ago. You're an only child. You don't smoke or use any drugs. You seldom drink and always socially. Your favorite color is yellow. You're a hard worker. And you're smart, but you lack self-confidence." He picked up a bread stick and chomped on it.

Rainey couldn't believe her ears. "How do you know all that?"

"Loose-lipped Lilly. She talked about you all the time."

"Okay, what about you? I don't know a thing about you except that you're a hopeless flirt."

"Okay, okay, I'm a fourth-generation native of Edmonton, but I prefer to live in Bragg Creek. I have twin brothers, both married, and three nephews. I love to ski. I love to fish. I love to fly. I went to college but didn't quite graduate." He grinned. "So many parties, so little time."

Right, Rainey thought. So many women, so little time.

"I don't smoke or use any drugs," he continued, "but I like a brandy on a cold winter night." He fell silent and gave her a dreamy, almost melancholy look. "Did I tell you, Rainey Miller, that you're a knockout?"

She shot him a warning look. "You're doing it again, Beck."

"Darn! I don't know what's wrong with me. Maybe we should talk business."

"Okay. What do you know about running an inn?" Rainey meant to sound merely inquisitive, but somehow the words came out sounding like a challenge.

"Less than nothing," Beck admitted with a shake of his

head. "But I'm willing to learn. What do you know about fixing one? I expect you've had a look around the Haven."

Rainey nodded. "What on earth happened? That inn was Lilly's pride and joy."

With a shrug, Beck replied, "Well, partly, she just got old, I guess. Lost her enthusiasm for it. And partly, I think she just wanted to have a little fun before her time was up." Rainey gave him a questioning look, and he explained, "I may be wrong, but I think she borrowed some money against the inn last year, to buy a few personal pleasures."

She asked what kind of pleasures, and Beck told her about some of the crazy stuff Lilly and her cronies had done.

"Her cronies?"

"Yeah. There's a service club in town called the Women of the Wapiti," he explained. "They raise money for charity, visit the sick…"

"Women of the *what?*" Rainey's laugh startled the nearby diners.

"The Wapiti. It's a big deer. They're all over the roads here. Anyway, Lilly was a member. My grandmother is a member. So is Freda Norman." His eyebrows shot up. "Have you met Freda?"

Rainey rolled her eyes. "I had the pleasure this afternoon."

He snorted. "Yeah, well, don't be too quick to judge her. She's actually the sanest employee there." Ignoring Rainey's frown, he continued, "Anyway, the three of them blew a bundle last year and the year before on trips. Caribbean cruises, little jaunts to Cancun, that sort of thing. There was other stuff, too, but you'll know about it soon enough. I suspect Lilly paid for all those trips."

Before Rainey could digest that information, their food arrived. "Hope your steak is okay, Beck," the waitress purred. Once again, she ignored Rainey. With nothing more than a curt nod, Beck said he was sure it would be fine. Ooh, but he was smooth. They obviously knew one another. Rainey could just smell a history coming off them. But Beck was with another woman tonight. Like all poker players, he knew which card to play.

Between bites of the delicious, perfectly cooked food, they talked about the repairs that needed to be done, and about the vacancy problem. Rainey commented that an inn like the Haven should be fully booked all year round. Some fresh marketing strategies would have to be developed.

"You know, you're right about that," Beck said. "I don't know much about marketing, but just for starters, don't you think the name Honeymoon Haven is a little dated? I mean, it's kind of corny, isn't it?"

Pleasantly surprised, Rainey nodded. That very thought had occurred to her just this morning. Obviously there was more to Beck than just dazzling good looks and a beautiful body and a simmering sexiness that could reduce a woman to mush in two seconds flat. Maybe, just maybe, this partnership thing was going to work out after all.

Then again, maybe not. Time would tell.

When the meal was over, Beck ordered two brandys for them, then sat back and searched Rainey's eyes. She returned his soul-searching gaze and the air grew thick around them. Finally he ventured, "So, ah, I guess this business partnership thing sort of rules out other kinds of partnership, huh?" He gave her a look of such hangdog disappointment that Rainey nearly laughed. Instead, she replied, "I don't get involved with colleagues, Beck." *Or with hustlers like you.*

"Hmmm." He tilted his brandy snifter from right to left so that the gold liquid, so much like his eyes, sloshed gently from side to side. "Maybe you should buy me out," he murmured in the soft, seductive tone he had obviously mastered. "Then I can devote myself to trying to get you into bed. Seems like way more fun than running an inn."

Rainey was instantly grateful for the dim lighting; it concealed the hot blush that spread up through her skin like wildfire. It wasn't hard to imagine making love with Beck. On the contrary… But it was out of the question. Working with Trevor after their breakup had been a miserable experience, but at least she had been able to get away from him by climbing on a plane and coming west. How would she get away from this guy?

Because as surely as he was drop-dead gorgeous, Beck Mahoney would break her heart. He had said it himself: A tiger can't change its stripes.

"Don't you ever quit, Beck?" she asked with a weary sigh.

"I guess not. Maybe I *am* hopeless."

It was time for ground rule number two. "Beck, I think we need to do more than stop flirting. For the sake of the partnership, I think we should agree to keep our business and personal lives separate."

For a second, he looked devastated. As usual, he recovered at the speed of sound. "Well, that'll be tough in Bragg Creek, Rainey. It's a small town. Everybody's in bed with everybody else, so to speak."

Rainey laughed. After Toronto, small-town life was definitely going to take some getting used to.

On the way to her car, she informed him of the meeting tomorrow morning with Hollis Harriman, and warned him not to be late. If there was one thing she couldn't tolerate, it was tardiness. He accepted the warning with a lazy shrug. She sensed he had something else on his mind.

Sure enough, as she searched for her keys, he ventured, "So, I guess we can rule out that massage too, huh?" He chuckled.

"It was never going to happen, Beck."

"Okay, then, how about a simple handshake to seal our partnership?"

"Of course." Rainey grasped the keys in her left hand and stuck her right hand out. Beck ignored it. Instead, he gently cupped the back of her head with one hand, leaned down and lightly touched his soft lips to hers.

"Beck Mahoney!" she cried when he pulled away, grinning like a frat boy who had just got to first base. "Didn't you hear a word I said in there?"

"Hey, lady, that's how we shake hands in Bragg Creek. You should see what happens when we hug!"

On the drive home, all Rainey could think about was how right she had been about him. He *was* delicious.

"TWO HUNDRED thousand dollars!" Rainey and Beck shrieked in unison.

Eyes flaring, Rainey motioned for Beck to close the door leading to the lobby, and he quickly complied. The reservations clerks working just outside the Haven's administrative office didn't need to hear this; they were jumpy enough. The place was abuzz with gossip about the new owners, and the air was thick with tension.

"Ah, that's right," Hollis Harriman confirmed with a violent twitch of his right eye. "That's what she borrowed."

Rainey stared across the meeting table at him, dumbfounded. In his midsixties, Hollis was a tall, perilously thin man with a few wisps of gray hair lacquered and stretched across a shiny skull. He had a funny little heart-shaped mouth and blue eyes so light they looked like the surface of a swimming pool. In addition to the twitch, he had a tremor in his left hand and whenever he stood his right knee buckled.

For the better part of two hours he had painstakingly gone over the Haven's books with them. Now they were poring over a list of things Lilly had cheekily labeled Extraordinary Expenses. Hah! They were extraordinary, all right. Hot air balloon rides. Helicopter tours over the mountains. The trips Beck had mentioned last night.

A mind-boggling item at the bottom of the first page caught Rainey's eye. "An aromatherapist?" she cried. "On *retainer?*" No sooner had that bowled her over than she spotted another doozy. "Please," she said to Beck, "tell me she didn't hire a psychic to conduct a seance."

"'Fraid I can't do that," he replied. "I think they were trying to call up the spirit of her dead father."

Rainey groaned. "I can't believe she wrote these things off as business expenses!"

"Oh, she definitely had a talent for numbers," Hollis declared with a twitch and a tremor. He chuckled nervously. To Rainey he seemed perpetually anxious, as if disaster were lurking around every corner. Of course, it might just be these darned books.

She looked at Beck. Ever since that silly kiss, she had found it unnerving to make full eye contact with him. Whenever their eyes did meet, he did something goofy—like wink at her, or raise his eyebrows several times very quickly. Oh, what a mistake that darned kiss was!

Still, she was grateful for him this morning. How on earth would she deal with all this stuff by herself?

Reading her thoughts, Beck stepped in and asked for the bottom line. Hollis explained that while the inn wasn't exactly bankrupt, it was barely breaking even. Occupancy was down to fifty percent, even in peak season, and the loan payments were eating up what little profits could be made. Not only that, major repairs needed to be carried out. He handed Beck a list of critical items. To Rainey he said, "Frankly, the staff are starting to be concerned about their jobs. They hear things."

"No one's going to lose their job," she declared with

fierce determination. ''But where on earth will we get the money to do the repairs? We can't borrow any more, and there's no cash on reserve.'' She bit her lower lip and began to pace back and forth.

A grin slowly spread across Beck's face, and a frustrated Rainey wondered if he'd lost his mind. There was nothing funny about any of this. First of all, he had been fifteen minutes late for the meeting—*fifteen* minutes. Secondly, he had so far showed precious little interest in their situation. He was going to have to buck up, start taking things just a little more seriously.

''I know where we can get it,'' he murmured like a boy who knew where secret treasure was buried. He smiled politely at Hollis. ''Would you kindly excuse us for just a moment?''

After Hollis shuffled out of the room, knee buckling slightly, a still-grinning Beck turned to Rainey. ''I have an idea, but you won't like it.''

''Try me.''

''Okay, but you have to promise me that you'll stay calm.''

''Oh, for heaven's sake, Beck. What is it?''

He leaned forward and whispered, ''I think we should get married.''

4

"I'D RATHER HAVE a third eye in the middle of my forehead!" Rainey stormed into her apartment, Beck nipping at her heels.

"Oh, now that's great!" he exclaimed as the door bounced off the wall and crashed into him. "You know, you're not a very nice person, Rainey Miller. You've got a nasty streak!"

"Nasty streak?" Seething, she tromped ahead of him into the tiny kitchen with its scarred pine table and rustic appliances. "Give me a break! I don't even know if I can work with you, and now you want to marry me? Forget it, buster!"

"Oh, now, wait just one minute there. My name's not buster—though I'm starting to think it should be. And, hey, what would be so bad about being married to me? I'll have you know that lots of women would kill for the chance. Hundreds. Thousands even!"

"I think you just answered your own question."

"Oh, baloney! I like women. So sue me."

Bristling, Rainey rummaged in the cupboards for the kettle. Tea. That was what she needed. A nice cup of tea. She had been in Bragg Creek all of twenty-four hours. So far, she had been cheated out of half her inheritance and been saddled with a crumbling, nearly bankrupt inn. She had lost her living quarters and acquired a flaky flirt of a business partner she didn't want. And now she was being asked to *marry* the flake? Good grief—what was next?

"Just hear me out." Beck plopped down at the table. "See, I have this trust fund. My grandfather left it to me when I was three. He set it up to be paid out in two installments. I got the first installment when I turned twenty-one, but I can't touch the rest until I turn thirty-five or get married, whichever comes first." He lowered his voice. "Rainey, there's enough money in that fund to turn this place into a palace."

"I don't want to marry a—a playboy! I don't want to marry anybody, at least not right now." Darn it, where was the kettle? Surely Lilly and her "cronies" drank tea.

Beck threw his hands in the air. "Oh, c'mon, Rainey. Why do you think I'm such a hit with the ladies? I'll tell you why. There isn't one woman in this town, for that matter in this region—what the hell, make it the entire province—who doesn't know about that trust fund."

Arghhh! Despite her determination to blow off steam for as long as humanly possible, Rainey felt her resolve weakening. She fought the little smile that tugged at the corner of her lips, but in the end it won. Over her shoulder, she joked, "Are you saying they're not after you just for your good looks and dazzling personality?"

He nodded vigorously. "That's exactly what I'm saying."

She turned and confronted him. "But you flirt with all those women!" Good grief, she sounded like a jealous wife.

He shrugged. "It's a pastime, nothing more. And you're not listening to me. I'm not suggesting that we get *married* married—you know, with bridesmaids and babies and a minivan and all that junk...."

"Those things aren't junk!"

His expression softened. "You're right. They aren't junk. I'd like babies myself, someday."

Surprised by the warmth and sincerity of his tone, Rainey

searched his eyes to determine if he was being serious or just goofing off, as usual. She saw nothing to suggest he wasn't being completely honest.

"You would?" She couldn't imagine Beck with a house full of kids. She couldn't even imagine him married to just one woman. And yet...somehow she could.

"Yeah, I would," he replied softly. Seeing the skepticism in her eyes, he heaved a sigh and insisted, "I really would, Rainey."

Oh, no. It was happening again. She felt herself involuntarily melting, succumbing to his charm—for exactly as long as it took for him to flash her one of his "gotcha!" grins. Before she had time to react, he winked garishly. "If you don't believe me, try me."

So much for warm sentiment. "Not in this lifetime, buster. I'd rather have a giant wart on the end of my nose!"

His smirk rapidly vanishing, Beck opened his mouth to retort, but nothing came out. For a moment, they just glared at one another. Then, despite the tension in the air, or maybe because of it, they both cracked up. Between howls, Beck cried, "Gee, Rainey, I don't know if I could look at a big wart every day!" Rainey laughed until tears sprang to her eyes.

"Look," he continued when their laughter finally petered out, "all I'm saying is, it would be the ideal solution to our problem."

Still searching in the cluttered cupboards, Rainey shook her head. "There has to be another way, Beck. It's—it's too crazy. It's too *extreme*."

"Okay. What's your solution?"

Well, okay, he had her there. Based on that list of urgent repairs, it was going to take a lot of money to fix up the inn. Rainey couldn't ask her retired parents for that much cash, and all she had was her meager savings and the proceeds from the sale of her condo in Toronto—hardly enough money to buy a new furnace.

"We'll borrow against your cottage," she suggested with cheeky aplomb. Darn it, maybe there was no kettle. Who had a Ouija board but no kettle?

Beck threw back his head and howled. "Not a chance, lady! I bought that cottage with the first installment of my trust. It's all I have in the world, and I'm not risking it."

The kettle—a battered tin thing with a whistling spout—finally materialized. Rainey took it to the sink. Lost in thought, she absentmindedly filled it to overflowing, then poured the excess water down the drain and set it down on a burner.

"The thing is," Beck argued while she searched for tea bags, "we've got big trouble here. If we don't bring this place up to snuff, we'll go bankrupt."

"Hah! You mean *I'll* go bankrupt. You'll be no worse off than before, Beck. And besides, if we use your money, you'll have more invested than I do. It will be your inn."

When he didn't respond immediately, Rainey looked sharply at him. His expression had gone soft and dreamy again. Another zinger was coming. True to form, he murmured, "You know, I really like it when you say my name."

"Enough already!"

"Okay, okay!"

"You're not listening to me, Beck."

"You can pay me back out of your share of the profits."

Arghhh! He had an answer for everything. He must have stayed up all night, working out the details.

"What's more," he continued as she finally found the tea bags and dropped them into Lilly's old ceramic tea pot, "after we convert this apartment into a wedding chapel, where are you going to live?"

"I'll get an apartment."

"There are no apartments in Bragg Creek, Rainey. You'd have to move to Calgary and commute. Have you seen the traffic on the Trans-Canada?"

She sat down across from him, folded her arms and adopted a stubborn pout. "Then I'll live in one of the suites here." She was clutching at straws now, and she knew it.

"Uh-huh, and how long do you think it will take for you to get sick of that? About a week, that's how long."

The wall phone rang, startling them both. Grateful for the distraction, Rainey jumped up and grabbed it. "Hello!" she belted into the receiver.

"Rainey?" an all-too-familiar voice tentatively asked. It was Trevor. Wonderful. Just what she needed.

"Trevor," she snapped. "I don't have time for you right now." *Or tomorrow, or the day after, or the day after that.*

"Rainey, I just want to talk to you for a few minutes—" he pleaded. "After you ran out like that—"

"I didn't run out, Trevor. I moved west. There's a difference. I have to go now."

"We need to talk, Rainey. Clear the air..."

Sighing impatiently, she glanced over her shoulder at Beck. He was watching her with wide eyes and thinly veiled curiosity. To Trevor, she roared, "There's two thousand miles of air between us, and it's all very clear to me! Goodbye!" She slammed the receiver down and sat down again, hard enough to bruise her tailbone.

A moment later, Beck asked, very casually, "Ah, who's Trevor?"

"Nobody. Just an old boyfriend." Oooh! How dare Trevor call her after what he had done! The *nerve.*

Beck's eyebrows shot up. "Your old boyfriends call you long-distance?" From his tone and body language, it was clear to Rainey that he was trying not to seem too interested, but failing miserably. An alarm bell sounded in her head. Her past was none of his business. "I don't want to talk about it."

He nodded and waited. When it finally became clear that she really wasn't going to say more, he cleared his throat. "Okay, then, back to us. Let's look at our options." He raised his right index finger in the air. "Option Number One. We do nothing. We continue running the Haven as is, until we go under."

"That's not an option. That's a disaster!" The kettle whistled. Rainey jumped up, moved it to a cold burner, and sat down again, forgetting to make the tea.

"Okay, then. Option Number Two. We sell the inn, split the profits, if there are any, and go our separate ways."

She gasped. "No way! I've worked my whole life for this opportunity."

Beck nodded. "Right. And for me this is a terrific business deal. So what does that leave us with?"

Rainey chewed on her lower lip and stared into space. Oh, darn. What did it leave them with? Nothing, that's what. Good grief, what a mess! How could she marry a total stranger she had vowed just yesterday to avoid at any cost? It was utterly insane. Every instinct she had told her to grab her still unpacked bags and get out of there as quickly as possible. Forget she'd ever heard of the Honeymoon Haven and Bragg Creek and Beck Mahoney. But where would she go? Back to "Tronna" and Trevor?

After a long silence, she sighed wearily and muttered, "Okay, tell me what you have in mind."

Excited, Beck leaned forward and gave her his thoughts. They would have Nate Frome draw up a prenuptial agreement. They would marry quietly and stay married only as long as necessary—six months, a year at the most. Then they would start to make noise about trouble in the marriage...

"Well, at least that part will be true!"

He ignored her sarcasm and continued. They would live in his cottage....

"In separate bedrooms, of course."

"Of course," he agreed a little too quickly.

Rainey eyed him suspiciously. She smelled a rat.

In the meantime, Beck concluded, they would renovate the Haven from top to bottom, step up their marketing efforts and reel in the profits. Simple.

Energized by the sheer absurdity of the situation, Rainey rose and began to pace back and forth in the confined space. She felt like a wild animal caught in a trap. Something told her it just wasn't going to be that simple. There would be all kinds of problems. Rules would have to be established. Scores of issues would have to be resolved. She struggled to mentally list them and consider each one separately.

Okay, for one thing... Whirling around like a prosecutor about to pounce on a hostile witness, she demanded, "What if you meet somebody three months from now, who you really would like to marry? What then?"

"I don't think that will happen." Beck's eyes slid over her from head to toe and back again. Rainey involuntarily blushed. Darn it all, why did he have to do that? Why did he have to stir up so many mixed feelings in her? Like, dislike, amusement, exasperation, rage, sympathy, lust.

Startled, she realized for the first time that she was, maybe, just maybe, a little attracted to the guy. Oh, what a dreadful thought! She pushed it away and tried to concentrate on the situation at hand.

"Besides," he added with a wry smile, "there's nobody in this town I can trust with my heart, Rainey. With you, at least I would know that you only married me for my money."

Her jaw dropped. "Beck Mahoney, that is the craziest thing anyone has ever said to me."

He shrugged. "It's a crazy situation."

Sighing, Rainey glanced out the window at the Haven's half-full parking lot. It was a hazy day and the majestic blue spruce trees surrounding the lot had taken on a bluish-green hue. Something on the far side of the lot caught her eye. What the...? It was a man and a woman, scrambling into the back seat of a car. They looked suspiciously like Freda Norman and Hollis Harriman, but from this distance it was hard to tell. Why on earth would those two be jumping into a parked car together?

A sense of defeat suddenly overwhelmed her and her shoulders slumped. All my life I've worked for this, she thought sadly. To run this inn, to live in this beautiful place, to be happy. Aren't I entitled to a little happiness?

Oh, well, maybe the Rainey-gets-a-new-life program would just have to wait another year. Beck was right. They had no options.

She fixed a stern eye on him. "Okay, I'm not agreeing to anything just yet, but if we do get married—and I'm only saying *if*—everyone will have to be told that it's strictly a business arrangement."

Beck bared his dazzling white teeth in a grimace. "Ah, well, there might be a little problem with that."

Yup. She was right. Problems already. "Really? Why?"

"Well, it's my grandmother, see. She'd be horrified if she thought the marriage wasn't real. From her standpoint it would violate the spirit of the trust. I think my grandfather meant for me to be happily married."

Good grief. Rainey dropped her chin and looked at him the way she might look at a teenager who'd just tried teenage logic on her. "Call me crazy, Beck, but wouldn't you be violating the spirit of the trust anyway? I mean, we're not exactly smitten here, you know."

The question caught him off guard and he hesitated. Alarm surged through Rainey like an electric jolt. Oh, no.

Surely he wasn't attracted to her in a serious way. How could he be? They had just met yesterday.

A playful smile played across his luscious lips. "I don't know. Maybe. Maybe not."

"What are you really saying? That we have to pretend to be smitten, for your grandmother's sake?"

"Yup, for hers and everybody else's. This is a small town, Rainey. People talk."

"That's ludicrous. How are we supposed to keep that up?"

He helped himself to another full-length appraisal of her. "I don't know about you, but I won't have any trouble playing my part." He glanced at her breasts. Licked his lips. Grinned like a monkey.

"Look, Beck," she warned him with narrowed eyes, "you mustn't get any ideas about me. I'm here to run an inn, nothing more. Understand?"

"Perfectly," he agreed with all the sincerity of a snake oil salesman.

Ooh, he was maddening! How on earth was a woman supposed to know when this guy was being real?

"Besides," Rainey added, regretting it almost immediately, "I'm...I've just been through...I'm a little vulnerable right now. You have to respect that." Darn, now why did she go and say that? It was way more than he needed to know.

Beck's eyes widened, but he had the sense not to press for an explanation. "Okay, I will," he agreed solemnly.

What a bunch of bunk. The man was as phony as a three-dollar bill, and Rainey didn't trust him as far as she could spit. Oops, what had become of the tea? She went to the stove and turned the burner on again. Beck rose and came up close behind her. Before she could turn around, he placed his hands flat on the countertop on either side of her and closed her in.

"What *would* be so bad about being married to me?" he murmured into her hair. "You might actually like it."

His taut body was just inches away from hers, and Rainey felt the heat coming off it. He smelled like sandalwood again. What was it? Soap? Aftershave lotion? Intermingled with his own natural scent, it was heady stuff. A lonely woman could easily fall prey to Beck, she realized. It would be *sooo* easy.

But it wasn't going to happen to her. No way. Loneliness had caused her to make one stupid choice. She couldn't let it happen again. Especially here, where she had no escape route. What would she do—move to Vancouver? Sheesh, at this rate, she could end up in Japan.

Lips pursed, she peeled his right hand smartly off the counter and turned around. Bad move. He just replaced it and closed her in again, face-to-face this time. Before she could react, he leaned down and brought those tantalizing lips very close to hers.

Flustered and trembling, Rainey assumed he was going to kiss her again. He didn't. Instead, he merely brushed his cheek against hers. His whiskers were bristly, his skin warm. His breath was hot on her face. In sheer defiance of her will to resist him, a wave of desire washed over Rainey and her lips parted in anticipation.

"It could be so good, Rainey," he whispered as she fought a powerful urge to put her arms around him. He was so close, so gorgeous, so sexy. One little kiss. What was the harm, really? After all, they'd kissed once before and the world hadn't ended.

Just as her fingertips made contact with his muscular sides, he abruptly pulled back. "Take a few days to think it over. Then get back to me."

A slow burn crept up Rainey's face and she flinched. How dare he treat her that way? Oh, what a fool she was! To think that...

Then, without so much as a backward glance, he strutted out of the apartment, whistling—so sure of himself that she wanted to scream.

Seconds later the kettle whistled, too. "Oh, for heaven's sake!" she snapped.

5

FOR THE NEXT three days, Rainey briskly went about the business of becoming general manager of the Honeymoon Haven.

On the morning of the first day she introduced herself to every member of the staff, in each case offering reassurances that despite whatever they had heard, all was well at the Haven. To her surprise, most of them were more interested to know how she felt about working with Beck than about the security of their jobs. Smiling tightly, she insisted she was thrilled, simply thrilled, to have Beck Mahoney as a partner. There was a lot of whispering behind her back, a little snickering and some blatant laughter.

"Humph! So it's going to be the two of you now, is it?" Mrs. Norman shouted at her. The women were close enough to touch, and Rainey almost fell backward. Before she could regain her footing and muster a reply, the head housekeeper said "Humph!" again and marched away.

Hollis was more succinct. "So, it's you and B-b-beck," he commented, adding a stutter to his already impressive collection of quirks.

Passing her in the corridor at noon, Beck leaned down and whispered, "Have you thought it over?"

"No!" Rainey snapped. She was still hurt and humiliated and, darn it, she was staying that way as long as possible!

After the lunch crowd cleared out, she had the plants removed from the dining room and spent a breathless afternoon helping the kitchen staff to rearrange the heavy tables. Then she called each of the inn's suppliers and formally introduced herself.

Before heading home, a sweaty, fatigued Beck poked his head into her office. All day he had been struggling alongside Hollis to temporarily repair one of the inn's two ancient furnaces. The weather had turned cool, and the guests had been forced to don sweaters. Moaning and grumbling, they repeatedly conveyed their displeasure to Rainey.

"Have you thought it over yet?" he asked yet again.

"No, I haven't. Get lost!"

"Certainly." He bowed deeply as he backed out of the doorway. Oooh, he was such a pain! She wasn't giving him the satisfaction of a laugh.

On day two she cleared the clutter from Lilly's office and went through dozens of bulging files, sorting the wheat from the chaff. There were documents dating back ten years or more, some on crumbling, yellowed paper. One file held the sticky remnants of a half-eaten butter tart.

In the bottom drawer of the file cabinet, at the very back, she found a folder labeled "Rainey." What the devil? Brows furrowed, she opened it and pulled out a single sheet of mauve, floral stationery—a letter addressed to her from Lilly.

My dearest darling niece,

   I expect that by now you have recovered from the shock of my recent decision and are getting on with things. I apologize for leaving the inn in such a poor state. I confess that lately I have left the running of the place mostly to Freda and Hollis. I am confident they will be a big help to you and Beck as you work to make the Haven everything it can be. He is a fine

young man, and was very sweet to me. Best wishes
for a long and happy partnership.

Sincerely,
Aunt Lilly

P.S. Don't forget about my party.

Stunned by its brevity and businesslike tone, Rainey sat
back on her haunches on the worn carpet and read the letter
again. That was it? No explanation of why Lilly had reneged on her promise? Just a reminder about the party?
Well, at least Rainey understood now why Mrs. Norman
wasn't exactly thrilled with the new arrangement. She was
used to being in charge.

Lilly was right about one thing. Whatever it took, she
and Beck were going to drag the Haven kicking and
screaming into the new millennium. With sound manage-
ment and a little spit and polish, the inn was going to be a
model of gracious hospitality and corporate efficiency. Rainey suddenly envisioned herself on the cover of one of
those glossy hotel trade magazines, smiling under the ban-
ner: Honeymoon Haven Voted World's Best Hotel. It was
going to happen. Yes, sir!

From time to time, Beck came by to check up on her.
Each time he asked if she'd thought it over, and each time
she said no. Good grief. Why was he in such a hurry? After
all, it wasn't going to be a real marriage. Uh, that was, if
it happened at all.

Marriage. Hmm. Her brain was still cycling crazily
through the list of potential problems. For one thing,
wouldn't marrying Beck mean spending altogether too
much time with him? Living with him, working with him.
Even the best of real marriages would buckle under that
kind of strain.

At the end of day three, weary from placating chilly
guests and a little cold herself, Rainey poured a hot bath
in Lilly's claw-footed tub and sank into it with a sigh of

relief. For the first time since his call, Trevor popped into her head.

Why had he called? Surely he didn't have any illusions about getting back together? How could they, anyway? He was an urban yuppie who detested small-town life. One week in Bragg Creek and he'd be whining, "What? No avante garde theater?" And Rainey was never going back to big-city life.

Never. As she luxuriated in the hot, soapy water, the sheer finality of that word hit her like a slap in the face. She was here and she was staying. Forever. Whatever it took to keep her in this beautiful place, she would do it.

Ah, even if it meant marrying the town hustler? Yes, she realized, even if it meant that.

Sighing, she looked around the bathroom, at the chipped paint on the wood wainscoting and the cracked, rippling mirror above the pedestal sink. Lilly's personal items were still in the medicine cabinet. Thank heavens Rainey didn't have to redecorate. There was, of course, still the matter of where she was going to live.

Hmm. A light flashed on in her head and she abruptly sat up, splashing water over the side of the tub. What would Trevor think if she married Beck? Hah! Wouldn't it just serve him right? Wouldn't it just *frost* him? She could just see the look on his bland face. Total shock. Oh, how she would love to see it! Of course, if she did marry Beck, she would have to settle for Trevor's reaction over the telephone. But even that would be worth it.

Oh, yes, she realized with maniacal glee, it would be *well* worth it.

Laughing like a lunatic, suspecting that she had lost her marbles but somehow no longer caring, and knowing full well that it was going to be a disaster, she scrambled out of the tub and called Beck at home. When he answered, sounding tired, she exclaimed, "Okay, buster, I've thought it over. Let's do it!"

"YES, LADIES and gentlemen," Beck intoned in his best impersonation of an infomercial pitch man, "it's the first, the only, free-trial offer of its kind. Try a wife! Satisfaction guaranteed or your money back. If you're not happy with the product, just return it after six months—a year at the most—and get a full refund."

Chuckling aloud, he dipped Lilly's ancient hand razor in the sink and took another careful swipe at his five o'clock shadow. He wanted to look his best tonight. He was about to make the biggest, and definitely the strangest, announcement of his life: I'm getting married, Grandma, to a woman I met five days ago. She doesn't love me, Grandma. Hell, she doesn't even like me much, but who cares? She's a babe!

His eyes, glassy and a little crazed looking, stared back at him from the mirror above Rainey's bathroom sink. "You've gone mad," he said to them.

"Beck, what on earth are you doing in there?" Rainey asked from outside the door. She sounded tense, rattled.

"Nothing," he answered in the high-pitched voice of a kid just about to shave his head and put a ring in his nose.

Moments later he heard an anxious sigh followed by the click-click of her heels retreating down the hall. He decided to keep his thoughts to himself.

Wasn't it just the deal of a lifetime? A *suiteheart* of a deal, he thought, choking back a laugh. How many guys could just try a wife on for size? Marry with the option, right up front, to just walk away if things didn't work out? None, that's how many. Nate Frome would be green with envy. He already had two messy divorces behind him.

Ah, wait a minute. He couldn't tell Nate the truth—not right away. If their little scheme was to work, everybody had to believe that he and Rainey were crazy in love. No exceptions. Dammit, he would love, just love, to see the look on old Nate's mug.

Distracted, he nicked himself. Terrific. Now he was going to be stuck with a nerdy square of tissue on his chin.

Of course, it wouldn't be a *real* marriage—not in the biblical sense, anyway. Rainey had made that pretty clear the other day. Separate bedrooms. Yeah, well, he'd just have to see about that.

And that stuff about being vulnerable. What was that about? Obviously, Trevor, whoever he was, had broken her heart. Beck wanted to kill the guy. Mostly for hurting Rainey, but also partly for giving Beck one more damned hurdle to jump. Loving Rainey was starting to feel like a four-hundred-yard relay.

He dabbed at the cut with a tissue. Hey, wait a minute. *Loving Rainey.* Now where had that thought come from? Stay cool, he silently warned his reflection. Stay cool, old boy.

He heard her banging around in the living room. Nervous and jumpy, she had changed her clothes about nine times in the past hour. Beck could just imagine what she was wearing now. One of those prim, high-necked blouses she seemed to have an endless supply of. A straight, knee-length skirt. Probably panty hose, too. You'd think she was still working at the Royal York Hotel, or something. He didn't have the heart to tell her that no woman in Bragg Creek wore panty hose if she could possibly avoid it.

Cool. Yeah, well, that was going to be tough. 'Cause no matter what kind of getup she wore, Rainey Miller was just about the most delicious piece of womanhood he had ever seen. Those eyes. Those curves. Those legs.

After that stupid move he'd made in her kitchen the other day, Beck had gone home and cursed himself three ways to Sunday. She had just issued a plea for mercy, and what had he done? Drooled all over her, that's what. Like it or not, he would just have to summon a little restraint. Keep his greedy mitts off her—except, of course, when it served their crazy purpose.

Yes, sir. The bedroom thing, the wardrobe thing, the anal-retention thing—all would be addressed in good time.

His thoughts drifted to Francine. Should he tell Rainey about her? Last spring they had gone out exactly three times—twice to dinner and once to a movie. Six whole months had passed and she was still bitter about their "breakup." What Beck didn't understand was, how could they have broken up when they never got together in the first place? They had nothing in common and couldn't dredge up enough conversation to get through a meal. Why, they hadn't even…

Anyway, maybe he should just leave it alone for now. Francine was smart and sensible. She'd come around eventually.

Another thing he wasn't about to tell Rainey: that despite his reputation he hadn't gotten down to business with *any* woman for nearly two years. He was hungry for a woman's touch, her taste, her scent. But not just any woman…

Lord knew it wasn't for lack of opportunity. It was just that…hell, there just wasn't anybody he wanted to be with. Meaningless, short-term stuff. Man, he was tired of that routine. The mindless chitchat over dinner. The slow buildup to the big question: So, when do you get your inheritance, Beck? And by the way, exactly how much money is it? Not that I'm *interested,* or anything.

And then, worst of all, the hurried, halfhearted sex that left him wanting more. What more he wasn't exactly sure— but there had to be *something* more.

The last of his whiskers shed, Beck washed his still-bloody face, rinsed the razor and put it away. Whistling, he raked a comb through his hair and donned a pair of clean khakis and a turtleneck sweater. Satisfied that he was at least passably presentable, even with the goofy tissue paper, he stepped into the hall.

And came face-to-face with an angel.

Grimacing and wringing her hands, Rainey stood before him in a long green linen dress. Sleeveless and collarless, it fell in a straight line from her slender shoulders to the tops of her thin-strapped black sandals. From there it was slit up both sides to her bare knees. A black enamel pin and a slender black bracelet completed the ensemble.

"Wow!" he exclaimed.

"Oh, Beck." Her expression was tortured. "Do you think it's okay? I mean, it's really a summer dress…"

"I think it's more than okay," he confirmed with an appreciative nod. "I think it's spectacular."

"Oh, Beck." She managed a small smile. Her hair shone and her lips glistened with a pale-pink glossiness. Despite her anxiety, she had a girlish glow on. It was just about the most beautiful thing he had ever seen.

Before he could stop them, his eyes took a good long look at the swelling of those more-than-generous breasts beneath the pale green sheath, and the graceful curves leading down to those luscious hips. He had no trouble picturing her without the dress. No trouble at all.

Restraint, he silently reminded himself. *Restraint, Beck.*

"You look wonderful, too," she said sweetly.

Beck eyed her suspiciously. In the past three days she had swung all the way from snarling at him to almost treating him like a human being. What was going on?

The doorbell sounded and he winked at her. "It's show time!" Rainey took a sharp breath and expelled it slowly.

"Beck, darling," his tiny, feisty grandmother chirped as he let her into the apartment, "you're as handsome as ever!" As usual, she was overdressed and over-coifed, her mauve suit, pink shoes and blue-tinted hair a medley of clashing pastels.

"Thanks, Grandma," he said as she brushed past him and made a beeline straight for Rainey. Smiling as sweetly as only a crafty old lady can smile, she held out her jeweled hands and clasped the sides of Rainey's bare arms. "Why, aren't you just the prettiest thing!"

Rainey beamed—and relaxed. "Thank you."

"I'm delighted to meet you at last. Your aunt Lilly always said such nice things about you. I can see now that she wasn't exaggerating." With that, her watery eyes clouded over with sadness. "Oh, I miss her so much," she said, her voice cracking slightly. "A stroke. And she was only eighty-four. It's tragic."

Beck rolled his eyes. He loved his grandmother, but her penchant for melodrama bordered on being insufferable.

Rainey, immediately smitten, murmured, "I miss her, too, Mrs. Mahoney."

Old Flo pursed her lips. "Oh, please. Call me Flo. We don't need formalities here."

"Oh, I couldn't do that!" Rainey cried. "It wouldn't be right."

Flo's frown quickly gave way to a sugary smile. "Well now, isn't that just the mark of a well-raised young lady. I'll tell you what. Call me Grandma then." She flashed Beck a disgusted look. "These Mahoney boys, they just don't seem to be able to produce girls. It will be a pleasure to have you as my granddaughter."

Beck nearly gagged. "Tea, ladies?"

"Only if there's a little gin to go with it," his grandmother replied as she and Rainey moved into the living room.

Beck sauntered into the kitchen and looked around for the kettle. Dammit, where had Rainey put the stupid thing?

If they couldn't manage a pot of tea, how were they going to manage a marriage and a renovation?

After a tedious search, he finally found it, along with the tea bags. Standing at the sink, he overheard the women chatting amiably about the weather, and Rainey's dress—so flattering!—and her new responsibilities. And, of course, the Women of the Wapiti. Rainey simply would have to join the club as soon as possible. They needed some young blood.

Leaning against the counter, Beck took a deep breath. Good Lord, how were they going to broach the subject of the marriage? And how about that five-day engagement, huh? Hell, in Flo's day, two years were considered scandalous. No doubt about it, the old girl was going to be appalled. Not to mention highly suspicious. After all, she was the trustee. She controlled the cash—and Beck along with it.

As the kettle began to whistle, his conscience finally kicked in. Man alive, how could he lie to his own grandmother? What kind of cad did that? Of course, he rationalized, he wasn't really lying. Not totally, anyway. He was attracted to Rainey and he did, for whatever warped reason, want to marry her.

Summoning all the courage he could muster, he went into the living room, sat down across from the women, and cleared his throat. They stopped chattering and stared expectantly at him.

"Ah, Grandma," he began, his throat suddenly dry, his palms sweating, "Rainey and I have something to tell you. We've, ah, we've…" Desperate, he glanced at Rainey for help, but she looked away and nervously licked her lips. "We've—we're—we've decided to marry!" He braced himself for the explosion.

It didn't come.

Instead, before his very eyes, Florence Mahoney's funny

little face lit up like a neon sign and she gasped—with sheer delight. "Oh, my, now isn't that just the best news I have ever heard! Let me be the first to congratulate both of you."

"Wh-whaaat...?" Beck stammered.

"Thank you." Rainey's green eyes widened in disbelief. From behind Flo's back she locked eyes with Beck, shook her head slightly and silently mouthed words he couldn't decipher. He had warned her to expect the worst. Now she was just as baffled as he was.

"Um, as you know," Beck blundered on, "we met just a few days ago...."

"Oh, don't bother to explain," Flo urged with a dismissive wave of her hand. "It must have been love at first sight. How wonderfully, delightfully romantic!"

Okay, Beck was thunderstruck now. How many times had she warned him that there was no such thing as love at first sight? About a million times, that's how many.

Flo made a big show of checking her watch. "Oh, my, would you just look at the time." In defiance of her advanced years, she sprang to her feet like an athlete and sprinted for the door. "I have to run along now, children. The club is meeting tonight to plan the winter festival."

"It was lovely to meet you," Rainey called out to her retreating back.

"It was lovely to meet you, too, dear," Flo replied.

The moment he closed the door behind her, Beck spun around and whispered harshly, "I don't get it! Something funny is going on here."

"I know," Rainey said. "You're bleeding."

6

"WHO HAS THE RINGS?"

The marriage of Rainey Ann Miller, only child of Laura and Jonathan Miller of Toronto, to Beckett Lee Mahoney, youngest child of Martha and Earl Mahoney of Edmonton, took place at 4:00 p.m. on the third Saturday in September, in Rainey's apartment. The bride wore beige silk. The groom wore gray flannel. There were no flowers and no bridesmaids. There would be no babies, and definitely no minivan.

Charles T. Longhorn, chief commissioner of the town of Bragg Creek, officiated. Freda Norman and Hollis Harriman, also of Bragg Creek, served as witnesses. When Mr. Longhorn asked if anyone present could say why this young couple should not be joined in holy matrimony, Rainey and Beck simultaneously spun around and glared at the witnesses.

Withering under their collective heat, Mrs. Norman and her twitching sidekick struggled to maintain straight faces. Hollis quickly lost the battle and collapsed into a fit of giggles. Scowling, Mrs. Norman jabbed him in the ribs. "Get a grip there, Holly!" As he doubled over in pain, a little smile tugged at the corner of her own lips.

"Who has the rings?" Mr. Longhorn asked again. Beck fished in his pocket for the plain gold bands they had hastily purchased that morning at the local jewelry shop. Fumbling slightly, they managed to get them on.

When Mr. Longhorn announced, "You may now kiss

the bride,'' Rainey turned nervously toward Beck. *Make it good,* her eyes told him. *People are watching. In truth, she didn't care who was present. If ever she had an excuse to kiss Beck, this was definitely it.*

All too happy to oblige, he put his arms around her and drew her close. She followed suit. While the others smiled benevolently, they joined lips, gently at first, then insistently. Beck's right hand came up to cup the back of her head, and his tongue snaked into her mouth. Rainey moaned softly. Oblivious of their bug-eyed audience, they let the kiss go on for a very long time.

At one point, Beck actually pulled back for air, then, moaning and whispering gibberish, kissed her again, even more deeply than the first time.

Out of patience, the commissioner cleared his throat and solemnly intoned, ''I now pronounce you man and wife.''

The bride and groom ignored him. They were drowning in the depths of something so strong, so powerful, that when they finally did pull away, it left them both panting and trembling.

''Wow!'' Beck exclaimed. ''Maybe we should get married again tomorrow!''

In the front of her mind, Rainey thought, *Hmm, now that's a kiss.* In the back, she thought: *Take that, Trevor! You rat!*

After the ceremony, Mr. Longhorn offered best wishes for a long and happy life together, which prompted another round of giggles, then showed himself out. Mrs. Norman and a still-twittering Hollis went back to work. Alone with Beck, Rainey suddenly grew self-conscious.

''Well,'' she stammered, avoiding his eyes, ''I guess it's time to clear out of here.'' She walked into the bedroom and began to gather her loose things. As she was dropping them into the biggest of her two suitcases, Beck leaned against the doorjamb and folded his arms.

"So," he said, utterly, predictably, true to form, "we're on our honeymoon."

Rainey looked up sharply. She had been expecting this little scene—though not quite this soon. "Oh, no, we're not, Beck Mahoney. This is strictly a business arrangement. You know that."

"Hmmm." He went on watching her, his eyes sliding provocatively over every inch of her. Rainey could feel them undressing her, even from across the room. Goose bumps formed on her skin.

"You know, I'm not opposed to mixing business with pleasure," he said quietly.

Okay, that was enough. "Look Beck, we made a deal. Separate bedrooms. You agreed."

He snorted. "Well, I don't know, Rainey. I mean, *agreed* is a pretty strong word. I went along with it. I'll give you that."

"Uh-huh, and you're going to continue to go along with it."

"Tell me you're not attracted to me," he teased.

With an exasperated sigh, Rainey closed the suitcase, picked it up and walked toward him. "Beck, there isn't a woman alive who isn't attracted to you."

He wagged a finger at her. "That's not an answer." He took the suitcase from her and set it down behind him, barricading both of them into the room.

Hands on hips, she stared him down. "Okay, then, I'm not attracted to you."

"Liar." He grinned.

"I am not lying!" Actually, as much as Rainey resisted the idea, she *was* attracted to him. Hopelessly. But so were nine-tenths of the women around here. And, attraction could be a deadly thing. Nobody knew that better than she did.

He nodded toward the living room. "We generated a

little heat in there, Rainey. You felt it, too. I know you did.''

Oh, for heaven's sake. Was there no limit to his arrogance? Maybe they shouldn't have just plunged into this thing. Maybe, in addition to the prenuptial agreement Nate Frome had drafted, they should have drawn up another contract. One that spelled out the guidelines. Defined the parameters. Laid down the rules. Of course, how could they? As far as Nate and everyone else was concerned, there were no rules.

More importantly, hadn't she asked Beck to play easy with her heart?

Fighting tears, she said, "I'm lonely, Beck. I'm in a new town and I don't have any friends here. I've got a new job, and I don't even know if I can do it. And I got married today, to a man I hardly know.''

"Hey,'' he said softly, his arms reaching out for her. Anguish clouded his handsome features. "I'm sorry, Rainey. I didn't mean to rush you like that.''

Functioning on autopilot, Rainey walked into his arms and sighed as they enveloped her. She put her arms loosely around him and he stroked her hair. "It's okay, Rainey,'' he murmured. "I'll be your friend. And I know you can do the job. I have complete confidence in you.''

She relaxed against him. There was nothing carnal about his embrace. On the contrary, it was friendly and soothing.

For about two seconds.

Before either of them knew what was happening, the heat they had generated earlier regenerated itself with even greater intensity. Slowly and sensuously, Beck began to stroke Rainey's silk-clad back, his fingertips skimming downward from the tops of her shoulder blades to her waist and back again. Rainey felt a stirring in her loins, and before she could stop them her hands had begun to caress his back.

"Rainey," he whispered hoarsely against her hair.

Mesmerized, she tilted her head upward to receive his kiss. When their lips were just whispers apart, Beck ran the tip of his tongue across the full width of her upper lip, then her lower. From there, he trailed across her cheek. When he landed, soft and wet and warm, on her earlobe, Rainey's breath caught sharply in her throat.

Not even the shrill ringing of the telephone got through to them—until the answering machine clicked on and Rainey heard Dana's chirpy voice. A blast from the past, it brought her smartly back to reality.

"Dana!" she yelped, abruptly pulling free from Beck. Sidestepping the suitcase, she ran into the kitchen, Beck close on her heels. Her shaky hand paused near the telephone. She looked at Beck. "Oh, no! What I am going to tell her?"

Beck was flushed and disheveled, still in a trance. "Who's Dana?"

"My best friend!"

Caught up in her panic, he cried, "I don't know! Tell her the truth!"

While they eyed one another with frenzied uncertainty, the message played on. "Rainey? Are you there? If you're there, pick up, sweetie. Sorry it's taken me so long to get back to you. I was away at a conference and—"

"But what *is* the truth?" Rainey pleaded.

"Tell her you got married this afternoon."

"I can't do that! She'll think I've gone mad!"

Calmer suddenly, Beck folded his arms and declared, "Well now, that is pretty close to the truth, isn't it?"

Her hand still hovering above the receiver, Rainey made a sour face at him. Arghhh! Obviously she should have thought this through a little better. Trevor she definitely planned to tell about the marriage. But what about the others? In her rush to make her ex jealous, she hadn't paused to consider that, sooner or later, everyone would have to be told about the ludicrous pact she and Beck had struck. Her mom, her dad, her best friend. Everyone!

Oh, dear. It would have to be later. She just couldn't deal with it right now.

"Anyway, sweetie, it's obvious that you're not there," Dana said as Rainey stared helplessly at the machine. "Call me when you get the chance. I miss you. Bye now."

The machine clicked off and Rainey looked at Beck. He was grinning. "When at first we do deceive..."

"You're not being very helpful!"

"And you're not being very realistic. Call her back. Tell her the truth."

"I can't. Not—not yet, anyway."

Beck shrugged. "It's your call, so to speak." With that, he went into the bedroom and retrieved the suitcases. On his way back, he paused in the kitchen doorway. "I'll meet you in the car. Call her, Rainey. Call her right now."

After the apartment door clicked shut, Rainey took several deep breaths to calm herself and dialed her old friend's number. Dana picked up after the first ring and sang a cheerful hello.

"Dana!" Rainey practically shrieked. Oh, dear, she had to get a grip. This was going to be hard enough.

"Sweetie! How are you? I miss you so much."

"I'm fine. Terrific, really. I'm—I'm sort of in the middle of something right now, and I can't talk for long. I just wanted to let you know that I'm okay." *Actually, I just married a perfect stranger. But don't worry, I'm fine.*

"I'm so glad to hear it. I won't keep you. I just...Rainey, there's something I..."

"Dana," Rainey interrupted, "I'm moving. Today. To a house."

"Really? Why? I thought you had an apartment at the inn."

"I do. Er, I did. It's kind of a long story. And, ah, I'm going to have a—a roommate!"

"You're kidding. Boy roommate or girl roommate?"

"Boy. His name is Beck Mahoney. He works here at the inn. He's a masseuse."

"A masseuse. How convenient. Is he cute?"

Despite everything, Rainey laughed. "Oh, yeah. He's cute, all right." *He's a hunk, Dana. You have no idea.*

"What's your new number?"

Rainey recited the number. As Dana was jotting it down, she glanced anxiously out the window and spotted Beck putting her suitcases into the trunk of the Fairlane.

"Listen, Dana, I really have to run. He's waiting for me."

"Okay, okay. It's just that…there's something I really want to talk to you about. In fact, I was thinking about coming out there."

Coming out here? Oh, no! "Dana, that's not a good idea. Not right now. I've hardly had time to get settled. My new job, this move, honestly, everything is crazy right now."

There was a brief pause. "Ah, sure. I can come out later, I guess."

Was it Rainey's imagination, or did her old friend sound a little anxious? Maybe even frightened. They knew each other through and through. Oh, well, whatever was troubling Dana, it would just have to wait. "Can I call you later, Dana? Honestly, I'm rushed."

"Okay, I give. Take care, sweetie. And do call me."

Rainey promised she would.

After hanging up, she took a few moments to gather her wits, then took one last look around the apartment. She would be seeing it again, but not like this. Soon, Lilly's things would be cleared out and the renovation would begin. This felt like goodbye.

Her whole life was starting to feel like that.

RAINEY GASPED. "Beck Mahoney, you call this a cottage!"

"Well, it was a cottage, originally. I've added a little space to it over the years."

A *little* space? Rainey couldn't believe her eyes. All along she had pictured a cozy cabin with two rooms and a thatched roof. Something Goldilocks and the Three Bears might inhabit. This was a house and a half.

Laughing with delight, she scrambled out of the Fairlane and gazed up at it with awe. It was a two-storey mansion of Laurentian design, similar in many ways to the inn. Built of cedar and stone, with tall windows and steeply pitched gables, it easily competed for glory with the tall, ancient spruce trees surrounding it.

The trees swayed gently in the wind, birds chirping from within the depths of their wide, sweeping branches. Casting her eyes downward, Rainey spied a rabbit, half white, half brown, making haste to evade the sudden intruders.

"So what do you think?" Beck asked, his voice full of pride.

"I can't wait to see it!" Rainey cried with a little more enthusiasm than was appropriate under the circumstances. She glanced nervously at Beck, but he, too, was looking at the house with awe. Rainey understood now why he couldn't risk losing it. It was everything to him. In a way, it was the love of his life.

On the ride here, he had been strangely quiet. Shy, almost. He seemed stunned. Blown away, Rainey assumed, by the fiery passion that had welled up between them this afternoon. Heaven knew she was surprised.

Could two people with practically nothing in common get caught up in the throes of a physical attraction so powerful it rendered them both deaf, dumb and blind? Sure they found each other attractive. But Beck was the hunk of the century; that was Rainey's explanation. What was his? He had more women than Carter's had pills. Surely there was nothing special about her?

Oh, boy. Beck's women. Now *there* was a problem she hadn't even considered.

"Let's go in," he suggested, breaking into her thoughts.

Inside, the house was even more impressive than outside. The living room soared to the full height of the structure, along with the massive stone fireplace that formed its magnificent centerpiece. Overlooking the living room was a big, open kitchen with stainless steel appliances and a generous work island. Behind it, Rainey found two small bedrooms, a laundry room and a half bathroom. Beck was using one of the bedrooms as a store room, the other as an office.

Looking around, she saw that most of the furniture was old and cheesy. Real guy stuff. A retro, plaid sofa. Mismatched chairs. A wobbly kitchen table that looked like it had been salvaged from a junkyard. The wagon wheel coffee table was just about the ugliest thing she had ever seen. Men. Honestly.

"Your room is upstairs," Beck said. "Across from mine."

Rainey braced herself for the inevitable smart remark. Normally, Beck would make the most of announcing something like that—wink at her, or poke her in the ribs, or do that goofy thing he did with his eyebrows. Not this time. His face was blank, his manner strangely remote. He grabbed her bags from their resting place by the front door and carried them up the wide staircase. Rainey followed him, her eyes helplessly glued to his adorable butt.

The two bedrooms on the second level were huge and shared a big bathroom. A very messy bathroom. Terrific, thought Rainey. A bathroom slob. Frankly, the whole house was dusty and messy, though she sensed that Beck had scrambled to tidy up for her benefit.

"I hope you don't mind sharing the bathroom," he said

in the flat, impersonal tone of a boardinghouse landlord renting out a room. "It's a long hike downstairs in the middle of the night."

"I don't mind at all," she replied. Good grief. The way they were acting, you'd think they really were just roommates. Well, of course, that's what they were. Oh, dear, surely she wouldn't have to remind herself of that?

While Rainey unpacked and took in the stunning view beyond her bedroom windows, Beck went into his own bedroom to change. She heard him whistling and breathed a sigh of relief. Once again, he sounded like the happy, overgrown kid he was.

Lord, she was exhausted. The past few days had whizzed by in a blur. It was amazing, she marveled, how much preparation even a meaningless wedding required. She looked forward to a long, hot bath, followed by a quiet evening. Maybe they could light a fire and enjoy a snifter of brandy together. Get to know each other a little better. After all, they *were* married—for real or not. Humming softly to herself, she changed into jeans and a baggy sweater and bounced down the stairs.

In the living room, she stopped dead in her tracks. Beck, too, had donned jeans and a sweater. But he was also wearing a jacket. Avoiding her eyes, he scooped up his car keys and put them in his pocket.

Rainey was appalled. "Surely you're not going out!"

"Actually, I am." He fidgeted unnecessarily with the zipper on his jacket, then raised his guilty eyes to hers. "I thought I might head up to Banff. Play a few hands with Nate and the boys."

"A few hands?"

"Yeah. Poker. Five card stud. Winner takes all. Or, in my case, loser gives all." He chuckled lamely.

Rainey didn't laugh. "But—but it's…" She trailed off there, awash in feelings she didn't understand and couldn't explain. She had almost said, "It's our honeymoon." But that was just nonsense.

"Look, Rainey," Beck grumbled. "You said it yourself. It's not a real honeymoon. So it shouldn't make any difference if I stay or go. Right? Besides, don't you want to relax? Get settled in?"

Anger welled up inside Rainey, but it was stupid, inexplicable anger. She struggled to get it under control. Beck was right. It wasn't real. Any of it. "It makes no difference at all," she lied.

Beck left and Rainey went to the window overlooking the driveway. As the Fairlane pulled away, spitting gravel, she suddenly recalled the fuming redhead who had screamed at him on the street that day in Banff—the day they had first met with Nate Frome.

"Humph!" she snorted, steaming up the glass. "Poker, my foot!"

7

"HOW MANY CARDS?"

Beck looked up. Someone had just spoken to him. Who was it? For one dizzy moment, he thought it was Rainey. But it couldn't be. He was here in Banff, hunched over Nate Frome's dining room table. She was alone in his cottage, doing heaven only knew what. Probably burning his clothes by now. Cutting up his furniture. Trashing his office.

"Beck?" came the bewildered voice again.

Beck snapped to attention. Okay, it was Nate Frome. At first glance he had actually looked like Rainey. Her face had somehow been superimposed on his—on all three faces at the table, in fact. Nate's. Arnie Hutchinson's. Pete Wilson's. They all looked just like her—minus the knockout body and the long legs, of course.

"Beck!" Nate repeated. He sounded more worried than impatient. "How many cards do you want?"

"Ah, I'll take three," Beck replied. Wait a minute. Was it three? How many cards did he have in his hand? Oh, yeah. Two. "I'll take three," he repeated dumbly.

A look passed between the others. Catching it out of the corner of his eye, Beck muttered, "Sorry, gentlemen. I'm a little off tonight."

"Yeah," Pete snorted. "Off the planet."

"Gentlemen, let's play cards," Nate said wearily.

Brows furrowed, lips pursed, Beck tried to concentrate on his hand. Okay, he had the jack of spades, the seven of hearts, the nine of diamonds and two sixes—a club and another heart. Nothing. "What's wild?" he asked, risking more ridicule.

"You being here on your wedding night," Arnie dead-panned.

Beck struggled to arrange his facial features into something resembling intelligence. "Rainey's getting settled in," he explained. "I'm just killing a little time." It sounded lame, but what else could he say? *I can't go home yet, guys, 'cause I'm hot for my wife—I just can't keep my hands off her.* Yeah, sure.

"Fives and tens," Pete said.

Beck frowned. "What?"

Shaking his head, Pete leaned across the table. "Fives and tens are wild, Beck. Listen, buddy, maybe you should just head on home now."

Beck peeked at his watch. It was only eight-fifteen. If he went home this early, he'd probably find Rainey awake and shredding his photo collection.

Damn that woman! She had been hotter than hell when he left, but she wasn't having it both ways. No, sir. Either it was a real marriage, or it wasn't. Either they were going to get down and dirty, or they weren't. And she was adamant that they weren't. So why was she upset? Women. He loved them, but he would never understand them.

"I'm out." He tossed his cards facedown on the table. Grumbling, Nate and Pete did likewise, and Arnie took the pot.

Restless, Beck jumped up and poured himself a cup of the strong coffee that helped the boys to stay awake, sometimes until dawn. It was probably a mistake. Sooner or later he would have to go home, and the last thing he needed was to lie awake all night thinking about how good it would be...

Nate cleared his throat. "So, ah, Beck, tell us how you

and Rainey fell in love overnight.'' A chorus of snickers rose up from the table. Beck ignored it—along with the annoying smirk on Frome's face.

Coffee in hand, he sat down again. His friendship with Nate had always had an edge to it—a friendly rivalry. After that little episode two years ago, it had gotten downright nasty. But hey—how was Beck supposed to know that Nate had been dating that woman? *She* certainly hadn't mentioned it.

"I don't know, Nate," he replied off-handedly. "I'm as surprised as you are."

"Okay, gentlemen," Pete announced, "it's kings and little ones. You don't need the king to make the little one wild."

The boys exchanged looks, but Beck stayed where he was.

Summoning all the concentration he could muster, Beck managed to get through the next hand, and the one after that. Between losses, his mind drifted back to Lilly's bedroom—to the embrace that had rocked his world.

How had Rainey managed to get him worked up so quickly? Sure she was sexy. But so was Francine. And Linda before her. And Maryann before her. They were all babes, but none of them got his hormones cooking the way Rainey Miller did. None of them sent his libido into hyperdrive whenever she touched him.

Francine. Linda. Maryann. Beck could have any one of them tonight, he knew. Yup, even on his wedding night. One phone call was all it would take. But he didn't want them. He wanted Gorgeous Green Eyes. Badly.

"So," Arnie ventured, "I don't suppose there's a connection between your recent marriage and your inheritance, is there?"

Momentarily stunned by the sheer audacity of the question, Beck glanced around the table at the others. Their faces were impassive, their eyes glued firmly to their hands. What the hell. There was no point in getting riled. Obviously he was going to have to get used to this kind of stuff.

He rearranged his own cards. "No connection at all, Arnie. As you know, I was going to get the money, anyway."

"Hmm." Arnie pretended to be fascinated by his hand. Beck knew that more was coming. Sure enough, two hands later, Arnie added, "Yeah, but not for another three years. Isn't that right?" That launched another round of snickers. Pete eventually laughed so hard he spit a mouthful of coffee clear across the table onto Nate's Polo shirt.

Okay, that was it. "I'm outta here!" Beck snapped.

"'Bout time." Nate said with a laugh. He dabbed at his shirt with a napkin. "If I had a woman like that in my bed, I would have been gone hours ago."

As Beck was nearing the door, Pete called out from the table, "Hey, buddy. Don't forget, you promised to help me build my garage. I really want to get it done before the snow flies. Can I still count on you?"

"Of course," Beck replied without hesitation. Actually, he'd completely forgotten about it. "Just call me when you're ready."

"Terrific. Thanks."

On the forty-minute drive home, Beck concentrated on the ribbon of pavement in front of him. It was just after ten, but the sky was already black. Winter was coming. How the hell was he going to get through a long, cold Alberta winter with the hottest woman he'd ever met sleeping in the room right next to his?

Yeah, well, like it or not, he would just have to bide his time. Rainey was "vulnerable." There would be no rushing her. And Lord knew the last thing he wanted to do was scare her off. After all, what if she did turn out to be the perfect woman for him?

As he pulled into the driveway, it occurred to him that

what he needed was a coping strategy. Hmm. Maybe if he kept busy, day and night, and kept Rainey busy, too, they would survive this ordeal intact. The inn would use up their days, but that left the evenings and weekends. Something would have to be done about them.

What a waste, he thought sadly. Killing time when they could be making love, talking, snuggling, making love, cooking, watching TV, making love, reading, hiking, making love...

Mercifully, the house was dark. Inside, he tiptoed into the living room and turned on the halogen reading lamp next to his favorite chair.

And blinked.

The room was spotless. He soon discovered that the entire main floor of the house had been scrubbed to within an inch of its life. He chuckled to himself.

Yup. Keeping busy. It was the only way.

"RISE AND SHINE, sleepyhead. It's seven o'clock."

Rainey peeled one eye open and peered up at Beck. When his fuzzy face finally came into focus, she muttered, "You mean, like, in the morning?"

He laughed. "Yes, ma'am. I mean, like, in the morning."

Groaning, she rolled over and burrowed deeper under the blankets. Ten years of working the night shift had turned her into a night owl. She didn't do mornings. Last night, however, she had hit the sack early, then tossed and turned for hours. In fact, she had been wide-awake when Beck got home. Just after ten—10:23, to be exact. Not that she cared, or anything.

"C'mon, woman." He jabbed at the blankets.

"Go away!"

"Okay, I'm leaving, but if you don't get up in the next two minutes, I'll be back with a bucket of ice water."

Ice water? A chill ran down Rainey's spine and she shivered violently. "You're mean. Go away!"

"Two minutes, woman."

She poked her head out from under the warm down comforter. "Why do I have to get up this early on a Sunday?"

He grinned. "I have plans for you."

"What kind of plans?"

"You'll know soon enough. Now get up. Your breakfast is waiting."

Breakfast? He had to be joking. Rainey ate breakfast when most people had already eaten lunch, lunch when they were just plopping down in front of the television, and dinner when they were undressing for bed. No way was she putting food in her stomach at this ungodly hour.

After Beck backed out of the room, counting backward from 120, she crawled out of bed, donned her terry cloth bathrobe and pulled a comb through her tangled hair. Still half asleep, she stumbled downstairs, only to be assaulted by the noxious odor of bacon and eggs. Yuck!

"How about cereal with skim milk?" she suggested hopefully. Yawning, she poured a cup of steaming hot coffee and slumped down at the kitchen table.

"Eat up," Beck commanded, setting a plate of the cholesterol-heavy food down in front of her. "We've got a big day ahead of us, and you're going to need more than cereal."

"Who ever needs more than cereal?"

"You do. Your cappuccino and croissant days are over. You're a mountain woman now."

While Rainey picked at her food, Beck, astonishingly, dropped to the floor and cranked out twenty push-ups. Her mouth fell open. What the devil? Surely he wasn't this hyper every morning at seven? *Puh-leez.* Immediately afterward, he sprang to his feet and did a dozen jumping jacks. Then, flushed and panting, he ran on the spot for a while. It was only five minutes or so, but it seemed much longer to Rainey.

Still running, he barked at her like a drill sergeant. "Hey! Eat those eggs. If you don't, I'm going to make you drop to the floor and give me ten."

She cocked an eyebrow. "How 'bout I give you ten dollars to get lost?"

"Not funny. Down the hatch, woman."

Before Rainey knew what had hit her she was in the Fairlane, hurtling down the sun-dappled highway at breakneck speed. Fir trees flew by in a blur. Small wildlife entered her peripheral vision only to vanish milliseconds later. All the while Beck chattered nonstop, switching wildly from one topic to another. He had to be on drugs.

Last night, she had gone to bed cursing him but had quickly come to her senses. For one thing, this was strictly a business deal, and wasn't it she who had insisted they keep their business and personal lives separate? It might be tough under the circumstances, but it wasn't impossible.

For another thing, she just couldn't seem to stay mad at the guy for long. Why was that? Of course, she might just be influenced this time by the fact that he had come home pretty early last night. Obviously he hadn't been with a woman, as she had assumed. Maybe he couldn't find one. Oh, yeah, sure! Beck Mahoney—unable to find a woman? The guy would find friendly female flesh in a nunnery.

From time to time, Rainey stole a sideways glance at him. In profile he was treacherously handsome, his aquiline nose and sculptured lips perfectly aligned between his strong forehead and square, manly chin.

As he babbled on about fishing rights in the national parks, she stifled the urge to reach out and touch his cheek. *Oh, Rainey,* she silently chastised herself, *don't get all sweet on the guy. There's nothing in it but a broken heart. Besides, things are complicated enough.*

When Beck stopped yapping long enough to catch his breath, she demanded to know, once and for all, exactly where they were going.

"Up," he finally admitted. "Straight up the Galatea Trail in Kananaskis Provincial Park, the most beautiful place on earth."

He was right. It was beautiful. Breathtaking, actually. Soon after they turned south off the Trans-Canada Highway onto a secondary blacktop, the forest hugging both sides of the road grew taller and denser and more varied. It was an explosion of green, punctuated here and there by startling bursts of pastel. A light breeze whistled through the trees, and the sky above was a perfect robin's egg blue. Rainey sighed with pleasure—until she realized what Beck had just said.

"What do you mean by *up?*" she asked. "Exactly how far up are we going? And how are we getting there?"

"Eight kilometers, on foot. That's about five miles, if you prefer the linear to the metric measurement."

Eight kilometers? Good grief! Rainey struggled to recall the last thing she had climbed. Oh, yeah. The little ladder astride the bunk beds in Dana's bedroom. Twenty years ago. Terrific.

"Please tell me we're not going to be rappelling off the side of anything!" she cried.

He shook his head. "Not today. That's next week. Today we're just hiking. That's about all you city types can handle on a first run."

In the public parking lot at the mouth of the trail, they encountered two of the giggly young clerks from Nate Frome's office—a petite blonde with a Kewpie doll mouth, and a lanky brunette who couldn't peel her eyes off Beck for a second. Looking clear through Rainey, she whined,

"Is it true what everybody is saying, Beck? That you're married?" She made *married* sound like *poisoned*.

"'Fraid so, ladies. This is my wife, Rainey." Beck draped his arm around Rainey's shoulders and drew her close. She put her arm around him, and they both beamed foolishly at the young women.

"How do you do, Mrs. Mahoney?" the blonde asked politely. Rainey blinked. *Mrs. Mahoney?* Maybe they should have talked about that name thing, too. Oh, well, it went with the territory, she supposed.

"Very well, thank you," she replied.

The women immediately dismissed her and started to chatter at Beck. Relieved, Rainey slipped out from under his arm—it felt a little too right—and took another look around.

"You know, you're putting a big dent in my fan club," Beck joked after his admirers bounced off in the direction of the trail.

Rainey rolled her eyes. "Oh, yeah, some dent!"

Laughing, Beck fished his backpack out of the trunk. He had made sandwiches for them, and brought fruit along, too. While Rainey appraised the steep, tree-lined cliffs facing them, he took something out of the backpack. "Rainey?" He tossed it to her. It was a necklace—a whistle, actually, suspended from a long shoelace.

She eyed it suspiciously. "What's this for?"

"Bears," he said without looking at her. "The trail will be nearly deserted today. Every now and then, we'll give it a blow, just to let them know we're here."

Rainey gasped. "Bears! Beck Mahoney, you didn't say anything about bears!"

"Ah, don't worry about it," he said as if she were a hopeless worrywart. "It's just a precaution, that's all."

She nodded and murmured, "Uh-huh." She didn't believe that for one minute!

They began the long, slow ascent. Beck went first, occasionally reaching back to help Rainey step up to a high ledge, or get over an outcropping of sharp rock. The mountainside was steep in some places, mercifully flat in others. Whenever they reached a level place, Rainey fell to the ground, gasping for air and begging for mercy.

"Buck up there, woman!" Beck teased. "It's a long way up."

Between the infrequent plateaus conversation proved impossible. It took every ounce of breath Rainey had just to blow the whistle. Beck had been right; the trail was seldom used at this time of year. But once in a while, when they stopped to rest, small groups of hikers overtook them.

At the halfway point, two stunning women about Rainey's age passed by. They were moving at a good clip, and neither of them had so much as broken a sweat. Rainey, on the other hand, was drenched. Long ago she had peeled off her sweatshirt and tied it around her waist. Her skimpy T-shirt was damp, her face smudged, her upper arms scratched and bloody from numerous encounters with prickly branches.

She wanted to kill the women. Especially when one of them drawled, "Hi, Beck. Let me know if it doesn't work out," before tossing her chestnut mane in Rainey's face and continuing along the trail. Beck's only reaction was to check Rainey for her reaction. Seeing the stunned disbelief in her eyes, he threw back his head and roared.

The climb took nearly four hours. At the top they paused and surveyed the scene. Rainey's jaw dropped.

A lush, green meadow stretched out before them, dotted with wildflowers in every color of the rainbow. Beyond it lay Mirror Lake, a shallow body of water so clear, so pristine, it seemed immoral even to look upon it. The nearby adjacent mountain peaks were perfectly reflected in the calm surface of the lake. It was an upside down photo, flawlessly framed and focused by nature itself.

Overcome with emotion, Rainey could barely speak. "Oh, Beck," she finally managed to whisper, "I had no idea." She squinted up at him. "Thank you for bringing me here. Thank you."

He beamed. "My pleasure."

They found an isolated, grassy slope near the water and lay down, side by side. The air was cool at that elevation, but the sun was hot—a phenomenon of mountainous areas, Rainey knew. She closed her eyes. Sometime later—time had ceased to exist—she opened them again. Beck had turned onto his side and sat up on one elbow. He was gazing dreamily into her eyes.

"I've always wanted to kiss a beautiful woman up here," he murmured softly.

Rainey cocked an eyebrow. "You mean you haven't?" Surely he was joshing. Surely he had brought other women here—and kissed them all soundly.

"No, I haven't," he insisted.

He was telling the truth. She knew it.

"Well, you've got plenty of women to choose from up here." She chuckled nervously. "I think I saw—"

Before she could finish, his right hand slipped under her back, inside her T-shirt and along her bare skin to rest between her shoulder blades. His mouth came down softly on hers.

When he pulled back, moments later, she gulped. "Beck, nobody is watching. You don't have to—"

He silenced her with another kiss, longer and deeper this time. While Rainey moaned, his hand eased around to make light contact with the side of her firm, bare breast. When his thumb grazed her swollen nipple, a small cry escaped from Rainey's throat and that darned throbbing started in her lower belly again. Unable to resist, she raked her fingers through his hair.

So what if they had no audience? So what if he had a stable of women? He was one gorgeous man.

"Actually, someone *is* watching!" came a harsh female voice from behind them.

Beck's head snapped back. Blushing like crazy, Rainey pushed him away, scrambled to a sitting position and hastily rearranged her rumpled T-shirt. They both climbed to their feet. A woman stood behind them, feet planted firmly apart, arms folded, eyes spitting fire. It was the redhead from Banff.

"Hello, Francine," Beck muttered.

"Hello, Beck," the woman snarled. "Long time no see." Her eyes slid over Rainey as if she were pond scum. Addressing Beck but still glowering at Rainey, she said, "I hear you got married. A bit sudden, wasn't it?"

"Not at all." He gestured between the women. "Rainey, this is Francine Yates. Francine, my wife, Rainey."

"How do you do?" Rainey asked politely. The woman didn't respond.

"Does this mean you're out of circulation now?" Francine asked Beck.

"That's exactly what it means, Francine."

She snorted. "Sure it does." She appraised Rainey from head to toe. "Watch your heart, lady."

Anger welled up inside Rainey. Anger at the impertinence of this bitter creature, anger at Beck for finding her buttons and pushing them and anger at herself for being weak and stupid, as usual.

"Well you needn't worry. I won't trouble you further," Francine huffed, then marched off toward the picnic area. They watched her retreating back until it was just a dot on the landscape, then Beck moved toward Rainey, smiling hopefully. "Now, where were we?"

She backed away and held up her hands. "Look, Beck, this is too much. Your life is way too complicated for me."

Astonishingly, he stomped his foot. "Ah, c'mon, Rainey! She's a reporter for the *Banff Cragg and Canyon*. She came to Nakiska Ski Lodge last winter to write a piece on the ski patrol. We went out a few times. That was all."

Shaking, Rainey sat down again and reached for the backpack. "It's time for lunch. I'm starving."

"Rainey!"

Before she could censor herself, the question she was dying to ask slipped out of her mouth. "Tell me something. Did you and she…?"

"No, we didn't."

"Well, it doesn't matter anyway, does it?" It didn't matter. Really it didn't. Did it?

Beck started to laugh. "Obviously it matters to *you*."

"Does not!"

"Does too!"

She sighed. "It's okay, Beck. Honestly. Let's just eat."

8

THE NEXT FRIDAY afternoon, Rainey sat at her desk, in a stupor. She was so tired she couldn't find the energy to move the stray lock of hair dangling before her eyes. Every once in a while she blew at it, hoping it would vanish. Finally she grabbed a pair of scissors from the drawer and cut it off.

After returning home from their hike on Sunday, Beck had insisted they dine out and go to a movie—a comedy Rainey had mostly slept through.

On Monday night he dragged her, kicking and screaming, to a darts tournament in Calgary. There she drank two beers and passed out, facedown, on their table.

On Tuesday night he took her to a hockey game at the Saddledome, where she lost her purse and spent two tedious hours searching for it.

The next night he insisted they go shopping for skis, boots, bindings and poles. Rainey's legs were so sore from the hike, the store clerk had to lift them and drop them into the boots.

Last night he had the nerve to come home with two brand-new mountain bikes strapped to the trunk of the Fairlane. Rainey begged and pleaded with him to stash them in the shed, but he insisted a short ride would be good for her pain.

In retrospect the hike up the Galatea Trail had been a cakewalk. The real nightmare had been the descent. Jumping from ledge to ledge. Landing hard on her sneakered feet. Bending and straightening her creaky knees. At least the pain was down to a dull ache now.

Painkillers were useless. What she really needed was a kneecap transplant.

She picked up the laundry services contract on her desk and examined the fine print at the bottom of its first page. She had a ton of paper work to do before heading home for the weekend, but concentration eluded her. It was partly the exhaustion, she knew, and partly the constant shuffling and scraping overhead. The crew Beck had hired to pack Lilly's things and put them in storage was nothing if not noisy.

Still, she couldn't complain. Next week the wedding chapel conversion would begin. Now *that* would be noisy.

It was also partly Beck. Something had to be done about the guy.

"Mrs. Mahoney!"

Startled out of her wits, Rainey tossed the laundry contract in the air and groaned as its half-dozen pages separated and flew off in different directions. Scowling, Freda Norman tromped into the room and began to collect them. Her previously gray hair, now midnight black, was a veritable explosion of red plastic bows. Combined with a new shade of bloodred lipstick, they made her look just like Bette Davis in *What Ever Happened to Baby Jane?* Only crazier.

Rainey closed her eyes and pinched the bridge of her nose. "You know, Mrs. Norman, you *can* call me Rainey. I won't be offended."

"I wouldn't dream of it! The furnace for the west wing has quit again. I thought you should know."

"Is Beck around?"

"No. He's gone to Calgary to meet with those *bankers*."

Rainey cringed at the housekeeper's vitriolic pronunciation of the word *bankers*. The inn was a hotbed of whispered speculation about the marriage—and, by extension, the money. One version of the story had Rainey as an evil vixen who had, from thousands of miles away, cleverly targeted poor, sweet Beck Mahoney as a sucker. Another labeled Beck as the villain, a lying, scheming rogue who had ruthlessly seduced poor, sweet Rainey Miller just to get his hands on the booty.

It was amazing, she thought, how quickly gossip circulated in a small town, and how quickly people put their own spin on it. She hated it—hated having so much attention focused on her. She had enough to worry about.

"How many suites in that wing are presently occupied?" she asked Mrs. Norman.

"Only four."

"Okay, then. Let's move those guests over to the east wing and give them free room service for the evening. And please advise the night clerk not to book anyone else into the west wing tonight." She reached for the phone. "In the meantime, I'll have the furnace people come by and look at it right away."

"Very good, Mrs. Mahoney." With that, Baby Jane—ah, Mrs. Norman—turned smartly on her heel and disappeared. Rainey arranged for a service call, then tried to focus on the laundry contract again. It was a blur.

Beck. What the devil was she going to do about him? He just couldn't seem to keep his hands off her. After their tense encounter with Francine Yates, Rainey had gone out of her way to avoid physical contact with him. But it was tough. They lived together. They worked together. They occupied the same space almost all the time.

And, as much as she wanted to deny it, it wasn't all Beck. Yes sir, a touch, a glance, it didn't take much to get them both hot and bothered. They were fine at a distance, but the moment they got close, the air between them heated up like a blowtorch.

Rainey knew that in her case it was lust fueled by loneliness. With Beck, of course, it was just plain old lust.

Francine's warning to watch her heart echoed in Rainey's head a hundred times a day. It was sound advice, straight from the horse's mouth. *Take the advice!* her brain urged. *Ignore it!* her hormones countered. *Make love with the guy, just once, just to see what it would be like. You know you want to.*

Beck's solution to the problem—to the extent that Mr. Cocky thought it was a problem at all—was to keep them both busy. Moving all the time. And preferably away from the house. He was trying to be a good guy. Rainey knew that. She had told him she was vulnerable, and he was doing his best to give her space. But, honestly, couldn't he find a better way? He was wearing her out.

Rainey was flattered by his desire for her. What woman wouldn't be? But her attraction to him was nothing short of disastrous. He had too many women, and none of them seemed to care one bit that he was married now. They would always be available to him. She understood that perfectly. It did little to quell her desire for him, but she knew it meant trouble.

She simply had to get strong again. Before she did something stupid. Something à la Trevor.

"Mrs. M-m-mahoney?"

Rainey looked up. It was Hollis this time.

"What can I do for you?" She wondered what new calamity he and Mrs. Norman might have spawned. Yesterday the housekeeper had sent him out to buy hair conditioner. Instead, he came back with an *air* conditioner. "How," Rainey had asked Beck, "could he possibly have mis-heard that woman?" Beck had laughed his head off, but Rainey didn't find it funny.

Hollis's right arm jerked involuntarily. "It's Cindy, the

reservations clerk scheduled to come in at six. She just c-c-called in sick. Would you like me to fill in for her?''

"Oh, would you, Hollis?'' Rainey gave him her best smile. For all the eccentricities, Hollis was a very sweet guy. She made a mental note to do something nice for him—get him some theater tickets, or a gift certificate for the Steak Pit.

"I'd be glad to.''

"Thank you, Hollis. I won't forget it.''

Hollis and Freda. Rainey was so grateful for them! They did far more than their jobs demanded. Of course, Mrs. Norman believed the Haven was rightfully hers, and Hollis, for whatever reason, did whatever the housekeeper asked him to do. But Rainey didn't mind one bit what motivated that pair. The results were wonderful.

Her thoughts bounced back to Trevor. Five times she had called the jerk since Monday, three times at his office and twice at home. Each time she had gotten only his voice mail, and each time she had quickly hung up. There was no way she was simply leaving her name and a brief message and the time she had called. Where was the fun in that? If she couldn't see Trevor's reaction to her news, she was at least going to get the satisfaction of hearing it.

Yesterday morning, on Beck's insistence, she had finally called her parents to give them the news. "They'll find out sooner or later,'' he lectured, reinforcing what she already knew but somehow couldn't get her brain around. "Wouldn't it be better if they heard it from you?''

"Why do they have to know at all?'' she argued. "We're getting divorced in a few months, anyway.''

"Rainey…'' His eyes urged her not to be so damned childish.

"Oh, Beck, you just don't know what they're like. If they thought I got married without inviting them to the wedding, they'd be horrified.''

"Then tell them the truth."

"What? That I got married for money? That's even worse!"

"You have to tell them something."

She pouted. "What about your parents, huh?"

"I've already told them. They were shocked at first, but they came around." He paused and stared over her head for a moment, pondering something. "Rather quickly, come to think of it."

"Oh, all right then!"

After twenty minutes of lip-chomping indecisiveness, she had finally dialed her parents' number in Toronto, only to get their usual, cheerful recorded message. Determined to get it over with, she called their next-door neighbors and was told the Millers had gone to Belize for two weeks. It was no surprise. They traveled often these days.

She still hadn't told Dana about the marriage. Worse, she hadn't told Beck that she hadn't told Dana. He assumed she had. Or, wait a minute, was she just assuming that he had assumed that she had? Anyway, as far as Rainey was concerned, ignorance was bliss. When you got right down to it, what Dana didn't know, and what Beck didn't know that Dana didn't know, wouldn't hurt either of them.

That's it, Rainey thought. I've lost it. I'm certifiable.

As she tidied her desk and prepared to leave for the weekend, a silly notion popped into her head. What if Beck really did have feelings for her? What if his attraction to her was more than just animal attraction? Something deeper, more meaningful. More…long-lasting.

It *was* possible. Sometimes she caught him looking at her in a way that suggested more than just a casual, physical interest. Did he look at other women that way? She tried to recall an instance, but nothing came to mind. For that matter, she wasn't with him every minute of the day. Heaven only knew what he was doing on his own time.

Lost in thought, she went to the window and stared out at the parking lot, the trees, the gray sky. Nah, he didn't care for her, not really. It was just her imagination setting her up for another disaster. Beck Mahoney could have a different woman every day of the week. Why would a man with that kind of selection settle for her? For any one woman, for that matter?

Too bad she couldn't just come right out and ask him. Many a woman had gotten exactly what she deserved after asking that question: a vague but deceptively positive response, noncommittal but just strong enough to give false hope. Or worse, an outright lie: *Sure, I love you.*

But what if...

No, it was sneaky.

Then again...

No. It was worse than sneaky. It was risky.

But still...

Okay, already! What if she suggested he continue to see other women? If he jumped at the chance, wouldn't she find out if he really did care for her? Wouldn't it settle the issue once and for all? Not that it needed settling, of course. It wasn't like she was in love with the guy, or anything.

"Mrs. Mahoney?"

Rainey turned around. A young man in denim coveralls came into the room, clutching an envelope. One of the workers from the moving and storage company.

Rainey eyed the envelope. "What can I do for you?"

He handed it to her. "We found this in one of the kitchen cupboards. It's addressed to you." Rainey turned the sealed envelope over in her hand. Her name was scrawled across its face—in Lilly's shaky handwriting. What the devil? Another letter? She thanked the young man and waited for him to leave.

Brows furrowed, she opened the envelope and pulled out a single sheet of Lilly's floral stationery. The letter read:

My dearest darling niece,

I am sure that by now you have had the chance to get to know Beck a little. I am also sure that you have some reservations—no pun intended, dear—about him. You will have noticed that Beck is very attractive to members of the opposite sex. Don't let this bother you. Beck may seem as flaky as puff pastry, but I assure you he is really a man of substance. I am confident you will come to realize that.

> Good luck and God bless,
> Your Aunt Lilly

Rainey was dumbstruck. Why, she wondered, would Lilly have speculated that she might be alarmed by Beck's prowess with women? It didn't make sense. Unless, of course, Lilly knew from experience that all women, her niece included, eventually lost their hearts to the guy. But if that were the case, why wouldn't she have advised Rainey to be careful, the way Francine had? It was almost as if Lilly *wanted* Rainey to fall in love with Beck.

She debated for a moment whether or not to show the letter to Beck, then decided against it. He would just make some sarcastic remark about Rainey heeding good advice when she read it. She resealed the envelope and put it in her top desk drawer.

On her way past the walk-in linen closet in the main corridor, she paused. For a second, she thought she had heard laughter coming from inside the small room. The linen closet wasn't exactly a funny place.

"Freedy, sweetie, you really do it for me," a male voice whispered hoarsely. It sounded like Hollis.

Rainey frowned. *Freedy, sweetie?*

"Holly, honey, you charmer, you. Come to mama."

Holly, honey? Come to mama? Rainey heard smooching

sounds followed by muffled giggles. Little moans and sighs. Hollis and Freda. What a hoot!

Choking back a laugh, she debated whether or not to crack the door and poke her head into the room. She tiptoed on past and kept going.

At the end of the day, she decided, some things were better left alone.

WHEN RAINEY arrived home, the house was dark.

Grateful for the solitude, she took a long, hot shower, relishing the heat and the steam filling up the glass enclosure. The week's exertions slid off her and ran down the drain, leaving her clean and relaxed. Afterward she donned a long, loose cotton nightgown and her slippers and bathrobe. If Beck wanted to go out tonight, he would definitely be going alone.

Just moments after she curled up in the corner of the old plaid sofa and opened a book, the Fairlane pulled into the driveway. Rainey set the book down and braced herself for one of Beck's dramatic entrances. Sure enough, he bounded into the house like a cat on the fly.

In the foyer he grabbed an umbrella from the stand and, wielding it like a cane, danced his way into the living room. "We're in the money," he sang. Rainey laughed. His singing voice was awful.

"You mean *you're* in the money," she reminded him.

"Hey, not just me, babe. You, too." He went to the kitchen and poured himself a glass of water.

Rainey blinked. *Babe?* Say what?

"So," he said before she could react to that outrageously inappropriate endearment, "what say we go out and celebrate tonight? Dinner at the Steak Pit? Maybe a little dancing? Whaddaya say?"

Rainey gasped. "Not on your life, Beck Mahoney!"

He winked at her. "Gotcha!" Laughing and sighing all

at once, he collapsed into the chair across from her. "Relax, I was just kidding. I couldn't dance at my own funeral tonight."

"Well, that's good, because I haven't got the energy to kill you. The desire, maybe, but not the energy."

Ignoring her sarcasm, he took a deep breath and released it slowly. Rainey saw how tired he was. All week he had alternated between giving massages at the inn and meeting with bankers and lawyers and architects and engineers and renovations contractors. Mind you, he was late for all the meetings, but he did manage to show up for them.

He sat up and rubbed his hands together. "What say we order a pizza, turn on the tube and chill out?"

"No problem. I can chill till your little heart desires."

While Beck took a shower, Rainey ordered the pizza and fetched some firewood from the bin on the front porch. In the blink of an eye the sky had gone from gray to black and a strong wind had come up. A storm was moving in. What a perfect night, she thought, for a pizza, a little TV and a crackling fire.

After Beck came back downstairs, looking handsome and smelling like sandalwood—it was a soap, she now knew—they talked quietly for a while. He told her about his meeting with the bankers—they would get their money on Monday—and about the cost estimates he had gathered. They had guessed right. Salvaging the inn wasn't going to be cheap.

Leaning across the work island, Rainey told him about the furnace problem, and he shrugged. Soon, he said, they would have new furnaces, new plumbing, new everything.

"Beck," she asked as he fetched two plates from the cupboard, "is there something going on between Freda and Hollis?"

He flashed her a look of incredulity. "You mean you didn't know?"

"No. How would I know?"

He shook his head. "Of course you wouldn't know." Affecting an exaggerated air of confidentiality, he glanced right and left as if spies were about. Then he leaned forward and whispered, "They're having an affair."

"I gathered that much. But what do you mean by 'affair?' They're not married—I mean, to other people—right?"

"Nope." He looked in the drawer for cutlery. "Hollis has never been married, and Freda's been widowed since the moon landing."

"Well, then, why don't *they* just get married? I mean, why all the sneaking around?"

He paused to consider the question. "Well, this is just speculation, but I think they like the thrill of it. I think it turns them on."

"How long has it been going on?"

"About twenty years."

"What?"

"No word of a lie. It's a local legend." Beck took a bottle of red wine from the wine rack and filled two glasses. He handed one to Rainey.

She rolled her eyes. "Okay. Whatever. And another thing. All those maladies Hollis has—the twitching and stuttering. What's that about?"

Beck dropped his chin. "I ask you—if you were sleeping with Freda Norman, wouldn't you develop a twitch?"

While Rainey entertained him with her thoughts on what sleeping with the buxom housekeeper would lead to, Beck got a fire started and turned on the television. An old movie was playing. Rainey peered at it for a moment, then started to laugh. It was *What Ever Happened to Baby Jane?*

Beck frowned. "What's so funny?"

"Nothing. It's a private joke."

The pizza arrived and they ate it with relish, sometimes

chatting, sometimes glancing at the movie. Between bites of her food and the occasional sip of wine, Rainey searched her brain for a way to present her suggestion. She had to know. But the timing wasn't right, somehow. It was a pleasant evening. The pizza was good, the fire warm and inviting. They were so relaxed, so…oh dear, she thought, so *content* together.

Then again, maybe she should just get it over with.

Taking her dish to the sink, she cleared her throat and began, "Ah, Beck…" Just then a sharp pain shot through her right knee and her leg buckled. As the wineglass fell into the sink and shattered, she grabbed the edge of the counter for support.

"Hey!" Beck quickly reached out to steady her. "Are those knees still bothering you?"

Rainey didn't want to be a baby about it, but yes, she admitted, the aching was still there.

"Don't move. I'll be right back."

Uh-oh, Rainey thought as he went into the small bedroom behind the kitchen, what's he up to? Moments later he emerged with a collapsible massage table. Whistling, he set it up in the middle of the living room. While Rainey stared at it, horror-struck, he went into the bedroom again and came back with a bottle of body oil, a big bath towel and a folded sheet.

"Okay, woman, out of those clothes," he ordered.

An alarm bell sounded in Rainey's head. "Oh, Beck, I don't think this is such a good idea." She licked her lips and swallowed nervously.

His tone and expression were deadly serious. "I do. Off with them. Now."

"But it's only my knees!"

"Now!"

"Okay, okay!" Rainey reluctantly went into the bedroom, stripped and wrapped the towel around herself. She returned to the living room and climbed up on the table.

Beck had turned the television off and placed the bottle of oil in a pot of hot water. He was busy twirling it. "On your stomach," he instructed, and Rainey turned over. He spread the sheet over her body, then reached under it and relieved her of the towel. Sheet or no sheet, she felt naked, exposed, helpless.

After rolling the sheet up to her knees he coated her right foot with the warm oil and gently began to massage it. "Relax," he murmured. Rainey, taut as a piano wire, went limp.

His fingers were magic. Simply magic. Smooth as butter, they slipped in and out of the gaps between her toes, along her arch, around her heel, up to her ankle and back again. Rainey's skin tingled from his touch. As he gradually moved upward and began to knead her calf, the tingling intensified and shot straight up her leg to...

"How does that feel?" Beck asked in a soft, low voice.

"Wonderful," she managed to mumble. It came out sounding like "womberfulb," but she couldn't help that. Her body and brain together had dissolved into mush. No wonder his clients at the inn raved about Beck.

As the fire crackled inside and the storm raged outside, he discreetly raised the sheet to the underside of her bottom, lifted her left leg and set it down again—a little to the left of where it had been. Rainey tensed and he urged her to relax again. It's all or nothing with this guy, she thought, total surrender or total resistance. She relaxed.

As his incredible hands worked their magic on her upper leg and thigh, Rainey felt the old stirring in her loins again. It was more than a pleasant sensation this time. It was an ache, a persistent, throbbing ache that threatened to rob her of all reason.

Finished with her legs, Beck draped the sheet over them

again, then folded it back from her shoulders to her waist. Rainey became acutely aware of her bare breasts pressed against the padded table. Of the skin on her back, her neck, her bottom. Whistling softly, Beck gently kneaded her back muscles, moving in a straight line from her neck to the sensitive curve of her waist, then from side to side. A soft moan escaped Rainey's lips.

When his hands moved to her sides, his touch became more sensuous than therapeutic. His fingertips grazed the sides of her breasts, then skimmed downward to her waist and back again. The sensation was so utterly, profoundly erotic that Rainey actually shuddered. Limp as a wet noodle, she melted into the table.

It would be so easy, so very easy, to just surrender to the man. In every sense of that word. Not just sexually, but mentally, emotionally, spiritually. All the way. It would be heaven on earth.

No man had ever made her feel the way this man made her feel. No man had ever done what he had just done.

If only it could be this way forever.

9

BECK STOOD BACK as Rainey, flushed and suddenly very, very pretty, slid sideways off the massage table to a standing position, holding the sheet around herself. She looked as though she didn't know whether to ravage him or run for the ski hills.

Half mad with desire, he took a tentative step toward her. The way she had just responded to his touch, the way she had aroused him... Wow.

He held out his arms. "Rainey, I..."

"Beck, I can't. It's not—not—"

His heart sank. "Not what? Not right? Not time? Or is it just not me that you want? Tell me, Rainey."

"I don't want to get hurt!" Her eyes begged him to understand.

"What makes you think I'm going to hurt you?"

"What makes you think you're not?"

Exasperated, he threw his hands in the air. Surely her vulnerability didn't cut this deep? She was glaring at him, waiting for something. For what? A promise to leave her alone, once and for all? That must be it. She hadn't liked him right from the start, and she wasn't going to change her mind.

"Look, Beck, I know you're a man..." she began.

"Thanks for noticing!"

"Let me finish. I know you're a man and that you have, ah, needs. So, I've been thinking..."

"Thinking what? What have you been thinking?"

She hesitated, bit her lower lip. Behind Beck, the rain pounded the tall windows flanking the fireplace. A bolt of lightning shattered the night sky, momentarily startling them both.

"I've been thinking," she said resolutely, "that you should find another way to satisfy them."

"Find another way? What does that mean?"

"I'm saying, Beck, that just because we're married there's no reason why you should curtail your normal, um, activities. I mean, after all, we're not really married."

Beck was stumped. The only "activities" he could imagine now were the ones that involved the two of them—and a lot of noise and sweat. "Spell it out, woman."

She heaved a sigh. "Oh, Beck, you know what I mean."

When it finally registered, he let out a snort. "Are you nuts? Do you really want me to sleep with other women?"

Looking like a confused little girl, Rainey opened her mouth to respond, then closed it again. "I want you to be happy," she finally muttered.

Hey, now they were getting somewhere! "Okay, then. Make love with me, Rainey. I guarantee you it will make me happy." He grinned at her, sensing it was a mistake. Sure enough, it was.

Bristling, she tromped into the living room, her oily feet slipping on the oak floor, and burrowed into the corner of the sofa. "I told you I'm vulnerable. A decent man would respect that. He would…he would wait."

Before he could stop it, Beck's mouth spit out the first words that popped into his mind. "Are you suggesting that if I wait for you there will eventually be a payoff?" Rainey's immediate and sharp intake of breath could probably be heard in the town center. Damn. The words had sounded funny in his head.

"Beck Mahoney, I am not some slot machine!"

Gesturing wildly with his hands, he began to pace around

the room. "Okay then, what exactly are you suggesting? That I date other women? That I be seen around town with them? Don't you think there's enough gossip about us now?"

Her eyes grew so large Beck thought they might actually launch themselves into outer space. "I'm not suggesting that at all. I know...what we have to do. I was just thinking that...if you were, you know, discreet about it...say, if you went to Banff...or something..."

Okay, that was it. What the hell was going on here? She had stumbled over her words. Rainey never stumbled. Next to his mother, she was the most articulate woman he'd ever met. Rock-solid sure of every syllable she uttered. Could she actually be *bluffing?*

He took a hard look at her. Doubt clouded her eyes. She was nervous and jittery. Yeah, dammit, she *was* bluffing. She no more wanted him to see other women than to strip naked and streak through the inn. So why the bluff? It didn't make sense. But hey, if she wanted to play a game, then fine, he would play along. For a while.

"Banff!" he barked with no conviction whatsoever. "For Pete's sake, woman, where are you from? The big city? We're just as famous in Banff, you and me, as we are here. Discretion is a joke."

Rainey clutched at her sheet and adopted a stubborn pout. "Well, that will just have to be your problem!"

"Okay, fine then." He pretended to fume. "If that's what you want, that's what—" Stepping forward, he smartly stubbed his big toe on the leg of his reading chair. "Ouch!" he yelped, and reached down to grab it.

"Are you okay?" Rainey asked. "Does it hurt?"

"I'm fine," he lied. Grimacing, he fell back into the offending chair and began to rub his toe.

They fell silent for a moment, and the tension in the air

abruptly dissipated. Beck ventured a wry smile. "Where were we?"

Visibly relieved, she smiled back. "We were shipping you to another planet so you could sleep with other women."

"Oh, yeah, right." He dropped his foot and sat back. Heaved a sigh. "Has it occurred to you, Rainey that what I really want…"

Two bright lights suddenly danced across the wall. Frowning, Beck jumped up and hobbled over to the window. Rainey joined him. A car had pulled into the driveway.

He peered through the wet glass. "Oh, no!" He looked at Rainey, horror-struck. "It's my parents! What are they doing here?"

"I don't know! What should we do?"

He looked around frantically—at Rainey's toga, the massage table, the oil, the pizza box, the broken glass. His eyes traveled up the stairs. "The bedrooms! The separate bedrooms! Quick, we have to move your things into my room!"

"But why?"

"Because they've driven down from Edmonton. They'll want to stay overnight. Quick!"

In a flash they raced up the stairs, Beck flinching from the pain in his toe, Rainey clutching at her toga. Her feet slipped once on the hardwood treads, and she nearly toppled backward. Together they charged into her room. While she hastily pulled together her unmade bed, Beck yanked her clothes from the closet.

They heard the sound of car doors slamming, low voices, footsteps on the walk.

"Hurry!" Beck ran into his room, threw Rainey's dresses on the bed, and rushed back into her room. Still struggling to hold the sheet in place, Rainey hastily emptied her drawers and stuffed her things into Beck's outstretched arms. He shot next door again, leaving her to scoop up her jewelry and toiletries with one hand. Shrieking, she fumbled and dropped a few things. Beck skidded back into her room, dropped to his knees and rounded them up.

The doorbell sounded.

Beck scrambled to his feet, flew back into his room, threw the wayward items on top of the dresses, and reappeared, red-faced and panting, in Rainey's room. "Okay, you put some clothes on and I'll get the door." Before turning to leave, he asked, "Are we still fighting?"

"No!" Rainey wheezed. "We can't. It's show time."

"Good, 'cause I don't want to fight." He grabbed her around the waist and planted a fast, hard kiss on her lips. Then he dashed downstairs.

BECK PAUSED in the foyer and took a few deep breaths to slow his heart down. Man, oh, man. What was this about? Only twice in the twelve years since he had left home had his parents dropped in on him unannounced. It was totally out of character for them.

And talk about bad timing. He wasn't through with Rainey Miller yet. No sir. He had more to say to her—later tonight. If she thought he wasn't going to call her ludicrous bluff, she was sadly mistaken.

He pasted a smile on his face and opened the door.

His mother and father stood side by side on the porch, striking their usual odd contrast. Earl Mahoney was tall—six-three at least. Streaks of gray adorned his dark-blond hair. Since taking retirement five years ago, he had let it grow a bit long, and he looked more like an aging hippie than a distinguished senior citizen. His body, once powerful, was a little soft from too much rich food and television sports. Martha Mahoney was dark-haired, thanks to science, two heads shorter and a hundred pounds lighter.

"Beckett, darling!" Smiling sweetly and reeking of musky perfume, she reached up and gave him a suffocating hug. "Sorry we didn't call, but we wanted to surprise you."

"No problem," he lied. "It's great to see you, Mom."

Vibrating with her usual energy, she brushed Beck off and sailed into the living room. "Where's the *big* surprise?" She looked around, her eagle eyes resting briefly on the massage table and the body oil before going back on scan.

"Son." Earl Mahoney gave Beck a hasty, awkward hug. Before you could say ESPN, he was cross-legged in Beck's chair, his right hand inching ever so slowly toward the remote control on the coffee table.

From behind his back, Martha barked, "Don't even dream of it!"

Beck had to laugh. How did she *do* that?

A look of long suffering developed on Earl's face. "But, Martha," he whined, "there's a hockey game on tonight. The Flames and the Oilers."

She whirled around. "I don't care if it's the Greeks and the Turks! We're here to meet our new daughter-in-law." Turning to Beck, she asked, "Where is Rainey?"

"Upstairs, changing."

As if on cue, Rainey emerged and made her way gingerly down the stairs. Beck beamed, and not just for the benefit of their company. In pale blue jeans—snug but not too snug—and a soft pink sweater, she displayed a wholesome, girl-next-door kind of beauty. She had pulled her hair back and tied it with a pink ribbon, and donned little gold earrings and a matching bracelet. Any man would be proud to have her as his wife, he thought, any man at all.

Hmm. Maybe he should tell her that. Maybe he should pay her a compliment once in a while, instead of just drooling on her. Then again, compliments wouldn't count for much after he gave her what she deserved—later tonight.

Beck's father rose to greet her. His mother held out her arms and Rainey, nervous and self-conscious, Beck saw, went into them. The women hugged. Releasing her but still holding her at arm's length, Martha gushed, "Why, Beckett, she's darling, simply darling."

Rainey smiled politely. "Thank you, Mrs. Mahoney."

"Oh, don't be silly. Call me Martha."

Never one to gush, Beck's father stuck out his hand. "Pleasure to meet you, Rainey. How do you feel about hockey?"

"That's enough, Earl!" Martha snapped.

He sighed. "Just testing, dear. Just testing."

The elder Mahoneys made themselves comfortable at the kitchen table. Beck quickly disposed of the massage table and Rainey tidied up the kitchen. While Earl drummed his fingers on the table and gazed longingly at the television, Martha spewed an unbroken stream of small talk about their long drive down from Edmonton—the kamikaze traffic, the dreadful weather, the appalling restaurant food. It was all just a mindless preamble, Beck knew, to the real agenda.

Sure enough, as Rainey put a pot of coffee on and Beck sat down at the table, Martha, the poster girl for directness cut right to the chase. "Enough chitchat. I want the two of you to know how very disappointed we are in you." Her lower lip actually trembled.

Beck locked eyes with Rainey. *Here comes the disappointment,* he silently communicated to her.

You're on your own, she communicated back.

"Mom…" Beck began, then fell silent. Why bother?

Martha waved a meticulously manicured hand in the air. "Rushing off and getting married like that! Depriving us of a real wedding. Honestly, Beckett, how could you?" She made it sound as if he had robbed a little old lady at gunpoint.

"How 'bout if we just turn the set on and keep the volume low?" Earl asked hopefully.

Ignoring him, Martha continued, "Well, it won't do. You'll simply have to get married again, and properly this time." She gave the tabletop a resounding slap.

Seeing the horror on Rainey's face, it was all Beck could do to keep from howling. He could just hear her thinking: *Married? Again? I'd rather have shingles!*

"Ah, well, we're pretty happy with just one wedding," he told his mother. "Aren't we, Rainey?"

"More than," she drawled.

Martha sniffed. "Well, we'll see about that."

"Could I just check the score?" Earl asked.

"No!" Faster than lightning, Martha's scowl gave way to a toothy smile. "So, dear," she said to Rainey, "tell us all about your plans."

Caught off guard, Rainey stammered, "Ah…plans?"

"Yes, dear, your plans for the future. What about children?"

"Children?" Panicked, Rainey looked to Beck for help. He pursed his lips and looked away, whistling a tune.

"Yes, you know," Martha persisted. "Little ones. Grandchildren. We have three now, but they're all boys. We want at least one girl."

To Beck's absolute surprise and delight, Rainey rose to the occasion. "Well, actually, Martha, we were thinking that four would be a nice round number. Weren't we, Beck?" She grinned mischievously at him.

"Absolutely," he concurred. "Two boys and two girls."

Martha lit up like a firefly. "Perfect! And what about vacations? I assume we'll see you both at the cottage next summer?"

Earl cleared his throat. "You know, it's intermission now. I could just catch the last two periods."

Uh-oh, thought Beck. His mother closed her eyes tightly.

He knew she was silently counting to ten. "For… crying…out…loud…Earl. Turn the darn thing on!"

"Thanks, dear." He kissed the top of her shellacked bouffant and made a beeline for the remote control.

Beck ran a hand through his hair. "Actually, Mom, we're not sure where we'll be next summer. Are we, Rainey?"

"That's right." She dazzled him with a very wifely look. "But the cottage would be nice. Wouldn't it, sweetie?"

"It would." He blew her a little kiss.

The coffee machine gurgled and Rainey poured four cups, delivering one to his father in the living room. While his mother babbled on, Beck watched his wife move through the room. Man, she was a looker! That dark, shiny hair, that creamy complexion, that pouty mouth. It was too pink, though, too smooth. He wanted to see it all red and puffy from too much kissing.

Not tonight, though.

Rainey sat down and crossed her hands on the tabletop. Eager to change the subject, Beck said, "So, Mom, what do you think about Lilly Miller leaving me half the Honeymoon Haven?"

Something remarkable happened then, something Beck had never seen before. His mother, Martha Jean Mahoney, queen of the half-baked opinion, spinner of tall tales, ruthless wielder of maternal power, actually stalled. First Rainey, now her. Beck was puzzled. She'd had plenty of time to think about it, and was normally all too happy to throw in her two cents.

"Mom?" he asked.

Within seconds, her sharp features radiated a shaky confidence. "Why, it's wonderful! A bit surprising, though, don't you think?"

Beck nodded. "More than a bit, but then again, life is full of surprises, isn't it?" He gazed lovingly at Rainey, placed one hand affectionately over hers and caressed her knuckles with his thumb. Her skin was silky smooth. This show time stuff was okay. At least it gave him an excuse to touch her.

"Well, anyway," Martha blundered on, "Lilly was right. You're…" Reddening slightly, she trailed off there and looked around, as if for inspiration. Beck and Rainey exchanged a look.

When, Beck wondered, had his mother been talking to Lilly? And what about? They hardly knew one another. "Right about what, Mom? What was Lilly right about?"

Martha licked her lips. Beck could just see the little spiders in her brain, spinning a tale.

"Well, it was just, ah, just a good decision, wasn't it?" It sounded ludicrous and Beck knew that she knew it. "I mean, look at how well things turned out!" Oozing saccharine, she reached across the table and placed her hand atop Beck's hand, which still rested atop Rainey's hands. One more hand, Beck thought, and we'll have a huddle.

Clearly desperate to move along, Martha abruptly dismissed Beck and devoted her full attention to Rainey. It was just the excuse he needed to flake out on the sofa and exchange grunts with his father. Before making the move, he glanced at Rainey to make sure she was okay with it. His mother could be intimidating, and this had to be hard enough on Rainey.

But she and Martha had already linked hands and were head to head. He smiled. They made a nice picture. Two beautiful women getting to know one another. It was enough to make a guy mushy.

The women talked for over an hour. Getting drowsier by the minute, Beck kept one ear tuned to the game, the other tuned to their conversation. At one point he overheard his mother sniff, "I certainly hope you'll be redecorating, dear.'' Beck groaned. Terrific. There went his wagon wheel coffee table.

A century later it was finally bedtime. Beck was beat and knew that Rainey was, too. While she got ready for bed in his room, he got his parents settled in her room. Before closing the door, his mother gave him another spine-crushing hug. ''She's very sweet, Beckett. I wish you all the best.''

''Thanks, Mom.''

Alone in the hall, he paused to switch gears from half-crazy mother to certifiably nutty wife. For the life of him, he couldn't understand why Rainey would suggest he get his ''needs'' met elsewhere. It had to be some kind of test. That, of course, could only mean one thing....

He opened the door and eased into the dark bedroom.

She lay under the blankets, not making a sound. As his eyes gradually adjusted to the darkness, Beck spied the collar of her long cotton nightgown. Too bad. He'd kinda been hoping for a little bare flesh.

Then again, it was probably for the best.

He peeled off his sweatshirt, hiked up his sweatpants and crawled in beside her. She smelled like fragrant oil and perfume, and her body gave off an intoxicating heat. He hoped she would come to her senses in the middle of the night and realize she loved him—then show him that she loved him. He might just let her.

''Beck,'' Rainey whispered, ''this is awful.'' She sounded distraught.

For one dizzy moment he thought she had actually read his mind. Then he realized she was talking about their *general* situation. ''I know,'' he whispered back. ''It's a mess.''

''We've lied to everybody.'' Her voice cracked a little.

''Hey, that's not true!'' He struggled to keep his voice down. ''We told Grandma we had decided to marry. That was true. Nate asked me how we fell in love so fast, and I said I didn't know. That was also true. We haven't told a single lie to anybody.''

"For crying out loud, Beck, we just told your parents we want four children!''

"No we didn't. You said four is a nice round number, and it is.'' *Besides, I want those babies. I want them with you.*

"That's not the point. The point is, when we file for divorce, people are going to be hurt, and it will be our fault.'' She sniffled.

Oh, man, if there was one thing Beck couldn't take, it was a woman in tears. But he was tired of this nonsense. He didn't want any damn divorce. He wanted Rainey, badly, and all the way. It wasn't his fault if she didn't believe that.

It was that jerk in Toronto. Devon or Kevin or Trevor, or whatever his name was. If Beck ever met the guy, he would strangle him straightaway. No handshake. No nice-to-meet-you banter. Just instant, ruthless homicide.

Then again, the logical part of his brain reasoned, the guy was partly responsible for bringing Rainey into his life. If he hadn't broken her heart, who knew where she would be right now? Married to the cad, most likely, and living in some suburb. In a way, Beck owed the man a debt of gratitude. Which he would graciously acknowledge, right before he killed him.

Rainey sniffled again. Beck fought a powerful urge to take her in his arms and comfort her.

He lost the battle.

"Come here.'' He lifted his arm so she could move next to him. Reluctant at first, she eventually snuggled up to him, resting her arm lightly across his chest. Her warm, bare skin felt wonderful against his.

For a few minutes, they lay quietly together, Rainey

whimpering, Beck wrestling with contradictory desires: one, to comfort her all the way; two, to make his stand and be done with it.

Dammit, he had planned to take her up on her ridiculous offer, but the timing wasn't right. It was one thing to be tired and fed up, another thing to be a complete jerk.

Not in a million years would he actually do it, of course. He didn't need to. What he wanted was right here beside him. But *she* didn't need to know that. It wouldn't hurt his cause one bit to have her think he was out with other women. Hell, she deserved it. It was *her* idea.

And who knew? It might actually spark a little jealousy. If it did, Beck would know, once and for all, how she felt about him.

Enough already! Tears or no tears, he couldn't wait any longer. He had to know now. "Rainey?" he whispered.

She started to snore.

10

CHOMP. Blow. Smack!

"A shtag party?" Rainey covered the receiver with her free hand and frowned at Beck. Looking incongruously sexy in paint-splattered jeans and a filthy, threadbare T-shirt, he slouched in the doorway to her office, blowing bubbles. Two weeks of working with construction crews had given him a few bad habits—cursing like a sailor, telling ribald jokes, drinking beer at lunchtime and chewing gum. The gum alone was driving her crazy.

"What on earth is a shtag party?" she asked him.

The giant bubble Beck had just blown erupted with a resounding smack and plastered itself across his mouth and chin. While Rainey watched, horrified, he used one grubby finger to stuff it back into his mouth.

"Ah, well, as near as I can figure, it's a cross between a stag party and a wedding shower. The point is, they're doing it today."

"Today!"

Beck raised the same dirty finger to his lips and shushed her. "Keep it down. We're not supposed to know about it." He glanced right and left down the hallway behind him.

Rainey groaned. How much more of this could she take? They had been married for three weeks now. Despite all the gossip, people stopped them everywhere they went to offer congratulations and best wishes for a happy future. Cards and flowers arrived daily at the house. Last week the Women of the Wapiti had thrown a tea party for Rainey and presented her with a scandalously skimpy white silk camisole and matching G-string. Which, she later learned, Freda Norman and Flo Mahoney had selected, giggling like schoolgirls.

Holding up one hand to stay Beck, she spoke into the receiver again. "Dana. I have to go. There's a crisis."

"Sweetie, this is ridiculous. Every time I call, you're in the middle of a crisis. What is it now?"

"We'll talk later. I really have to go."

"Rainey, I'm starting to get really worried about you. It isn't like you to be so stressed all the time. I'm coming out there. I'm booking a flight this minute."

"No! It isn't necessary!" Rainey lowered her voice. "Really, it isn't."

Beck came into the room and closed the door behind him. Chewing furiously, he plopped down on the chair across from Rainey's desk.

"Rainey, don't go yet!" Dana begged. "I really need to talk to you about something. It's about...poor Trev. Frankly, sweetie, I think you were a little hard on him."

Rainey blinked. *Poor Trev?* Since when was Trevor *poor Trev?* Since when was he anything to Dana? And what did she mean by "hard on him?" After what he had done? Puh-leez! "Listen, Dana, I can't talk about this right now. I'm sorry. I'll have to call you back."

Dana sighed. "Okay. It can wait a little longer. I guess."

After Rainey hung up, Beck shifted the huge wad of gum to his right cheek. The effect was that of a chipmunk storing nuts. He raised his eyebrows. "Brace yourself, babe. That was the good news."

She held her breath and waited.

"The bad news is, not only are they doing it today, but they're doing it at our house."

"What!" Rainey practically jumped out of her skin. "At our house?" Oops, when had she started thinking of Beck's house as her house? That had to stop. "But why our... I mean *your* house? Why not somewhere else?"

"Well, apparently, we have the only house in town big enough to hold everybody."

"Good grief, how many people are we talking about?"

"The rumor mill says fifty. Could be more, though."

Fifty people! Rainey closed her eyes and prayed for strength. "When?" She looked at her watch. It was four o'clock now. So much for a nice, quiet Friday evening at home.

Beck waved a hand in the air. "Take it easy. Word has it that it's going to be a sneak attack, around seven o'clock. We have plenty of time to get ready."

"Oh, Beck." Rainey slumped against the back of her chair. "If I'd known that things were going to get this complicated, I would have sold the inn and gone right back to Toronto!"

"What?" He gave her one of his phony hurtful looks. "And missed out on being married to me?" He grinned and blew another bubble.

"Beck Mahoney, take that gum out of your mouth right now!"

"Yes, ma'am." Looking sheepish, he rose and tossed it into the wastepaper basket. On his way to the door, he said, "Where's your sense of fun, woman? I don't know about you, but I'm in the mood for a party. I've been working my buns off."

Ooh, too good to resist. Tongue planted firmly in cheek, Rainey made a big show of appraising the adorable buns in question. "I don't know about that," she murmured. "They look fine to me."

His big amber eyes registered surprise. "Why, Rainey Miller, is it just my imagination, or are you actually developing a sense of humor?"

"Do I have a choice?"

"No, you don't." He paused in the doorway. "Tell you what. I'll help the guys clean up, we'll head home in about an hour, and when they show up we'll play dumb. Act like we didn't suspect a thing."

Rainey snorted. Acting. If they got any better at it, they'd be able to audition for the local Shakespeare Festival.

After Beck left, Rainey ran a hand through her hair and stared at the wall. She debated whether to indulge in a mild anxiety attack or just loosen up and make the best of it. Oh, darn, maybe she was being a bit of a stuffed shirt. It was a lovely gesture, really. And it wasn't the party planners' fault if she and Beck were a couple of shameless frauds.

But, oh, if the divorce was going to be as complicated as this darned marriage, rough times lay ahead.

Some things, she had to admit, were going well. Working flat out, six days a week, Beck had kept the renovation project right on schedule. The new furnaces were up and running, and the inn was toasty warm. The wedding chapel was in progress, and the west wing had been cleared in preparation for a complete teardown. It was mid-October. With any luck, they would be able to reopen that wing in time for Christmas, then close the east wing and renovate it in time for the spring wedding rush. The incessant pounding and drilling, the horrible throat-choking dust, the noxious paint fumes—all would cease and things would get back to normal. Whatever normal was in this crazy place.

Beck, she had discovered in the past few weeks, had less than zero interest in the daily operation of the inn. Couldn't distinguish an invoice from an ad flyer. Didn't know a clean towel from a paint rag. Couldn't care less whether the guests were comfortable or not. In fact, he regarded them as pesky intruders.

But that was okay. Rainey handled all those matters with

increasing ease, but she didn't know a thing about renovations. In a way, they made a good team.

Everything else was out of control.

Beck's family, just for starters. On the morning after their surprise visit, his parents had insisted on taking the newlyweds to Calgary for an expensive brunch. All through the meal, Martha had gushed over Rainey. So smart! So pretty! Beck was lucky to have her, and Martha was going to personally make certain that he never forgot it.

Then there was the issue of Rainey's parents. She still hadn't told them about the marriage, and, of course, she hadn't told Beck that she hadn't told them.

She reached into her desk drawer. Next to Lilly's cryptic letters was a postcard they had sent her from Belize:

Darling daughter,

Having fun in the sun. Hope you are enjoying your new life in the west. Please let us know when you are holding the party for Lilly. We can't wait to see you.

Love, Mom and Dad

Rainey couldn't believe she had overlooked this little detail. Of course, they would want to attend the party. Why hadn't she thought of that? It was because she was in full-blown denial, that's why. Until now she had been convinced that she could just slip the marriage right past them with no harm done. They would never know that she had once been married and divorced, and what they didn't know wouldn't bother them.

They were back in Toronto now. The smart thing, she knew, would be to call them and get it over with. But every time she summoned enough nerve to reach for the phone, some new and urgent matter arose that demanded her immediate attention. Anyway, she would get around to it. Really, she would.

As for the situation at home—ever since his parents' surprise visit, Beck hadn't laid a finger on her except when company was present, and even then his embrace was strictly platonic. Obviously he had found another place to park his hormones.

Six times in the past two weeks he had come home just after eleven, grabbed a shower and fallen into bed. He didn't say where he had been, and she wasn't about to give him the satisfaction of asking. She had been right about him all along. He was a hustler, a flake, no more capable of getting serious about her than about any of the women who trailed around after him with their tongues hanging out.

Anyway, why should she care if he'd found somebody? She wasn't exactly seething with jealousy. No way.

She nearly jumped out of her skin when he came tearing into the room again.

"Rainey," he whispered harshly. "We have to go home *now* and rearrange the bedrooms again!"

Calm, Rainey. Stay calm. "Why? Who's going to go upstairs?"

"Grandma. She likes a nip. Sooner or later, she'll want to lie down. Guess where?"

"Why couldn't she lie down in the spare bedroom downstairs?"

"On what? The massage table?"

Rainey envisioned tiny, feisty, blue-haired Flo Mahoney passed out and snoring on the narrow table. She laughed. "Okay, let's go. But I warn you, I'm never doing this again!"

THEY CAME IN the darkness, like marauders, only bearing gifts. Lots of gifts. Big, brightly wrapped packages with festive ribbons and bows.

They brought food. Heaping trays of cold cuts and

chopped vegetables with dip, paté and crackers and deviled eggs. Finger sandwiches. Desserts. Crates of wine and champagne.

Before you could say "party animal," they were all over the house, in the kitchen and living room, on the stairs, in the small rooms at the back. Someone had put a selection of CDs in the player and hit the shuffle button. Music and laughter echoed throughout the house.

"Everybody! Everybody! Could I get your attention?"

Flo Mahoney stood in the middle of the crowded living room, waving a heavily jeweled hand high above her head. She was two heads shorter than almost everyone else in the room, and all that could be seen of her was the hand, snaking out from her Day-Glo purple sleeve and clutching a full glass of champagne. Rainey watched, spellbound, as she waved the glass around without spilling a drop.

"Give it up, Grandma!" Nate Frome called out from the far corner of the room.

Muttering to herself, Flo grabbed Beck's arm as he tried to slip past her, and demanded that he make them listen. "Hey, everybody," he shouted, "my grandmother wants to speak!" The room abruptly fell silent.

"Folks," Flo said in a slightly inebriated drawl, "I would like to make a toast. To Rainey and Beck. May they live a long and happy life together."

"To Rainey and Beck," the crowd chimed, raising their glasses in the air.

Leaning against the work island, Rainey blushed and squirmed. Beck sidled up to her, put his arm around her and kissed the top of her head.

"Ah, isn't that sweet," someone sang out. Everyone laughed. A few people applauded.

"Tell us the story of how you met," Nate demanded. Rainey detected a little sarcasm under the request. Hmm. What was that about?

"We met in the dining room at the inn." Beck gave Rainey's arm a friendly squeeze. "Didn't we, Rainey?"

"That's right." She smiled sweetly up at him. *You were hustling a woman and I was redecorating the room.*

Nate let out a snort. "*Boring* story." Everyone laughed again.

"Was it love at first sight?" someone else asked.

"It was for me," Beck said softly. Rainey dared not look at him. The lie was so outrageous, she thought it best to just get past it.

With that out of the way, the guests quickly lost interest in the newlyweds and resumed their loud and scattered conversations. Rainey had already figured out that the marriage was just a convenient excuse for a party. But that was okay. Beck had been right. They needed this.

As the evening wore on, she grew more and more comfortable in the role of hostess. It was a role she had never played outside her job, and it was fun. Smiling graciously, she circulated through the rooms, chatting with as many people as possible. It was a mixed group. Employees from the inn. Teachers. Lawyers. Ski bums. Students. Shopkeepers. Some of the trades people Beck had hired.

Feeling more than a little guilty, she accepted their congratulations and thanked them for the gifts. Those gifts were a problem. She hadn't planned on opening them.

Oh, well. There was no sense in getting all wound up about it. She was getting used to this charade.

"Surprised?" Mrs. Norman barked at Rainey as she infiltrated the housekeeper's group. Heavily made up and sporting a chintzy tiara, she was huddled in the kitchen with some of the other staff from the inn. Hollis stood next to her, half-drunk and slobbering on her shoulder.

"Completely," Rainey lied.

"Wonderful!" Mrs. Norman shouted. Hollis mumbled something unintelligible, and Rainey moved along.

The party raged on. Around ten, some of the older folks offered best wishes and went home. A space was soon cleared in the middle of the living room, and a few brave souls began to dance.

Looking around, Rainey spotted Beck standing next to the fireplace, chatting with Nate and a short, balding man who had introduced himself as Arnie Hutchinson, one of Nate's two law partners. Apparently, Pete Wilson, the other partner, was away at a conference in Seattle.

For a while, she watched him, undetected. She had never seen him in a crowd before, and it was something to see. Beck was at ease around people. Happy, confident, comfortable in his own skin.

Not meaning to eavesdrop, she overheard Arnie tell Beck about a client whose ten-year-old son had lost both his legs below the knee in a terrible car accident last winter. The boy had been fitted for dual prostheses, and was determined to learn how to ski. Did Beck know of a good ski program for kids with disabilities?

"I've got a better idea," Beck shouted over the din. "Get me his phone number. When the hills open, I'll teach him myself."

"Just one thing," Arnie cautioned. "The family doesn't have much money."

"Don't be ridiculous. I wouldn't take a dime for it."

Pleasantly surprised, Rainey smiled. She, above all, knew how busy Beck was. He put in long, hard days at the Haven. Yet, whenever someone asked him for help with this or that, he dropped whatever he was doing and lent a hand. Even if it meant his own chores would extend late into the evening. She figured he could have referred the boy to any of several ski programs in the area, but he didn't.

Not only that, people stopped him everywhere—on the street, at the inn—to ask his opinion, then listened carefully while he gave it. They looked up to Beck. They respected him.

Something fluttered in her heart.

Suddenly, the thought of not seeing Beck every day, of not being here with him, in this house, at night, was horrible. Even on the nights he was out late, even when she agonized over his whereabouts, just knowing he would be coming home filled her with a kind of joy. Heaven help her, she couldn't imagine not being married to him.

There was no denying it any longer. She loved Beck. Really loved him. Her attraction to him had nothing to do with loneliness, and certainly nothing to do with revenge. She simply loved the man himself.

A lump formed in her throat. Oh, God, she had actually encouraged him to see other women! How could she have done that? Now she found herself looking at each of the women in the house and wondering: Is it you? Are you the woman my husband is dating?

Sensing her eyes on him, Beck said a few words to Nate, then strolled toward her, frowning. He took her by the elbow and directed her away from the booming floor speaker. "Are you okay? You look a little tense." He reacted with mild surprise when Rainey slipped her arms around him and melted against his chest.

"I'm having a great time," she declared with forced cheerfulness. She inhaled his wonderful scent, felt the body heat coming through his sweater, and wished he loved her.

"Good. You know, I've been looking around here tonight and thinking there's something wrong with this place."

"Really? What's wrong with it?" He loosened his grip and she grinned up at him. "I mean, aside from that horrible coffee table."

"Hey, I picked that out myself! But you're right. It wouldn't hurt to spruce the place up a bit." He tucked a loose strand of hair behind her ear. The gesture was so innocent, yet so intimate, somehow, it made her blush. "I was wondering, would you like to redecorate the house?"

Rainey couldn't believe her ears. "Oh, could I! Er, I mean, that would be fun." She smiled shyly. "How much can I redecorate?"

"As much as you want."

"Oh, Beck!" Caught up in the moment, she kissed him soundly. He returned the kiss with gusto. For one precious moment they were alone in the room.

He held her at arm's length and gave her a warning look. "All I ask is nothing floral or chintzy. Okay?"

She laughed. "No flowers, no chintz. I promise."

"Isn't love grand?" Waving a snifter of brandy around now, Flo sidled up to Beck, swaying a little on her bright-pink pumps. Her speech was slurred, her mauve lipstick smeared. Beck released Rainey and put his arm around her to steady her.

"Everything has turned out so well," Flo gushed, her eyelids drooping. "You're such a lovely couple. Just perfect for one another! I mean, we never thought you would actually get *married*, but..."

Baffled, Rainey furrowed her brows and locked eyes with Beck. He shook his head. Who knew what the old girl was talking about? She was a little drunk. But still...

Before they could question her, Nate swiftly materialized next to Beck and said, "Hey, Grandma, I think it's time for you to lie down now."

The old lady served up a sly grin. "With you, gorgeous, or by myself?"

Rainey managed to keep a straight face, but Beck howled.

Nate issued a weary sigh. "By yourself, Grandma, by yourself." He promised Beck he would take good care of

Flo, then steered her through the crowd. Beck turned back to Rainey. "Now where were we?"

The doorbell rang. Surprised, Rainey glanced at her watch. Even on Friday nights, Bragg Creek was an early-to-bed, early-to-rise kind of town. It was late for new arrivals. On her way to the door, Arnie Hutchinson touched her arm and said, "Hey, Rainey. Let me know if you get tired of you-know-who. If you do, I'm definitely available."

Rainey teased him with a promise. "I'll remember you said that, Arnie." Chuckling, she opened the door—and looked straight into the piercing, dark brown eyes of Francine Yates. The attractive redhead was wearing a black leather jacket, skintight jeans and her usual scowl.

"This is for you." She thrust a gift box into Rainey's hands.

Astounded, Rainey accepted the package and racked her brain for an appropriate response. What was this? Some strange local custom?

"Well, good night." Francine turned to leave.

Rainey hurriedly set the box down on the foyer table and went out onto the porch. "Francine," she urged. "Come in. Join the party."

Halfway down the walk, Francine turned around. "Not tonight. I have plans."

"Well then, thank you so much for the gift." Rainey called after her.

"You're welcome." Francine's dark eyes bored into Rainey's. "You know, I really did care for him," she muttered.

Rainey's heart melted. "Oh, Francine, I'm so sorry." She gestured behind her. "Are you sure you don't want to come in?"

Francine said she was more than positive she didn't want to. She tried to leave again, but Rainey called out her name once more. Heaving an exasperated sigh, she reluctantly turned around again.

"Francine, I...this sounds dumb with all these people here, but I really don't have any friends in this place." Rainey chewed her lower lip and waited. It was a risk, but some instinct told her it was worth taking.

The redhead snorted. "You've got Beck Mahoney and you need a friend?"

"I need a girlfriend," Rainey explained. "Someone who doesn't have smelly feet." She ventured a smile.

Now it was Francine's turn to look flabbergasted. She recovered quickly. Tossed her long red mane. Sniffed the air and pretended to give the idea serious but doubtful consideration. "I'll think it over." The faintest of smiles crossed her lips. "What makes you think *I* don't have smelly feet?"

Rainey laughed. "Trust me. Any odor would be an improvement!" She waved good-night and went back inside, shivering from the cold night air.

Near midnight, when the house was finally empty, Beck collapsed on the sofa, took a deep breath and released it slowly. Rainey flaked out in the chair across from him. They agreed the party had been a blast and debated, for all of two seconds, whether to start cleaning up now or leave it until the morning.

"What say we just sell the place?" he suggested. Rainey agreed that it was a terrific idea.

Grimacing, Beck raised up and felt the seat cushion beneath him. "There's a spring coming up through this thing. Good thing we're turfing it." He shifted one cushion to the left and glanced up the stairs. "I wonder if Grandma is okay?"

Rainey went up to check on her and reported back that the room was empty, the bed untouched. Their eyes automatically turned to the little bedroom behind the kitchen.

They found her there, passed out and snoring—on the massage table.

11

RAINEY SLIPPED a pillow under Flo's head, removed her shoes and covered her with a down comforter. Pleasantly weary, she turned the lights off and dragged her tired body upstairs and into the bathroom. Already half asleep, she brushed her teeth and hair, then absentmindedly stripped off her clothes and threw them down the laundry chute. The second they left her hand she remembered that her nightclothes were in Beck's room.

Arghhh! Panicked, she plunged her arm into the chute and tried frantically to retrieve her things, but it was too late.

Darn. She couldn't sleep naked. Had never been able to. Besides, it was chilly here at night. Flannel was mandatory. Either that or a warm body.

She looked around for something to cover herself with, but of course she had tossed all the big bath towels down the chute just before the party and hung two smaller towels in their place. Cursing under her breath, she wrapped one around her naked body as tightly as possible. It barely covered her breasts, and reached only to the tops of her thighs. Butterflies forming in her belly, she tapped lightly on Beck's door. He opened it, naked from the waist up.

"I need my nightgown," she muttered.

For a moment, he said nothing. In the dim light cast by the bedside lamp behind him, Rainey could just make out his amber eyes taking a stroll all over her. When he finally spoke, his tone was playful. "Why? I kind of like you just the way you are."

"Beck..." She licked her lips nervously.

He leaned against the doorjamb and crossed his arms. Helped himself to another generous look. When his eyes met hers again, they radiated mischief. "I'll give you fifty thousand dollars for that towel."

Oh, for crying out loud. Why had she even bothered to suggest he date other people? Obviously there weren't enough women in the world for Romeo.

She leaned against the wall and shook her head slowly. "You're some piece of work, aren't you, Beck Mahoney? You just don't give up."

"On you? Never."

"For the life of me, I don't understand what you want with me."

"I want to make love with you."

That almost got to her—almost. "Uh-huh, and then what?"

His eyebrows shot up. "Educated guess? I'll probably want to make love with you again."

"Is that so? Tell me something. Aren't you tuckered out? I mean, how much love can one man make in a week?" It was a pathetically obvious attempt to extract information from him, but Rainey didn't care. She was desperate.

He leaned slightly toward her and did that goofy thing he did with his eyebrows. "Wouldn't *you* like to know."

Yeah, she would like to know! Badly. "I mean, you've been out a lot lately. Surely you must be getting all the action you can handle."

He shrugged. "Maybe. Maybe not."

Something about his shifty body language and vague response gave Rainey pause for thought. Beck was never vague. Even when he was flirting with her, he was very clear about what he had in mind. So why the coyness? If he really was seeing other women, why didn't he just come right out and say so? After all, she had okayed it, hadn't she?

Could it be that he was bluffing? She was bluffing, too, of course, but he didn't know that. She eyed him suspiciously. For no accountable reason, he seemed nervous.

Why, that rascal! He *was* bluffing. He hadn't been stepping out at all!

Her heart soared, then fell like a rock. She couldn't be a hundred percent *sure* he was bluffing. Short of just coming right out and asking... Humph! Not a chance. Two could play this little game.

She gave him her sweetest smile. ``Well, I certainly hope you're getting some action. We can't have you doing without, now can we?''

``Speaking of doing without, I think you'd look terrific without that towel,'' he replied, neatly dodging the question. ``A hundred thousand. I can cut the check right now.''

Rainey couldn't help it. She laughed. ``Out of my way, you brat!''

Chuckling himself now, Beck stepped aside and let her pass. ``Two hundred thousand in cash. That's my final offer.''

``Not enough!'' After a hasty search Rainey located her nightgown and skittered into her own room. ``Good night, Beck.'' She started to close the door.

``Half a million, then. And worth every penny, I might add.''

``Go away. You're a pest!''

``Hey, let's start fresh here. Did I mention that you are absolutely stunning in a towel?''

She sighed. ``Beck Mahoney, when are you going to *get* it? How long is it going to take?''

His grin crumpled. ``It? What, exactly, is it?''

``Figure it out for yourself.'' She closed the door. Moments later, she heard him grumble, ''It. Define it.'' Finally, she heard the click of his door.

Her last thought before drifting off to sleep was: What's wrong with you, Beck Mahoney? Why don't you ask *me* out on a date?

A WEEK LATER, Beck told Pete Wilson everything—and swore him to secrecy.

''So, let me just get this straight.'' Pete walked across the concrete floor of the half-built garage, plugged the air gun into the portable power generator and handed it to Beck. ''You got married for the money, and you're planning to get divorced, and you're not in love with her, and you're not sleeping with her, and she thinks you're out three nights a week doing the wild thing with other women, and you *want* her to think that?''

''Yup,'' Beck replied, aware of how ludicrous it sounded. ''Three nights a week for the past three weeks. She doesn't know I'm here and I don't volunteer the information.'' He grinned. ''Ingenious, huh?''

Pete slowly shook his head. ''Becky, boy, that is the craziest thing I've ever heard.''

''No, it isn't,'' Beck argued, knowing full well that it was. ''It makes perfect sense.''

Pete snorted. ''Yeah! If you're already two beers shy of a six-pack!''

Beck took the rack of nails Pete held out to him, removed his gloves and loaded the air gun. When his bare fingertips made contact with the cold metal surface of the tool, he shivered. It was late October and the air was damp and chilly. In a way, he was grateful for the cold. It kept him alert.

''Okay,'' Pete continued. ''Let me ask you this, then. If you're not in love with her, and she's not in love with you, then why do you want her to think that you're out with other women? I mean, why bother trying to make her jealous? Seems like a lot of work for nothing.''

``Hey, I didn't say she wasn't in love with me.''

Pete laughed. ``You know, you'll make a great lawyer one day, Beck. You have no logic, but you have just enough arrogance to compensate for it.''

Increasingly taken with the notion, Beck insisted, ``She's nuts about me, Pete. Nuts. And besides, it was her idea. I'm just giving her what she deserves.'' He sniffed the air, puffed up his chest. Yup, he was a master strategist, all right.

The look on Pete's face was pure skepticism. ``Uh-huh, and what exactly is it that you want?''

``A little fun, that's all.''

``Yeah, well, it sounds to me like you're kinda stuck on her, too.''

``Nah,'' Beck lied, to his friend, to himself. ``She's nothing special. I had this dumb idea that she might turn out to be the perfect wife, but it's not working out.''

Pete positioned a stud and motioned for Beck to nail it into the bottom plate. Beck complied. They straightened it and checked it with a leveling tool, then Beck shot two more nails through the wood and into the top plate. They stood back and examined their handiwork. *Man alive,* Beck thought, *at this rate, it'll take us till spring to finish this thing.*

Between this commitment, his massage practice, the renovation project and the situation at home, he was starting to feel physically and emotionally drained. His earlier worries about keeping himself and Rainey busy had become a joke. She put in long days at the inn and still insisted on keeping the house spotless. Every night he came home late, exchanged a few perfunctory words with her, then fell into bed. Sleep came in minutes.

Yesterday the Springbank Airport had called and asked

him to start giving flying lessons again. He turned them down. He had already told Nakiska Ski Lodge to scratch his name off the list of instructors this winter. They could still count on him for the ski patrol—he considered that a civic duty—but his schedule couldn't accommodate much more. The massage practice he planned to keep, for a while anyway. He found it just as therapeutic as his clients.

Besides, there was no reason to kill himself. He no longer needed the income those jobs used to provide.

Selecting another stud from the pile, Pete asked, "So what's not perfect about Rainey? Nate says she's a major babe."

Secretly pleased with the compliment, especially its source, Beck smiled. "Major is an understatement, Pete. She's smart and pretty and classy and—"

"Sexy?" Pete interjected with a sly grin.

"Beyond your wildest dreams, my man. She's like sex in a bottle. Unfortunately, she's also anal retentive, childish, stubborn and bone-headed. She has no self-confidence, no sense of hah-hah, and she can't climb worth a damn."

"Oh, yeah! Major deterrents when you've got sex in a bottle!"

Overcome by self-pity, Beck set the air gun down on the floor and straddled Pete's sawhorse. "Oh, man, who am I fooling? I never thought I'd say this about a woman, but it's more than sex. I'm crazy about her, Pete. If I was any more in love with her I'd check myself into a loony bin."

Pete hooted. "No kidding."

The sarcasm sailed clear over Beck's head. "The worst thing," he complained, "is that she doesn't seem to *mind* my seeing other women. At first she was kind of snotty about it. Tonight she practically shoved me out the door. Told me to have a good time, even. What do you make of that?"

Clasping his stubbled chin with one hand, Pete pretended

to give the question deep, lawyerlike consideration. "Well, either she's craftier than you—and let's face it buddy, that's not much of a stretch—or she really doesn't care."

"Thanks." Beck made a sour face. "Thanks a lot."

"Sorry, man. The truth hurts sometimes."

Sighing, Beck rose and picked up the air gun again. Pete took it away from him and put it back in its carry case. "Look, Beck, if you love her, why don't you just tell her and see what happens? What have you got to lose?"

"Nah, it's hopeless." Beck shook his head. "Some guy in Toronto broke her heart and she's gun-shy. Besides, I made a terrible first impression on her. She thinks I'm a hustler and that she's just another target. She doesn't believe a word I say."

Pete dropped his chin and gave his old friend a withering look. "Beck, you *are* a hustler."

"Was," Beck emphatically corrected him. "No more. That's all finished."

Lost in thought, Beck absentmindedly lifted the air gun out of its case again and looked around blankly. He tried to focus on where he was and what he was supposed to be doing. Pete took it away again. Remotely grateful, Beck plopped back down on the sawhorse, oblivious to everything but his feelings.

"See that's the thing," he sheepishly admitted, while Pete gathered up his other tools and put them away. "I've been trying to hustle her from the minute I laid eyes on her. I ask you—how stupid was that?" He looked at Pete for confirmation that it wasn't stupid at all—just impractical, or something.

"Pretty stupid," Pete confirmed. "But not reversible. Why don't you just adopt another strategy? Women appreciate friendship. Try that." He grinned. "Even you might like it."

Beck shook his head. "We are friends. At least I think we are. But I can't help myself. I just want to touch her every minute of the day." Realizing how selfish that sounded, he quickly added, "At least I've been paying her more compliments...."

"Compliments are good. Women like compliments."

Beck groaned. "I don't know, Pete. Maybe I've been a hustler for so long I don't know how to be anything else."

"Have you ever asked her out on a date?"

"A date? But we're already married!"

"Yeah, but there was no courtship."

Beck searched his memory for something, anything at all, resembling a real date. "Well, I took her to a darts tournament once." It sounded lame, even to him.

"Nah, nah, I mean a romantic date. You know, dinner, dancing, the stuff women like."

Dating. Hmmm. It was a radical idea, but Beck had to admit it wasn't bad.

Darkness descended and the first snow of the season began to fall. Pete suggested they call it a night and walked Beck to the Fairlane. As Beck was fishing for his keys, Pete said, "Let me give you some free advice, friend. If the dating thing doesn't fly, write her off. Do what you have to do, get the divorce, and get on with your life."

Beck got into the car and rolled down the window. "Gee, Pete, I don't know if I should be taking marital advice from a guy whose wife has thrown him out three times."

Pete grinned. "Actually, Annie's turfed me four times, but who's counting?"

Beck laughed, then gave his friend a warning look. "Listen, this is just between you and me. Understand?"

"Perfectly," Pete replied with a straight face. "I won't say a word."

THE FOLLOWING THURSDAY, Rainey finally called Dana back. She told her everything and made her swear not to tell a soul, especially Rainey's mom and dad.

For a long time after she finished talking, nothing could be heard over the phone line but a little long-distance static and the sound of Dana going into shock. Rainey heaved a sigh. She knew it all sounded crazy, but honestly, it wasn't *that* big a deal. Not anymore.

"Dana," she asked impatiently. "Are you still there?"

"So—so let me just see if I've got this right," Dana finally said. "This guy, Beck, your, um, husband. He married you for his money, and you didn't love each other at first, but you do now, and you're living together but not sleeping together, and you want him to think that you think he's seeing other women? Have I got it right so far?"

"Yup, that's it in a nutshell." Rainey lay back on the bed and shifted the receiver to her other ear. Weeks ago, when the construction noise above her office had reached a fever pitch, she had moved her desk and computer into one of the empty suites in the west wing. It wasn't an ideal setup, but at least it was quiet. The bed was definitely a bonus.

So were the three dozen yellow roses on her desk.

"Sweetie," Dana said, "I'm going to count to ten, and when I'm finished the real Rainey Miller is going to get on the phone. Have you lost your mind? I'm worried sick about you. I'm flying out there tonight."

"Ah, don't be silly." Rainey waved a hand in the air as if Dana were in the room with her. "I'm fine. Besides, we're throwing a party for Aunt Lilly on—" she struggled to a sitting position and looked at her desk calendar "—November 23. Why don't you fly out a couple days before that and you can come to the party?"

There was another short silence. Rainey lay back again, gazed at the cracked and crumbling ceiling overhead, and hummed a tune under her breath.

"A party," Dana repeated dumbly. "Um, call me crazy, sweetie, but isn't your aunt Lilly, you know, dead?"

Rainey cleared her throat. "Ah, well, technically, yes. But the Women of the Wapiti are holding a seance before the party to call up her spirit. So who knows? She might actually show."

"The women of the *whaaat?*"

"The Wapiti. It's a service club. They inducted me last week. I had to wear a silly hat and swear an oath of allegiance." Rainey paused and racked her brain to recall it. "Um, let me see now—to serve and—"

"Rainey!"

"Oh, relax, Dana. I'm okay. In fact, I haven't had this much fun in years."

"Okay, about your, um, situation. So the two of you are living together and making like Ozzie and Harriet, but he goes out three nights a week?"

"Yup. Tuesday through Thursday, every week. He thinks that I think that he's seeing other women, but I know for a fact he's actually helping a friend build a garage."

"How do you know that?"

"I called our lawyer, Nate Frome, to ask him a question about the transfer of title on the inn, and he let it slip."

"That's not all that's slipping out there!"

Rainey cackled. "Check this out, Dana. Afterward he comes home and takes a shower so I'll think he's trying to get the scent of another woman off him. Isn't that a riot?" Rainey giggled. It was a thing of beauty. Truly.

"Yeah, it's a laugh a minute. But the part I don't get is, if you really do love each other, why are you playing this dumb game? And why are you so happy that he thinks that you think he's sleeping around?"

"Don't you see, Dana? It means that he really does love me. I didn't think he did. Then I sort of thought he might.

Anyway, this confirms it. He isn't seeing other women. He just wants to make me jealous.''

"Oh, yeah, that's what men do when they love you!" Dana sighed. ''Call me crazy, but the last time I checked there were easier ways to find out that a man loves you. Why didn't you just ask him? For that matter, why don't you just tell him the jig is up?''

"I'm just having a little fun with the guy," Rainey explained. "And besides, he deserves it.'' That sounded a little spiteful, she realized, but hey, spite was right—sometimes.

"Why does he deserve it, Rainey? What's he done?"

Rainey sighed impatiently. "You aren't paying attention, Dana. It's because he's letting me think he's been with other women.''

"But you said it was your idea!"

"Hey, I am occasionally allowed a bad idea.''

Dana hooted. "Oh, boy, I'm not going to touch that one with a cattle prod!''

"The best part of it," Rainey enthused, "is that he's changed completely. He's being really sweet, paying me all these compliments, buying me flowers, stuff like that. He's even letting me redecorate the house. Of course, I'm not sure whether to go with leather or fabric....''

"Rainey. Sweetie. You married a guy you'd only known for five days, and you're concerned about *fabric?*"

"Well, it's an important choice.''

"Whatever. You know, I've gotta tell you, friend, he sounds like an okay guy to me.''

Rainey turned on her side and switched the receiver to her other ear again. "Well, he's not perfect by any means. He's conceited and cocky and arrogant. He's late for meetings, if he bothers to show at all, and he's a slob around the house. On the other hand, he's really talented. He's supervising all the renovations at the Haven, and he designed the wedding chapel himself...."

"Wedding chapel?"

Duh. Now why had Dana pounced on that? What possible interest could she have in the wedding chapel? Before she could ask, Dana said, "The last time we talked, Rainey, you said he was cute. Define cute."

Pleasure coursed through Rainey's veins and she closed her eyes. "Mmm. He's more than cute, Dana. He's scrumptious. He's like...sex in a bottle."

"Rainey, for crying out loud, just tell the man you love him."

"What? And spoil all this fun? Don't be ridiculous!"

12

"UM, EXCUSE ME."

Rainey craned her neck and looked up. A tall, vacuous-looking creature with long hair streaked a dozen shades of blond slouched in the doorway, grimacing and wringing her hands. She was expertly made up and draped with fine gold jewelry. Her huge and annoyingly perfect breasts spilled out of a low-cut, skintight red sweater clinging to an even tighter pair of jeans.

Rainey asked Dana to hold on. "Yes?" she said to the blonde.

"Um, my name is Trish Mortimer," the creature said in a breathless, little-girl voice. "My boyfriend and I are staying here at the inn. We just bought the boutique across the street...."

"Yes?"

"Um, I have a problem." Her tortured expression suggested that the problem was no mere trifle.

Great, Rainey thought, what now? Another complaint about the noise? Another construction calamity?

Yesterday a pipe had burst on the second floor of the west wing, spewing hundreds of gallons of cold water through the ceiling below, into the suite of a young couple celebrating their honeymoon in the traditional way. The groom had emerged from the suite, half-dressed, angry, wet and shivering, to declare, "Excuse me, but I'm all through with cold showers."

Later in the day, one of the carpenters working in the

wedding chapel fell through an opening in the floor, miraculously landing flat on his feet on the reservations desk. An elderly gentleman standing at the desk gazed up at him and quipped, "Where's your cape, son?"

Rainey motioned for the blonde to wait and spoke into the phone again. "Dana, I have to go. There's a problem."

"Sweetie, your whole life is a problem."

"It's business, Dana. I have to go." She said a hasty goodbye and hung up.

Rainey quickly got off the bed and smoothed out her skirt. Darn. She had really wanted to ask Dana about their last phone conversation, specifically what she had meant by "poor Trev." More and more she suspected that something was going on between that pair. It was probably just her overactive imagination. But still…

"What can I help you with?" she asked the blonde.

Absentmindedly twirling a strand of her glossy hair, she said, "Um, that guy…the masseuse? I think his name is Beck? Do you know where he is? He gave me a massage this morning, but the effects have worn off, and I really feel the need for another one." She giggled.

Oh, it was just unbelievable. Rainey gritted her teeth and silently counted to ten. "*That's* your problem?" She struggled to stifle her contempt. She didn't want to be rude, especially to a guest, but honestly. Beck's fan club. She had just about had it with them.

The blonde seemed confused. "Um, well, *I* think it's a problem."

"My husband is not available right now," Rainey said, relishing the woman's stunned reaction to the word *husband.* "He'll be back on Monday."

"Oh! Oh!" The creature's impossibly long eyelashes fluttered. "He's your husband." Her big blue eyes swiftly appraised Rainey's high-necked blouse and knee-length skirt. Her panty hose and sensible, low-heeled shoes. Rainey could just hear her thinking: What's a hunk like that doing with a loser like this?

"You're one lucky woman." The blonde rolled her dinner plate eyes. "If I had a man like that... Ooh la la!"

Rainey smiled tightly. "Yes, well...Trish, is it?...as I said, Trish, he'll be back after the weekend."

Apparently unable to grasp the fact that she just wasn't going to be feeling those fantasy-inducing hands again until Monday, the woman lingered for a moment, bewildered and traumatized, before thanking Rainey and slithering down the hall.

Muttering to herself, Rainey closed her temporary office and went upstairs to check on the hands in question. With so much work on her own plate, she hadn't paid much attention to the wedding chapel project. Stepping into the room now, she gasped.

Beck had gutted the big apartment and reconfigured it into one enormous room, leaving only the bedroom and bathroom walls intact. The kitchen he had reduced to a single counter with sink, below a row of shiny new cupboards suitable for limited food preparation and storage. The new bay window in the living room afforded a spectacular view of the snow-covered grounds beyond. In front of it, he had built a platform where wedding ceremonies would be performed, and covered it with a soft gray carpet. The rest of the floor was being finished in a smoke-gray ceramic tile.

The walls were a pale creamy yellow—Rainey's favorite color.

"Hey, woman," he called out to her from the far corner of the room. Looking hunky as ever in his grubby work clothes, he strolled toward her. Rainey smiled. She had a new, secret nickname for him: Mr. It.

"Beck, it's simply beautiful," she gushed, and watched

him light up like a neon sign. She knew he was proud of the work, and pleased with her approval.

``It is, isn't it?'' Because the floor tile installer was present, he leaned down and gave her a cautious little kiss. Ever since the shtag party he had hardly touched her, preferring instead to constantly search her eyes for some clue as to what ``it'' might be.

``Thank you for the flowers,'' she said quietly.

``My pleasure.''

They walked around the facility for a while, chatting about the new fixtures and furnishings on order. Beck gave her the rough schedule for the west wing renovation, and Rainey brought him up to date on the project cost sheets Hollis had prepared for her that morning. Then she looked at her watch. It was just after five. ``I'm tired, Beck. I'm going to call it a day now.''

``Um, before you go...''

``Yes?''

Suddenly, miraculously shy, he shifted from one foot to the other and seemed uncertain of what to do with his hands. He looked, Rainey thought with amusement, like a teenage boy struggling to make conversation with the most popular girl in school. ``Um, I was wondering if you would do me the honor of being my date tonight.''

Rainey groaned. ``We're not going shopping for plywood again, are we?''

``No ma'am. I was thinking more like dinner, maybe a little dancing.'' He licked his lips and swallowed hard.

Wow. Dinner? Dancing? Maybe there was hope for the man after all.

``Mmm, I don't know,'' she said, knowing her indifference would drive him wild. ``I'll have to think about it.''

Beck glanced at the floor tiler, then grasped her elbow and led her out into the hall. ``Hey, I'm putting my ego on the line here. Do we have a date or not? If not, just say so. I'll understand.''

Sure you will, Rainey thought. *You've probably never been turned down for a date in your entire life!*

''Well, I must say I'm surprised,'' she teased. ''I mean, it's Thursday. Isn't *she* available tonight?''

He closed his eyes. ''C'mon, Rainey. There is no 'she.' You know that.''

''I know no such thing!'' It was a lie, but it was a fun lie.

''Then know it now. You're the only she I want to date, tonight or any other night. Okay?''

Rainey smiled inside. It wasn't exactly a declaration of love, but it might be the best she could expect. She let him squirm a moment longer. ''Well, okay then, it's a date.''

He beamed. ''Great! Ah, I have to put some more time in here. What say we get together around eight?''

Rainey said eight was fine. For one awkward moment, Beck seemed on the verge of kissing her, but then thought better of it. It was just as well. As far as she was concerned, his ration of kisses was used up—at least the ones he wanted.

''WHADDAYA MEAN, you don't know how to cook?''

Rainey reached across the kitchen island and tried to fish a slice of zucchini out of the big wooden salad bowl. Beck stopped chopping for a second, gave her a look of stern reproach and swatted her hand away. She made a face at him. Given that his idea of dinner and dancing had turned out to be a bag of groceries and a box set of Nat King Cole CDs, the least he could do was let her nibble.

''I mean,'' she replied, still eyeing the coveted zucchini, ''that I never learned how to cook.''

Mild disdain flitted across his handsome face. ''Nothing? Nada? Zip?''

``I can make scrambled eggs, and I do a mean tuna fish sandwich.''

``Rainey.'' He dropped his chin. ``A chimpanzee can make a tuna fish sandwich.''

``Hey, give me a break! I've been eating hotel food for the past ten years. Working at night and going to school during the day doesn't leave much time for entertaining.''

Beck diced an onion and dropped the pieces into the bowl. ``Didn't your mother teach you how to cook?''

``Not really.'' Rainey twirled the stem of her wineglass. ``She was forty-two when I was born, and my dad was forty-seven. By the time I came along, they were so set in their ways they just sort of went on doing everything themselves.''

Shaking his head sadly, Beck said, ``Do you realize, woman, that we've been living together for over a month and I hardly know a thing about you?''

``Ooh, are you saying that you've actually developed an interest in my mind?'' she teased. ``In addition to my body?''

``Hey, that hurts!'' When Rainey stopped laughing, he added, ``Besides, you should cut me some slack. It's kind of hard to ignore that body.'' He shielded his eyes with one hand, which made Rainey laugh. Beck chuckled nervously, too. Lately they had carefully avoided any reference to the powerful attraction between them. Too much was at stake.

``Do you really want to know me?'' Rainey asked cautiously. It sounded wimpy, but so what? Trevor had wined and dined her for six weeks without asking her a single question about herself. Just once in her life, a man was going to show an interest in something higher than her cleavage.

``Yes, I do,'' Beck replied softly. ``I meant it when I said that. You just didn't believe me.''

``Well, under the circumstances...''

Laughing, Beck turned and reached behind him for the bowl of sliced peppers beside the sink. Rainey quickly snatched the zucchini stick and bit into it. It was delicious. ``What kind of sauce did you put on this?''

Beck added the peppers to the bowl and tossed the mix. ``Mint sauce. That's the secret to making a good Greek salad.'' He pointed the sharp tip of the knife at her. ``And if you don't keep your hands out of it, I'm going to tie them behind your back.''

Ooh, wouldn't you just love to do that! Rainey thought.

His expression softened. ``You look very pretty tonight.''

``Thank you.'' Rainey had assumed they were going someplace fancy and had overdressed for the evening, in a long black skirt and a low-cut, white silk blouse—throwbacks to her glittery evenings out with Trevor.

``You know, you look pretty good when you get out of those school teacher skirts and blouses.''

Say what? ``What's wrong with my skirts and blouses?''

``Nothing. It's just that they're a little, shall we say, corporate for this part of the world.''

Rainey shrugged. It was true, she supposed. Certainly no one else around here dressed like her. Maybe she should go shopping. Maybe Francine would like to tag along.

Watching Beck work, Rainey felt a pang. He had been a perfect gentleman lately—and very sweet. Not just by flattering her, but by praising her in a way that made her feel she could do anything, be anything, that she wanted. It wouldn't hurt to return a little of that.

``Beck,'' she began, ``I haven't told you what a great job you've been doing at the inn....''

``Uh-uh,'' he interjected, ``I don't want to talk about work tonight. I want to talk about you.''

``Really?''

``Yeah, really. Tell me about your childhood.''

Rainey let out a whoop. "Oh, now, what's this? A man actually asking about a woman's childhood? You must be desperate to get my clothes off!"

To her absolute delight, Beck blushed. "Oh, man, I think I'll just leave that comment alone."

The timer on the convection oven sounded. While Beck took a pan of tarragon chicken breasts from it and moved them to a warm plate, Rainey added two logs to the fire and set the table. All around the house, snow fell in a soft steady stream. The fire was lovely, the table pretty, the man perfect.

If I lived in heaven, she thought, this is what it would be like.

Beck dimmed the lights, lit a few candles, and they sat down to eat. Between sips of wine and mouthfuls of the delicious food, Rainey talked about her upbringing in the Rosedale district of Toronto, a community of genteel red-brick mansions north of the downtown core. There was a lot of old money in the area, she told Beck, and some slightly frowned upon new money. Laura Miller had inherited Rainey's childhood home from her parents, then married a working man, so the Millers didn't fall into either category.

"What was it like, being raised by older parents?" Beck asked.

Parts of it were awful, Rainey said. Strict curfews. No noise allowed in the house, especially rock music. No makeup or dating until she turned seventeen. "It wasn't so much that they were older," she explained. "It was that they were so darned old-fashioned."

"They must be shocked. I mean, you're their baby."

It took Rainey a moment to realize Beck was talking about the marriage. Oh, dear, he *did* think they knew. "Um, yes, shocked," she stammered, hoping he couldn't smell the fear oozing out of her pores.

Apparently satisfied with her response, Beck asked her what it had been like to be an only child. She shrugged. ``It was okay. You don't miss what you've never known. Of course, my friendship with Dana was a big help.''

``You must miss her,'' he said softly.

Rainey nodded—and grinned. ``I do. But I'm trying to recruit Francine as a stand-in.''

``Oh, brother.''

Bored with her own ho-hum life, Rainey asked Beck about his childhood. He told her he'd grown up in a posh district of Edmonton, where there was a lot of new money and a little, slightly frowned upon old money. That made Rainey laugh. East and west. They truly were different worlds.

It was a privileged childhood, he said. His great-grandfather, Elias Mahoney had come to Canada from Ireland in the early nineteen hundreds and homesteaded on a section of farmland just south of Calgary. When the city limits reached his property, he sold all of it to the municipality for a small fortune. Some of that money had fueled a comfortable retirement. The rest had been shrewdly invested—in coal and diamond mines, and later, in oil and gas stocks. That was where Beck's trust fund had been born.

As the night wore on, he kept her in stitches with stories about the outrageous stunts he and Nate Frome and Pete Wilson had pulled off. Once, he confided, they had completely dismantled his parents' car while they were away on vacation, and managed to reassemble it just ten minutes before they walked in the door. He made her cross her heart and swear never to tell.

While Rainey chuckled, his eyes softened. He reached out and touched her cheek. ``You know, you're the most beautiful woman I've ever seen.''

Rainey blushed. ``Oh, Beck, I have ordinary looks.''

"Not to me, you don't."

"Thank you. You were saying…?"

"Oh, yeah. Right." Before retiring, he continued, his dad had worked as an oil patch engineer while Martha had worked at home and volunteered for charities. His brothers were a lot of fun, he said. Rainey would like them. They were both happily married, Ian with two sons, and Jake with one. He paused and gave Rainey one of those hangdog looks that always made her want to kiss him silly. "That's why Martha wants girls."

"Hmmm." She sipped her wine.

"Tell me something, Rainey. If you weren't in the hotel business, what would you be doing instead?"

The question was a pleasant surprise. From the age of ten, Rainey had focused on one goal—to run the Honeymoon Haven. Other interests she had were dismissed as trivial or unrealistic. But that didn't mean she didn't have them.

"Okay, since you asked, mom and dad gave me a camera for Christmas one year, and I discovered I had a flair for landscape photography. But nobody encouraged it, so I just sort of let it go." She took another sip of her wine and gazed into the fire, lost in the memory. She hadn't thought about that for eons.

Moments later she realized Beck was gazing at her expectantly. "What?"

"Aren't you going to ask about me?" He sounded like a little boy who'd been cut out of the adults' conversation.

Properly chastised, Rainey laughed. "You mean there's more to you than being a flake who drives women wild on the massage table?"

He pretended to be deeply offended. "Hey, who are you calling a flake? Seriously, I guess you've noticed that aside from the renovations I'm not much interested in the inn."

Rainey batted her eyelashes. "Why no, I hadn't noticed that at all."

"I'll forgive you that sarcasm. Anyway, it's not really what I want to do with my life. I'm grateful to Lilly for thinking of me, but what I'm really interested in is environmental law. In fact, now that I have a little money, I'm thinking of enrolling in law school next fall."

"You're kidding. What about your other interests? The skiing and flying?"

"Well, that's just it, see. Those things used to be my hobbies. Now they're just work. I want them to be fun again."

"Okay. Why environmental law? Why not criminal or civil law?"

Speaking quietly at first, Beck slowly mounted a rant about the greedy developers who, if left unchecked, would pave over every inch of the Bow Valley Corridor that wasn't protected land, turning it into one big playground for tourists. There would be horrible consequences, he said: erosion of the land, destruction of natural habitats and feeding grounds, congestion, pollution and increased crime. As he spoke, he grew more and more animated. His voice went up and he gestured wildly. Rainey jumped a little when he slapped the tabletop to make a particular point. Finally he ran out of steam and cried, "Don't get me started!"

Rainey was stunned—and a little ashamed. Beck was smart, sure. But she hadn't thought him capable of such concern, such passion.

As they gazed at one another with a new and surprising respect, the sweet harmony of Nat King Cole and his daughter Natalie issued from the speakers. "Unforgettable." It was a favorite of Rainey's. She closed her eyes and let the melody soothe her mind.

Beck stood and held out his hand. "Care to dance?"

Rainey opened her eyes. "Are you serious?"

"Yup. I promised you dancing, and dancing you're going to get. On your feet."

She gave him her hand and together they moved into the living room. Beck moved the coffee table to a corner, then turned around and held out his arms. She walked into them. They were timid at first, dancing a few inches apart like strangers at a wedding. But, little by little Beck pulled her closer. Rainey didn't resist. She didn't want to. It felt good to be close to him.

As if he had just read her thoughts, Beck pulled her even closer and she rested her head in the crook of his neck. She liked the way her breasts felt pressed up against his broad, muscled chest. His body was warm and hard. He smelled wonderful. If she wasn't careful, she would soon lose the little resolve she had left. It was tempting.

But not yet. Not just yet.

"Rainey," he murmured into her hair. "This is nice. I like being your date."

"Hmmm."

"May I walk you home later?"

She laughed with sheer delight. "Yes, you may."

As the fire crackled behind them and the snow landed softly on the trees beyond their windows, they swayed to the music, not so much dancing as making love on their feet. They felt so right together, Rainey thought. They fit.

"I should warn you in advance," Beck said. "I'm going to kiss you good-night at your door. And you're going to let me."

"Oh, am I now?"

"Yes ma'am, you are."

She pulled back and gazed up at him. His eyes were the same color as the firelight, a fierce, deep gold. She wanted to rake her hands through his hair. She wanted to kiss him, badly. But if she started kissing him now, she would never stop. All things considered, it would be best if... Oh, the hell with it! "Maybe we should practise. You know, just so it won't feel awkward later on."

Shock registered in his eyes, then quickly vanished. "Good suggestion."

They stopped moving. Beck took her head in both hands and lowered his mouth very slowly to hers. It was their best kiss ever. Long and slow and tender. The heat that threatened to consume both of them was there, as always, but there was no pressure now. Just sweet contentment.

When the kiss was over, they resumed their slow, hypnotic dance. Each sighed with pleasure, and they both chuckled softly.

"You know what?" Rainey joked as she fought a powerful urge to run her tongue along his neck. "I don't think we did it right. Maybe we should practise some more."

Their second kiss was even better than their first. It was more than a kiss, she thought. It was a celebration of something new and wonderful. It was a beginning.

"Rainey," Beck whispered hoarsely. "I…there's something I want to tell you."

"Yes?" *Say you love me, Beck. If you say it, I will, too.*

A car pulled into the driveway. Beck went rigid. "Oh, no."

They went to the window and peered through the wet, heavy snow. The car lights dimmed. A man climbed out of the vehicle and bolted up the walk. "That's Pete Wilson," Beck muttered. He looked at his watch. "It's ten-thirty. What could he possibly want at this hour?"

While Beck answered the door, Rainey turned the lights up and smoothed down her tousled hair. The afterglow from those sweet kisses rapidly vanished.

"PETE, THIS IS NOT a good time," Beck growled. "I repeat, *not* a good time."

While Beck glared at him, Pete removed his wet coat

and hung it in the foyer closet. "Forgive me, friend, but Annie has thrown me out again and I need a bed for the night."

"Not here you don't! What's wrong with a hotel room?"

Pete looked at Beck as if he were a blithering idiot. "It's the beginning of ski season, Beck. There isn't a single vacancy anywhere in the corridor. You know that."

"I don't care." Beck stood firm in the foyer. Pete was leaving. He was leaving *now*. "Couldn't you stay at Nate's place? Or Arnie's?"

"No. They're at a seminar in Vancouver."

"Then take your butt home this minute and kiss and make up!"

"You must be Rainey." Pete practically shoved Beck aside as he tromped into the living room. He extended his hand. Seething, Beck held his ground. Friendship or no friendship, Pete had exactly twenty seconds to clear out.

"I am." Rainey shook Pete's hand and then, gracious as a southern belle, offered him a glass of wine and something to nibble on. From behind Pete's back, Beck motioned frantically for her not to be so damned nice, but she ignored him and went into the kitchen.

Pete plopped down on the sofa, yelping when his butt got acquainted with the broken spring poking up through the seat cushion. "I guess I won't be sleeping here!" he said with a chuckle.

Fuming, Beck gave up and dropped into the chair across from him. His back turned to Rainey, he silently mouthed the words, "Out. Get...out." Pete ignored him. He was busy following Rainey's movements in the kitchen. Grinning, he leaned forward and whispered, "Nate was right. She *is* a babe."

Beck motioned to stand. "I'll call the Haven and get you a room there." *If I have to, I'll drive you there myself and tuck you in for the night.*

Rainey handed Pete his glass of wine and gently pushed Beck back down with her hand. "There's no room at the inn," she reminded him. "Besides, there's no reason why Pete can't stay here tonight, is there?" She smiled sweetly.

"I like this woman," Pete said. "She's okay!"

Beck clenched his teeth.

"I'll just go up and prepare the guest room." Her back to Pete, Rainey used her eyebrows to motion frantically in the direction of the stairs. Beck realized she was panicking over the bedroom arrangements. Dammit! Pete knew they were sleeping in separate rooms, but Rainey didn't know that Pete knew that, and Beck didn't want her to know that he knew.

Man, he was tired of this nonsense!

The second she was gone, Beck pounced on their guest. "Your timing couldn't possibly be worse!"

Pouting, Pete whined, "What's the problem? You said yourself, there's nothing going on here."

"That's not true. There was a helluva lot going on before you got here."

"Oh, yeah? Like what?"

"None of your business. Beat it. Get lost. Make tracks!"

Rainey whacked her elbow on the doorjamb of her bedroom and let out a muffled cry. Both men automatically looked up. She had an armload of dresses and shoes, and was trying to transfer them as quietly as possible from her room to Beck's. Good Lord, Beck thought, our lives have become a farce.

"What's she doing?" Pete whispered.

"Never mind." Beck pointed a finger sharply at his old friend. "You owe me for this, man. You owe me big time."

Pete had the gall to look incensed. "Excuse me, but doesn't this mean she'll be sleeping in your room tonight? It looks to me like I'm doing you a favor right now."

As Rainey tiptoed back across the landing, Beck struggled to keep his voice down. "No you aren't. I don't *want* her sleeping in my room tonight. I'm...courting her."

"Courting her?" Pete repeated dumbly.

"That's right. Courting her. It was your suggestion, and it was a damn fine one."

Pete's eyes lit up with the power of deductive logic. "Yeah, well, won't this make the courting just a little bit easier?"

"No, it won't. It'll make it harder."

"I don't understand."

"You're right. You don't."

After Rainey came back downstairs, she and Pete chatted amiably while Beck bristled and squirmed and repeatedly looked at his watch. Pete asked Rainey a dozen questions about herself, and she answered them all good-naturedly. He didn't volunteer why Annie had tossed him out again, and of course Rainey was too polite to ask.

Beck didn't care why. It had better be major stuff, though. If it turned out to be something trivial, like a failure to take the garbage out on time, he would kill Pete. Yes, sir. Pete and Trevor, or whatever his name was. He'd have two dead bodies on his hands—and all for the love of one woman.

One very desirable woman. But still...

Yawning, Rainey finally excused herself and went to bed. Sensing his imminent death, Pete quickly turned in, too. Beck killed a few minutes by loading the dishwasher and wiping down the kitchen table. He was still tighter than a guitar string when he crawled into bed beside the object of his enduring fantasies. Right up until she snuggled up to him and nestled her pretty head in the crook of his arm. He relaxed then. Completely.

"Beck," she whispered against his neck. "I'm sick of this."

A knock came at the door.

Beck groaned. "Do we own a rifle?"

Rainey laughed. "No, but maybe we should get one."

"What is it, Pete?" Beck called out. It had better be good. It had better be very, very good.

"Um, I need a blanky," Pete said in a little-boy voice.

"A blanky!" Rainey buried her face in the comforter and howled.

Beck hollered at Pete to look in the linen closet, then turned on his side, facing her. "What were you saying? Oh, yeah, you're sick of this. That makes two of us."

What she was mostly sick of, Rainey said, was switching rooms. She simply could not do it again. Would Beck mind if she just slept in here from now on?

Oh, man. Courtship or no courtship, exactly how much restraint could one super horny, crazy-in-love man reasonably be expected to summon? "I don't mind at all," he murmured.

"Beck…"

He shushed her. "I know. I understand. I'm just a dumb guy, Rainey, but I think I finally got it."

They fell asleep in one another's arms.

13

LOVE WAS IN THE AIR.

Four days before Lilly's party, Rainey strolled through the Haven, making a mental list of all the things that constituted happiness.

Happiness, first and foremost, was having God's gift to womankind come into your office six times a day and kiss you until your limbs turned to Jell-O.

Happiness was coming home late from work to a house full of yellow roses—and the same tall, gorgeous, charming, funny, sexy gift destroying the kitchen as he made your dinner.

Happiness was opening your wedding gifts with the husband of your dreams and knowing, even if you weren't ready to acknowledge it just yet, that you would be keeping every one of them.

Happiness was being led, blindfolded and giggling, to the little bedroom behind the kitchen, where a brand-new 35 millimeter, single lens reflex camera with a full set of lenses, a tripod and a carry bag, rested atop the massage table.

Happiness was lying in bed at night, beside your gift, caressing his cheek while he caressed yours and searched your eyes clean through to your soul.

Happiness was the slow, tantalizing buildup to what you both knew was coming but understood the need to earn.

Happiness was other things, too.

It was noticing, really noticing for the first time, the newlyweds who sat cheek to cheek in the inn's dining room, holding hands and smooching while their food got cold.

It was going shopping with Francine for new clothes, and then for furniture. A soft, tan leather sofa. A Persian rug in hues of gold and yellow and rust and brown. Walnut tables with beveled glass tops and rounded corners. Antique lamps with stained-glass shades. Cushions and throws.

It was having coffee with Francine in a restaurant in Banff and looking up, surprised, to see Nate Frome standing there. Best of all, it was introducing the feisty reporter and the slick lawyer and witnessing a spark of interest between them.

Oh, yes, love was definitely in the air!

Humming softly to herself, Rainey sailed into her office—it was functional again—and checked her phone messages. She frowned. Darn it. Once again there was no message from her parents. Ten days ago she had sent them an invitation to Lilly's party, then called to confirm that they had received it.

And to tell them, once and for all, about the marriage. As usual, Beck had been right. She should have told them right at the start. Talk about cowardice.

Regardless, her resolve turned out to be for naught. Having braced herself for a shrieking parent, all she got was a pleasant, recorded voice: "You have reached the Miller residence. We're not available at the moment, but..."

Once again Rainey called her parents' next-door neighbors on the off-chance that her mother, at least, might be there. But this time the family had no idea where the Millers had gone.

Was it just Rainey, or did they sound...insincere?

She picked up a spare copy of the engraved party invitation and read it again. Frankly, she was worried about her parents. It wasn't so much that they might miss the party, though that was bad enough. It was more that, well, it just wasn't like them to go so long without contacting her.

As she glanced out the window at the sun-dappled snow blanketing the inn's grounds, she realized that Dana hadn't called to RSVP her own attendance at the party. Had she confirmed it during their last phone conversation? Hmmm. She hadn't.

Rainey dialed Dana's office in downtown Toronto, and was told that she was away—for two weeks. From the way she stumbled over her words, you would think the receptionist *did* know where Dana was: she just wasn't telling. Rainey then called Dana's apartment, but got only her machine, too.

What the devil was going on here?

On a hunch, she went to the lobby and checked the reservations book, starting with Friday, November 22. Nothing. From there she scanned back through the week. Allen. Simpson. Melnick. Hardisty. Then, finally: McCallum. Dana McCallum of Toronto. The reservation was for Tuesday, November 19. Today!

Why, she wondered, would Dana have booked a room here? Why wouldn't she want to stay with her and Beck? Based on their last phone conversation, she might have deemed it best to stay out of the lion's den. But then again, it wasn't like Dana to be put off by a little soap opera. On the contrary.

Rainey looked at the book again. The reservation was for two people, for one night, yet only Dana's name appeared in the register. That was odd. The Haven's strict policy was to list the names of all guests, regardless of whether they were sharing a room or not.

``Did either of you book this reservation?'' she asked the two young clerks on day duty. She smiled to indicate the young women weren't in any trouble.

"No, Mrs. Mahoney," they chimed with wide-eyed innocence.

Rainey eyed them suspiciously. There was something shady about the way they had responded. As if they knew something she didn't. It was meaningless, of course. Almost everyone in this nutty town acted slippery at least half the time. She was used to it by now.

"Thank you, ladies. Carry on."

With lots to do before noon, Rainey went back to her office and buckled down to it. Her new furniture would arrive late this afternoon, and at some point—heaven only knew when—Dana would turn up with her mystery guest. Nothing would get accomplished after that.

After making a few calls to suppliers, Rainey reviewed the project cost sheets Hollis had prepared. They were of greater interest to Beck than to her, but as general manager she made a point of reviewing every document, authorizing every purchase and signing every check and voucher. When it came to money, Beck had no restraint. Left to his own devices, that man would install solid gold taps in all the bathrooms.

Sighing, she set the document down and drifted into a daydream. Beck. Oh, how she loved him! Mrs. Norman had commented more than once lately on the dreamy look on her face. "You must be in love!" she had shouted at Rainey yesterday morning.

"I am," Rainey replied with a wink. "Just don't tell my husband."

Struggling to banish him from her thoughts now, she picked up the inn's year-end accounting statements and scanned their long, tedious columns. Not surprisingly, the Haven had lost money this past year.

An item on the second page caught her attention. An entry for a cash reserve of $174,000.62. Rainey stared at the figure, baffled. First of all, it was a great deal of money, far more than could ever be overlooked. Secondly, when she had first reviewed the books with Hollis and Beck, there had been no cash on reserve anywhere. Where, then, had this huge chunk of money come from? And where was it now?

Finally, there was something strangely familiar about the figure itself. What was it? Reviewing the year's quarterly statements to determine what she had missed was way more work than she wanted to tackle right now. Besides, she was no number cruncher. That was Hollis's job.

Not at all sure why she was doing it, Rainey reached into the file cabinet for the list of items Lilly had labeled Extraordinary Expenses. She hadn't paid close attention to the list before, but some instinct told her to take a good look at it now.

The items were listed alongside their respective costs. Rainey flipped over to the second page and looked at the total. It was $25,999.38. For no particular reason, she added that figure to the mystery cash on reserve—and got a total of two hundred thousand dollars.

The exact sum Lilly had borrowed against the inn.

Stunned, she poked her head into Hollis's office. ``Can you explain this?'' she asked, startling him as he sat hunched over his computer. Glancing at the documents, his pale-blue eyes widened and his right eye started to twitch. Was it just Rainey, or did he seem even more nervous than usual? Why was everyone around here acting so weird?

Hollis said he couldn't s-s-solve the mystery, and suggested she check with Flo Mahoney.

``Why? What does Beck's grandmother have to do with this?''

He merely repeated the suggestion.

Rainey's mind raced. It looked as though Lilly had borrowed the money but spent only a small portion of it. Hollis obviously knew something about it but wasn't talking. Flo

Mahoney was somehow involved. Lilly and Flo had been best friends.

What was the connection?

With Hollis's wary eyes on her every second, she paced the room for a long time, struggling to make the pieces fit. When they finally came together, she threw back her head and laughed hysterically. Why those conniving old dames!

Oh, yes! Everything suddenly made perfect sense. Why Lilly had left half the inn to Beck. The letters. The funny way people behaved around she and Beck. The utterly inexplicable manner in which they had readily accepted the marriage, as if the union of two perfect strangers was entirely normal. It wasn't. Not even here.

Flo, Nate, Pete, Arnie, Mrs. Norman, Hollis, Beck's parents—they all had accepted it without question. The only people who hadn't were the people who didn't know what was going on—the inn's other employees, the townsfolk, Francine, Dana.

Nah, it was too crazy.

Then again...

``Thank you, Hollis,'' she said, startling him with a kiss on the cheek. ``I think I'll pay Grandma a little visit.''

Once again, it was show time.

FLO MAHONEY SNIFFLED. ``Oh, dear. I'm so very, very sorry to hear you say that.'' She fished a lace handkerchief out of her lime-green sleeve and dabbed at her tears.

Rainey sat beside her on the sofa, doing her very best to look emotionally shattered. It was tough, what with the gigantic laugh that wanted to erupt in her throat.

``I'm so very sorry to have to tell you, Grandma,'' she said, forcing her voice to crack a little. She tried to work up a tear of her own but failed. How in heaven's name did real actors do it?

``When did you know?'' Still sniffling, Flo got up to

draw the blinds against the dazzling winter sunlight streaming into the living room of her overdecorated house in Red-
wood Meadows. Before sitting down again, she lightly
touched Rainey's arm in a gesture of sympathy. Rainey
nearly lost it.

"I—I guess I knew almost from the beginning,
Grandma. As you know, Beck and I married on very short
acquaintance. I had just come from another failed relationship, so I sort of married him on the rebound. As for Beck,
well—" she rolled her eyes "—you know how impulsive
he is."

Flo snorted. "Don't I, though!" Noting the anguish on
Rainey's face, she quickly added, "Oh, dear, please forgive
me. This is no time to be flippant."

Nodding, Rainey pulled a tissue from the box on the end
table and dabbed at her own eyes. There was nothing to
dab at, but the effect, she figured, was the same.

"Anyway, we tried to make it work, Grandma. Really
we did. But we just don't have anything in common besides
the inn. I thought that would be enough, but, alas, I was
wrong." She hung her head in shame.

"There, there, dear," Grandma soothed. She patted Rainey's knee.

"And now," Rainey continued, getting more and more
worked up, "we have all these financial complications.
Beck has a lot of money tied up in the Haven, and I don't
have the cash to buy him out, and oh, it's just a terrible
mess!" Finally, she managed to work up a sob. It wasn't
much of a sob, but it wasn't half bad, either.

Flo looked like she was trying to pass a gallstone. "Oh,
dear, we hoped it wouldn't come to this."

"We?" Rainey batted her eyelashes a few times.

"Your aunt Lilly and I. We... Ohhh, I had hoped never
to have to do this, but I suppose there's no choice now."

Sighing heavily, Flo got up and left the room, returning

shortly with an envelope—Lilly's mauve, floral stationery. The final letter—it must be. She pressed it into Rainey's hand and sat down again. Feigning bewilderment, Rainey opened it.

My dearest darling niece,

If you are reading this letter, it must be because things have not worked out between you and Beck. Please forgive me for believing they would. I had good reason to do so. I know you as well as I might know a child of my own, and I have come to know Beck very well these past few years. He is a wonderful young man, despite whatever you may think of him now. In my heart of hearts, I believed he was your perfect match. Obviously I was wrong.

I expect you will want to repay the money advanced to him by his grandmother. Please do not hold any of this against her. Her only wish is to see her grandson happy.

The money you need has been placed in trust with Nate Frome. You need only ask him for it and he will comply.

Good luck and God bless,

Your Aunt Lilly

Struggling to keep a straight face, Rainey set the letter down on the coffee table and fixed her green eyes on Ethel Mertz, Lucy Ricardo's partner in calamity. ``I don't understand,'' she lied.

``Well, it was very simple, dear. Your aunt always maintained that you and Beck were made for one another. He was single. You were single. We thought that if we just...threw you together...that nature would take its course. We meant well. You must believe that.''

Oozing empathy, Rainey murmured, ``I'm sure you did,

Grandma. But the part I don't understand is, how did you know we would get married?''

Flo took a sharp breath. "Oh, but we didn't! We had no idea you would take such a desperate measure!"

Okay, Rainey truly was baffled now. "But how, then, would Beck have gotten the money from his trust fund?"

"I'm the trustee, dear. I have the authority to override the marriage clause. If he'd asked me to, I would simply have released the funds."

The laugh she had been holding back for so long finally exploded in Rainey's throat, startling poor Flo out of her wits. Oh, it was too rich! The money was available all along. They needn't have married at all.

Frowning, Flo sat forward. "I don't understand, dear. What's so funny?"

"You are!" Rainey pointed an accusatory finger at her. "You and my sneaky aunt. Shameless matchmakers, both of you."

"But…"

"Gotcha!" Rainey cried, enjoying the moment immensely.

"Huh?"

Rainey watched as the confusion on Flo's funny little face gradually gave way to full comprehension. "Why you little imp." This time she swatted Rainey's leg. "How dare you give me a scare like that!"

"Oh, c'mon, Grandma. You deserve it."

"Oh, you! I could just spank you."

"Grandma." Rainey shook her head. "I have to ask— if Beck and I were made for one another, why didn't you just introduce us and wait to see what would happen?"

She gasped. "And leave it to Beck? Land sakes alive, dear. That boy hasn't a lick of sense when it comes to women. Besides, he makes a terrible first impression."

Hah! Wasn't *that* the truth.

The women sat quietly for a moment, chuckling to themselves. Finally, Flo reached across and grasped Rainey's hand. "Just tell me one thing, dear. Do you love my grandson?"

"More than life itself, Grandma." Rainey jumped up and helped Flo to her feet. At the front door, she held out her arms and the tiny woman walked into them.

"Thank you, Grandma, for giving me Beck Mahoney."

"And I thank my good friend, Lilly, for giving me you. Even if you are a brat!"

LETTER IN HAND, Rainey sailed into the Haven. Beck would get such a kick out of this. She couldn't wait to see the look on his face. Total shock. And oh, what a story they would have to tell Dana tonight!

On her way past the reservations desk, Rainey paused to check on her old friend. Hmmm. No sign of her yet. From there, she went upstairs to the wedding chapel, but the room was locked. Recoiling from the appalling dust and noise, she then made her way gingerly through the half-gutted west wing. None of the workmen had seen Beck for over an hour. Finally, Mrs. Norman said she had spotted him a while back, going into the massage salon.

Fast running out of breath, Rainey adopted a slower pace through the lobby, down the main corridor, past the dining room and her office. As she approached the open door to the salon, she overheard voices coming from inside. Beck's and a vaguely familiar female voice. Darn. He had a client, and he didn't like to be disturbed during sessions. Oh, well, she would catch up with him later.

Turning to leave, she overheard the client say, "Are you free right now? If you are, I could be, shall we say, accommodating."

Rainey stopped dead in her tracks. She was used to Beck's legion of drooling admirers. They no longer bothered her. Women, she had finally figured out, wanted him for the same reason she did—because he was Beck. She couldn't fault them for that. But that voice, that whispery little girl voice. Whose was it?

"You should know that I'm a married man," she overheard Beck say.

"That's okay," came the breathless response. "I have a boyfriend. But he's minding the store right now. Besides, he can't hold a candle to you."

"What did you say your name was?" Beck asked.

"Trish Mortimer."

Of course. It was the creature with the gargantuan breasts, the blonde who had bought the shop across the street. Who had felt those exciting hands on her and couldn't wait to feel them again.

Taking care not to move a muscle or utter a sound, Rainey glanced sideways through the door, at the far wall of the salon. The shadows dancing there told her that Beck and the bimbo were both standing on the other side of the room, where they couldn't see her. From the look of things, the woman was wearing only a sheet. She had Beck backed up almost into the corner.

"Are you sure your boyfriend won't mind?" Beck asked in the playfully seductive tone of voice so familiar to Rainey. She stopped breathing. Her heart started to pound and real tears welled up in her eyes.

Please, Beck, she silently begged him. Please...

"What he doesn't know won't hurt him," the bimbo maintained. "The same goes for your wife."

Beck chuckled softly. "Is that so?"

"It is. You know, we could get a room, right here, right now, and have a little fun. I'd love to show you some new tricks." She purred like a lazy cat.

"Hmmm, sounds...interesting."

The tears erupted with full force now, spilling down Rainey's cheeks and onto her sweater. She swiped at them with the back of her hand. Oh, how could she have been so stupid! Humble or not, Beck was Beck and always would be. He had said it himself: A tiger can't change its stripes.

"Let me just go and take care of it," the bimbo generously offered.

Beck cleared his throat. "Yeah, well, there's just one little problem with that."

"Really, what's that, gorgeous?"

"You see, I'm not just a married man. I'm a happily married man, and you can't hold a candle to my wife. So I think you should just run along now."

"Fine!" the blonde snapped. "But you don't know what you're missing."

It took Rainey a moment to grasp what she had just heard. Then her heart filled up with an unspeakable joy. Before it could burst out of her chest, she scampered down the hall and into her office. She quickly closed the door and leaned against it, panting. When her nerves finally settled down, she put Lilly's letter in her purse, along with the others, and grabbed a tissue.

This is what happiness really is, she thought. It's knowing the absolute truth.

14

BECK BURST INTO the room. "Hey, babe! Wanna come to the hardware store with me?" Spying Rainey's red, puffy cheeks, he came around the desk, reaching out for her. "Hey, you've been crying. What's going on?"

She buried her face in his chest and let him hold her. "It's nothing. It's just been a very...emotional day."

"Oh, boy, is it one of those, you know, *female* things?" he asked awkwardly.

Men. If only he knew. "Yes, Beck, it's one of those female things."

He stroked the back of her head. "I know just the cure for it."

She smiled up at him. "Really? What's that?"

"Lasagna. How 'bout if I make a run to the hardware store, do a little grocery shopping and cook you a nice dinner tonight? Maybe we can go to a movie afterward. Whaddaya say?"

"Oh, Beck, we can't. My friend, Dana, is arriving sometime today. She booked a room here, but I'd really like for her to stay with us."

"Man, oh, man," Beck grumbled. "When do we get to be alone?" He brightened. "Hey, I've got an idea. Why don't we send her to stay at Pete's?" He cackled like a lunatic.

"Beck! She's my oldest friend, and I really miss her. Please understand."

"I know, Rainey." He smoothed her hair and kissed her forehead. "It's okay. She's welcome to stay with us."

Mrs. Norman materialized in the doorway. Her hair was copper red today. "Sorry to disturb the lovebirds!" she hollered at a level just slightly below that of a sonic boom. For once she actually smiled. Rainey was surprised to see that she had a nice smile.

Still hugging her husband—her husband!—Rainey asked what the housekeeper wanted. There was a problem at the desk, Mrs. Norman barked. A double booking. "We have an unhappy camper."

"That's my cue to buy drill bits." Beck kissed Rainey and made haste for the door.

"Wait!" she called out to his retreating back. She really wanted to show him Lilly's letters before Dana arrived. But he was gone. Oh, well.

Rainey instructed Mrs. Norman to cancel the room reservation for Dana McCallum, to give that room to the disgruntled guest, and to give Rainey's home address to Ms. McCallum, if and when she checked in. "I'm taking the rest of the week off," she concluded. "I have personal business."

"Very good, Mrs. Mahoney."

Moments after Rainey focused on the unfinished paperwork on her desk, she realized Mrs. Norman was still standing in the doorway. Smiling politely, she asked, "Is there something else?"

"You'll do just fine." The housekeeper's tone was almost normal.

Rainey blinked. Surely her ears had just played a trick on her. "I beg your pardon?"

"I said you'll do just fine. As a manager."

A silly lump formed in Rainey's throat. Oh, dear. In a day power-packed with emotion, this was almost more than she could handle. "Thank you, Mrs. Norman."

The housekeeper sniffed. "You may call me Freda, if you wish."

BARELY TWO MINUTES in the door, Beck hurled himself into the corner of the new sofa and plopped his feet down on the new coffee table. As Rainey approached, he ran his hands over the smooth leather of the sofa and looked around with awe. "Wow, you did a terrific job with this place."

Rainey beamed. Everything was working out so well. The house looked fabulous. The fridge was fully stocked with food and wine. Her best friend was coming to visit. If and when Dana showed, that was. It was just after seven, and there was still no sign of her. Rainey felt torn. Part of her couldn't wait to see Dana. Another part of her wanted to be alone with her man. Especially tonight.

Bursting at the seams, she sat down beside him and worked up her best you-won't-believe-this look. "Beck, I have something to show you. Something incredible."

Grinning, he draped his arm around her shoulders and drew her close. "I have something to show you, too. I want to show you how a beautiful woman should be kissed."

He showed her. Boy did he show her. He loved her with all his heart. Rainey knew that now. All her doubts, all her fears, had vanished. All she needed now was to hear the words.

As if he had just read her mind, Beck commented, "You're excited. It must be me. I have that effect on women, you know."

"I've noticed. But sorry, it's not you this time. Well, okay it is you. But mostly it's—" He stopped her with another kiss.

"Rainey, Rainey, Rainey." He pulled back and shook his head. "When are you going to stop punishing me?"

She teased him with a smile. "What makes you think I'm punishing you?"

"Gimme a break, woman. I'm smarter than I look."

"Good thing, too! Just one question. If I stop punishing you, will you stop buying me roses?"

"Would you like me to buy you roses every day?" He stroked her cheek with his thumb.

"I would," she kidded.

"Consider it done." He kissed her again and Rainey melted. Oh, what she wouldn't give to tear his clothes off right now, to run her hands over his magnificent body, to taste every delicious part of him.

Darn that Dana. Why couldn't she come *tomorrow* night instead of tonight?

"Rainey," Beck whispered against her lips. "Forgive me for being such a jerk. Let me make love to you." He kissed her again, not so gently this time.

Coming up for air, Rainey managed to sputter, "Beck, I have something…" But his mouth smothered hers again, and when he was kissing her there was nothing else in the world.

Faster than you could say "animal attraction," they were stretched out on the sofa, face-to-face, their bodies pressed together, their limbs entwined.

"Beck…" Rainey managed to whisper between kisses.

"Quiet, woman. She's not here yet."

Moaning softly, they tasted the inside of each other's mouths. They ran their hands through each other's hair, and roughly along each other's sides. The temperature in the room shot up ten degrees.

"Beck…"

"Quiet. You talk too much."

Laughing, they tumbled off the sofa and onto the Persian rug. Beck pinned Rainey down and kissed her so soundly her ears started to ring. When his hand slipped inside her sweater and found her bare breast, she gasped.

"Rainey," he whispered huskily, drawing a circle around her nipple with his thumb. She shuddered.

The shrill chiming of the doorbell startled the daylights out of both of them.

"What!" Rainey cried. No car had pulled into the driveway, no footsteps had sounded on the walk.

Giggling and blushing all at the same time, she scrambled to her feet and smoothed down her sweater and her tousled hair. When Beck had pulled himself together, she opened the door.

Dana stood on the porch. All five feet, two inches of her. Same short, sandy hair. Same pixie face. She wasn't alone. Trevor stood beside her. All six feet of him. Same expensive haircut. Same bland expression.

"Trevor!" Rainey cried as if he were alone. "What are *you* doing here?"

"Hello, Rainey," he said quietly. "Nice to see you again." They shook hands awkwardly.

"Rainey. Sweetie." Dana gave Rainey a quick hug, then peeled her coat off and thrust it into her outstretched hands. "We have to talk!"

"What about?" Rainey hung both their coats in the closet.

Dana spied Beck standing in the living room. Eyes bugging out of her head, she approached him, hand out. "No doubt about it, you're Beck. I'm Dana McCallum, Rainey's friend."

"Pleasure to meet you." Beck shook her hand and looked over her shoulder at Trevor. He returned Beck's gaze and they discreetly sized one another up.

"Dana, what's going on?" Rainey demanded. "What do we have to talk about?"

"Nice digs," Trevor interjected. "*Love* the sofa."

Her face twisting into a grimace, Dana said, ''Rainey, I swore I wouldn't tell, but I just can't do that to you. Brace yourself. Your mom and dad are here.''

''What!''

''They're here, at the Haven. We flew in with them this afternoon. They've got our rental car, and they'll be here any minute.''

''But—but they don't have a reservation at the inn!''

''Oh, yes, they do. They reserved under the name Hardy. Or Hardisty. Something like that. They wanted to surprise you.''

Hardisty. Of course. Rainey had seen the name in the register. ''But—but—oooh!'' She clasped the sides of her head and looked frantically at Beck. Oh, boy. Trouble loomed.

He furrowed his brows. ''What is it, Rainey? What's wrong?''

She whirled on Dana. ''Do they know?''

''Know what?'' Beck demanded, glancing between the two women.

''No!'' Dana yelped. ''You made me swear not to tell them!''

''Why didn't you call and tell me they were coming?''

''I did. I left messages for you every day this week, but you didn't call me back. I called here, too, but you're never home. Why don't you have a machine like everybody else?''

''Beck hates answering machines. And I didn't get any messages from you at work!''

Beck glared at Rainey. ''What don't they know?'' His rigid stance and low, harsh tone suggested that he already knew what they didn't know. The question was just a formality.

Rainey groaned. ''Oh, Beck, they don't know that we're married!'' She bit her lower lip and looked away.

``Oh, that's terrific!'' He threw his arms in the air. ``That's just terrific!''

``I tried to tell them. Honestly I did, but they were always away when I called.'' Whew, that was *almost* true.

He stared daggers at her.

``Okay, we have to be calm,'' Rainey declared, wringing her hands. ``Everybody just sit down.''

Everybody sat down. Everybody folded their hands in their laps. Everybody looked helplessly at everybody else. Beck was furious. Rainey could just feel him burning up. Trevor, on the other hand, was enthralled with the house. Admiring the fireplace, he asked Beck, ``Is that real river rock?''

A sucker for anybody, anybody at all, with an interest in his handiwork, Beck lit up like a firecracker. ``Yeah. I hand-picked every stone myself.''

The next thing Rainey knew, they were on their feet, taking a closer look at the darned thing. Men. The world could be going to hell around them, and they would find something to whittle.

Rainey grabbed Dana by the hand and dragged her into the small bedroom behind the kitchen. Closing the door, she whispered, ``What's going on? Why is Trevor with you?''

Dana spoke through clenched teeth. ``Trevor and I have been seeing each other since you left. I've been trying to tell you for ages, Rainey, but every time I call you're chin-deep in a crisis.''

Relief overwhelmed Rainey and her shoulders slumped. ``Oh, Dana, it's okay. Trevor and I weren't right for each other. I always knew you were his perfect match. I'm sorry I made such a fuss about it.''

``I felt guilty, too. You have *no* idea.''

The women hugged.

"I've missed you so much." Tears welled up in Rainey's eyes. Good grief. Never had she cried so much in one day.

"Me, too." Dana nodded in the direction of the living room. "I can't believe you've been living with that hunk and not sleeping with him. What are you? A Tibetan monk?"

"That's about to change. Ah, that is, if he's still speaking to me after tonight."

"By the way, you look fabulous," Dana nodded her approval of Rainey's loose-fitting sweater and long, flowing skirt. "Lust looks good on you."

"Thanks. I had some help."

Dana sighed. "Trevor and I are getting married, Rainey. We thought we might like to do it here, in your new wedding chapel. All I have to do is call my parents and they'll fly out for the ceremony."

"Oh, Dana, that's terrific! When?"

"We thought maybe Saturday, before the party. That is, if it can be arranged on such short notice. We're going to Banff tomorrow afternoon with your mom and dad, but we should be back by Friday night."

Rainey said she would make the arrangements in the morning, and the women went back to the living room. Beck and Trevor had cracked a bottle of brandy and were flaked out on the sofa, debating the merits of skiing versus snowboarding. Rainey circled around them, trying to make eye contact with Beck. Still hot, he flat out refused to acknowledge her.

Please, Beck, she silently communicated to him. *Please don't be mad at me. I love you.*

When the rental car pulled into the driveway, they all fell silent. Beads of sweat formed on Rainey's brow and her heart drummed crazily in her chest. This was going to be awful. Just awful. Her parents probably knew about the marriage by now. Someone at the inn would have let it slip.

Sure enough, the faces that greeted her at the door were frigid and tight-lipped. The blast of cold air coming off them had nothing to do with the weather.

``Mom! Dad!'' Rainey cried with false cheer.

``Rainey,'' Laura Miller muttered with about as much enthusiasm as she might muster for a liver transplant.

Rainey hung their coats up and hugged each of them fiercely. They looked older than she remembered. Her mother had finally stopped coloring her hair, and it was a soft, attractive gray. Her dad looked fit, as usual, but the lines in his face were more deeply etched than before. Of course, it might just be his mood.

Beck approached him. ``Sir, I'm Beck Mahoney.''

``Yes, I know,'' Jonathan Miller said in the firm, deadly tone Rainey recalled from all those nights she missed curfew. ``You're my daughter's husband.'' He ignored Beck's outstretched hand.

Beck flinched and Rainey nearly fainted. Oh, dear, this was going to be even worse than she had thought.

``D-dad…'' she stammered.

He pointed a shaky finger at her. ``Don't you `Dad' me, young lady. You've got some explaining to do.''

``Sir,'' Beck piped up. ``If I could just—''

``Not another word out of you, young man!''

Always the mediator, Dana ordered everyone to sit down and calm down, for heaven's sake. Rainey motioned to sit next to Beck but changed her mind and sat across from him instead.

The second they were all comfortable, Laura Miller confronted Dana. ``Young lady, did you know about this?''

``Yes ma'am, I did.''

``Did you know about it?'' she then asked Trevor.

Trevor glanced cautiously at Dana, then at Rainey. He cleared his throat. ``Ah, well I knew about it when Dana told me, um, when she knew…what I mean to say is…''

Laura dismissed him with a wave of her hand. ``That's fine. You've said quite enough.'' She turned to Rainey next. Rainey groaned inwardly. She knew what was coming.

``How could you?'' her mother cried. ``How could you just go off and get married like that? Depriving us of the opportunity to attend our only child's wedding. Honestly, Rainey. We're terribly disappointed in you.''

Squirming, Rainey whined, ``Oh, Mom! It's sort of hard to explain. It's…Beck and I…'' She glanced at Beck for help. No go.

Laura snorted. ``We know all about you and Beck. Shame on both of you. Marrying for a few pieces of silver. You could have asked us for the money. We would gladly have given it to you.''

``But—but—'' Wait a minute. Wait just one minute. Rainey narrowed her eyes. ``How did you know about the money, Mom? For that matter, how did you know about any of this?''

While Rainey watched, astonished, a smile tugged at the corners of her mother's lips. A foxy little smile that wanted to get bigger. Soon Laura was laughing uproariously. Rainey's dad tried to keep a straight face but quickly gave up. Beck and Rainey and Dana and Trevor exchanged a puzzled look.

``Mom?'' Rainey asked.

``Oh, my! This is even more fun than I thought it would be!'' Laura cried. She touched her husband's arm. ``Can you remember when we last had this much fun, Jon?''

Still chuckling, he thought it over for a second. ``Well, there *was* that unfortunate incident with the weed whacker.''

``Will somebody please tell me what's going on?'' Beck pleaded.

"We knew all along," Laura told him. "Lilly called months ago and told us all about her little plan."

Rainey's jaw dropped. No wonder they hadn't been in touch with her. They had known all along what she was doing.

"Plan?" Beck wailed. "What plan?"

Sighing, Rainey fished Lilly's letters from her purse and handed them to Beck. Brows furrowed, lips moving, he read them, then flashed her a disgusted look. "*Puff pastry?* I resent that remark."

"Beck!"

"I still don't get it," he muttered, and began to read the letters a second time.

"It was a matchmaking scheme," she told him. "And everybody was in on it, everybody except you and me." While he listened, flabbergasted, she told him about her visit with Flo, and about the money held in trust with Nate.

No one said a word as Beck's mind raced back through the events of the past two months, putting two and two together, just as Rainey had done earlier that day. "Oh, man!" he finally cried. "You mean to tell me that Nate and Pete and Arnie knew about it all along?"

"Yup, every single one of them," Rainey replied. Turning to her mother, she asked, "How did you find out about the marriage? It wasn't part of their little scheme."

"Simple dear. We had a contact here, a liaison if you like."

Rainey closed her eyes and nodded. "Let me guess. Freda Norman. Right?" It was Freda who had booked the room reservations and withheld her phone messages from Dana.

"She's the one," Jonathan confirmed with a chuckle. "Peculiar-looking woman, I must say. Come to think of it, she looks just like Bette Davis in *What Ever Happened to Baby Jane?*"

Rainey rolled her eyes.

``Just one question, son,'' Jonathan said to Beck. ``Is this just about the money, or do you love my daughter?''

Rainey inhaled.

Slower than molasses, his eyes slid sideways to rest on hers. His gaze was soft but reserved. ``Yes, sir,'' he said. ``I love her very much.''

Rainey exhaled.

Jonathan sat forward and extended his hand to Beck. ``That's good enough for me. I'll shake that hand now, son.'' He sat back and smiled at Rainey. ``Now on to more important matters. Daughter, is there anything to eat in this house? I'm famished.''

``Just one minute.'' Laura held up one hand. ``Rainey, do you love this young man?'' She gestured toward Beck.

Gulping back tears—again!—Rainey looked at Beck. ``Yes, Mom. I love him with all my heart.''

``Good. Then all we ask is that you get married again. We won't be cheated out of a wedding. Understand?''

Dumbstruck, Beck and Rainey simply nodded.

``Let's eat,'' Jonathan insisted.

Hours later, after Dana and Trevor had turned in and Rainey's parents had gone back to the inn, Rainey and Beck sat in opposite corners of the sofa. Well fed, a little drunk, and numb from the sheer craziness of it all, they regarded one another warily.

``Are you still mad at me?'' Rainey asked shyly.

Beck nodded. ``Damn right I am. You are the most maddening woman I've ever met. You're spoiled, you're childish, you're stubborn and you're cowardly.'' He draped his arm over the back of the sofa and gestured for her to come closer. Giddy with relief, she slid over and turned sideways to face him.

``Did you mean what you said earlier?'' She idly fingered the neckline of his sweater.

He looked amused. "What? You mean about loving you?"

Oh, he was insufferable! "Don't do me any favors, Beck Mahoney!" She tried to get up, but he held her down. Taking her face in both hands, he said, "I love you, Rainey Miller."

"Well, you could of said so earlier!"

"Oh, yeah? And what about you?"

"I love you," she said simply. It was the truest thing she had ever said.

For a while they sat quietly together, gazing into one another's eyes. Then Beck started to laugh. "I don't believe this. I don't believe we were set up by a couple of crafty old dames. I don't believe we never had to get married. I especially don't believe that your ex-boyfriend, Trevor the cad, is sleeping in my house."

"With my best friend to boot!"

He shook his head. "You know, Trevor is a pretty nice guy, Rainey. I'm having a hard time believing he callously broke your heart. What exactly did he do?"

Rainey hesitated. Oh, dear. At the time, it had been devastating. Now it just seemed silly. She cleared her throat. "Well, he said…"

Beck stiffened. "He *said* something?"

"Yes. He said… Oh, darn. He said he thought Dana was special!"

Faster than lightning, Beck sprang to his feet, sending Rainey sprawling onto the rug. "That was *it?*" he whooped, helping her to get up again. "That was all the poor guy did? Oh, you are something else!"

Breathing fire, he advanced toward her. "Give me a break!" she snapped as he circled around her. "He was my first real boyfriend since high school."

Beck threw back his head and roared. "I don't believe

this! All this time you let me think it was something serious."

Oh, he wasn't getting away with that. "Excuse me, buster, but I didn't let you think anything at all. You're responsible for your own thoughts."

Still circling, he wagged a finger at her and grinned mischievously. "You're mine. Understand? All mine."

Rainey gulped.

He came up close to her. Looked her boldly, nakedly up and down. "You see this pretty mouth? It's mine." He kissed her hard. "You see this beautiful body? It's mine." He ran his hands over the front of her sweater, down her sides and around to her back. Rainey quivered. Consumed by raw, pulsating desire, she barely managed to whisper, "Kiss me. Please…"

Beck abruptly stepped back and pointed his finger at her again. "You're going to be kissed all right. Tomorrow night it's you and me, and I'm in charge. Understand?"

She smiled inside. "I understand perfectly."

"Good."

"I could be yours tonight," she suggested hopefully. What the heck, it was worth a shot.

He snorted gleefully. "No such luck, sweet thing. What I have in mind for you is going to be noisy. No guests allowed. Now get those gorgeous buns upstairs to bed. Now!"

Rainey danced along ahead of him, yelping when he smacked her smartly on the buns in question.

15

WHEN BECK let himself into the house the next night, Rainey was calm and happy. As calm and happy as a woman could ever hope to be.

She had donned the white silk, button-down camisole and G-string given to her by the Women of the Wapiti, and covered them with her fluffy bathrobe. Then she had dimmed the lights, put Nat King Cole in the CD player, and started a fire. A snifter of brandy sat on the work island. Beyond the living room's tall windows, night fell, clear and cold.

Beck dropped his keys on the foyer table and strolled into the room. Seeing her curled up in the corner of the sofa, he paused and looked around. "Are we alone?"

"Yes, we are."

His eyebrows shot up. "You're sure there's no one hiding in the house?"

"I'm positive."

Sighing wearily, he sank into the opposite corner of the sofa. "What a day. Freda sent Hollis out to buy airplane glue. Guess what he came back with?"

Laughing, Rainey got up and fetched the brandy snifter, and handed it to him. "Don't tell me. I don't want to know." She sat down again, one cushion closer than before. Beck took a sip, set the snifter down on the coffee table, and eyed her bathrobe with frank interest. "Did our guests get away on time?"

"Yes. We went out for brunch this morning and had a nice visit. Trevor and Dana seem very happy."

"Hmmm." He gazed at Rainey for a long time, the firelight dancing in his eyes. Finally, he asked, "Do you have any idea how much trouble we're in?"

She nodded. "I know. Everyone expects us to get married again."

He reached out and ran his index finger along the sensitive curve of her neck. "Almost seems a shame to disappoint them, doesn't it?"

Oh, dear. This was more than she had hoped for. "I agree. Absolutely."

"Of course, it'll be hard to explain a divorce after *two* weddings." He chuckled lamely.

Rainey inched closer to him. "Well, I can't speak for you, but I've sort of been having second thoughts about that divorce."

His eyes twinkled with amusement. "You have?"

"I have. I've sort of been thinking I don't want a divorce." She said the words casually, as if she had simply changed her mind about the decor.

He shook his head. "You know what, Rainey? I never wanted a divorce."

"Beck, I have some things I want to say to you...."

He shushed her. "You don't have to say a word. Just love me." He reached for her.

She held him off. "There are no words to say just how much I love you, Beck Mahoney. Right now, I need to say these things." She took a sharp breath. "I married you under false pretenses, Beck. I mean, in addition to the false pretenses we *already* had. I had this dumb idea that I could make Trevor jealous by marrying you. It wasn't just the inn and the money. I married you out of spite, and I'm ashamed of it."

"Oh, yeah? I can beat that. I actually thought I could

just try you on for size, and dump you if it didn't work out.''

"I'll go you one better. I was only bluffing when I suggested you see other women. I was testing you. It was shameless.''

"I know. I can't believe you did that.''

"I can't believe you went along with it.''

Beck sighed. "Rainey, I never saw any other women. I didn't even consider it.''

"I know. You spent all those nights helping Pete to build his garage.''

His mouth fell open. "How did you know that?''

She told him about her phone conversation with Nate.

He threw back his head and laughed. "Nate. Maybe I won't kill the guy after all.''

"In a way, we're indebted to him. To all of them, especially Lilly and your grandmother.''

"Speaking of Grandma, you know what occurred to me today? You're the only woman I've ever known who's never asked about the money. Don't you want to know how much there is?''

"No. I never cared about the money.''

"Well, I'm going to tell you anyway.'' He quoted a figure and Rainey gasped. It was more money than they could spend in three lifetimes.

A hot coal flew out from the fireplace and landed on the Persian rug, startling them both. Rainey went over, scooped it up with the little brass shovel, and returned it to the fire. Then she put two more logs on the burning pile. Beck came up close behind her and put his arms around her rib cage, under her breasts. She leaned against him.

"I have some things to say to you, too," he said in a firm but quiet voice. "Now I'm only going to say this ten times a day for the rest of your life, so listen up. I love you. I've loved you from the minute I laid eyes on you. I want you and only you.''

"Oh, Beck..."

"Quiet. I want to go to sleep with you at night, in our bed, and wake up with you in the morning. I want to see your beautiful face across the breakfast table. I want to reach for you whenever I feel like it, and I feel like it all the time. I want to make babies with you. Four of them, just like we said."

"Beck," Rainey whispered, her heart overflowing with all the love, all the tenderness, all the passion she had held back for so long.

His voice became hoarse, ragged. "I'm going to make love to you now, Rainey, and when I'm done you'll be mine forever."

She couldn't speak, so intense was her desire for him.

His breath hot on the back of her neck, Beck undid her bathrobe and eased it off her shoulders, let it drop to the floor and pushed it away. Then he gently cupped the undersides of her silk-clad breasts, his thumbs grazing over her swollen, aching nipples.

"You're so beautiful," he whispered into her hair.

While Rainey trembled, he undid the top button of her camisole. "I'm going to tell you what I love about you, okay?"

"Mmmm. Please do."

"I love the way you look in the morning. All sleepy and rumpled. Sexy."

Rainey sighed.

He undid another button. "I love the way your gorgeous green eyes light up when I walk into the room."

She moaned and writhed against him.

He undid another button. "I love the way you're good at everything you do, but don't see it."

"Beck..."

"Quiet." He undid the last button. "I love this exquisite body. I want it. I want it all for myself, tonight, tomorrow night, every night."

She trembled as he slowly peeled the camisole back until she was fully exposed in the firelight. Breathing raggedly, he slipped it off her shoulders and threw it away, then cupped her breasts fully, his incredible hands moving sensuously over them. When he gently squeezed her nipples, Rainey's breath caught sharply in her throat. Every bone, every muscle, every nerve in her body caught fire.

"Tell me you want me," he whispered huskily into her ear. "Say the words."

Rainey's head lolled back, her lips parted. "I want you. I want you." She had never wanted anything or anyone so much in her entire life.

"Say my name. Tell me you love me."

"I love you Beck, very much." How much could a woman possibly love a man? This much, obviously. This much.

His fingertips trailed down her tummy, whispering over her G-string, to caress the tops, the insides, of her thighs. Waves of unspeakable pleasure washed over Rainey, and a small cry escaped from her throat.

Whispering endearments, Beck slipped one hand inside her G-string and inched ever so slowly down to the spot that was already hot and wet and ready for him—had been ready for him for a very long time. When he made light contact with her throbbing flesh, Rainey feared she might collapse from desire.

He let his fingers rest there for an agonizingly long time before gradually increasing the pressure. When they finally slipped inside her, she cried out.

She turned around and helped him out of his clothes. All the while they kissed, wildly, passionately, in a frantic need to devour each other wholly.

When Beck was finally naked, Rainey gasped. He was beautiful. Long and lean and silky smooth. And, oh, my...huge and shiny and hard as granite. For a long time they just kissed and caressed one another, both of them trembling with anticipation.

While the fire raged behind them, Rainey dropped to her knees and gently encircled him with her lips. Relished the taste of him. Every beautiful inch. Trilled her fingertips down the back of his taut, muscled thighs and over his calves.

Beck moaned and raked his fingers through her hair. Soon a guttural sound issued from his throat and he pulled her away, panting. "Not yet, Rainey. Stay with me."

He followed her to the rug, their limbs already entwined. Rainey gasped when Beck reached down and tore her G-string away. They used their fingers then, and their mouths, to give each other more pleasure than either of them had ever thought possible. When Beck's tongue snaked along the inside of Rainey's wet thigh on its way home, she shuddered for the first of many times.

They said one another's names over and over again. They tasted each other's wet, salty skin. They whispered gibberish. They were gentle, then rough, then gentle again. They could not get enough.

When Rainey thought she could bear it no longer, Beck positioned himself above her and, cupping the back of her thigh, brought her knee up and made them one person—a single entity, moving together in a rhythm as old as mankind.

He moved slowly at first, just inside, teasing her, tormenting her, making her beg for mercy. Then a little faster. A little deeper. Until, finally, there was no telling where he ended and she began.

As Beck moved deep within her, Rainey raked her fingernails across his back and cried out again and again and again. It was too much. It was unbearable. She was in a new place. She was alive. She was the best she could ever be.

He was right. She was his. Forever.

At long last, Beck arched his back and cried out her name one last time.

For a long time afterward they lay quietly in one another's arms, drenched in sweat and breathing softly. Rainey could not believe what had just happened. In her wildest fantasies, she hadn't imagined how truly awesome it would be. Never had her body responded to a man that way. It went beyond mere coupling. It was heavenly, spiritual, sublime.

It was final, she knew. For the rest of her life, there would be no man but this one.

When the fire finally died, they went upstairs, arm in arm, and crawled into their bed. And made love again. And again. And again. Many hours later, when the sun peeked in through their window, Beck propped up on one elbow and, gazing into her eyes, murmured, "Now I know what *more* is."

"What does that mean?"

"Never mind." He kissed her forehead, her eyes, her lips.

"Rainey," he said when she was almost asleep.

"Mmm."

"What we were talking about earlier. About getting married again?"

She opened her eyes. "Yes."

"I was wondering. Would you do me the honor of being my wife? I mean, for real?"

"I don't have a choice," she informed him. "The arrangements are already made."

He hooted. "Oh, yeah? Who's cocky now?" He reached under the bed and came up with a small, blue velvet box.

Inside was a slender gold band supporting a big, square-cut white diamond, surrounded by smaller, yellow diamonds in a raised setting. It was exquisite.

"Oh, Beck!"

"I figured we should do things right this time."

Rainey put the ring on and admired it. "Question. Can you get engaged to be married when you're already married and about to get married again?"

"Don't *complicate* things, woman!"

THE SECOND WEDDING of Rainey Ann Miller, only child of Laura and Jonathan Miller, and Beckett Lee Mahoney, youngest child of Martha and Earl Mahoney, took place on the third Saturday in November, in the wedding chapel at the Honeymoon Haven. The bride wore a white silk gown with a veil and a long train. The groom wore a black tuxedo with tails, and a bow tie.

Charles T. Longhorn, world-weary chief commissioner of the town of Bragg Creek, officiated. Trevor Thorland of Toronto served as best man. Dana McCallum, also of Toronto, served as maid of honor. Freda Norman and Flo Mahoney made history as the world's oldest, and definitely most colorful, bridesmaids.

A hundred guests were on hand for the occasion.

Mr. Longhorn eyed the bride and groom suspiciously. "Haven't I married you before?"

Beck and Rainey beamed at one another, then at Mr. Longhorn. "Not really," they chimed.

He peered at them doubtfully for a moment, then cleared his throat and looked out over the crowd. "Fine then. Can anyone here say why this young couple should not be joined in holy matrimony?" All one hundred guests stood up and applauded. Martha Mahoney, who had wept softly throughout the ceremony, let out a wail.

Mr. Longhorn sighed. "Whatever. I now pronounce you

man and wife. You may kiss the bride.'' Three minutes into the kiss, he clasped his chin with one hand and narrowed his eyes to slits. ``I'm sure I've married you before.''

When the brief ceremony was over, the groom and best man swapped places. The bride and maid of honor did likewise. Within minutes they had concluded the marriage of Dana and Trevor.

Three minutes into their kiss, Mr. Longhorn mumbled, ``Must be the drinking water around here.''

Without further ado a dozen big round tables were hustled into the room and draped with white linen. Vases of red, white, pink and yellow roses appeared on the side tables. Soon there was food and drink and laughter and loud conversation. A band of musicians set up near the altar and tuned their instruments.

The seance to resurrect the spirit of Lilly Miller had failed to produce results, so a toast was declared instead. ``To Lilly!'' Nate Frome cried, rising to his feet. Francine stood with him.

``To Lilly,'' the guests sang out.

Around midnight, Beck whispered into Rainey's ear, ``This is fun, but I'm thinking we should head home and get started on baby number one.''

She put her arms around his neck and gave him a coy smile. ``Beck Mahoney, are you trying to hustle me?''

``Yes, ma'am.'' He nuzzled her neck. ``Every day from now on.''

Epilogue

One year later

"HEY, BABY," Beck called out from the door. He dropped his load of books on the foyer table and breezed into the kitchen.

Seated uncomfortably, as usual, at the kitchen table, Rainey tilted her head up to receive his kiss. Her gorgeous green eyes shone. "Hi, sweetie. How was school today?"

He made a face. "Contract law. Yuck. I can't wait to specialize."

She laughed and let him kiss her, once, twice, three times.

"How's Lilly?" Beck reached down and ran a hand over Rainey's enormous stomach. Soon. Very soon.

"Lilly," she replied dryly, "is a pain in the butt. Literally."

"Not much longer."

"That's easy for you to say!"

Over her shoulder, Beck examined the eight-by-ten color prints spread out on the table. Spectacular shots of mountain vistas, rippling streams, dense, dark forests. "Wow, these are terrific."

"Thanks." Rainey glowed with pride. Francine had secured a contract to write a history of the Bow Valley Corridor and recruited Rainey to shoot the accompanying pictures. Rainey was drunk on the experience.

``How are things at the Happiness Inn?'' she asked, knowing he had stopped in at the newly refurbished—and renamed—hotel on his way home.

``Never better. It looks fabulous and we're booked solid until well past Christmas. Freda and Hollis are doing a terrific job of running things.''

``I'm so glad. If darling Lilly is going to be the handful I think she's going to be, they'll be running things for a while.''

``That was a stroke of genius you had—putting them in charge.''

``Really?'' Rainey grinned. ``No word of a lie?''

Beck put his arms around his wife's shoulders and kissed her soft cheek. Could he love her more? Yes, he could. A little more each day.

``It's the truth, babe. You can trust me.''

My Place or Yours?

Wendy Etherington

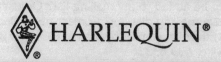

HARLEQUIN®

TORONTO • NEW YORK • LONDON
AMSTERDAM • PARIS • SYDNEY • HAMBURG
STOCKHOLM • ATHENS • TOKYO • MILAN • MADRID
PRAGUE • WARSAW • BUDAPEST • AUCKLAND

Dear Reader,

I grew up wanting to rule the world—or at least to be the CEO of Coca-Cola. Then I discovered two literary giants: Harlequin romances and Louis Grizzard. (For those of you above the Mason-Dixon line, Grizzard was a famous—or was it infamous?—writer and Southern humorist.) Who knew these three passions would someday blend together into a career? These days I get to create a world I rule with my keyboard, and write about enduring love with a comedic twist.

The inspiration for *My Place or Yours?* came from a real-life experience. My poor house in Atlanta endured a lot before passing into new ownership, including plumbing problems and the somewhat disconcerting day I came home from church (on Easter Sunday) to find termites munching on the floorboards in my dining room. Needless to say, my stress inspired much trouble and fun for Alex, Rebecca and Moose.

The real Moose, by the way, is probably looking down from Cat Heaven—at least, I'm assuming he's looking down rather than up; with Moose anything's possible—and thinking, *The least you could have done was make me a posthumous size six.*

Want to be added to my mailing list? Or just share your own moving disaster? Contact me online at WendyEth@msn.com or by mail at P.O. Box 8, Cottleville, MO 63366.

Wendy Etherington

To my editors, Susan Pezzack and Brenda Chin,
for making this book something special.

Special thanks to my husband, Keith,
and my children, Caitlyn and Grace,
for their support. And thanks to my friends
and fellow writers for their critiques and advice—
Anna Adams, Adele Ashworth, Jacquie D'Alessandro,
Carmen Green, Jenni Grizzle, Stephanie Bond Hauck,
Rita Herron and Jennifer LaBrecque. I could never
manage this crazy business without you!

1

THE CAT WAS PISSED.

Rebecca Parsons stood in the foyer, warily eyeing Moose, her twenty-plus-pound Persian. His bushy tail beat in a series of decisive thumps against the bottom step of the wooden staircase. His round, golden eyes stared unblinking at the envelope tucked beneath her arm.

"Forget it. We're still moving."

She set her briefcase at the base of the steps, then walked into the kitchen.

And gasped.

The fifty yards of bubble wrap she'd bought the day before lay in mangled bits scattered across the floor. Ripped pieces dangled from the overhead light. One long strand hung off the kitchen table, the formerly round bubbles of air designed to protect her breakables during the move reduced to old, deflated balloons. Her normally pristine yellow-and-blue kitchen—the only room Mama had let her bring out of the nineteenth century—was a disaster.

"Moose…"

Slapping the envelope containing the sales contracts on the table, she turned to face him, certain he'd followed her into his favorite room. "The buyer will be here any minute. How could you?"

Moose nonchalantly washed his paw.

She stomped to the sink, then grabbed the trash can from

the cabinets below. "Do you have any idea how much that stuff cost?" She stooped on the white-tiled floor and gathered the mess, tossing the ruined plastic in the can. "I bet you'd adopt a new attitude if I starting buying you the twenty-cents-a-can cat food, instead of that gourmet sixty-five-cent stuff."

Moose sent her a malevolent stare. One did not mess with Moose's meals.

Too bad, buddy. She couldn't afford to toss the expensive bubble wrap—just another reminder of her sad financial state. If this sale didn't go through… No, she wouldn't even consider the possibility. Too much was riding on her successfully unloading The House.

Sighing, she crawled under the table to reach the last of the plastic. Moose's obvious resentment about the move only deepened her guilt. Mama would never have approved of the step she was taking. Mama had loved this house. Every turret and rotunda, every inch of gingerbread trim, every piece of antique furniture and every ornate—as well as mismatched and tacky—decoration.

Though completely impractical, her mother had clung to her kooky house, the house where Rebecca never felt she fit in. She'd lived in the shadow of the extraordinary, beautiful Angelina Parsons all her life, and now it was time to consider the future. Her future.

Since Mama had passed away, Rebecca didn't see any reason to continue to live on the edge of bankruptcy in this town full of eccentrics just so she could keep The House. A big-time New York City law firm had offered her a job so today she had closed her small law office for the last time. In a city of that size she was bound to find a place where she belonged, not just as the quiet, brainy offspring of her mother. She couldn't wait to experience the excitement of the city—plays, restaurants, coffee houses, art galleries. Plus her financial crisis would finally be over.

Though if Moose continued expressing, in such expensive ways, his displeasure over leaving, she might never be solvent again. What she needed was a wealthy buyer with a mission to preserve the past. According to her real estate agent, stockbroker Alexander Carlisle fit the bill.

Rebecca knew little about him beyond what Pam had told her—he was a charming negotiator, had a sexy phone voice and was rich as sin. Pam had been known to greatly exaggerate a man's assets, so Rebecca didn't take her too seriously. Except the rich part. As long as he had enough money to buy one slightly used Victorian house...

As if on cue, the doorbell chimed. Her stomach fluttered in anticipation.

After shoving the now-full trash can under the sink, she hurried down the hall, her hand automatically smoothing the French twist she'd wrangled her curly hair into. She paused to glance in the beveled glass mirror—with gold-leafed cherubs dancing along the frame—and brushed a strand of beige cat hair off her conservative navy pantsuit. Objectively, she absorbed her reflection. Though blue-eyed and dark-haired like her mother, she didn't have the up-turned, catlike eyes, or luxurious, sexy hair a man longed to bury his hands in. She was plain. The most ordinary person she knew. Hell, she was the *only* ordinary person she knew.

Rolling her shoulders, she opened the front door...and found herself staring at a broad masculine chest.

Rebecca tipped her head back to meet a pair of bright green eyes. He stood over six feet and wore a tailored charcoal suit that whispered power and probably cost more than her car. His jet-black hair waved in the front and looked so soft, her fingers tingled with the urge to run her hands through it. His jaw was square, his face sculpted.

Sexy phone voice? Wait'll Pam got a load of the visual effects.

Then he smiled.

The expression transformed his whole face from merely handsome to breathtaking, causing every practical, professional thought in her brain to pack their bags and retire to Florida. Warmth rolled off him, bathing her in a glow like the sun breaking through the clouds after a rainstorm.

Good grief. Poetic after one smile? A lawyer used to reside in her body, but where she was at the moment, Rebecca had no idea. Maybe Orlando.

His green gaze locked on her face, then slid down her body so thoroughly she was almost certain he'd touched her. Male appreciation heated his eyes, making her knees wobble. Had any man ever looked at *her* like that? The way men always looked at Mama?

"Rebecca Parsons?" he asked in a deep, husky voice that sent a thrill racing down her spine, proving, for once, Pam hadn't exaggerated.

"Uh-huh." She leaned against the door frame.

He extended his hand, enveloping hers in a smooth shake. "I'm Alex Carlisle."

"I, uh—yes." Rebecca ducked her head. God, how long had she stood there gaping at the man? Baffled by the instantaneous chemistry, she pulled her hand from his then stepped back, holding the door wide. "Please, come in."

He walked inside, leaving a whiff of spicy cologne drifting through the air. She lifted her nose to catch more of the scent. Good grief. She probably looked like Moose, following the scent of tuna fish.

Get a grip, girl.

He gazed around the two-story foyer, the chandelier raining shimmers of light on the dark-stained solid oak floor, then studied her face again. "It's quite...lovely."

"Thank you." Rebecca dug deep for a businesslike attitude, and, blessedly, found it. He probably stared at every woman that way. She'd seen enough of her mother's charming boyfriends in her life to recognize a natural flirt when she saw one. "I was a bit surprised when your offer came in without you ever seeing the house." It was certainly something *she* wouldn't have done.

"The pictures your agent sent were enough." He smiled again, casting the glow in her direction. "I make decisions about things—and people—on gut instinct."

And what did he think of her? she wondered, then couldn't believe she cared. He was here to see the house, not her. It was just that he made her feel so oddly center-of-attention-like.

She just hoped his gut instinct could see the house beneath her mother's eccentric—polite translation of tacky—decorating.

As she directed him into the front parlor, with its dainty, curvaceous, pink Victorian sofa, she noticed the way he stroked the furniture's crushed velvet upholstery. He didn't sneer or even blink at the lavender walls. His eyes drank in his surroundings, as if amazed to be in the presence of such beauty. She'd seen that same look on her mother's face every time she'd spotted an antique she just had to have.

Alex Carlisle was looking better and better.

"Would you like the full tour?"

His gaze skimmed down her figure. "If you're the guide."

Nodding, she wondered how he made a simple sentence sound like an indecent proposal.

He walked toward her, not stopping until their chests nearly brushed. The ridiculous idea that he might pull her into his arms raced through her mind. Seconds ticked by—with her holding her breath—then he slid his hands into the pockets of his slacks. "Lead me on," he said finally, his eyes gleaming.

Her breath whooshed out at the loaded suggestion. What in the world was wrong with her? She didn't touch perfect strangers, and she certainly didn't *pant* in anticipation of one touching her. *He's just different,* she told herself. Junction Gap, Georgia, didn't raise too many charming, sexy, sophisticated men. And certainly no one like him had ever given her a second glance.

Stepping to the side, she pointed to the portrait in the large, gilded frame above the fireplace and began her tour. "Antonia Millford, my great-great-grandmother, built this house with her husband just before the turn of the century. She was fascinated with Victorian England, hence the decorative style and architecture."

He slid his hand across a heart-backed chair, also upholstered in pink. *Mauve,* Mama would have corrected. "It's very feminine," he said.

"Yes, well, you may want to redecorate." Her agent, in fact, had encouraged her to do so before putting the house on the market. While Rebecca couldn't afford to, she also couldn't bring herself to paint over her mother's hard work. The buyer could change whatever he wanted, but she didn't want to witness the change. "The house has passed through the female side of my family," she continued as she led him into the dining room and suppressed a wince at the tangerine-colored walls. "It's a family tradition to keep the furnishings intact." *As well as not breaking your flamboyant mother's heart.* "The plumbing and wiring have been updated, of course."

He pulled out a chair—upholstered in purple paisley. With barely a glance at the fabric he pushed it back, then walked around the enormous mahogany table.

She'd been prepared to defend Mama's eccentric taste, but it didn't seem like there was any need. Either he planned to repaint or his taste was equally hideous. As long as he signed the papers he could dance naked in the foyer if he wanted to.

Hmm…maybe she should find that pen and get him to sign. The sight of broad-shouldered Alex Carlisle naked was a sight she'd like to—

"If it's such a tradition, why are you selling?"

Appalled at her line of thinking, Rebecca tried to remember what she was selling and why. Oh, yeah. The House. "I've accepted a job out of state."

His gaze met hers. "You could rent it out."

She shook her head. "A buyer will take better care of it."

"It seems a shame to break such a long-standing family custom."

"Yes, well…" His curious gaze made her squirm. And just when she thought she'd beaten back the guilt. "Lucky for you, huh?" She cleared her throat. "This table chandelier is one of the items I'll be taking with me."

He ran his finger down one of the over nine hundred glowing, multifaceted crystals. "It's beautiful."

And Mama's favorite. Pushing aside the melancholy, she said, "Let's go back across the hall."

She showed him the study and library—decorated in candy-apple red and lime green respectively—and he lingered over the curved, solid oak staircase leading to the second floor.

Rebecca remembered the summer she and her mother had refinished the staircase themselves, since they didn't have enough money to hire a carpenter. That summer had been hard work but refreshingly lacking in Mama's endless stream of boyfriends, as she'd given up men—again. Most of her mother's attention was focused solely on Rebecca, making the memory more precious for its rarity.

So many memories here, Becca, Mama had said. *I know you think I'm too sentimental, but you'll understand when you're older.*

But Rebecca had never really understood, and she'd known even then that hanging on to The House just wasn't *practical.* Mama didn't even know the definition of the word. Yet, as Rebecca watched Alex Carlisle run his hands reverently over the railings and newel posts as another man might touch a beautiful woman, she knew he understood.

After leading him upstairs, she showed him the gilded guest bedrooms, then walked past the closed door to the master suite.

"What's in here?" he asked from behind her.

She bit her lip. Damn. That was a room she probably should have found the money to redecorate. "Just another bedroom," she said as she faced him.

He angled his head. "Can I see?"

"Of course." She walked toward him, holding her breath as he turned the brass doorknob.

He strode into the room, then suddenly ground to a halt. Rubbing his chin, he stared, blinked, then stared again. "It's...well...uh..."

"An exact replica of a nineteenth-century whorehouse."

He whirled, a slow smile spreading across his face. "No kidding?"

Was it possible to make up something that humiliating? She looked around at the red walls, red carpet, gold drapes, heart-shaped four-poster bed and mirrored ceiling. "No kidding."

"Cool."

It was her turn to blink and stare. Did he just say *cool?* He wasn't horrified? He wasn't going to run from the house crossing himself and muttering rosaries under his breath like that couple from Louisiana? Clearly, Alex Carlisle was made of stronger stuff. And what attractive stuff it was.

She was half tempted to show him the portrait she'd hidden in the attic—a full-length nude of Mama painted during a brief affair with an Italian artist—just to see his reaction.

"This is the master suite," she said, still watching him closely.

His smile widened. "Yours?"

"God, no—" She cleared her throat. "My room's at the other end of the hall."

He crossed to the bed, then plopped down, leaning back on his elbows to stare at the mirror overhead.

Rebecca didn't have a difficult time picturing him naked, ebony hair mussed from a woman's fingers, in flagrante delicto beneath the red satin sheets. In fact, she was enjoying picturing him that way. Desire stole over her, warming her blood, sending tingles through her limbs.

Waggling his eyebrows, he patted the space next to him. "Join me?"

Now *that* was the most interesting offer she'd had all week. Actually, all month. Okay, year. Maybe years. It was also impulsive and wild—not at all like her.

With some regret, she turned away. "I'll just wait in the hall."

He joined her moments later, seemingly unaffected by her refusal. Of course, his offer hadn't been serious. A man like Alex could have any woman he wanted.

Her room was decorated in white and pale yellow, with simple pine furniture and clean lines. Alex looked around with interest, as if trying to glean the meaning behind the contrast of this room and the others. His large frame nearly filled the small cupola she'd turned into a sitting room. The floor-to-ceiling windows revealed the wooded view and cloudless azure sky. Afternoon sunshine streamed through the yellow and orange leaves of the tremendous oaks shading the backyard.

"I'll be taking these furnishings, as well," she said, then headed toward the bathroom. She stopped just inside the French doors, letting him brush past her, and she again inhaled his alluring cologne. Having him stare at her toothbrush and lotions—as well as her smiling gargoyle toothbrush holder—added to the intimacy of the moment.

He pointed at the clawfoot tub. "It looks refinished."

"Yes. All the porcelain and tile has been either replaced or reglazed within the last ten years."

"It must have cost a fortune to keep everything up."

Rebecca nodded, staring at the white-tiled floor—hand-laid by her and her mother. "My grandmother left a sizable inheritance." Which hadn't been nearly enough, but he didn't need to know that.

"You included the furniture in the price?"

She nodded. "Except for the items I've mentioned."

They continued to the attic, then walked down the back stairs leading to the hall beside the kitchen. At the cellar door she paused, gripping the knob, feeling ridiculous because of the way her heart doubled its beat. There wasn't any truth to that old dead-body-buried-under-the-stairs story stupid Tommy Mackenzie had told her in the third grade. Mama had only laughed when Rebecca had questioned her about it, and who knew what *that* meant? Then there was that small dog-size rat she'd seen last summer.

You went to law school, for God's sake. You can handle a rat or two.

"Another bordello room?" Alex Carlisle questioned from behind her, his breath stirring the hairs on the back of her neck.

She glanced at him over her shoulder, trying to decide if he looked hopeful. "Uh...no." She swallowed. "Just the cellar. Did you want to see it, too?" she asked, trying to make the idea sound unreasonable.

"Yes," he returned, stepping around her and opening the door, "but you can stay up here if you like."

Who said chivalry was dead?

He was back upstairs a few minutes later. "Your wine collection is excellent. I'm an enthusiast myself."

"Really?" He'd fit in *perfectly* in Junction Gap, she thought sarcastically. The only thing most men around here knew about wine was the convenience store price of Mad Dog 20/20. She was half tempted to convince him he'd be bored senseless inside a month if he moved here, though the lawyer in her killed that idea quickly. *Don't try to read the jury before the verdict is even in.*

Rubbing his chin, as if deep in thought, he said, "The house is terrific."

"Yes, it is," she said, practically holding her breath in anticipation of his decision.

"A lot of responsibility, I imagine."

She swallowed. "A bit." *Liar, liar, pants on fire.* The

House being "a bit" of responsibility was like saying Mount Rushmore had taken "a bit" of chiseling. "How about some coffee?" she asked. Maybe he would be impressed by her modern kitchen and convenient, no-hassle appliances.

"Sure."

She led the way down the hall and into the kitchen. Perched on the table, his furry body sprawled in abandon, Moose blinked his gold eyes. Halfheartedly, Rebecca shooed him off. She knew some people felt weird about cats in the kitchen. As a neat freak herself she could sympathize, but there was no keeping Moose off the counter and table.

After wiping the table, she pulled out a chair for her buyer. "Have a seat, Mr. Carlisle."

"Alex, please," he said, smiling up at her as he lowered his lean body into the chair.

"And I'm Rebecca." She stepped away from the glow of his expression, retreating around the bar to add water and grounds to the coffeemaker, but deciding she liked that mischievous smile, as if everything in his life was amusing and fun.

"Another modern room. You have some interesting contrasts around here."

As always, she found herself making excuses for Mama's odd—she bit her tongue on the word *tacky*—sense of style, even though she'd gotten used to it long ago. "Mama and I were a contrasting pair."

His eyes twinkled. "So the bordello..."

"Was completely her idea." She paused before adding, "She died six months ago."

"Oh." His expression lost its animation briefly.

She hoped he wouldn't ask how, as a lot of people did.

She didn't want to discuss Mama's brief fascination with bungy jumping.

"I'm sorry," he said simply. "I would have liked to meet her."

"Thank you." She smiled inwardly at the image of Angelina Parsons meeting a man like Alex Carlisle. She would have had the sales contracts signed and his undying love wrapped up inside five minutes.

She started the coffeemaker, then pointed to the envelope on the table. "My agent drew up the contracts," she said, working hard for a matter-of-fact tone. "I've already signed them."

His gaze slid to the envelope, then back to her. "Right."

Rebecca's stomach fluttered—at being the focus of his attention and worry over whether he'd changed his mind. Finally he withdrew the papers and began to read. Pretending not to care that her whole future was riding on his decision, she busied herself pulling mugs from the cabinets and wiping the already-spotless countertops.

"Meow."

Alex looked up from the papers, then down at Moose, who sat silent beside the table, glaring back at the stranger. "I think your cat's calling you."

The meows continued to echo rhythmically. "That's the clock," she explained. "Another item I'll be taking with me."

He angled his head, listening until the last meow rang out. "Cute." He went back to the contracts.

She should have thrown out that silly clock years ago, she supposed, but it and Moose had been a twenty-third birthday present from her mother. The two were forever tied together.

As the coffee hissed into the pot, Alex withdrew a pen from inside his coat pocket and scrawled his name.

Rebecca let a sigh of relief escape. *That was easy.* Too easy, in fact.

"It looks like we're all set—after the buyer's inspection, of course," he commented lightly as he signed the other copies. "It's scheduled three weeks from now?"

"Yes." Way too easy. With The House, she'd never known three days to go by without something going wrong, much less three weeks. Wasn't there a patron saint of house protection? She'd seen those white statues in other people's yards. She should probably invest in one. "We only have one certified inspector in Junction Gap, and that was the best he could do." She poured them each a mug, then set his on the table. "Do you need cream or sugar?"

"No." He caught the mug between his hands, studying the contents. Then he looked up and flashed that heart-stopping smile.

Her knees buckled, forcing her to brace her hands against the table, or else flop into an undignified heap on the floor.

Pushing his coffee aside, he leaned toward her, his gaze locked on her face. "I suddenly feel like celebrating." He stroked the tips of her fingers with his thumb. "If I buy a bottle of wine from you, will you join me?"

Rebecca's stomach trembled, then tightened. His touch was hypnotic…enticing, making her wonder how his touch would feel on other parts of her body. Men as appealing as Alex Carlisle ought to come with warning labels: "The Surgeon General strongly advises you to keep your distance. This man is a professional heartbreaker."

She briskly reminded herself how many charming men her mother had gone through since Rebecca's father had deserted her before she'd been born. They promised plenty and delivered little.

"It's barely noon."

"So we're being…bad," he said, his voice deep, his smile sexy as hell and his thumb still gliding back and forth over her skin.

He was a charming negotiator, all right—provided the other party happened to be a woman. They probably fell prostrate at his feet and did whatever he asked. But being the smartest Parsons in decades, she knew Alex's interest in her was just an instinctive reaction to his love 'em and leave 'em persona.

She pulled her hand away, gathering his coffee mug. "One glass."

"For now."

Turning away, she crossed the room, dumped the coffee in the sink, then opened the refrigerator. "I have a California Chardonnay. Will that do?"

"Perfect."

Good, since there was no way she was retrieving a bottle from the cellar. Her neighbor's husband performed that task whenever she needed. Glasses, bottle and corkscrew in hand, she returned to the table. That was the moment she noticed his pants.

2

TEETH CLENCHED, Rebecca stooped at Alex's feet, brushing the thick beige hair clinging to his pant leg. "I'm so sorry. Your beautiful suit. That cat is so—"

Leaning down, he stilled her hand. "It's fine."

Her pulse raced as she stared at him, a lock of black hair grazing one eyebrow. She fought the urge to brush it back. She had to get a hold of herself.

Not get a hold of him.

She rose, breaking their tenuous bond and glaring at Moose, who proceeded to jump into Alex's lap. Beyond embarrassed, she nudged the cat's backside, then shook her finger in his face with a sharp "No!" Moose simply turned his back, brushing his tail across her face before he stalked from the room.

"That cat," she muttered, noticing Alex's lap was now covered in beige fur. She brushed briskly. "He's not happy about the move. I guess he figures if he makes you mad, you won't buy the house." She grabbed a particularly stubborn hair between her fingers. "Silly, I know, but he's always seemed more human than feline, so—"

"Please stop," Alex said, his voice sounding strained.

"What?" She glanced at his face, noting the tension there, then back at his lap—where she'd been brushing her hand for the last several moments. *Why can't this loony house have a trap door in the floor? One that can open and swallow me whole?* Mortified, she plopped into a chair, mumbling, "Why don't I just pay to have your suit cleaned?"

He winked. "Don't worry about it. I pretty much enjoyed the entire experience."

He was teasing her, trying to ease her embarrassment. And though her face was probably still the shade of an overripe tomato, she relaxed. Besides that great smile, he was smooth. Way too smooth for someone like her.

"Let's enjoy the wine," he said as he opened the bottle and poured a small amount for tasting. "Excellent," he said after a sip. He filled both glasses. "You have great taste, in wines as well as houses."

"Thank you." She clinked her glass against his, the peal of the crystal lingering as their gazes locked.

He didn't sip from his glass. Instead, he stared at her. His eyelids closed halfway. His gaze shifted to her lips. Drawn to that slumberous, desire-filled look, she leaned toward him, wondering how he'd taste.

Did he want to kiss her? He could have any woman he wanted. Men like Alex pursued women like her mother. He couldn't possibly be attracted to her, though she couldn't deny her attraction to him. Part of her fought to rationalize the idea of being drawn to a man so quickly, while the rest of her reveled in the hunger trembling in her belly, the longing flowing through her veins. She'd never experienced anything like this. She'd always watched flaming attractions objectively, from the outside. Was it finally happening to her?

Alex dipped his head.

Wouldn't Mama be thrilled?

She jerked back, spilling wine over the rim of her glass. Heart racing, she jumped to her feet. "I'll just— Let me get a cloth." After she managed to mop up the mess, she chanced a glance at him, noting with irritation he still looked cool and relaxed, leaving her to wonder how many women he'd kissed—and more—after knowing them less than an hour.

Retreating behind the bar with her glass and pretending she didn't desire him more with every breath, she asked, "What brings you to Junction Gap anyway?"

"An impulse," he said. "My grandparents own a Victorian-style house in upstate New York. I thought it would be fun to try it myself."

Fun? She nearly choked on her wine. *If you're loaded, it's probably a blast.*

"What a coincidence," she said. "My new job is with a law firm in New York, in Manhattan, though."

"Really? I live in Manhattan most of the year."

"Most of the year? Where else do you live?" Maybe he had more money than she thought. She should have raised the price of The House. At least enough to cover the cost of bubble wrap.

"I own several houses in addition to the brownstone in New York, but I've never lived anywhere for long. I like moving around." He paused. "At least until recently."

"What happened recently?"

"I turned thirty-five and realized I had places to live, but no home. My grandmother says that's because I'm always 'flitting about.'" He wiggled his fingers, and Rebecca could easily imagine Alex's grandmother giving sensible advice to her jet-setting grandson. "Anyway, an historical house represents permanence and stability, right?"

Permanence, yes. Stability? Well, that depended on the planets aligning just right with The House.

Before she felt compelled to comment, he continued.

"My grandparents live in a small community, so they suggested I try small-town life. If I like it, I may settle here permanently."

Here? she almost gasped. She managed to bite back the question. The man knew what he was doing. In more areas than just real estate, too. She wondered if she should warn him about her matchmaking neighbors, though. If he wasn't already thinking that "settle" meant wife, kids and PTA, he would shortly.

"Well, you've picked a nice town." *Good grief, Rebecca. Now you're the town's tourism bureau?* She grabbed the mugs from the sink, then opened the dishwasher. And stopped cold.

Ground-up food had splattered the inside. Lettuce leaves, leftover spaghetti, tomato sauce, onion, bits of mushroom and green pepper. Everything she'd put in the garbage disposal the night before caked the racks, sides and top of the appliance. How in the world—?

"Everything okay?" Alex asked, rising from his chair.

Her heart leapt. "Oh, uh— Fine. Sit, please." She shoved the mugs inside and clanged the door shut. If Mr. Jet-Setting, Rich Buyer thought the appliances weren't in working order, her big sale could be history. "I just...uh, remembered I have to be in court."

"Court?"

"Yeah." Lying made her nervous and snippy. "You know, that place with the judge and jury box, attorneys defending their clients against injustice." She rounded the bar, then stood impatiently next to him until he finished his wine. When he did, she snatched the glass from his fingers. "We have big cases here in Junction Gap. We're the county seat. Just last week my client received a settlement from a Fortune 500 company."

She didn't mention the settlement was only ten dollars, the exact amount of the candy bar and postage it had taken to mail it back to the manufacturer. Her client had thought the chocolate tasted old.

"I see." Eyeing her as she sprayed glass cleaner on the crystal, he stood and walked to the counter. "Is that why you're suddenly hopping around here like a spooked rabbit?"

She lifted her chin. "I simply realized I have another engagement. If the contracts are signed, I'll just take them to my agent."

Looking amused, he scooped the envelope off the table. "I'll take them. I'm on my way into town anyway."

She lined up the glasses on the counter. "I'll show you out." Leading him down the hall, she ran through the solutions to this latest problem. She knew nothing about garbage disposals or dishwashers. How could the disposal pipes be crossed with the dishwasher pipes? Could she find a repairman on a Friday afternoon? Could she afford a repairman?

At the open front door, she held out her hand. "It was nice to meet you, Mr. Carlisle."

He grasped her hand, his thumb gliding across her wrist. "You, too…Rebecca."

Her name rolled off his lips like the caress he'd just given her skin. She went hot, then cold, then very hot.

"Bye." He strolled down the steps, looking almost as good from the back as from the front.

Breathing hard, the memory of those intense green eyes still flashing in her mind, Rebecca slammed the door and slumped against it. Even if she knew how to fix a garbage disposal, she was absolutely certain she wouldn't remember now. The man had managed to short out several million brain cells.

Moose padded into the hall, and Rebecca could have sworn she saw him smile.

ALEX PULLED his Mercedes into an end spot in the diner's parking lot. Stepping out of the car, he remembered the contract copies he'd stuck in his jacket pocket. As he slid them into his briefcase, he again contemplated Rebecca Parson's no-nonsense scrawl, as well as the lady herself.

The conservative lawyer living in a house with a bordello bedroom.

He had less than a month. Could he manage to uncover the secrets behind her deep blue eyes, the curvy body beneath her perfectly pressed suit? He'd certainly accomplished that much and more in less time, but the lovely Miss Parsons hadn't exactly fallen into his arms. Frankly, he was used to women chasing him, not the other way around. Her wariness presented an obstacle.

Then he recalled the smokey look in her eyes as they'd toasted with their wineglasses. He'd been about to kiss her, and she'd come close to letting him. He'd wanted her lips on his—more than he probably should. In fact, he'd *never* wanted to kiss a woman so badly. Theirs was a chemistry he just had to explore. *With a little effort on my part…who knows?*

With a slight spring in his step, he strode toward the entrance of Mack's Diner. He should probably be worrying about where he was going to sleep tonight, since the apartment he'd rented for the month was suddenly unavailable. When he'd stopped by to pick up his keys, a sign was hanging on the building manager's door. It literally said Gone Fishin'.

After several frustrating rounds of knocking on doors, Alex had learned—from a very helpful female resident—that the manager was indeed fishing, wasn't due back until Monday and no one had a set of keys to Alex's apartment. After lunch he supposed he'd have to start hitting the motels.

A bell jingled above his head as he pushed open the diner's door. The conversation level dimmed, and several people turned their heads and stared.

Alex smiled, ignoring the burst of nerves. He'd been the new guy in town many times before. He'd lived all over the world, belonging nowhere, yet he'd learned to charm his way into many a good grace. His father claimed it was genetic.

But he'd obviously inherited some domesticated genes, as well, since some of the happiest times in his life had been summers at his grandparents' house. Their settled lifestyle and homey neighborhood made him question whether he was missing something important. Frowning, he wondered if that was the reason behind his intense attraction to Rebecca. "Settled" equaled a wife and children, he supposed, and though he really hadn't thought that far ahead, he'd bet Nana Carlisle had.

Sorry, Nana. Homeownership was enough permanence for him. A wife was vaguely ahead in the future. Way ahead.

To divert himself from these thoughts, he studied the diner. It wasn't fancy, decorated in dated fifties style with red vinyl booths lining the windows, chrome bar stools resting beneath the counter and gray linoleum floors.

A buxom waitress dressed in jeans and a red-checked shirt sashayed toward him. "Just one, sugar?"

Smiling—though at only about half the wattage he'd focused on Rebecca—he nodded.

She stared at him for a full ten seconds before leading him to a table, where she handed him a plastic-coated menu. "You see anything you like?" she asked after a few moments, leaning toward him and giving him a generous view of her cleavage.

Oddly enough, he found himself unmoved by the sight. Instead, he envisioned unhooking the brass buttons on Rebecca Parsons's blue suit. He wondered if the creamy skin at the base of her throat was as soft as the underside of her wrist. Would her pulse race as he trailed his lips down her neck, his tongue dipping into—

"Ya memorizing it?"

Alex jerked his gaze to the waitress, unnerved by the depths to which he'd sunk into his fantasy. "Uh, no." With considerable effort, he managed to focus on the menu long enough to order the blue plate special.

The waitress scribbled his request on her pad, then tucked the menu beneath her arm. "Not from around here, are ya?"

From moving around most of his life, he didn't have a distinctive accent, which naturally stood out in the South. "No, but I'm in the process of moving here."

The waitress's eyebrows nearly disappeared into her curly blond hairline. "Really? You got relatives who live here, or somethin'?"

"No. I'm looking for a place to stay, though."

A wide, inviting grin appeared on her mouth.

"Temporarily," he finished.

Her grin never faltered.

An expert at diverting attention without insulting, he cleared his throat and asked, "Is there a motel in town?"

The waitress tapped her pencil against her lips. "Sort of. There's Bill's Rooms."

"Bill's Rooms?"

"Yeah. Just let me put this order in." She sauntered behind the long counter, then shoved a slip of paper underneath a metal wheel. "Order up, Mack!"

When she returned, she pulled out a chair and sat opposite him. She had a cute, round face and beaming smile, but again Alex found himself comparing her with the elegant Rebecca Parsons.

"Name's Sandy, by the way," the waitress said, sticking out her hand.

"Nice to meet you. I'm Alex Carlisle." He shook her hand. "I'm buying a house on Forest Street."

"Rebecca's place?"

As he nodded, a male customer shouted, "Hey, Sandy, can we get some iced tea back here?"

She waved her hand. "In a minute."

"Come on, Sandy. We gotta get to the lake."

"Oh, damn." Giving Alex a regretful look, she rose from her chair. "I forgot the fishing tournament. Bill's Rooms are probably booked."

Alex sighed. "Great."

"Sorry. You picked a bad weekend to come into town."

"Sandy…" the customer called.

"I'm comin'!" To Alex, she said, "You might try the Motel Six in Hopeville." After one last provocative look over her shoulder, she rushed off to attend to her customers.

Alex retrieved his cell phone from his inside coat pocket. Several small towns like Junction Gap dotted the highway. Surely one of them would have an open room. Macon was the closest large town, but it was nearly two hours away.

He pushed the power button on his phone. The words *No Service* appeared on the screen.

Alex frowned. No service? What was that all about?

"Dead air space," Sandy said, nodding at the phone as she passed by his table.

"You're kidding." How in the world was he going to check his voice mail? Call his secretary?

"Nope. Whole town's that way." She nodded toward the back of the diner. "We have a pay phone by the bathrooms."

"Hell."

Sandy smiled. "Welcome to the country, Alex Carlisle."

REBECCA PUSHED OPEN the diner's door, praying she could find a handyman inside. Mack's place was the hangout, the nerve center of Junction Gap. If she couldn't find help here…well, she'd apply herself harder toward figuring out the owner's manual for her garbage disposal. Since it was written in Spanish, she didn't hold out much hope on that front.

She responded to several waves as she walked inside, then strode directly to the counter. "Hey, Mack," she called.

Mack's thin, scowling face appeared at the opening to the kitchen. "Yeah?"

"Can I talk to you?"

"No." His bushy gray eyebrows drew together as he gestured to the diner. "Afternoon rush."

Rebecca glanced around. Immersed in her own problems, she hadn't noticed the crowded restaurant.

"What's going on?"

"Fishing tournament," Mack said. "I'm swamped."

"Of course." Rebecca sighed and scanned the diner

again. Any potential repairman was probably throwing his rods and reels in the back of his pickup about now. And the phone call to her usual handyman hadn't produced promising results. He'd gotten married and run off to Florida for a two-week honeymoon.

The nerve of some people. Didn't he realize the inspector was coming in three weeks, and the sale to Alex was contingent upon a favorable review?

Her gaze halted on the back of a dark-haired man. He turned, his electric-green gaze zeroing in on her.

"Whoa," Rebecca whispered.

She did her best to ignore the fluttery nerves in her stomach and walked toward his table, hoping she'd exaggerated his disconcerting effect on her.

"Hey," she said, stopping next to him, noting he'd removed his jacket and loosened his tie. The gorgeous executive on a break. Her palms broke out in a sweat. Nope. No exaggeration anywhere around here. "I see you found Mack's."

He stood, then pulled out the chair next to him. "Have a seat."

"Me? Uh, no." *Wow, Rebecca. Talk to any men lately?* No. At least not anyone she was so intrigued by.

He smiled. "Come on."

She needed to find a repairman, but with Alex in the diner, she could hardly accomplish that task. "Um, okay."

He waited until she slid into the chair before returning to his seat. "How was court?"

"Brief, for once." *Liar, liar,* her conscience chanted.

"Well, you arrived just in time."

His husky voice and half smile continued to work their magic on her senses. "I did?"

"Yes. I'm in something of a bind." He gestured to his

glass. "Would you like something to drink? Sandy recommended the sweet tea, and I think it's growing on me."

"No, thanks." So…he and Sandy were on a first-name basis and already discussing Southern traditions such as sweet tea. She could hardly fault the waitress for her excellent taste. Alex, no doubt, had a powerful effect on every woman within his vicinity.

"Anyway, my problem," he said. "The apartment I rented has been given to someone else and the fishing tournament has filled all the motels in the area. I was wondering if you have any ideas."

"You don't have anywhere to stay?"

"No. And I think people are irritated at me for monopolizing the pay phone." He tapped a cell phone laying on the table. "Do you know you have dead air space?"

He looked so confused—and cute—Rebecca had to hold back her smile. "So I've heard." She cocked her head. "You tried Bill's Rooms?"

Brows drawn together, he nodded.

On impulse she laid her hand over his. "Don't feel too bad. You're not missing much."

His gaze locked on their touching hands. A tremor started from Rebecca's fingertips and bounced up her arm.

Wrong man. Wrong time. Definitely wrong time. Definitely wrong man.

His sensual assault on her senses was too overwhelming. She couldn't think straight when she was around him. She had a move to accomplish and a house to hold together. Besides, no matter how often he smiled at her, he couldn't be truly interested in her.

As casually as possible, she lifted her hand and rested her chin in her palm. "So, uh, how about the Motel Six in Hopeville?"

He stared at her as if he had no idea what she was talking about, his eyes glimmering with a sensual light.

"Motel?" she prompted. "Hopeville?"

He blinked, his long, inky lashes hiding the green fire for a brief moment. "Right." He cleared his throat and sipped tea. "They're booked, too. Along with the Super Eight and Red Roof Inn in Bolton."

"You can't very well sleep in your car. What are you going to do?"

He shrugged, his head ducked. "I have no idea."

"Why don't you stay with me?"

Rebecca looked around for the little devil who'd pushed her to utter such a ridiculous suggestion.

Alex's head jerked up. He was obviously trying to look surprised by her offer, but the gesture didn't quite come off. "With you?"

Wondering if she'd been manipulated by a master, she waved her hand. "Dumb idea, I know. Forget I said it."

"Did you mean it?"

"Well, I—" *Earth to Rebecca. Don't you have a household repair issue to deal with?*

Alex leaned forward, his expression earnest, his thousand-watt smile firmly in place. "It would only be for the weekend. I'm sure I can get in my apartment once the manager comes back from the fishing tournament. You'd really be saving me."

Yes, but who's going to save me from home ownership hell? Who was going to fix her possessed garbage disposal and convince her cat that New York was a real swell place to live? Who was going to save her from the urge to rip this man's clothes off and have her wicked way with him?

"I would insist on paying rent, of course."

She stared at him. "You would?"

"Absolutely. How does two hundred dollars a day sound?"

Her eyes widened. "Two hund—" It sounded like a Mozart symphony.

He laid his hand over hers and smiled. "Please?"

Oh, boy.

Knowing this move could land her in a heap of trouble, but also knowing how much the cash could ease her repair problems, Rebecca forced a smile. "Just for the weekend."

3

ALEX STARED at Rebecca's flushed cheeks and damned himself for exploiting her generosity. He couldn't help it.

Sleeping in a bed, rather than the cramped back seat of his Mercedes, was critical—especially to his back. But more than that, he found himself irresistibly drawn to the woman sitting across from him.

"So…" He smiled. "Do you prefer the left or right side?"

She propped her chin on her fist. "Of the house, or the bed?"

Heat shot to his groin. Rebecca's amused blue gaze remained locked on his face. "Either," he managed to say.

"I pretty much sleep in the middle of the bed—and you'll be sleeping in the west wing." She grinned, and his heart thumped hard. "You'll have your own bathroom and sitting area, too."

"The sky-blue room with hot air balloons painted on the ceiling?"

"Exactly. You paid attention during the tour."

"I always pay very close attention."

Her pupils dilated. Pleased he'd affected her so well, caught in the moment, he reached for her hand.

"Hey," Sandy said, approaching the table to pour tea in Alex's glass.

Alex leaned back in his chair, remembering they were in

a busy diner. Rebecca made him forget anyone else was around. She overwhelmed his senses, and he couldn't think straight in her presence. Maybe getting involved with her wasn't the wisest move. At least in the long term. But, then, he'd never been a long-term guy.

"Need anything, Rebecca?" Sandy continued.

"No, thanks." Rebecca stood. "I have to get going." She looked at Alex. "I'll see you later."

"Yeah. Thanks." He rose from his chair, wanting to say more, itching to yank her into his arms, but didn't see how with Sandy and half the town looking on.

Rebecca disappeared out the door with a backhanded wave, and Alex sat.

"How was everything?" Sandy asked.

He forced a smile, his mind still focused on Rebecca and the troubling idea of just how much he wanted her. "Terrific. Thank you."

He should be grateful for Rebecca's hospitality, and their attraction could be fun, but even thinking the words *long term* was a development he didn't like. "Play the field," his mother often said. She and his father, who divorced when he was five, certainly did.

As he retrieved his wallet, he noticed Sandy's home phone number scrawled in bright red marker across the bottom of the check. On any other day, he might have called her. But today he'd met Rebecca.

He left Sandy a generous tip instead, then walked outside into the late-afternoon heat. Squinting into the sun, he decided he should check on office space for rent. If he was going to live here, he'd need to open a Southern branch of his business.

He slid into his car and pulled away from the diner. He drove down Main Street where trees lined the road, their branches forming a tunnel of shade, the sunlight struggling to peek between the foliage.

Along a side street, he slowed to a crawl by the pond. Thin pines mixed with ancient oaks, similar to the ones in Rebecca's backyard, lined the water's edge. The green oak leaves were tinged with yellow, just beginning their dramatic color change, and Alex looked forward to watching the show. The only concrete was the sidewalk around the pond, the tallest structure a telephone pole.

Different? Yes. But he smiled, feeling the rightness of his decision. The impulsive ones were always the best. If there were any other kind.

His colleagues thought he was nuts for the spontaneous way he bought and sold stocks. He didn't spend his days researching companies on the net, or his nights at the library. He took clients to lunch and ladies to dinner. He listened to people talk. He networked. He paid attention.

As he continued down Main Street toward the real estate office, he decided he shouldn't show up at Rebecca's empty-handed. Wine. He knew Rebecca liked wine.

After handing over the signed contracts to Rebecca's agent, Pam, he asked about a wine store.

She smiled slyly, her artfully made-up eyes crinkling at the corners. "We have Piggly Wiggly."

They have what?

Obviously noting his confusion, she stepped closer to him, wrapping her hand around his arm. "If you're looking for a drink, I'm sure I've got what you need."

Again, he found himself comparing a woman to Rebecca. The glint of interest and confidence in Pam's eyes was no match for Rebecca's beauty and grace. "I need directions," he said to the agent.

She gave them, along with her home phone number— again—her beeper number and her cell phone number.

When he arrived at a strip mall of stores, the largest one on the end bearing a giant pig's head, he laughed. He liked this town's sense of humor, making him think again of Rebecca and her whimsically decorated house. The contrasts between her and her mother's tastes were obvious, but he wondered if Rebecca realized how telling the cat clock and the gargoyle toothbrush holder were. Rebecca had inherited a few rebel genes.

After passing through the grocery store's automatic doors, he walked around the crowded check-out area, then wound through the aisles, passing a display of Budweiser cases in the shape of a football goal post, before arriving at the wine section.

The selection was sparse: a red, a white and a rosé in gallon jugs with screw-off tops, a few bottles of champagne and something called Mad Dog 20/20.

"I don't think so," he said under his breath.

"Need any help?" A redheaded teenage girl dressed in a blue apron with the Piggy Wiggly logo bounced toward him.

Alex smiled—giving her the low-wattage one reserved for underage girls and women over sixty. "I'm looking for a bottle of wine."

She stared for a few seconds, blushed, then ducked her head. "It's right there."

"I was hoping for something more…exotic. What about in the storeroom?"

"Well…" She glanced over her shoulder. "I'm not really supposed to let any customers back there."

Alex turned up the wattage a bit. "Just this once? I'm in something of a bind."

"Well..." She grinned. "The manager does special-order some other kinds."

Twenty minutes later, he'd purchased a '95 Sonoma Valley Chardonnay, a '94 Napa Valley Merlot and a bouquet of yellow roses. Whistling, he slid into his car and headed to Rebecca's.

As he pulled in the driveway of the mint-green Victorian house, he let satisfaction roll through him. The turrets rose and fell in fanciful, but somehow balanced, peaks. Three pointed cupolas showed off the round, windowed rooms that afforded the house its spectacular wooded view. The left side of the wide, white wood porch formed a gazebo with white gingerbread trim.

The house looked homey, solid...permanent. Would he spend the rest of his life here? Could he really settle down? He liked spending summers in New York, winters in Florida, a few months here and there in San Francisco. But he was enticed by the idea of becoming a permanent part of a community, of investing in something besides stocks.

As he rang the doorbell, he realized the similarities between this house and Nana's made a future here seem right, maybe even fated.

When the door opened, he smiled at Rebecca. "Hi."

"Hey." Though the smile she gave him in return was a bit strained, it didn't detract from her natural beauty. Curly locks of her hair had come unpinned and fell around her face. She'd changed from her suit to a peach-colored knit top and jeans, both of which did wonderful things for her feminine figure.

She looked positively delectable.

"Come in." She held the door wide.

He brushed by her, setting the grocery bag with the wine

on the floor, then pulled the roses from behind his back. "For you."

Her eyes brightened as she took the flowers, but her smile still wasn't genuine. "Thanks."

His lovely landlady looked troubled. He angled his head, studying her. "Are you all right?"

Her gaze leapt to his. "Of course. Why wouldn't I be?"

Settling his hands at his waist, he walked around her...slowly, studying the womanly curve from her breast to her hips, the gentle swell of her bottom, the pale skin at the nape of her neck. As he faced her again, he cocked his head right, then left, saying nothing.

"What?" she asked finally, obviously exasperated.

"You look...luscious." Grinning, he quickly pulled her into his arms, twirling her around the foyer.

She braced her hands against his chest. "What do you think you're doing?"

"Dancing."

"Why?"

"In addition to looking luscious, you also seemed stressed."

She eyed him suspiciously. "You dance to relieve stress?"

"Of course. Don't you?"

"Who would I dance with? The cat?"

"Mmm. I guess living alone is a problem." Though it never had been for him. "No boyfriend, lover or friend you'd like to become a lover?" he asked as he dipped her back over his arm.

"No—to all three," she said, scowling.

Was the scowl for him, or the lack of a boyfriend? He shrugged, knowing he could handle both, or either. The men in this town must be nuts, he decided, but at least he knew she was available. As he pulled her up, he took the opportunity to draw her closer to his chest, then continued his seduction—er, waltz. "So how do you relieve stress?"

"I take a bath."

"Why, Miss Rebecca Parsons," he said in a bad Southern accent, "what a scandalous offer."

She smiled, this time with enthusiasm. "Why, Mr. Carlisle, I do believe you're not a gentleman."

"Definitely not." He stopped suddenly, noting she wasn't quite steady on her feet. *Perfect.*

He lowered his head, inhaling her flowered scent. *Damn, he wanted her.* Beyond time, place and reason. He got hard just thinking about her, imagining them together in a tangle of limbs and laughter. That image shot blasting heat through his body. And now she was just where he wanted her—in his arms, watching him with a mixture of confusion and curiosity.

He placed his mouth over her glistening, peach-painted lips. *Just a taste,* he told himself.

But when she sighed into his mouth, her hands grasping the front of his shirt, he hardened further, his adrenaline surging. Pulling her against his chest, he settled one hand over the curve of her bottom as he angled his head, deepening the kiss. He swept his tongue inside the warmth of her mouth, and when she answered his caress, his heart jumped, then pumped harder, then raced.

Without his usual finesse or any semblance of gentleness, he thrust his tongue into her mouth over and over. He couldn't seem to stop himself. She'd unleashed an untamed part of his soul he hadn't even known existed. His hands roamed her body, molding her against his erection. She thrust her arms around his neck so quickly, his shirt jerked from his pants. Moaning, she molded her body to his, burying her fingers in his hair.

With her breasts pressed against his chest, he imagined their bodies connecting intimately...skin to skin, her legs parting, inviting him into her warmth. He wanted to strip off her conservative clothes, show her the wild side of life...of sex. He wanted to join with her, discover her, know her.

He had no idea how or why, but some part of his brain started blinking a red neon warning sign, overriding other—usually more determined—body parts. Lifting his head, he stared down into the most beautiful, slumberous, desire-filled eyes he'd ever seen.

Oh, man. His erection throbbed.

She blinked. Then, as realization hit, her face flushed. Her hands slid from his hair, her arms dropped to her sides.

Be cool, he said to himself. Especially to his body.

He forced what he hoped passed for a carefree, lopsided grin. "Let's eat." He turned away from her, picked up the grocery bag, then strode into the kitchen. Though he hoped he moved with the casual confidence of the experienced, maybe even jaded, man he was, inside he was a wreck. He'd only intended an easy, get-to-know-you kind of kiss. He sensed he needed to take things slow and steady with Rebecca. He didn't want to scare her off.

So how the hell did "easy" turn into if-I-don't-have-you-this-minute-I'm-going-to-die?

Glancing over his shoulder to see if she'd followed him, he noted she was still standing in the foyer, scowling. Damn, he hoped he hadn't blown it. He wanted Miss Rebecca Parsons. He also didn't want to spend the weekend sleeping in his Mercedes.

"I even brought wine," he said, smiling and pulling the bottles from the bag.

She returned his smile.

Maybe everything was going to be okay.

She started toward him, and he found himself hypnotized by the sway of her hips as she moved. Brushing past him into the kitchen, she said quietly over her shoulder, "Your hair's standing on end, and your shirt's untucked."

"It's— What?" He glanced down to realize she was right about the shirt. After straightening his clothes, he tunneled his hand through his hair, noting the strands did seem to be out of place. *Well, hell.*

How had he lost control so thoroughly? Shaking his head, he crossed to the refrigerator, where he stored the white wine, then set the red on the counter. "Have you eaten?" he asked as she approached the long bar that separated the cooking area from the sitting area.

Looking a bit dazed, she shook her head, and he wondered if he had that same "what the hell just happened?" look on his face. "Have a seat." *Way over there at the table, where I might not be tempted to attack you again.* "I'll handle everything. I'm a great cook."

"That's convenient," she said. "I'm not."

He decided on a red sauce after noting the plump, ripe-looking tomatoes—what color were her nipples? That shade of red? More raspberry? Or peach?

"I can at least open the wine," she said from behind him.

Startled from his thoughts, he banged his head on a shelf. "Oh, uh—" He rubbed his head. "Sure."

"Are you okay?" She raised her hand as if she intended to check his head for a lump.

He ducked out of her reach, grabbed the bottle of wine

from the counter, then held it out to her. "I could use a glass about now."

She didn't look at him as she nodded briskly and muttered, "Me, too," leading him to think she probably didn't make out in her foyer with men she'd just met and was just as baffled about their intense combustion as he was.

While she took care of the wine, he threw together a quick basil, tomato and garlic sauce to serve over some angel hair pasta he found in the pantry. As dinner simmered, he sipped the Merlot. She stood on the opposite side of the bar, staring into her own glass. He was glad the tiled counter separated them. An urge to stroke her cheek, explore the creamy expanse of her neck surged through him.

The cat suddenly leapt onto the tiles.

"Moose…" Rebecca said in a warning tone, planting her hands on her hips.

The fat feline blinked his big, golden eyes.

After moving his wineglass beyond the reach of the animal's bushy tail, Alex grinned. "Moose?"

Both Rebecca and the cat lifted their noses in the air and glared at him.

"Sorry," Alex said, biting back further amusement.

"He's a bit temperamental," Rebecca said, scratching the cat behind his ears. "Does it bother you to have him on the counter?"

Though Alex wasn't keen on cat hair in his pasta, he figured Moose served as a good bodyguard for his owner. "He's not bothering me."

They sipped their wine in silence a few moments. For the first time in—well, never—Alex found himself awkward around a woman. Should he apologize? He wasn't sorry. Should he even bring up the subject? Maybe the best thing to do was what he always did—roll with the punches and grab opportunity when it presented itself.

Reaching into his back pocket, he retrieved a check from his wallet. "The promised rent," he said as he handed the money to Rebecca. "I really appreciate you letting me stay here."

She tucked the check in her pocket. "No problem."

More awkward silence. The cat yawned.

"Surely that sauce is ready by now," Alex said, crossing to the stove and feeling like an idiot. As he set the meal on the table, he hoped she'd be impressed by his cooking skills, since his ability to hold a conversation seemed to have deserted him.

"This looks great." Rebecca forked up a bite of pasta, holding it in front of her parted lips. She chewed slowly, her jaw working, her eyes rolling back. "Wow." She licked her lips and twirled another bite on her fork.

Alex's forehead beaded with sweat. How much would a woman this enthusiastic about food enjoy sex?

"Aren't you going to eat?"

He shoved a bite in his mouth, barely tasting the food, never budging his gaze from Rebecca's half smile, the light sheen of oil on her lips, the curls draping against her cheek.

She sipped her wine, her blue gaze penetrating his. "Listen, about what happened earlier—"

The room was suddenly plunged in darkness.

"What the hell..." Alex half rose, then realized he couldn't see more than two feet in front of his face. "Rebecca?" he asked into the inky black, fumbling across the table until he grasped her hand.

"I don't believe this," she said, sounding irritated.

Moose meowed in protest.

''I wonder if the neighbors' power is out, too,'' Alex said.

''Stay here.'' She let go of his hand, and he sensed her moving away from the table. Her footsteps shuffled against the floor, then he heard a whirring sound—the blinds being raised. Pale moonlight glowed through the glass panels of the back door.

Rebecca peered into the backyard. ''They have lights on next door.''

Alex rose from the table to stand behind her. ''It's probably just a blown fuse. Where's the fuse box?''

She sighed. ''The basement.''

''What about candles or a flashlight?''

''I think I have some candles in the china cabinet.'' She left the room, her footsteps echoing down the hall.

Alex gazed at the sliver of moon hanging in a black sky, breathing deeply to catch a whiff of her light, flowery perfume and wondering again why she affected him so much.

Need for her crawled through his body like a hot rash.

''Found them.''

Alex dismissed troubling thoughts and simply enjoyed the sight of her, walking toward him with two glowing tapers, the beauty of her face heightened by the soft candlelight.

She handed him one of the dainty silver candlesticks. ''Why don't you finish your dinner? I'll check the fuse container.''

He smothered a laugh. ''It's fuse *box,* and how about I tag along, just in case you need an assistant?''

Even in the low light, he could tell she was relieved by his offer. She turned and headed down the hall, leaving him to follow.

A whiff of cool, musty air brushed Rebecca's face as she

opened the door leading to the basement. She held her candle aloft and peered into the gloom. *No way.*

Gulping, she flattened her back against the wall. "Go ahead. I'm right behind you."

Alex chuckled, and the halo illuminating his face flickered. "Scared of the dark?"

She sucked in a breath. "Of course not." As long as big, strong Alex Carlisle preceded her down those shadowy steps.

"I promise to protect you," he said, his face within an inch of hers.

Thinking the moment didn't really call for joking, she shoved his shoulder. "Just go already."

With his lips crooked up on one side, and looking way too adorable, he turned, then started down the stairs. She stuck as close to his back as she dared without setting his shirt on fire. When he halted at the bottom, she stumbled, bracing her hand against his shoulder to keep from falling.

He reached back with one hand and enveloped hers. "Stay close behind me, so you don't trip on anything," he said over his shoulder.

She jerked her head in a nod and held on with all her strength.

"It's kind of spooky down here," he said.

Kind of? She moved closer to Alex. "The fuse box is over there," she said, pointing toward the left, thanking heaven the electricity had managed to stay intact until this moment. She never would have made it down here by herself, as her irrational fear seemed unwilling to budge itself. Of course, having her buyer witness this latest problem couldn't be good, either.

With none of her hesitancy, he strode in that direction, then opened the metal box. "Aha." He held the candle up, and she saw a series of switches, one of which exposed a section of red. "Just as I thought. It's tripped." He flipped the switch and pale light pushed away the darkness.

As relief rushed through her, Rebecca blew out her candle. "Thank goodness."

Alex's hand hovered over the switches, his green gaze intent on hers. "I thought the candlelight was romantic."

She grabbed his hand. "Don't."

He was so close, she could feel his breath on her face, smell his spicy cologne. Still glowing, the candlelight from the taper danced across the angles of his handsome face. She could hardly believe they were standing here this way, with her gazing into his eyes like a long-lost lover, wondering if she could manage to draw another breath before she threw herself into his arms.

As flattering as it was to have a man like Alex interested in her, this whole attraction was hopelessly impractical. They'd both gotten caught up in the moment. She was just a moment in Alex's life, a blip on his romantic radar. No doubt she would be risking major heartbreak.

You decided you wanted New York excitement, didn't you? Could anything else be quite this good?

Setting the candlestick on top of the fuse box, he turned, then cupped her cheeks in his palms. He rubbed his thumb across her bottom lip, just watching her. "About earlier..."

Just like before, she was mesmerized by his touch, the sound of his voice. "Uh-huh?"

"Wanna do it again?"

Rebecca melted like warm wax. She felt no fear, only longing for his touch to settle against her. His lips brushed hers once, then twice. As if his touch were already familiar, her heart pounded, her body heated.

Then she grabbed him.

Like a crazed animal in heat, she jerked him to her by the front of his shirt. Her parted lips clung to his, dying for the moment his tongue would tangle with hers. When she felt the stroke, her knees wobbled.

She imagined a more intimate tangling—his body with hers. Wrapping her legs around his hips, inviting him inside where only he could ease the ache of her longing. Gripping his waist, she marveled in the firmness of his muscles, the underlying strength he possessed.

He backed her against the basement wall, his lower body pressed against hers, trapping her against his heat and arousal. He trailed hot, openmouthed kisses beneath her jaw, then down her neck, and she fought for breath and sanity.

She'd had sexual encounters—well, two—but nothing she'd ever experienced equaled this. Men didn't move this fast with her. She'd never wanted them to. She'd always left the wild men and wilder impulses to her mother. Alex's hands slid beneath her top, his fingers fumbling with the catch of her bra, and she pulled up his shirt so she could feel his warm skin. *No wonder Mama was always smiling,* she thought deliriously.

"Rebecca?" a familiar voice called down the stairs.

Breathing hard, Rebecca jumped away from Alex.

"I was washing my dishes when I looked out the window and saw all your lights were out. I nearly killed myself groping through the kitchen when—"

Her next-door neighbor, Linda, ground to a halt at the base of the steps. Her lips broadened in a smile as she took in the scene.

Rebecca squeezed her eyes shut.

"Well, it's about time you did something worth interrupting, Honey!"

4

As she and Alex followed Linda up the basement steps, Rebecca fought to straighten her clothes, her unhooked bra giving her the most trouble.

"Allow me," Alex whispered in her ear, his hot breath searing the back of her neck.

"Fix your hair and your shirt," she muttered back.

And all this behind the watchful eye of one of her closest friends. This is what she got, she supposed, for forgetting she didn't engage in empty affairs with near-strangers. Mama had filled the Parsons quota for that activity for at least three more generations.

God only knew what her neighbors and clients would say about smart Rebecca Parsons getting involved with a man like Alex. *"Now that her mama's gone, she thinks she's the man killer, poor thing."* She didn't think she could bear the humiliating, sad shakes of their heads.

In the kitchen, she performed the introductions. "Alex Carlisle, this is Linda Mason, my neighbor." She scooped their dirty plates off the table, then headed to the sink. "Soon to be your neighbor, I guess."

Linda's mouth fell open. *"You're* buying the house?" She turned to Rebecca. "You have a contract already? I can hardly believe it. I mean you just put it on the market and you know I don't want you to move anyway. How in the world did all this come about so quickly and without even telling me the moment it happened?''

With her nerves already shot on account of Alex, Rebecca had a harder time than usual following Linda's rapid, seemingly unpunctuated speech. ''Alex is the owner-to-be as of this afternoon,'' she said.

Linda clapped her hands. ''Well, that's just wonderful. I mean I don't want Rebecca to leave but, well, she wouldn't listen to me. No matter how many times I talked to her about it.'' She fluttered around the table, waving her hands as fast as she talked. ''Everyone in the neighborhood has been so worried, I mean you just never know *who* will move in.'' She cocked her curly, red-topped head, her gaze raking Alex from head to toe. ''But you look okay, not homicidal or anything, so now that you're here you simply *must* come to the fall block party. It's a going-away party for Rebecca, too. Oh, you will come, won't you?''

Alex opened his mouth, but Linda whirled to face Rebecca. ''Talk him into it.''

Talk? Honey, those lips are for kissing.

Alex smiled. ''I'd love to come.''

Linda's eyes glazed over as if she might faint from that killer smile, but Alex valiantly grabbed her arm and held her steady.

Tamping down an unexpected twinge of jealousy, Rebecca ran water in the sink. Linda was happily married. Almost everyone, except two widowed cousins who lived at the end of the street, was married. Just another reason why she didn't fit in around here. She saw an exciting, prestigious career in her future, not rocking on her front porch with her husband.

Her cheeks flushed to the color of her hair, Linda asked Alex, ''So, I take it you're not married?''

"No, I'm not."

You will be soon enough, Rebecca thought. Finding Alex a wife would probably become a neighborhood project.

Suddenly he was beside her, taking a pan from her hand. "Let me do that."

"You cooked." She took back the pan, thinking of her still-broken garbage disposal, and knowing she couldn't handle him standing so close. "Sit down. Pour yourself another glass of wine. Would you like one, Linda?"

Her neighbor stood dazed and frozen in the center of the kitchen. Obviously shocked into silence over a gorgeous man who not only cooks, but offers to clean, too.

Yep. Alex's bachelor days were numbered.

"Alex, pour her a glass, please."

With Alex occupied, Rebecca loaded the last fork into the dishwasher to keep up the pretense of having working appliances.

"Psst." Linda leaned against the bar, her glass tipping precariously toward the pristine white countertop. Rebecca pulled it from her hand and set it on the tiles. "We need to talk," Linda said, her voice low.

"We do?" Rebecca glanced at Alex, who had filled his wineglass and was staring out the French doors into the backyard. "About what?"

Linda jerked her head toward Alex. "Later."

"Ah." More advice about not moving. Dire warnings about a woman alone in New York. And now with Alex in town…well, Rebecca could see where this conversation was leading.

"I'm going to get a few things from the car," Alex said, walking to the counter and setting down his glass. He winked at Rebecca, as if he knew she and Linda needed a moment alone. And why the hell didn't he look as flustered as she felt? He probably groped women in basements on a regular basis. The man was way too smooth for her, no doubt about it.

Linda's gaze remained glued to Alex as he walked from the room and down the hall. As soon as the front door shut behind him, she whistled. "My, oh my. I had no idea they still grew them that hunky."

"Amen, sister."

Linda sipped her wine. "My Jake is no slouch, but that smile, those shoulders...wow." She fanned her face.

With Rebecca's thoughts already leaning in a carnal direction, listing Alex Carlisle's many assets didn't seem like a good idea. "You needed to talk to me?"

"Oh, right." Linda was suddenly serious. "I think you'd better find someone to take a look at your roof."

Rebecca swallowed. "Roof?"

"Well, you know these nasty wind gusts we've been having lately?"

Rebecca nodded, not trusting her voice.

"This afternoon I was raking leaves, and the wind swept a whole bunch of your roof tiles into my yard. They sailed right over my head. I stacked them by my back door but they look pretty worn. That's a bad sign, don't you think?"

"Definitely." Rebecca could feel a monster headache beginning just behind her eyes.

"The way these afternoon thunderstorms crop up, you need to see about it right away. What if there's a leak?" She cast a glance toward the hall. "I didn't want to say anything in front of your buyer. Well, come on, I'll show you."

As they walked outside into the cool October night, Rebecca concentrated on putting one foot in front of the other and trying not to panic. This wasn't a big deal. A few roof tiles. How hard could it be to get a ladder and hammer them back into place? Easy as pie.

At the back corner of the house, on the side closest to her property, Linda stopped and pointed up. "There."

Rebecca craned her neck back, way back. The three stories and turrets seemed a mile high. "Above or below the balcony?"

"Above. It took a long time for them to float down."

Right above her bedroom. *This gets better by the minute.*

"Wow, that's really up there," Linda commented. "Do you think they even make ladders that high? Maybe you'll have to find someone with one of those bucket thingys the telephone company uses."

Rebecca could see her checkbook register turning red. Her stomach churned.

Linda shrugged. "It'll be fine, I'm sure. You always manage to find a solution. And I should get going and let you get back to—" she raised her eyebrows "—whatever it was you were doing."

"If I knew, I'd tell you, believe me."

Linda yanked her into a tight hug. "We're going to miss you so much. I can't believe you're really leaving. It's just too awful."

Before Rebecca could respond, Linda turned and trotted away. To her surprise, Rebecca felt tears prick her eyelids. She had to move. She had to find her own place in the world. Leaving her friends, though, might not be as simple as she'd thought.

Wondering if roofers made weekend calls, she turned toward the house. Alex was peeking out the back door. Hell. How in the world was she going to fix anything with him in such close quarters? A garbage disposal was one thing. A roofer and a bucket thingy was quite another. She'd have to wait until after the weekend to call for help.

Her guilty conscience tried to remind her she was unscrupulously deceiving Alex, but her internal accountant tamped down that emotion. Besides, the house was still her responsibility—at least for another three weeks.

Pasting on a smile, she walked up the four steps to the patio. "Linda just had to show me her, uh…the new mums she planted."

He glanced at his watch. "At this hour?"

"I agree, but it's not wise to argue with Linda."

"Hard getting a word in?"

"You got it." She brushed by him into the house. Damn. Why did he have to smell so good? She walked a few steps, then turned. Damn. The view was better than his scent. Facing him, knowing they were alone again in the house, quickened her pulse. Why him? Why now? She really wasn't emotionally equipped to face this…thing and deal with the house, too.

His eyes darkened as he stepped forward. "Rebecca—"

"No. Don't say it. I know." She held him off with her hand. "We made a mistake. I'm moving. You're moving. We're strangers. It doesn't make sense."

He captured her hand. "It doesn't have to make sense."

His touch heated her blood, made her forget why she had to pass up a relationship with him. She wasn't savvy enough, experienced enough…anything enough to come out of an affair with Alex unscathed. He was definitely too risky.

With the pad of his thumb, he caressed her wrist. And way too tempting, she decided, biting her lip.

He groaned. "Don't do that. It makes me want to bite back."

She tugged her hand free and backed into the hall, even as her heart pounded. "Why don't I show you to your room?"

He smiled, his eyes gleaming with sensual interest. "Lead on."

Halting, she planted her hands on her hips, hoping bravado would keep her from grabbing him. *Hey, you're not a hormonal teenager. What's stronger, Rebecca? Your body or your mind?*

She let her gaze rove Alex's body. Sweat broke out on her brow.

You don't have to answer that right now. You have to compare your English-Spanish dictionary with your garbage disposal manual.

"You're a smart guy," she said, fighting to sound casual. "I'm sure you can find your way to your room by yourself." She turned and strode up the stairs.

When she was halfway up, he called, "Rebecca."

She glanced over her shoulder to see him leaning against the newel post, one foot propped on the first step—carpeted in salmon with white polka dots.

She grit her teeth. Did he *have* to look like a Greek god? Couldn't he do *something* about that damn grin of his?

"You know where to find me...if you want me."

Well, I don't. So there. But as she retreated upstairs she knew she was lying.

ALEX AWOKE COLD, but smiling.

Cold because he'd taken three icy showers during the night. Smiling, because they hadn't done a damn bit of good. Rebecca had followed him into his dreams, renewing his determination to have her. He especially liked the one where she brushed cat hair off his lap, naked…both of them.

But recalling his fantasy caused him to harden. Painfully. Again.

He supposed he'd have to get used to being in this state around Rebecca. His interest and erection seemed to have no end beyond the moment he finally managed to get her into his bed, naked, flushed and wanting him in return.

He swelled. Okay. It was time for distraction. Or another cold shower.

Pale sunlight streamed through the bay window across the room. Flopped on his back, he stared at the puffy white clouds decorating the sky-blue painted ceiling. A smiling sun adorned one corner. Touches created by Rebecca's mother, no doubt.

He rolled out of bed, then showered—cold, but not icy—contemplating his plan of attack for the day. Maybe some distance was in order. Rebecca didn't seem the type to jump into bed with every man she met, and in the light of day, she'd probably be more determined to resist the attraction between them. Since he needed to find office space, he could be a gentleman—for a few hours anyway.

For clothes, he selected a black Armani shirt and slacks. Maybe Rebecca liked the dark, mysterious type. As he walked to the door, still shrugging on his shirt, he listened carefully for any sign of movement in the house.

With his ear pressed to the door, he didn't hear Rebecca. He heard rumbling. A low, ground-shaking rumbling that drew closer and closer. The sensation was almost earthquakelike, but he didn't see how that was possible in Georgia.

Curious, he opened the door, then stepped into the neon-yellow-and-turquoise-painted hall.

Rebecca stood at the top of the stairs, her brow furrowed as she stared at something she held in her hand.

"What's that?"

She thrust the object behind her back. "Nothing."

The roaring increased in volume. He raised one eyebrow.

She held out the object. "You mean this, uh..."

Distracted from the noise, he looked down. "That's a wrench."

She snapped her fingers. "Right. Wrench."

"What are you doing with it?"

"Umm..."

"Is something broken?"

She shook her head, her dark ponytail whipping her cheeks. "No. Of course not."

He waved his hand. "I'm not interested in the wrench. What's that noise?"

"What noise?"

Thankfully, the roaring increased in volume. He didn't want to voice the earthquake theory. "*That* noise."

"Oh, that." She rolled her eyes. "That's just Jake and his tractor."

"Tractor? As in one of those big yellow vehicles with giant wheels and a scooper on the front?"

"Uh-huh. Jake is Linda's husband. He stops by every Saturday to see if anybody needs any plowing done."

"Plowing? For what?"

Rebecca shrugged. "Anything you like. He came in handy last spring with planting my azalea bushes." She stood in front of him, staring, her head cocked. "What is it with you and your shirts?"

Glancing down, he realized he hadn't finished buttoning his shirt. He grinned at her briefly, then started buttoning. "Around you they have a mind of their own."

When her gaze locked on his chest, he forced himself to slow the movements of his fingers. She was definitely interested, and he took the opportunity to return her thorough stare. She wore a pale pink sweatshirt and blue jeans that molded her hips and thighs. Her dark ponytail accentuated her delicate bone structure. Little makeup covered her face—just a bit around the eyes and a glossy pink on her lips.

She continued to watch him, passing the wrench from hand to hand. He could always put breakfast on hold....

But as he stepped forward, the spell broke and she stepped back.

Distance now, progress later. "I'm heading into town this morning, but if you don't have plans later, how about I take you to dinner? To thank you for letting me stay."

"You're going into town? For how long?"

She'd miss him. How sweet. And promising. "Most of the day probably. I'm looking for office space."

"Oh. Good."

Good? Not promising. Better double the effort. He flashed her his brightest smile. "What about dinner?"

"Oh. Sure." She tapped the wrench against her palm, seeming distracted. "Hey, do you know any Spanish?"

"Spanish?"

"You know, *adiós,* et cetera."

When he shook his head, she frowned, drawing his attention to her lips again. "Well, I'll see you later." She continued down the hall.

"Have you had breakfast?"

She didn't pause as she opened the door at the end of the hall, revealing a set of wooden steps. "Yeah. Yogurt." She started up. "I've got to get something from the attic. See ya."

Alex rolled his shoulders, then headed downstairs. She obviously had other things on her mind besides seduction. He'd fix that.

"A LEG CAST? You can't be serious." Rebecca clutched the phone receiver. A clap of thunder shook the windows, ominously confirming the weatherman's first correct prediction this decade. So much for waiting to address this problem until Alex left on Monday.

"Yes, ma'am. I fell off my garage roof last week," said the roofer—the only roofer currently not fishing or working on the new subdivision at the edge of town.

Rebecca winced. "Does that happen often?"

He laughed. "No, thank goodness."

How was she supposed to determine the damage to her roof? There was no way she was climbing a ladder—even if she could find one tall enough.

A streak of lightning slashed across the sky, thunder rattling the windows. Oh, hell, no. She wasn't going out in that.

"How about a temporary fix? It's already thundering here."

The phone line remained silent for several seconds, and Rebecca held out hope that the roofer had a brilliant backup plan in mind.

"Well, ma'am, you might want to run down to Wal-Mart."

Her heart rate spiked. "They have a repair department?"

"No, ma'am, but they've got buckets, and you're gonna need a whole lot of 'em."

Rebecca hung her head. A dial tone buzzed in her ear.

How was she going to hide buckets in her bedroom and keep them hidden from Alex? *Not that he'd be spending any time in there.* She'd settled all that yesterday. Too over-whelming, too smooth, too risky, et cetera, et cetera.

Another bolt of lightning slashed across the sky as the rain began.

"Back to buckets," she said as she trudged down the hall and up the stairs.

She halted at the door to her bedroom, her gaze frozen on the ceiling. Water dripped from at least four different places around the room, one of which was dead center above her down-filled comforter.

"This just gets better and better."

She rushed into the bathroom, yanked a towel off the rack, then raced around the bedroom, wiping away the water before it ruined the solid oak floors. After scouring her bathroom and the hall closet, she found four plastic buckets and placed them under each leak.

Moose padded in the room and jumped on the bed, look-ing with grave interest at the bucket.

"Don't start," she told him.

He gave her an unconcerned glance and propped his paws on the lip of the bucket. As usual, Moose's pudginess was his downfall. Weighing more than the bucket, Moose tipped it over, splashing water over the top of his head and onto the comforter.

Outraged, he hissed and ran under the bed.

"Serves you right." With a towel, Rebecca sopped up the mess and righted the bucket. "If I had any sense, I'd join you under there until this nightmare is over."

Hands planted on her hips, she looked around the room at her quick-fix efforts, and, deciding it would have to hold for the moment, she called Jake. Even with rain pouring in sheets, he said he would meet her at the back of the house.

Bless good neighbors.

Clad in her rubber gardening boots and holding an umbrella, she darted out the kitchen door and into the storm. Thunder rumbled. The dark gray sky flickered with lightning as if the angels were turning a switch on and off.

With nothing but a baseball cap to shield his head, Jake stood at the corner of the house. He craned his neck back. "That roofline's pretty high."

She really wished everyone would stop saying that.

"No way my ladder will reach, but a buddy of mine works for the phone company. I think his brother has some roofing experience."

"Those bucket thingys."

He smiled, water dripping off his chin. "Right."

Rebecca rolled her shoulders. "Call him then. But keep it quiet. My buyer is staying at the house for the weekend."

"He's living with you?"

"He's not *living* with me, living with me. He just needed a place to stay until—" She broke off when a sly smile broke across Jake's mouth. "Never mind."

"Hell of a storm."

Rebecca glanced over, where Alex was leaning halfway out the back door. His silky black hair shined, soaked through from the rain. Water droplets trickled off his face. He looked exhilarated by Mother Nature's show. Exhilarated and sexy.

Rebecca sighed. He was going to find out about the house, then he would retract his contract and leave.

She also considered the legal ramifications. He could sue her. Of course, at the time she signed the disclosure statement nothing was wrong, and she would make sure everything was repaired and had a warranty. Her intent was honorable.

Oh, *that* would go over well with a jury when he sued her blind.

Broken dreams, heartache and more plastic buckets all lay in her immediate future.

She slogged through the rain and mud to face the music.

5

PINE STRAW IN the gutters, huh?

Somehow, Alex thought there was a bit more to Jake's presence in Rebecca's backyard during a roaring thunderstorm, but he didn't question Rebecca's story. He didn't want to start an argument. Especially since the weather had provided him such a romantic indoor setting—dinner with Rebecca in an old house, rain pattering on the roof, thunder rumbling in the distance.

"How's your dinner?" he asked her.

She licked her lips, and he clenched his fork. "Delicious. Thanks. You were great earlier, by the way."

He waved that away. "Sending Jake on his way wasn't any big deal. Convincing you I could still salvage dinner...that required finesse."

"And thanks for picking up dinner and bringing it back here. It's not a great night to go out."

He leaned toward her, lowering his voice. "Don't thank me too much. You might find yourself in debt."

"Any more than I already am?"

"What do you mean?" Frowning, Alex chewed a bite of the tangy barbecue pork. Her family had owned this house for generations. How was she in debt?

She glanced up at him, eyes wide, as if she'd admitted something she didn't want him knowing. "What I meant to say is…moving, moving is so expensive. Especially to New York. Everything costs so much up there.''

"Yes, it does. Before you go, I'll help you plan an investment strategy to recoup your expenses. I got this great tip the other day on a technology stock.''

"Mmm. I've heard they're doing well.''

"Volatile, but profitable.''

She dabbed her napkin over her lips.

Man, he really wanted to be that napkin. She'd let down her hair—literally—tonight, the soft, curly locks falling to her shoulders. He longed to bury his hands in her hair, lose himself in her kisses. The distance he'd maintained during the day had done nothing but heighten his need for her, leaving him to wonder, again, why she'd invaded his thoughts so thoroughly, so quickly.

He liked women a great deal. He enjoyed their delicate skin, teasing smiles and laughter. But he didn't crave them. Not like he craved Rebecca.

The thunder rumbled closer this time, then a bright streak of lightning crashed so close to the house, the silverware jumped.

"Damn, I hate that.'' Rebecca rubbed her hands down her arms.

Frankly, Alex was glad to be startled from his thoughts. "Do you think we should go to the basement?'' he asked, rising from the table to look out the back doors.

"I've got a weather radio. Let's see what the forecasters say.'' After pulling a small, cubed-shaped radio from the cabinet, she flipped it on and set it on the bar. Though a tornado watch was in effect until 5:00 a.m., none had been spotted. For the moment, all they had to deal with were severe thunderstorms.

Alex stared out the windowed back door, the dark gray

sky sending a shiver down his spine. He'd never experienced a tornado and didn't really want to start now. "Maybe we should head to the basement, anyway. Just in case."

"Storms make you nervous?" she asked with a teasing grin.

He had the feeling she was making fun of him, so he said importantly, "Of course not. It's the one-hundred-mile-an-hour winds ripping houses off their foundations that scare me."

She retrieved their iced tea glasses from the table and handed him his. "We're okay during the storms. You're in trouble when everything goes still."

Hoping she knew what she was talking about, he sipped his tea and tried to regain his light mood and seduction plans. Though how in the world he'd seduce her in the middle of a tornado he had no idea.

"How did your search for office space go?" she asked.

"Great. A health food store just closed down on Main Street. The property owner offered me a great deal and said I was lucky to find such a premium spot."

"Uh-huh."

Something about her tone had him narrowing his eyes. "It's not a premium spot?"

"Well, yes. As premium as any spot can be in Junction Gap. The owner just may have exaggerated about the 'just closed down' part of the health food store."

"Exaggerated?"

"It's been gone about three years."

Alex recalled the buyer—an older man who snapped his suspenders, assuring him in his slow, Southern accent he'd discovered a gem of an office. *Men,* he thought in disgust. You couldn't trust 'em. "Three years, huh?"

"That group of offices is in a good location, though. The barbershop on the corner is gossip central. They'll spread the word about you faster than any advertising you could buy. The insurance office next to yours handles every farm in the county. The owner will be a good business contact." She bit her lip, obviously fighting back a smile. "And then there's Sylvia—two doors down from you. If you're ever uncertain about a stock, she'll be glad to help out." Rebecca's eyes watered with the effort to contain her mirth.

"She's a broker?"

"No, she's a psychic. You know—crystal ball, Tarot cards, palm reading. Mama swore by her, and she helped one of my neighbors find her dog last spring. Of course, the leftover pot roast Linda set on her back porch didn't hurt."

A smile crept to Alex's lips. Junction Gap might be sleepy and settled, but it would never be boring. He made a mental note to thank Nana Carlisle for encouraging him to give small-town life a try. Maybe he really could live here permanently.

"You're not upset?" Rebecca asked, surprised, then quickly continued, "Of course not. This is the man who said, 'Cool' after seeing the bordello bedroom."

"A psychic brings color to the neighborhood."

"I could use a little less color in my life, thank you."

Boom!

Alex jumped away from the door at the simultaneous crack of thunder and lightning. His glass slipped from his hand, shattering on the tile floor. The lights flickered, then went out.

"Not again." Rebecca sighed in obvious disgust. "Stay here. I'll get the candles."

He linked his hand with hers, her warm, soft skin sending

a ripple of desire through his body. He'd just found his break. "I'll come with you. Knowing where the candles are is a necessity in this house." He guided her around the broken glass, considering the gift Mother Nature had handed him.

Dark, spooky, old house. Thunderstorm. Danger and electricity crackling in the air. Heroine in distress. Hero conveniently available. He smiled, puffing out his chest as they shuffled from the kitchen to the dining room.

"Here we go," Rebecca said, and he heard her open a drawer.

From the lustrous moonlight coming through the window, he could just discern her profile. The outline of her full lips, her dark hair framing her pale face. The wind and rain pounded against the house, rivers of water cascading down the glass panes.

She released his hand to strike a match and touched the small flame to a taper. Her face glowed in the soft light as she handed him the candle, then retrieved one for herself. Hunger for her clawed at his gut. They'd been alone for nearly two hours, and the only touching they'd accomplished was holding hands.

They were *way* behind.

Each carrying a silver candlestick and flickering candle, they returned to the kitchen where they cleaned up the broken glass and spilled tea. Alex decided he liked how much smaller the world seemed by candlelight. Unable to see beyond the kitchen doorway, it seemed as if he and Rebecca were the only people for miles.

"I guess we should head to the basement and check the fuses," she said, sounding none-too-pleased at the idea.

"I'll do it." He didn't want those lights back on just yet. After grabbing his candlestick, he pulled out one of the kitchen chairs. "Why don't you relax?" He glanced out the back door, noting they were again the only ones without light. "It's probably just another tripped switch."

On his way down the hall he stumbled over something. Something that hissed. Holding his candle aloft, Alex leaned down to find Moose staring up at him accusingly. "Sorry, big guy."

The cat turned his back, twitched his tail in Alex's direction, then sauntered down the hall.

Chuckling, Alex continued to the basement. At the fuse box, he discovered tripped switches controlling power to the kitchen, dining room and library. Nothing serious. He could have the lights back on in seconds. But what Rebecca didn't know wouldn't hurt her, and it just might give him the atmosphere he needed.

He swung by the wine racks, then grabbed a bottle of cabernet sauvignon, whistling as he made his way up the creaky basement stairs.

"I don't know what's wrong," he said to Rebecca as he entered the kitchen. "I guess we'll have to call an electrician in the morning."

Scowling, she tapped her fingernails against the table. "Great."

Not a lie. Just an exaggeration. Not a lie. He really didn't know why the switches continued to trip, and she should consult with an electrician about the problem.

"We'll make the best of it. Look what I found." He showed her the wine bottle.

Even by pale candlelight, he could see suspicion creep into her eyes. "What are you up to, Alex Carlisle?"

He grinned devilishly. "Would it really be so bad? Wine by candlelight…with me?"

"It's not the wine or the candlelight I'm worried about."

They were way behind. Time stood still for long moments, long enough for him to realize how disappointed he'd be if she brushed him off. His emotions were tangled in Rebecca more than he was completely comfortable with. An odd feeling he might have called worry—if he were the worrying type, that is—nagged him.

Before he could give the sensation too much credit she tossed back her hair and said, "Oh, what the hell."

Just the right attitude, Alex decided. He opened the bottle, poured two glasses, then settled in the chair next to hers. "To thunderstorms," he said, tapping his glass against hers.

He was rewarded with only half a smile. "Oh, yeah. They're a laugh a minute." She sipped her wine, then played with the stem, a contemplative look on her face. "Mama loved storms. Of course, she loved anything that was loud and flashy."

"The house certainly has a distinctive stamp. Were you two really so different?"

"Night and day." She paused, then added, "She was very beautiful."

Alex didn't see how that made them different. "And you didn't get along?"

She looked up at him, surprised. "Of course we did."

"But you disagreed about the house."

"Sometimes." She shifted in her chair, obviously uncomfortable, but Alex wanted to push for more. He was curious why a few mismatched walls and a racy bedroom bothered her so much. "Okay a lot," she added. "She was all the family I had, though. My father left her before I was born, and she spent her whole life pretending he hadn't broken her heart."

"Everybody deals with pain in a different way."

"Dating half the male population in Georgia seemed a bit extreme."

But it had probably been fun, Alex thought, though he figured he shouldn't make the comment aloud to Rebecca. "Well, I see a lot of similarity between you two."

She rolled her eyes. "Like what?"

He tapped her nose. "A gargoyle toothbrush holder?" He nodded at the clock hanging on the wall beside the refrigerator. "A cuckoo clock that meows?"

"Those are just…things."

"Uh-huh." Very telling things. He held out his hand. "Let's dance."

"Dance?"

"You know, moving your feet back and forth in time to music." He grinned and stood, pulling back her chair. "Arms around each other. Bodies touching." He tugged her hand, bringing her body flush against his chest. Her heart hammered against his, as she stood silent, staring up at him, her blue eyes wide.

"Do you really think we should—"

"Absolutely." Look what happened last time they'd danced. He moved his feet back and forth. "Do you have a radio—with batteries?"

"In the parlor."

Bad idea. The parlor had power. But if one of the lights was already on, surely they would be able to see the light filtering down the hall. He grabbed the candles, then nodded toward the kitchen doorway. "After you."

She stared at him for several long, seemingly interminable, seconds. Was she going to tell him to back off? Had he ticked her off by comparing her to her mother? What the hell did he know anyway? Why was he questioning himself? He never did that.

Taking one of the candles, she said, "I like jazz, not classical," then walked down the hall.

SHE WASN'T TURNING into her mother, was she?

Rebecca stood in the center of the dimly lit living room while Alex set the radio on one of the solid cherry end tables. While part of her wanted to retreat to the safety of her bedroom and brood over her financial problems and house repairs, another part hungered for—actually craved—his touch.

It didn't make sense. It wasn't practical. It was impulsive and exciting and wild.

She *was* turning into her mother.

After all this time she finally understood Mama's need to have a man notice her the way Alex did, like he couldn't look long enough. Like she was the most interesting person he knew. Like he wanted to kiss his way up her extremities.

She should be examining the reasons why he seemed so determined to flirt with her. She should be worried about the possibility of falling for a playboy.

A soft, bass clarinet ballad echoed through the room, and Alex turned from the radio. His green gaze raked her from head to toe. He was so beautiful, standing there in his tailored clothes, his black hair just brushing his collar, his whole being totally focused on her. His gaze shifted to her lips, and she sucked in a much-needed breath.

She could examine and worry later. Right?

As he drew her smoothly into his arms, the spicy scent clinging to his shirt enveloped her in a sensual dream. She slid her hands up his broad chest and linked them behind his head. The chemistry between them had erupted quickly, not giving her time to consider her actions. Now that she had time, she still she let herself go, welcoming this slow, graceful fall into desire.

Another song began, and Alex moved his hands from her sides to span them across her back, his fingers gliding against her shirt. Rebecca longed to feel his touch against her bare skin. If he moved his hands just a little lower, he could slide his hand beneath the edge of her shirt, caress her skin, pull her harder against his body.

Oh, boy. She had to find conversation before she did something rash. "You've neatly managed to avoid telling me anything about yourself all night, while I've been spilling my guts."

"Have I?"

"You said you've lived in a lot of places, and your grandparents are in New York. What about your parents? Where are they?"

He shrugged his shoulders, his muscles rippling beneath her hands. "A little bit of everywhere. They've been divorced since I was five. Right now Mom's in Monte Carlo with husband number three, and my father's going through a golf phase on Amelia Island."

"That's in Florida, right?"

He nodded. "Near Jacksonville. That's how I found out about your house. My grandparents told him I was looking for an historical house, so he e-mailed me when yours went on the market."

"Historical houses, like the Victorian one your grandparents own." When he simply nodded, she became curious. *Aha.* Mr. I-see-a-lot-of-similarity-between-you-two was about to have his own life dissected. "So you've decided to give up jet-setting for Junction Gap."

His brow furrowed. "Well, not exactly…maybe."

"So what *exactly* are you going to do with my house?"

"Your house? You're certainly protective all of a sudden."

She simply stared at him, waiting for an answer.

"I told you, I *may* settle here permanently."

"Uh-huh." Rebecca ducked her head to hide her smile. Since the moment Alex Carlisle had swept through her front door, she'd never seen him have an uncertain moment—other than that bit of nerves at the thunderstorm—but she'd swear he was not only confused by his sudden interest in settling in a small town, but also at odds on what to do about those feelings.

Then he lifted one black eyebrow in a gesture so cool and sexy she nearly forgot how to work her tongue. "Is the inquisition over, Miss Parsons?"

She stared into his eyes, deciding talk, even for a lawyer, was highly overrated. "For the moment." She dropped her gaze to his neck. The strong, tanned column beckoned her lips, as if asking her to press her mouth against the pulse rapping beneath his jaw. She leaned forward, wondering how sophisticated Alex Carlisle would look with a hickey.

His thumb skimmed along her cheekbone. "You're exquisite."

Exquisite? Her breath froze in her throat. She started to look around to see who had come into the room. She wanted to shake her head or argue, but the honesty and desire in Alex's eyes stopped her.

Before she had time to consider his words further, he lowered his head, his lips brushing hers with just a whisper of warmth against her mouth. She angled her head, inviting him to sink his tongue past her lips. As he explored her mouth, she tightened her grip on his neck, tunneling her fingers through his silky hair.

He slid his hand beneath the edge of her shirt, and her

body hummed for more. His nimble fingers teased her waist, traveled up her back. She pressed her chest against his, her breasts heavy with desire. She wanted the barriers between them gone, wanted him beyond all reason and logic.

Could she really sleep with a man she'd just met? Invite him to her bed?

Wait. Her bed…with a water-filled bucket square in the center of the comforter.

She dragged her mouth from Alex's. His considerable kissing skills had scrambled her brain into forgetting the current hell her life had plunged into. She had a leaky roof, a noncooperative garbage disposal, an angry cat and now electrical problems.

He cupped her head between his hands. "God, I want you."

His head descended again, and he nibbled gently at her lips. Her mind fogged. His warm, persuasive mouth coaxed her lips apart, stroking her tongue with his, igniting fires of desire, tempting her to forget all that stood between them. He sank his fingers into her hair, angling her head back, so he could trail kisses down her throat. His hands slid beneath her sweatshirt, finding the clasp on her bra. When her aching breasts were free, he stroked his thumbs across her nipples, sending shimmers of desire through her body.

She fought to catch her breath. Every sensible, practical thought in her head vanished when he touched her. All sensations pooled between her legs, pulsing, demanding to be satisfied.

He shoved up her sweatshirt and bra, exposing her to the air. Her nipples budded tighter. She dropped her head back and sank her hands in his hair as his tongue flicked across each aching point in turn. Her head spun. She had to brace her hands on his shoulders. He alternately laved and blew on her breasts until she thought she'd faint.

She clenched his shirt in her hands, wanting to get closer to him, needing to feel his skin. Desire gnawed at her, making her fingers tingle and her pulse pound. She slid her fingers between the buttons—and ripped it open.

She gasped. He jumped back.

"What the hell—" he began, then glanced at his shirt, then back to her. He grinned, yanking her against him and backing toward the sofa.

Rebecca knew she should be horrified by what she'd done, but she was too busy rubbing her hands across the light sprinkling of hair on his muscled chest. Alex flopped back on the sofa bringing her down with him. She moaned, her stomach meeting the hardness between his legs. The pressure alone sent pleasure spiraling through her. Sitting up, she slid her legs on either side of his waist, then rolled her hips over him.

"Oh, man." His eyes closed, his hand jerking to her hips to hold her in place, obviously savoring the sensations.

Then Moose jumped on his bare chest.

Alex jackknifed up, sending the cat tumbling to the floor as Rebecca tightened her hold on Alex's hips with her thighs.

Groaning, Alex wrapped his arms around her. "I'm really beginning to hate that cat."

Moose meowed—the disgruntled meow. The one that proceeded the pissed-off big-time meow. The one he gave when he was hungry.

She dropped her forehead on Alex's shoulder. "I forgot to feed him."

They both looked down at the cat, who sat in front of

the sofa, his tail twitching. The exasperated look on his face said it all—*What the hell could you two possibly be doing that's more important than my dinner?*

Rebecca cast Alex a regretful look. "Sorry. I'd better take care of him."

Alex's lips tipped at the corners. "Probably."

He looked so darn cute sitting there with his shirt in tatters, his hair sticking out on the sides, his chin smeared with her lipstick. They'd gone and done it again. Lost control, lost all sense of time and place, lost their minds.

She reminded herself she didn't get involved with love 'em and leave 'em types. She observed too many of Mama's confusing, unproductive and, ultimately, painful affairs. She'd nursed Mama through too many broken relationships to risk heartbreak of her own.

She loved her cat, her mother and her sole pair of Manolo Blahnik shoes. But love a man? No way. Not in this house, or this town, and certainly not Alex.

Climbing off him, she tugged her sweatshirt back into place as she stood, then flipped on the floor lamp.

He grabbed her hand. "You're coming back, aren't—" His gaze shot to the brilliant light, then back to her face, his neck flushing a deep, guilty red.

The brilliant light? She'd turned it on out of habit, forgetting about the power outage.

She stared down at him. "Why is the power on in here?"

"Uh, well…" He looked everywhere but at her. "Maybe it came back on?"

Crossing her arms over her chest, she said, "Try again, smart guy." *We'll have to call an electrician,* he'd said. Add that to her list of plumber, roofer and God only knew what else before the inspector arrived with his clipboard and sharp eyes.

He stood, spearing his hand through his hair, mussing it further. Now it stood up on top, too. "Okay. Look, when I checked the fuse box, I found a couple of tripped switches. Probably from that bolt of lightning so close to the house. We had candles, the moonlight, and I—"

"Blatantly lied so you could attempt to seduce me," she finished.

"You have to admit it was a pretty damn good attempt."

She couldn't argue with him there.

And while she knew she'd told her own lies about the house, at least *she* hadn't turned his body against him, and *she* hadn't tossed out empty compliments. Exquisite, indeed. Ha!

Anger rolled through her, anger that allowed her to regain control of her mad desire for him. This proved to her that they were completely wrong for each other. He was flashy, she was plodding. He was imaginative, she was practical. He was staying, she was leaving.

He laid his hands on her shoulders. "I'm sorry. Truly. I just wanted to heighten the atmosphere. I thought it would be fun."

She shrugged off his touch, pacing away from him. "You need special effects to get a woman into bed?"

A muscle ticked along the edge of his jaw. "Not usually."

She flung her hands out, waving at the room. "I'm sure there are dozens of women around you wouldn't have to go to nearly so much trouble to have."

"I want you," he said quietly.

For the moment. Until she left—if even for that long. Maybe just for one night. She'd seen Mama go through too many men in that same blasé, "see you around" way.

She'd sworn she wouldn't do the same. Why did Alex have to tempt her to break that vow?

She needed time to think. She couldn't concentrate with Alex staring at her, desire so plainly reflected in his eyes. "This doesn't make sense," she said finally, knowing she'd expressed the same frustration yesterday. "*We* don't make sense."

"Sense doesn't apply anywhere in our relationship."

"But I want it to. It *has* to." She turned away—from him, from her feelings. "Would you blow out the candles? I'm going to bed."

"Alone?" he asked.

So afraid the sight of him might change her mind, she didn't turn around. He'd be moving into his apartment in two days, then she probably wouldn't see him at all until the closing. She could stay in control, keep her heart intact, whip this crazy house into shape and get on with her life.

"Alone," she said, then ran to her room.

6

On Monday morning, Alex peered through soap-stung eyes at the sudden lack of water streaming from the showerhead. "You've got to be kidding."

Swiping the back of his hand over his face to remove the soap, he twisted the knobs back and forth. Nothing. He glared up at the nozzle, poking his fingers in the holes. "What the hell is going on?"

Shampoo suds rolled down his face, one stream pooling in his ear, one rolling off his eyelashes. Cursing, he rubbed his eyes, then tilted his head to one side, hoping the suds would run out. While keeping his eyes closed—he was strictly a no-more-tears man from now on—he fumbled around the shower curtain for a towel. Nothing. "I just can't get a break," he muttered. He made do with the plastic curtain, then flung it aside and stepped out of the shower.

With the soap drying rapidly, he jerked a towel from the rack by the sink, trying to wipe off the remaining suds, but they clung to his skin like glue. He itched. His eyes burned. And his reflection in the mirror—with his hair standing on end in clumps and with his bloodshot eyes—wasn't a pretty sight. He needed water. He turned the knobs above the sink.

Again, no water. Not a drop.

As he flung the towel around his waist, his thoughts turned to Rebecca, much as they had all day yesterday while she'd avoided him. He'd smiled, attempted to engage her in conversation, even offered to cook. She'd announced she wasn't hungry and closed herself in her room, claiming she needed to pack. He finally got so frustrated he'd gone shopping for office furniture.

He supposed he couldn't blame her for her lack of enthusiasm toward him. Not only had he lied, he'd also done a damn poor job of seduction Saturday night. He hadn't shown her how special she was, how uniquely and completely she affected him. He didn't slowly tease her to the heights of passion. No, he'd taken greedily, so overwhelmed from touching her he'd thought he might lose complete control of his body several times. He wasn't sure what was wrong with him, but he had to get back on track today.

Why did the water have to die now? Why did it have to happen while he was in the shower? He rubbed his hand through his hair, still staring at himself in the partially fogged mirror.

Why, indeed?

Frustrated, eyes stinging, he marched from the bathroom, heading directly to the basement. One look at the main water valve confirmed his suspicions.

Someone had shut off the water.

Shaking his head, he jogged back upstairs. ''That little vixen.'' She'd probably spent half the day yesterday plotting this bit of revenge for his power outage scheme.

He stopped at her bedroom door, tapping on the wood. ''Rise and shine, Sleeping Beauty.''

Moments later, her dark head peeked around the edge of the door.

He leaned one shoulder against the door frame. ''If you wanted me naked and soapy, all you had to do is ask.''

She glared at him, opening the door wider, cinching the belt of a fluffy pink robe around her body. "What in God's name are you talking about?"

He took a step toward her, pleased when she backed up a step. "You're adorable in the morning." He glanced down, smiling at the fuzzy orange cat slippers she wore. "I especially like the slippers."

"Why are you pounding on my door dressed—" she lifted one dark eyebrow "—or perhaps I should say *undressed* like that?"

"I was taking a shower."

"And you lost your clothes?"

He grinned, then paused to scratch his chest. "The water shut off. Imagine that."

She looked at him blankly.

"Oh, come on, Rebecca. You got me back for the other night. Turning off the water was really original." He leaned toward her. "I had no idea you were so...inventive."

She angled her head, staring at him as if he'd lost his mind. "You're saying I just tiptoed into the bathroom, yanked back the shower curtain, turned off the water and ran back to my room before you noticed?"

"No. You turned it off at the main valve."

"I—" Her mouth dropped open. "What? I did no such thing."

He scratched his stomach. "Right."

She finally seemed to realize he was serious. "Alex, the main water valve is in the basement."

He scratched the back of his neck. "So?"

"I don't go to the basement."

True. A trickle of alarm inched its way up his spine. He scratched. "*Somebody* turned off the water. I just went down to the basement and turned it back on."

"Maybe it shut off by itself. Like the power."

He shook his head. "A knob doesn't turn itself." Only seconds ago he was certain the culprit was Rebecca—after all, she was the only person in the house besides him. But he hadn't considered her fear of the basement....

"Someone's been in my house," she said suddenly, her tone hushed.

Spinning away, he grabbed the edge of the door. "Stay here and lock the door. I'm going to check this out."

"Not without me you're not."

Not only did he not want her coming along, he'd rather have her out of the house until he got to the bottom of the whole incident. "No."

"No? Excuse me, did you say no?" She wrenched the door from his hand and held up an aluminum bat with the other. "I keep it behind the door," she explained as his gaze darted from her to the bat and back again. She huffed, looking impatient. "It's my house—at least for another couple of weeks."

Arguing with a woman holding a weapon aloft was not Alex's idea of a good move, so he stepped aside to let her out of the room, but he took the lead down the hall.

After checking all the bedrooms and finding no one lurking and nothing missing, they headed for the stairs. When they reached the bottom, Alex heard a faint meow. "Moose?"

"He was in my room earlier, but that's not him. It's the clock."

Six more meows echoed down the hall, before the house fell silent again.

Bright sunlight streamed through the windows in the front of the house. The foyer's wooden floor gleamed—a product of Alex's labors yesterday in an attempt to gain

Rebecca's attention. The parlor's purple carpet was fluffed to perfection—he'd vacuumed, too. Everything seemed normal.

In this house that was a very bad sign.

Drawing a deep breath, Alex tucked Rebecca close behind him. They crept down the hall, scanning the interior of the rooms they passed. They saw no one. Nothing moved.

"Do we really have to go down there?" she whispered in his ear when they reached the basement door.

He fought to ignore the sizzle of excitement both her sweet breath and the element of danger added to the moment. "That's the only place we haven't checked."

"Besides the attic."

"We'll go there next." Since he'd already been to the basement, he didn't really think they would find a homicidal criminal with prankster tendencies down there. But that was the scene of the crime, so to speak. "Let me hold the bat."

She handed the weapon to him without objection as he opened the basement door. The old hinges creaked, echoing like a shriek in the quiet house. He winced, not remembering the noise before, and peered into the darkness.

Though he tried to tell himself no one could possibly be lurking about after his earlier trip down there, his heart rapped against his ribs in a rapid staccato. He glided his hand up the wall until he felt the light switch, then flipped it on.

"At least we're not in the middle of a power-robbing thunderstorm," Rebecca said dryly from over his shoulder.

"Very funny." He turned his head, only to encounter her face inches from his own. Why did the woman have to possess the softest, best tasting lips on the planet?

She didn't trust him and, after Saturday night's fiasco, he could hardly blame her. She'd run away from him. She'd spent all day yesterday avoiding him.

He'd been many things to many women, but desperate wasn't ever one of them. So why couldn't he stop thinking about her, wanting her, needing her?

Her gaze dropped to his lips, her eyes going smokey.

He swallowed hard, recalling Saturday night, the moment she'd straddled him, rubbing the cleft between her legs against his erection. At this rate, he was going to need a bigger towel.

"Are we going or not?" she asked.

He cleared his throat and looked away, holding the bat in front of him. "Absolutely. Why don't you go upstairs and call 911?"

She grabbed him by the waist, but when her hand encountered the towel, she jerked her hand back. "I'm sticking."

Fearful that the towel wouldn't, he fought for control of his body. This situation was serious. Maybe even dangerous. And in truth, he didn't have much experience with prowlers. A top-notch security system guarded his brownstone in Manhattan. He'd never even been mugged. But here, in this sleepy Georgia town, he was prepared to encounter God-only-knew-what in Rebecca's basement.

"Do you have ghosts?" he asked, stalling.

Her disbelieving gaze fell on him. "Ghosts?"

"The guy at the furniture store said a lot of the these historical homes have them."

"No. I don't have ghosts."

"Well, then, let's proceed, shall we?"

"Let's."

Before anyone moved, however, a furry ball charged

through Alex's legs. Heart racing, he jumped. "What the hell?"

Moose sat at his feet, long, bushy tail gliding across the wood floor, big gold eyes staring at them.

"Oh, Moose." Rebecca waved her hand. "Go, go. Some guard kitty you are. Of course, you didn't help me with that rat, either."

Alex coughed. "What rat?"

"The big one I saw in the basement six months ago."

"Oh." Alex walked down one step, then stopped, staring at her over his shoulder. "Just how big?"

"Bigger than Moose."

Alex clenched the bat tighter and started down the stairs. But after a thorough search they determined the basement was deserted, so they crept to the attic.

They had to work around the dozens of paint cans and some old trunks, but found nothing there, either. "Well, we seem to be alone." Alex said, glancing around.

Rebecca blew out a breath, stirring the bangs against her forehead. "I guess so."

Noticing a closet on the far side of the room, he headed toward it. He'd just shoved the doors aside, when Rebecca grabbed his arm. "There's nothing in there."

He didn't turn around because a large object had caught his attention. He tilted his head sideways, staring at the painting, then whistled. "Is that who I think it is?"

Rebecca sighed. "Yes."

Grinning, he looked at her. "*You* posed for a nude portrait?"

"Of course not." She stared at him oddly. "That's Mama."

Alex picked up the painting, turned it upright, then leaned it against the wall. He ran his gaze over the woman's smokey blue eyes, her glistening, full lips and her wavy, dark brown hair—just a bit longer than Rebecca's. He took his time studying her body, as well—the beautiful, creamy skin, the ripe swell of her breasts, the seductive curve of her hips, the dark triangle between her long legs and the bright pink nail polish on her toes.

The woman looked so much like Rebecca—with his lascivious, male imagination filling in most of the naked parts—his blood heated. "Whoa, baby."

"Do you have any idea how humiliating it is to hear grown men say that?"

Confused, he turned to her. "Why?"

"She's my *mother*."

"So, she's supposed to stop being sexy?"

She huffed. "Well, she didn't have to flaunt it."

"You're sexy. Do you think you flaunt it?"

Eyes wide, her mouth opened, then shut. "Uh...no. To both."

Both? As in she didn't flaunt her sexuality and *what?*

He recalled their conversation about her mother's beauty and their differences. Did Rebecca not think she was sexy? While she wasn't the Victoria's Secret type in low-cut blouses and short skirts, she was breathtakingly lovely, elegant, subtle and—his gaze slid from the painting to the woman as he considered the curves beneath her bathrobe—hot as hell.

How could a woman as terrific as Rebecca not see her own appeal?

He returned the painting to the closet, then dropped one arm around her shoulders. "Rebecca, honey, your mother couldn't have concealed her sexuality any more than you can." He stared directly into her startled eyes, determined to make certain she didn't miss his intent. "But just for the record, I prefer you any day of the week and twice on Sunday. You're beautiful, smart, enticing, and I've never—'' he stopped himself, brushing a lock of hair off her forehead ''—I'm crazy about you.''

He watched her throat move. "I am? You are? But—"

He laid his finger over her lips, not ready to articulate more than that simple fact as he guided them toward the door. "I do have a question, though. Just how physically similar were you and your mother?"

She glanced at him out of the corner of her eye.

"It was kind of dark the other night, so I didn't really get a good look—"

"Alex Carlisle!" She lightly slapped his arm, though he could tell his curiosity pleased her. "I might have a prowler, and you're thinking about sex."

"I'm a man. It's difficult not to."

"Try," she suggested briskly.

They convened in the kitchen to plot their next step. While Rebecca fed Moose—who stood by his bowl with an extremely put-upon look on his face—Alex poured them each a piping hot cup of coffee.

"There's no way this could happen by accident?" she asked, sitting across from him at the kitchen table.

Alex blew on his coffee, then sipped. "I don't see how. You saw the knob."

She sighed. "I guess I should call Dwayne."

"Dwayne?"

She sighed again, deeper this time. "The sheriff."

"You don't want to call him?"

Her lips quirked upward behind her coffee mug. "Let's just say having a point-oh-one percent crime rate has its disadvantages."

"So, Dwayne is—"

"Fond of his uniform, his salary, charming the ladies at the beauty shop and washing his patrol car."

Alex raised his eyebrows. "In that order?"

"Unfortunately."

"And the safety of the locals?"

"Falls somewhere south of shining his boots." She paused, considering. "Though he's been known to help the occasional damsel in distress."

Alex leaned forward, resting his elbows on the counter. "I see." He didn't much like the thought of Rebecca here alone with not even a decent police department for protection.

"You know, it's okay for you to get dressed now. I think the danger's passed," she said into the silence.

He glanced down at the towel around his waist, then up again, surprised to see her eyes narrowed with annoyance.

"Aren't you cold?" she asked.

"No." Cold was never a state he found himself in around Rebecca. In fact, he'd been hotter than a fire poker since the moment he'd laid eyes on her.

Rebecca ran her gaze over Alex's broad, damp bare chest. She needed a big glass of ice water, not hot coffee. Didn't the man have any decency? How was she supposed to resist that beautiful body?

She frowned, considering. Maybe that's what he wanted. *Look what you passed up, baby.* Why else was he calmly sipping coffee as if he had a right to prowl her house practically naked? Why else was he telling her she was beautiful—which she knew very well she wasn't—and making her heart flutter by saying things like *I'm crazy about you?* She tried to remember he just wanted to use her for sex until she left. They had no future, and she didn't engage in empty affairs, though he no doubt did—and frequently.

He set down his cup, then crossed his arms over his chest, drawing her attention to his well-defined muscles. "I was supposed to move into my apartment today, but I think I should stay."

"Here?" Rebecca asked incredulously.

"Of course here. You shouldn't be alone until the police find out what's going on."

With Dwayne on the case, the solution to the water prank could be twenty minutes away or just short of never, depending on how long it took the culprit to confess. No way was Rebecca having that luscious, tempting, hard body under her roof another second. Not to mention she had a roofer coming to check out her leaks, and a plumber to fix the garbage disposal.

She shook her head vehemently. "No."

He'd started to pick up his mug again, but set it down at her refusal. And he had the nerve to look downright shocked. "What?"

"You heard me. *No*. I extended my hospitality for the weekend, so you wouldn't have to sleep in your car. As of this morning, the weekend is over."

"You're asking me to leave?"

Wrapping her hands around her coffee cup, she shrugged. "Yes." *You thick-headed, gorgeous dolt.*

He watched her in silence for a few seconds, then smiled.

Damn, he knew what that smile did to a woman. After the power outage incident, she should have known he didn't play fair.

"Is there some reason you're so anxious to get rid of me?" he asked.

"I'm not the least anxious. It's just time for you to go."

He leaned forward and gestured at her with a wave of his hand. "You look anxious to me. Your eyes are dilated, you're breathing hard and if you grip that mug any tighter, it's going to break.''

She relaxed her grip. She didn't like his proximity one bit. ''It's been a stressful morning,'' she said indignantly.

''Which brings me back to my original point. You shouldn't be here alone with a prowler on the loose.''

''I can take care of myself.'' He merely lifted one eyebrow, raising her anger further. ''Do we have to have this conversation with you dressed like that?''

''What difference does it make what I'm wearing?''

''It distracts me, and—'' She stopped, realizing what she'd admitted.

His eyes glowed like bright green gems. ''Do you like the view, Miss Parsons?'' he asked huskily.

All the air in the room suddenly dissipated, and Rebecca found she couldn't catch her breath. The clean smell of soap and man rose from his bare chest, and she couldn't help noticing the towel had parted on one side, revealing one muscular, male thigh. His black hair had dried into messy spikes, but she had to admit he was by far the most appealing sight she'd ever seen in her kitchen. Or anyplace else in her life for that matter.

His innate sensuality rolled off him in waves, and she realized his elegant clothes concealed a predatory nature she had just barely glimpsed. What would it really be like to hold all that energy, sexiness and confidence for longer than a few minutes? Carnal ideas zipped through her mind, heating her face and turning her muscles soft with longing.

And he isn't even touching me, she thought with a hint of desperation.

She stood, taking a physical and mental step backward. ''This is what I mean. We can't even have a simple conversation without all this…*stuff* getting in the way.''

He rose, as well, leaning over the table, until his face was just inches from hers. "I happen to like this stuff. I like it a great deal."

Honestly, she did, too. Except when her stomach was churning with confusion, or the logical side of her brain was butting in. Like now.

"You should go, Alex. Please," she added when he didn't so much as twitch a muscle. And she was giving those incredible muscles a close inspection, so she would have noticed.

His eyes darkened with what might have been hurt, but they danced again quickly. He turned, then strode casually across the room, only pausing when he reached the doorway and glanced back at her. "I'll see you around. Soon." Whistling, he walked down the hall, the floor creaking as he made his way up the stairs.

Moose leapt onto the table, swishing his tail and looking more satisfied than he should—even after a meal.

Rebecca wished she could be relieved by Alex's exit, but she only felt depressed.

Moose purred.

"Oh, shut up."

"MA'AM, I NEED YOU to check out the work before I go."

Leaning forward on her kitchen counter, her pen poised above a blank check, Rebecca stared at the roofer Jake had recommended. "I trust you. My neighbor says you do fine work. How much do I owe you?"

He shook his head. "I'm sorry, ma'am. I have to insist."

She didn't really have time for this. After fixing the garbage disposal, the plumber had left a horrible mess in the sink. She was waiting for the sheriff to actually respond to her call, and thanks to Alex Carlisle's presence, she hadn't packed one box all weekend. "And just how in the world am I supposed to examine work done to my roof?" He continued to stare at her silently. "Oh, no," she said. "Not that bucket thingy."

"Bucket truck, ma'am."

"Right." She tried to smile. "I'm sure it's perfectly safe. After all, you were up there all afternoon. I just don't think—"

"It's safer than any ladder."

Deciding now was not the time to tell her able-bodied handyman that because of her mother's daring nature she'd never stood on a ladder taller than her own body in her life, she sighed in resignation. She certainly didn't want to spend another night like Saturday, sleeping beside her bed on the hard wooden floor, waking up every two hours to change buckets full of rainwater and burning out her hair-dryer as she dried the water stains on the ceiling.

She followed the roofer out the back door and into the yard. Attached to a small truck was a long mechanical arm. The bucket thingy dangled from the end of it, three stories up, at the edge of her roof. *No stinkin' way.*

"This way, ma'am."

"I don't think—"

But the roofer kept walking toward the truck, ignoring her protests. He climbed into the control seat, then slowly lowered the bucket.

"I don't think this is such a good idea," she continued, her heart lodged in her throat.

"It's perfectly safe," he said, looking toward the darkening sky. "Please, ma'am. This storm could come back anytime, and I have other jobs."

Stalling as she struggled to find her backbone, Rebecca glanced at the black cloud hovering over her backyard. At least if it rained she'd have a full test of the repair work. She forced her legs to move and approached the bucket hovering a few inches off her lawn. Hiking her leg over the side, she dropped into the contraption, bracing her hands on the sides.

With a lurch, the arm swung into motion. Rebecca kept her eyes focused on the roof—she didn't dare look down— and hoped she could handle this development with the restrained professionalism she possessed before this nutty house began tumbling down around her ears. It could be worse, she supposed. The pipes in the *basement* could spring a leak.

By the time the bucket reached the edge of the roof, she'd closed her eyes and convinced herself she was on an airplane ride at the county fair.

"How does it look?" the roofer called from what seemed like a great distance.

Rebecca made a show of turning her head right, then left, as if she were giving his workmanship great consideration. While the bucket swayed in the late-afternoon wind and her stomach bottomed out, she reminded herself this was the part of the ride where she flew through a pretend storm. "Fine," she said, eyes still closed, imagining her cute little plane with pink wings. "I think this will do just fine. Yep. No holes that I can see."

"I do excellent work," he called back.

"You certainly do."

"I'll bring you down now," he called again.

"Okay." She managed to smile, picturing her plane gliding down for a landing.

This visualization thing was working quite well. She wondered if it would work with Alex. Doubtful. The man could seduce her without even being around. When she was in the kitchen, she thought of the meals he'd made. When she was in her room, she thought of him appearing at her door in nothing but a towel. When she was in the parlor, she thought of their dance, his hot kisses, his firm muscles....

Whew. She fanned herself. What a relief it would be to move out of The House, to leave behind memories of Alex, as well as those of her mother.

Well, she didn't really want to leave Mama's memories behind, she just didn't want to wake up to polka-dotted carpet, paisley chairs and the bordello room. She needed a place that was hers. One where she fit in.

"You're down now, ma'am."

Rebecca opened her eyes and stared at the roofer, wondering how long she'd stood there, deep in thought. "Of course." She climbed out of the bucket, proud to find her legs decently steady.

She took two steps, then ground to a halt. "Dwayne."

The town's one-and-only full-time lawman hooked his fingers around his gun belt—though the mayor required him to carry his pistol unloaded—and rolled his thin shoulders. "Miss Parsons."

"Dwayne, we've known each other since kindergarten. I think it's safe to call me by my first name."

He frowned. "This is business. Serious business. I understand you've had some trouble out here."

Rebecca resisted the urge to roll her eyes at his dramatic tone. "Maybe. It's been an interesting morning."

And she just didn't mean the suspected prowler. Again, she pictured Alex Carlisle, his naked, muscular chest glistening with droplets of water.

"I'll get to the bottom of it," Dwayne said.

Somehow she didn't think Dwayne was capable of getting to the bottom of her attraction to Alex, so she merely nodded, leading him and the roofer into the kitchen.

Wincing as the roofer tracked his muddy work boots across her white-tiled floor, she filled out his check and sent him on his way.

Two catastrophes—the roof and the disposal—down. Only one more to go.

She eyed the skinny, self-assured, khaki-clad lawman who'd settled himself at her kitchen table with a cup of hot coffee. "Just help yourself, Sheriff," she said, not bothering to keep the sarcasm out of her voice.

Dwayne glared at her over the top of his mug. "I need fortification. It's life or death in the law biz. You need quick wits, catlike reflexes."

"Uh-huh." Rebecca watched Moose pad into the room. He stared at Dwayne with a gleam in his golden eyes.

Then he leapt onto the table.

Dwayne—quick wits and catlike reflexes included— jumped, smashing his knee on the table and sloshing his coffee down his sleeve.

Fighting to hold back laughter, Rebecca dashed to the counter to grab a dishcloth. She offered it to Dwayne, whose face had turned beet red. Moose, satisfied with his work, laid his pudgy body on the table.

Dwayne spun away from the cat, then leaned against the bar. "Let's get down to business. What happened this morning?"

"Someone turned off the water from the main valve in the basement," she said as she refilled his coffee.

Dwayne pursed his thin lips. "Someone, huh?"

"Yes. As I'm sure you know, the main water valve doesn't shut off by itself."

"Well, I heard about this one case…" he began importantly.

"Dwayne. Sheriff. Please." She handed him the coffee mug. "Let's stick with my case."

"Right. Right." He frowned, then sipped his coffee. "Just who is this *Yankee* who's been living here?"

She ground her teeth, wondering what a nearly two-hundred year-old prejudice had to do with anything. "He's not living here," she felt compelled to clarify. "His name is Alexander Carlisle, and he's a successful stockbroker who's contracted to buy my house. He arrived in town late Friday and because of the fishing tournament he found himself without a place to stay. Naturally, I offered to let him stay here.

"Mr. Carlisle is a very nice man. He's intelligent, courteous, friendly, gracious and—" She stopped herself from saying "sexy."

"And the only person besides yourself in the house."

Rebecca ground her teeth. Surely they had *real* cops in New York. "Alex didn't shut off the water."

Of course he'd lied about the electricity on Saturday night, her conscience reminded her. But she waved that away. He'd been in the shower when the water shut off. He would hardly subject himself to such an inconvenience. She said as much to Dwayne.

Dwayne rocked back on his heels. "Uh-huh. In the shower?"

"I wasn't an actual witness to the shower, of course," she said quickly. "When he came to my bedroom to tell me about the water, he'd obviously just gotten out of the shower."

Looking horrified, Dwayne set his mug down with a bang. "He was in your bedroom?"

Rebecca was surprised not to see steam rising off her flaming cheeks. "Only when we searched the house." God, she was just digging herself deeper. "He was wearing a towel," she added lamely.

Dwayne yanked a notebook and pen from his shirt pocket, then began writing frantically. "I need his name, rank and serial number. A description, too. We should put out an all-points bulletin right away."

While she didn't date often, surely a towel-clad man in her bedroom wasn't *that* big a cause for alarm. And wouldn't the ladies at the beauty shop just love to hear about her fugitive lover? Even Mama never dated a criminal.

"Wouldn't you like to investigate the basement?" she suggested quickly, anything to dissuade Dwayne from humiliating her and arresting Alex.

Dwayne stopped scribbling in his notebook and cocked his head. "The basement?"

"That's where the water valve is."

Pocketing the notebook and pen, Dwayne followed her down the hall. "Of course. The crime scene, so to speak."

As they headed down the creaky stairs, Rebecca reconsidered her big investigation idea. The thought of some unknown individual skulking around her basement creeped her out in a big way, especially with only Dwayne and his unloaded gun for protection.

While she bit her lip and tried to convince herself that scurrying noise was just the wind, Dwayne ambled around the room, looking at everything, touching nothing.

"Shouldn't you take fingerprints, or something?" she asked impatiently.

"You've been watching too much TV, Miss Parsons."

Oh, that's right, she thought. *The police actually* solved *crimes on TV. Silly me.*

Dwayne tapped the side of his head. "All I need is what I've got in here and my catlike vision."

Rebecca started to remind him it was his reflexes that were catlike when he stopped suddenly by the door leading to the backyard.

"I think I found something."

Rebecca leapt to his side. "You're kidding."

He looked at her askance, then back to the floor. "Looks like a footprint."

She supposed she saw a vague outline of dried mud. "Can't you take an impression or something?"

Rubbing his chin, he said, "I'm not sure. The guy from the cement company used to do that. But he passed on about two years ago. Besides, I think that only works on soft ground."

"Can you at least tell what kind of shoe? Is it a man's or a woman's? We should eliminate my shoes and my buyer's."

Dwayne hitched up his belt. "Slow down, missy. I've got this entire investigation under complete control."

Rebecca crossed her arms over her chest. "Sure."

If she could just survive the next three weeks without being murdered in her bed by some intruder, Alex would inherit this whole mess. In fact, his grandchildren would probably be dealing with this mess someday.

Dwayne crouched next to the print. "It looks like a work boot. Put your foot over here." Rebecca placed her black leather flat where he indicated. "Well, I think we can safely eliminate you." Then Dwayne set his own foot beside it. "I'm guessing a man's, about the size of mine. I think I've got a camera in my squad car. We could take a picture of it."

Knowing he needed all the encouragement he could get, Rebecca said, "Absolutely. Great idea, Sheriff."

Since she had no intention of hanging out in the basement alone, she followed him upstairs, refreshing his coffee while she waited for him to retrieve the camera and take the picture. She even shooed Moose from the room.

A few minutes later, he strolled back into the kitchen, setting the camera on the table. "All done." He rolled his shoulders back. "I've got a lot of cases on the go, so I should have the rest of this roll taken sometime in the next week or so."

"Next week!" Rebecca paused in the act of handing him a full cup of coffee. "Why don't you just advance the roll and develop what you have?"

Shaking his head, Dwayne settled himself in a chair. "No, no. Can't do that. Waste of the taxpayer's money."

"Waste of—" Great. Just perfect. A criminal could be on the loose, she was alone in the house with only Moose and a baseball bat for protection and the sheriff was worried about a three-dollar roll of film. She practically slammed the coffee mug in front of him and intended to give him a piece of her mind about all the water he wasted washing that damn patrol car of his when he jumped in with another bomb.

"Miss Parsons, I think you should know I already have a prime suspect in your case."

She raised her eyebrows. "Really?"

"You betcha."

She waited for him to explain. "Well, who?" she finally asked impatiently.

Dwayne sipped his coffee, obviously enjoying the suspense.

"Are you planning to tell me *today?*"

"You're not going to like it too much," he warned.

She didn't like anything about this whole situation. How could whatever he said—

"That man you're living with."

"He's *not* living with me. He just stayed here—" She cut herself off with a wave of her hand, then yanked back a chair and plopped into the seat. "Never mind. We've already been through this. Alex didn't shut off the water."

Dwayne pulled out his notebook again. "Just how long have you known this man?"

Rebecca tapped her nails against the table. "Three days."

Dwayne nodded in an I-told-you-so kind of way. "I'm going to have to question him."

"Good grief." She couldn't believe she'd actually contacted this man for help.

"Do you know where he is?"

She shook her head, glad she could be truthful. She didn't want to be responsible for exposing Alex to Dwayne's investigative techniques. The man probably still advocated public hangings for Yankees. "He left here early this morning. He's renting an apartment until we close on the house."

Dwayne frowned. "I thought he was living here."

"Just for the weekend." She sighed, not bothering to correct him again.

"I see," he said, though clearly he didn't. "Well, what does this fellow look like?"

"About six-two, around two hundred pounds, black hair,

green eyes, broad shoulders…'' She trailed off, getting warm just thinking about her description.

''Okay, that's—'' He stopped, his gaze locking on something over Rebecca's shoulder. ''Well, it looks like I can start my questioning sooner than I thought.''

Swallowing, she turned, knowing Alex had picked that inconvenient moment to arrive. She didn't ask why he'd come back; instead her foolish heart beat ridiculously hard at seeing him again.

''I knocked, but no one answered,'' he said, his gaze sliding from her to Dwayne.

He looked sexy and confident in the same worn jeans and blue T-shirt he'd left wearing that morning. When he smiled in her direction, Rebecca's palms broke out in a sweat. Why hadn't she jumped into bed with him? She seemed to remember having a good reason. She wracked her brain, but came up blank in the reason department. Surely she had one. She hadn't given up *that*—she let her gaze linger on Alex's broad, muscled chest—without some rational, practical, systematic decision making.

''Pull up a chair, buster,'' Dwayne commanded, breaking into her thoughts. ''You have a lot to answer for.''

Of course, since Dwayne was bound to arrest him at any moment, the reason might be pointless.

7

IGNORING THE WEIRD sensation tightening his chest—an emotion he'd call jealousy if he didn't know himself better—Alex strode into the room. "You must be the sheriff."

"You bet I am, buster. Dwayne Hubbard. I have some pretty serious questions for you about this water business."

Rebecca rose, casting the sheriff a hard glare. "Innocent until proven guilty, Dwayne." She smiled at Alex. "Would you like some coffee?"

"Sure, thanks." His gaze followed her as she retreated behind the counter, her jean-clad backside swaying with every step. God, the woman had some kind of walk.

The sheriff cleared his throat.

Alex tore his gaze from Rebecca's sensuous curves to find the sheriff glaring at him. He wasn't sure what he'd done to provoke the lawman's irritation, but knowing he was innocent of everything except desiring Rebecca, he slid casually into a chair. "Any progress with the investigation?"

"It's coming along." He poised a pen over a spiral-bound notebook. "I understand you were in the shower when the incident occurred."

"Yes. The water just shut off suddenly. Rebecca and I discovered the main valve had been shut off," he said as the sheriff scribbled.

"You own a pair of work boots?"

The sudden shift in conversation had Alex frowning. "A pair of hiking boots."

Rebecca set coffee in front of Alex, then narrowed her eyes at the sheriff. "Dwayne…" she said in warning.

Dwayne ignored her. "Can I see them?"

Rebecca's face flushed red, from anger or embarrassment, Alex couldn't tell. Something odd was going on here. "I suppose. Mind if I ask why?"

"Just get the boots, please," Dwayne said, his brown eyes giving nothing away.

"I'll come with you," Rebecca said as Alex rose.

"Miss Parsons, I need you to stay here, please," Dwayne said.

Rebecca flung her hands out. "This is ridiculous, Dwayne! Alex didn't do anything."

"It's okay, Rebecca," Alex said, squeezing her hand briefly before he left the kitchen. He realized Dwayne had jumped to the same conclusion Alex had earlier that morning. With only he and Rebecca in the house, one of them was the most likely culprit, and Dwayne had decided Alex was his man. How the boots came in, however, he didn't have a clue.

He retrieved the shoes from his bag, wondering how Rebecca would react when she discovered he still had his luggage in his car. Would she even believe the manager who'd "gone fishin'" had already rented Alex's apartment to someone else? He'd claimed that Alex hadn't shown up on time on Friday and rented the place to another tenant.

The whole turn of events was positive, Alex had decided philosophically on the drive over. Romancing a woman from miles away wasn't his style. He liked the personal, within-touching-distance approach.

He returned to the kitchen and handed the sheriff his

hiking boots, hoping they weren't due to become evidence. After all Rebecca had said about Dwayne, he wasn't sure he liked the idea of the Junction Gap Police Department taking possession of his six-hundred-dollar boots.

Dwayne frowned as he studied them, but Rebecca's eyes lit like blue flames. "Aha!" she exclaimed. "They're too big."

Alex leaned one hip against the bar. "Do you two mind telling me what's so interesting about a pair of boots?"

"We found a shoe print in the basement, near the door. It appears to belong to a man's work boot." She gestured with her thumb toward the sheriff. "Dwayne here thought you shut off the water."

Alex shrugged. "I figured as much."

Obviously disappointed, Dwayne set the boots on the table, then leaned back in his chair. "Well, we don't know for sure the print even belongs to the intruder."

Rebecca groaned. "Dwayne…"

Dwayne rose slowly to his feet, hooking his thumbs around his gun belt. "Now, Miss Parsons, I'm the law in this town—"

A spurt of laughter burst from Rebecca. She held her hand to her mouth, trying to contain her mirth, but her eyes watered and her face glowed. "Dwayne, you've been watching way too many John Wayne movies."

The sheriff huffed. He turned to Alex. "What are you doing back here, anyway? I thought you were renting an apartment."

Alex watched Rebecca, not the sheriff. "When I went by today to move in, the apartment manager had already rented it to someone else."

"Oh, I'll bet he did," the sheriff said as if that were the

lamest excuse he'd ever heard. "So, you're here to further impose on Miss Parsons's hospitality."

Alex grinned. "I doubt you're aware of the depths of Miss Parsons's hospitality."

Rebecca's face flushed. Dwayne scowled.

Obviously, the sheriff didn't like the idea of Alex staying with Rebecca. Well, too bad. She only had three weeks left, and Alex planned to occupy each one of those days, so it looked as if Dwayne the lawman was out of luck.

"How do you feel about him staying here, Miss Parsons?" Dwayne asked.

Rebecca picked up the sheriff's coffee cup, then strode around the bar, dumping the contents in the sink. "How I feel about that doesn't concern you, Sheriff. I'm sure you have better things to do than butt into my personal life." She smiled sweetly. "You'll let me know about any new developments in my case, won't you?"

Dwayne snagged his camera off the table, then headed toward the door. "Of course. I'll have a deputy watch the neighborhood, just in case anyone is hanging around." He glanced over his shoulder at Alex, as if warning him not to step out of line. "Let me know if there's any more trouble."

Rebecca joined him in the doorway. "Of course. I'll see you out."

While she escorted the sheriff to the door, Alex picked up his previously untouched coffee and took a sip. Surely, if she planned to throw him out, she would have done it along with the sheriff. He really needed a place to stay. And he really wanted to be with her. He *needed* to be with her, and he—

Wait. He wasn't nervous, was he? Hell, he really had

flipped over her. He sank into a kitchen chair, propping his feet on the table, trying to act relaxed.

When she returned, pausing at the threshold, he flashed her a smile. "Do you ever get the feeling we're destined to be together?"

She planted her hand on her hips, but her lips twitched. "No apartment, huh?"

"Apparently one of your fellow citizens has been thrown out by his wife, and he showed up Friday just as the apartment manager was leaving for the fishing tournament."

"And just like that—" she snapped her fingers "—you're out and he's in?"

"It looks that way." He looked up, giving her his best you-can-trust-me expression. "So...is my room still available?"

"Yes, but—"

"Of course, I'd insist on continuing to pay rent...."

"Hmm. But you're staying until the closing?"

"It would be simpler, don't you think? Especially with this prowler still on the loose...."

"I suppose so. But—"

"Great." He dropped his feet to the floor, then rose. Crossing to her, he pulled her into his arms. "Why don't we seal the deal with a kiss?"

She flattened her hands against his chest. "Wait a second, Slick. I just remembered all my rational, practical and systematic reasons."

"Your what?"

"Reasons why us getting involved is a really bad idea." She stepped back, ticking them off on her fingers. "You're impulsive, I'm plodding. You're flashy, I'm practical. You're staying, I'm leaving."

He stroked his thumb across her bottom lip, pleased

when her mouth trembled. "We don't need logic, darling. We have chemistry."

"Exactly my point." She picked up his hand, then carefully dropped it by his side. "You can stay, but no touching."

"No—" He blinked, certain he'd misunderstood.

"You heard me right. No stroking, no hugging, definitely no kissing and not even any hand-holding."

"You can't be serious."

She crossed her arms over her chest. "Take it or leave it."

How the hell was he supposed to seduce her without touching her? Even for him that was a tall order. It truly amazed him that after all the time he'd spent with women, he still had no idea what went through their minds. Rebecca had melted in his arms—when she wasn't busy ripping off his clothes.

And now she suddenly didn't want him touching her.

He paced away from her, puzzling through this baffling development. She was conservative, he reminded himself. And sensitive. And embarrassed by her mother, who flaunted her sexuality and had lots of affairs. Maybe Rebecca didn't think they could have a brief relationship without attachments or hurt feelings. He'd done so plenty of times before, but he figured Rebecca hadn't.

Did his past experiences turn her off? Scowling, he had to admit that comparing his past liaisons to his desire for Rebecca seemed cheap. She had so much…*more* than any other woman he'd ever known. The thought of never touching her again made him sweat. The thought of never seeing her again made his stomach hurt.

He had to find a way around this latest obstacle. Until then, he'd bow to her rules. What other choice did he have?

You could give up, find another woman to pursue.

No way. He wanted Rebecca. If he knew nothing else these days, he knew that.

Rolling his shoulders back, he walked over to her. Her blue sweater matched her eyes, the cotton material clinging to her womanly curves. Curves he wanted to stroke.

No stroking.

She looked troubled, her delicate brow furrowed. His arms ached with the need to hold her.

No hugging.

And, sweet heaven, if she didn't have the glossiest, most tempting lips on the planet.

Definitely no kissing.

He extended his arm. *Not even hand-holding.* He pulled his hand back, shoving it in his back pocket. "Deal."

IN THE SHOWER, Rebecca tilted her face toward the hot, pounding spray, wishing she could wash away her troubling thoughts as easily.

Alexander Carlisle is living with me—again.

Even with her practical reasoning back in full force and the "no touching" rule in place, she knew she'd really screwed up this time. Though The House had decided to hold together the last few hours, that could change at any moment. Meanwhile, she'd be tripping over Alex and his delectable body every time she turned around.

In a way, she wished she was the kind of woman who could have a romantic fling, then move on without missing a beat. People did it all the time. Why not her?

Well, she hadn't been asked very often, for one thing. In school, when guys had problems with their homework, they came to her. When men had legal problems these days, they came to her. But when they wanted a date, they looked elsewhere.

And that was certainly fine by her. She was proud of her brains and the professional respect she'd garnered, which was destined to increase at her job in New York. She wasn't just an object of desire. She didn't want to be just a blip in someone's love life. Even Alex Carlisle's.

As she applied shampoo to her hair and scrubbed the solution into frothy suds, she smiled. She couldn't deny, however, the thrill that raced through her body whenever Alex complimented her, or looked at her like she was special and beautiful. He'd even told her he preferred her to her mother. Though he couldn't possibly understand how vibrant and captivating Mama had been, Rebecca somehow believed him. Since the moment he'd arrived on her doorstep, he'd been focused on her. She'd told herself he could have any woman he wanted, but he hadn't looked elsewhere.

"He wants *me*," she said aloud, trying out the words as she rinsed her hair.

But not only was she leaving, succumbing to the temptation of Alex would lead straight to major heartbreak. Too risky, she decided firmly.

She washed her body, rinsed, then stepped out of the shower, flinging one white towel around her body and one around her head. Leaving with darn good reason, too. She wiped the steam from the mirror so she could look herself in the eye. "You are out of money. You are tired of having a punch line for a house. You do not want eccentric friends and neighbors you have nothing in common with. You're tired of people who consider you a pale imitation of Mama."

As she dressed in blue sweats and brushed her hair,

though, she considered the idea of never seeing The House or her friends and neighbors again. Had she really thought through that decision?

She padded to the sitting room alcove and looked out the cupola's bay window to the large expanse of front yard. Maybe she craved a bit of normalcy and a place to fit in, but she certainly wasn't going to find a view like this in an apartment in New York City. Would she miss the old wood floors? The grand staircase? Her quirky neighbors? Knowing the town sheriff had eaten Play-Doh all through kindergarten?

Shaking off the odd sensation tightening her chest, she left her room and tramped down the stairs. Earlier, with a working dishwasher, she'd cleaned her china to prepare the dishes for packing. She didn't want the irreplaceable plates going into the boxes covered in dust. She needed to start another load and pack the clean ones.

Just outside the kitchen, she paused, hearing Alex's voice, obviously speaking to someone on the phone.

"Yes, I know, Alice," he said. "But I want this deal to happen."

Rebecca frowned. She didn't want to intrude or eavesdrop, but she wasn't sure how to gracefully avoid doing so.

"Can I afford to let the money ride again?" He laughed. "What the hell. I can survive bankruptcy, can't I?"

Bankruptcy? She swallowed. Alex had plenty of money. Didn't he? She tried to brush off the idea as ridiculous, thinking of his houses, expensive clothes and car. But then, there were plenty of people in the world who had those things and were in debt up to their eyeballs. Any minute the balancing act of debt and profit could send the facade tumbling down.

How much did she really know about Alex Carlisle?

She knew he was smooth. He was a great negotiator. He was charming. He could convince anyone of anything. Just look at the way he'd neatly managed to move back in. She might have thrown him a bit with the "no touching" rule, but she was certain he never had any doubts about her letting him stay. Had she been seduced more than she thought by that smile? And hadn't he proved he could be sneaky that night the lights went out?

As far as his financial situation went, she only had his word and her real estate agent's assurance he'd secured financing to purchase the house.

So what could he possibly gain by turning off the electricity and the water?

She tapped her lips, considering. Wasn't it odd that these incidents had begun just as he'd arrived? If he confronted her with the house's troubles, then he would be in the stronger bargaining position. He could possibly even sue her for breach of contract...*fraud.*

She was hiding the repairs. Was he deceiving *her,* as well? If so, he had some nerve. Well, she wasn't going to feel guilty for one more second about concealing the repairs. She conveniently shoved aside the realization that she'd never felt guilty. After all, she wasn't planning to take advantage of him, or use her deception for financial gain. In fact, she never planned for him to find out anything that was going on with the house.

Just one more reason they were completely wrong for each other—she was forthright, he was sneaky.

"You bet." He laughed again. And damned if he didn't have a great laugh. Not a tee-hee-hee giggle, but a good, from-the-heart *honest* laugh. "See ya." The phone clanged into its cradle.

Alex wasn't going to sue her. This prowler business and

Dwayne, with all his accusations, had made her paranoid. Alex would never be so underhanded, she decided as she strode into the kitchen.

And ground to a halt.

Alex sat at the table, a laptop in front of him, his briefcase open, papers strewn about. Shirtless. She blinked. No, this wasn't some midnight fantasy. His tanned chest, lightly sprinkled with black hair, gleamed under the bright kitchen lights. Muscles rippled over his shoulders and down his arms.

He leaned back—giving her an excellent view of his washboard abs—and smiled. "Good shower?"

She planted her hands on her hips. "Where the hell are your clothes?"

He glanced down at himself, as if he'd forgotten he was half-naked. "Oh. I was hot."

"Hot?" She fanned herself. Yep. It certainly was hot. "I can turn down the heat."

Picking up a pen, he wrote something on one of the papers in front of him. "That's okay. I wouldn't want you and Moose to be cold."

He wouldn't want— Not underhanded, huh? Dwayne had made her paranoid, right? Ha! She stomped to the dishwasher, unloading a stack of plates.

"I'm going to check all the door and window locks later, if that's okay with you."

"Sure. Whatever." She wondered if he planned to do *that* shirtless, too. Of course, if he was the one who'd shut off the water that was a bit like letting the fox guard the hen house, wasn't it?

Looking way too pleased with himself, he directed his attention back to the papers in front of him.

Rebecca reminded herself she wasn't some gullible,

helpless female and decided for the moment to put aside the problem of Alex the Exhibitionist. She had packing to do. Once she'd finished unloading the dishwasher, she carried the stack of plates into the dining room. She set them on the large mahogany table, then remembered she'd hidden the bubble wrap in the sideboard, away from Moose and his happy claws.

She knelt in front of the sideboard, but a movement along the baseboard caught her attention. Peering closer, she saw several odd-looking bugs. They looked like black ants with wings.

What in the world? Moose didn't have fleas. The cat had never put so much as one pampered paw outside the house in all his life.

Then, from somewhere in the recesses of her memory, she recalled the exterminator who inspected the house prior to putting it on the market. He'd given her a pamphlet titled *If You See This* with several different types of pests pictured. She'd seen a bug just like these printed on that paper.

Termites.

She screamed.

Alex charged into the room. "What's wrong? Rebecca?" He grabbed her shoulders. "What happened?"

She swallowed hard. "I—uh…"

How could this be happening? Termites, for heaven's sake. Alex would back out; she'd never find another buyer for this expensive, tacky, handyman's delight; she'd go bankrupt; the bank would get the house… The implications flashed through her mind like a tragic nightmare.

Alex shook her slightly. "Rebecca, what is it?"

She swallowed again, looked up into his worried green eyes—and lied. "Nothing. It's silly." She stepped out of his reach and waved her hand. "A spot on my china."

He angled his head. "A *spot?*"

Snatching the top plate from the table, she licked her thumb and rubbed the imaginary speck. "I need to get these into boxes right away."

"You screamed over a spot?" he asked, his tone revealing his incredulity.

Knowing how ridiculous she sounded, but desperate to hang on to her ruse—at least until she could contact the exterminator and find out how bad the problem was—she smiled weakly. "Silly, I know. I'm a little neurotic about the china. It was my grandmother's."

He raised one black eyebrow, as if neurotic was an extreme understatement.

"Did I interrupt your work?" She winced at the forced innocence she tried to inject into her voice. *You're scum, Rebecca Parsons, pure scum. Yeah, but he's sneaky and half-naked.* "I'll keep quiet from now on. I'm just going to pack."

"If you're sure you're all right..."

She put down the plate, then made a shooing motion with her hands. "Go, go."

After he turned and left the room, Rebecca sank against the table. This couldn't be happening. Termites. She shuddered. Was the whole house going to tremble and fall into a big pile of worthless glass and wood and purple carpet like in a cartoon?

The image forced her into action. She rushed into the kitchen, grabbed a small plastic bag and the cleaning supplies, holding up the latter for Alex to see. He barely glanced at her before turning his attention back to his work. She squirted the dreaded bugs with the glass cleaner—surely the ammonia would kill them—then squashed them for good measure with the paper towels. When she was sure the little suckers were dead, she dumped their bodies in the bag, then stuffed it in the sideboard underneath the pillar candles.

No. Bad idea. Who knew if the power would go out again?

Instead, she hid the plastic bag between the tablecloths. Then, on her hands and knees, desperately hoping Alex didn't make another surprise appearance, she inspected the baseboards, the table legs and china cabinet. She could find no evidence of damage.

"Please let that exterminator have a twenty-four-hour emergency number," she muttered. Thinking of the two repair checks she'd already written that day, she added, "And reasonable emergency rates."

How in the world she was going to hide an exterminator from Alex, she had no idea, but she'd worry about that when the time came. Maybe she could hold off the termite invasion with glass cleaner and paper towels until morning. Surely Alex would head to his new office—if he could manage, long enough, to get dressed, that is. He must have files to organize, maybe office equipment to buy. And if he had a few customers…

Hmm… Now she had two phone calls to make.

Upstairs in her bedroom, she found the exterminator's pamphlet. Sure enough, the sketches on the front labeled "termite" matched the icky winged things she'd found in the dining room. When she called the office number listed, she had to leave a message for a return call after 9:00 a.m. the next day.

Then she called Miss Nettie and Miss Francine, the elderly cousins who lived at the end of the block. Alex Carlisle might think he was sneaky, but he hadn't met Miss Nettie Sims. She could con you into doing anything and make you think you were doing yourself a favor at the same time. As a bonus, Miss Nettie could find out if Alex was having money or any other kind of troubles.

"Hello," Miss Nettie said after a couple of rings.

"Miss Nettie, this is Rebecca Parsons."

"Oh, hey, dear. I understand you have a buyer for your house. A stockbroker, I believe. Quite a handsome one, and he's living there, too."

No doubt she already knew his mother's maiden name, his social security number and his blood type. "Yes, ma'am. Alex Carlisle. You'll like him."

"The question around here is—do you?" As she sighed dramatically, Rebecca vowed to cuss out Linda at her first opportunity. "What a shame it would be to let a man like that get away."

You mean a sneaky, underhanded, doesn't-play-fair, half-naked Greek-god-like— She stopped herself just in time and said neutrally, "Mmm. I guess."

"Miss Nettie, get off that phone this minute," Rebecca heard Miss Francine shout in the background. "It'll give you cancer."

"That's the microwave," Miss Nettie shouted back calmly.

Rebecca held on to her laughter. "How is Miss Francine today?"

"She thinks she has leukemia."

"Oh, boy." For most people this pronouncement would have elicited something closer to "how tragic" or "I'm sorry," but Miss Francine had claimed to have every disease, from mad cow disease to the bubonic plague. "What brought this on?"

"She got a paper cut yesterday, and it took a full two minutes to clot."

"Aha."

"Rebecca, did you take your vitamin C today?" Miss Francine shouted.

"Tell her I did," Rebecca said to Miss Nettie, though it was a wonder she wasn't peeing orange from the thousand-milligram pills Miss Francine had foisted on her. Once Miss Nettie had relayed the message, she steered the conversation back to Alex. "With Mr. Carlisle being new in town, he doesn't have any clients yet. Are you still looking at options for investing your brother's money?"

"Well, you know, ever since I converted the Ladies' Quilting Circle to an investment club, we've done quite well on our own."

"Of course," Rebecca returned smoothly. "But some professional advice couldn't hurt, could it?"

"I suppose not."

"Miss Nettie, get off that damn phone and help me find my fish oil capsules."

"What's that for?" Rebecca couldn't help asking.

"To treat her coronary artery disease."

"Be sure and tell her my heart's doing just fine." Rebecca had no intention of swallowing any fish oil. "You sound busy, so I'll let you go. When you see Mr. Carlisle, I'd appreciate you not mentioning I called you. I don't want him to think—"

"Something's wrong with the house, and you need to get rid of him for a while."

Leave it to a con to know when she's being conned. "Something like that."

"I can be discreet."

When it served her purpose. But since Rebecca had gotten what she wanted, she wasn't about to complain. "Just make sure you check out all his references before you give

him any money," she reminded Miss Nettie. She couldn't
live with herself if the ladies lost their considerable assets
because of her.

"Of course, dear. I'll see you at the block party on the
twentieth. Bye."

Biting her lip, Rebecca set the phone in the cradle. She'd
forgotten about the fall block party. Because of her depar-
ture, her neighbors were pulling out all the stops, planning
a more tremendous feast than usual. Today was the fifth,
the closing on the twenty-second. Why did that seem too
soon?

She waved that thought away and rushed back downstairs. She had a lot of packing left to do. At the doorway
to the dining room, she ground to a halt. Shredded bubble
wrap littered the floor, draped over the dining room table,
hanging limply from the chairs.

And the sideboard doors stood wide open.

"Moose…"

8

ALEX SMILED across his brand-new mahogany desk at the two elderly women—his soon-to-be neighbors and first customers. "How much is the estate worth?"

Tall and thin, Miss Nettie—as she'd insisted he call her—served as the spokesperson for the cousins. She was decked out in a yellow polka-dot dress and clutching her black patent leather purse as if it held the national debt. She had big, innocent blue eyes, enhanced by the fluttering artificial lashes she wore. She angled her head, the just-curled silver strands bobbing. "Oh, around twelve mil I should think. Does that sound about right, Miss Francine?"

Miss Francine was a tiny woman with suspicious hazel eyes and wore a pantsuit the color of a robin's egg. She, too, held a black patent purse, but it was half as big as she was and bulged with its contents. He already knew it contained a full-size spray can of Lysol, since she'd sprayed down his office the moment she walked in the door. "About that," Miss Francine confirmed.

"Of course, my brother only had about six when he passed on." Miss Nettie leaned forward, as if imparting a great secret. "But we've done very well with Microsoft stock."

"Really?" Alex handled big-money clients all the time, of course. He just hadn't expected to find such a large portfolio in Junction Gap. "And you want me to handle the entire estate?"

Miss Nettie blinked, then glanced at her cousin. "Yes, I believe so. Miss Francine?"

Miss Francine nodded.

"Great." Obviously, his charm was in complete working order, despite Rebecca's continual unappreciation of him.

Then Miss Francine narrowed her eyes. "You're not sick, are you?"

"Sick?" What did that have to do with their investment portfolio? "Uh, no."

Miss Francine rummaged in her bag. "I'd better check. Lots of bad stuff going around these days."

When the object emerged, Alex's jaw dropped. He knew women carried around some strange stuff in their purses, but he had to admit he'd never seen anyone with a blood pressure cuff.

As if it were the most natural thing in the world, Miss Francine rose from her chair, rounded the desk, then proceeded to wrap the cuff around his arm.

Alex looked to Miss Nettie for help, but she shook her head, saying, "It's best just to humor her."

Minutes later, Miss Francine briskly pronounced his blood pressure excellent. The small machine went back into the bag; then she withdrew a bottle, which she plopped on his desk. "I recommend these, though. For your heart. You're in a high-stress profession."

Alex squinted to read the label. *"Fish oil concentrate."* Uh-uh. He had no intention of swallowing fish oil anything, but he smiled at Miss Francine. "Thank you."

She blushed.

"Now, back to your estate." He pulled a stack of papers from his desk drawer, then handed copies to both ladies.

"My references are listed there, as well as my credentials. Once you fill out the application, we'll make an appointment with the bank to transfer the money into a brokerage account. When it's convenient for you, we also need to discuss your goals and investment style. I'm a pretty aggressive investor, but not all my clients are the same."

As Miss Nettie filled out the necessary information, Alex typed into his laptop. "If your brother had such a large amount in his estate, he must have had an excellent investment strategy. Maybe you would like to continue with his plans?"

Miss Nettie stopped writing and looked up, then she burst into laughter.

Caught by surprise, Alex stared at her as tears of mirth rolled down her softly powdered cheeks. Even stoic Francine cracked a smile.

"Oh, Mr. Carlisle, forgive me," Miss Nettie said, wiping the lingering tears from her eyes. "If only you knew my brother, you would understand my amusement." She glanced at her cousin. "We really must tell that one to The Circle."

Miss Francine nodded.

Miss Nettie laid her delicate, blue-veined hand on top of the investment forms. "You see, Mr. Carlisle, my brother was the biggest cheapskate the South ever birthed. He'd argue with the hardware store clerk over the price of a ten-cent nail. He rationed water, lit candles to save electricity bills and was generally a pain in the butt to all who knew him. His estate was large because he never spent any money."

Alex coughed. "I see."

Miss Francine leaned forward, studying him. "When did that cough begin?"

"About ten seconds ago."

"Uh-huh." She rooted in her bag.

If she pulled out a needle or a throat swab, twelve mil or not, Alex was getting the hell out of there.

She pulled out a book—a large book. At least three inches thick. *The Physician's Desk Reference.* Opening it, she ran her finger down the page. "Hmm. Cough. Sudden onset." She glanced up. "You're pale, a little sweaty."

He was nervous.

"Whooping cough."

"Uh, Miss Francine," he began, not wanting to hurt her feelings, but pretty sure whooping cough only occurred in children and had been practically eliminated from the general population of the United States. He looked to Miss Nettie for advice. She just sighed and shook her head.

"Anyway," she began with a sharp look at her cousin, "about my brother's odd ways with money. We only convinced him about five years ago to actually put the money in the bank. He kept it under his mattress, for heaven's sake."

Alex tried to focus on Miss Nettie, but Miss Francine had returned the book to her bag and was pawing through the contents again. "Really."

Miss Nettie waved her hand. "It was so embarrassing, especially since I'm president of the Ladies' Investment Circle."

After watching Miss Francine zip her bag, Alex met Miss Nettie's gaze. "What's that?"

"We're a group of ladies who plan investment strategies for ourselves and the community interests." Miss Nettie snapped her fingers, as if a great idea had just popped into her head. "You'd be an excellent guest speaker at our next meeting."

Alex leaned back in his chair. "You think so?" At least somebody appreciated him. Rebecca had politely declined his offer of advice.

"We've been muddling along on our own up to now. The Circle even bought a World War II memorial for the town, but we can make a real difference with an expert consultant around. The high school needs a new stadium, and we need big bucks to accomplish that goal. What do you say, Mr. Carlisle?"

In a blink, Alex realized he'd been flattered into not only serving as a guest speaker, but also becoming the new consultant for the Ladies' Investment Circle. That sounded like a commitment.

"As long as we're at this," Miss Nettie continued, blinking her baby blue eyes, "I'm sure our soccer team could use a new field, and, of course, the library always needs new books. Imagine what we could accomplish."

A long-term commitment. Well, he'd already committed to preserving a historical home. How hard could it be to attend a couple of meetings?

He patted her hand. "Glad to be on the team."

Miss Nettie's eyes flashed with triumph, then she sighed, her shoulders slumping. "I just wish you weren't coming to us just as Rebecca is moving. She's a lovely girl, don't you think?"

He wasn't really sure where this tangent was leading, but was willing to go along, figuring Rebecca's longtime neighbors could give him some insight. Clearly, he was doing something wrong. He'd bought work-out equipment and asked Rebecca if he could use the study as a temporary gym. He'd flexed and lifted until he thought he'd pass out. He'd spent the last two days wandering around the house without a shirt. Instead of jumping his bod, Rebecca had turned down the heat.

Alex finally said to Miss Nettie, "She's very lovely."

"It's such a shame she's leaving us. I'm afraid she's always thought of us as a bit eccentric." She cut her gaze in her cousin's direction, who had her head buried in her bag again. "You know."

"Hmm. Yes. She seems a bit conservative."

"She can be a lot of fun, too. She's just kept kind of to herself since her mama died."

"What was her mother like?"

Miss Nettie tapped her lips in consideration. "Miss Francine, how should we describe Angelina?"

"The sixteenth birthday party," she said without looking up from her bag.

"Oh, yes." Miss Nettie smiled with remembrance. "Angelina threw a huge party for Rebecca's birthday, inviting all her high school friends, plus all us neighbors. She hired a band, cooked for a week and hung decorations everywhere. Of course, Angelina had found some great sale, so the decorations were a combination of St. Patrick's Day, Valentine's Day and the Fourth of July."

Alex winced. He could picture a red-faced, teenage Rebecca, not knowing how to explain her mother to her friends.

"By the time the party got underway, though, nobody really noticed the decorations. They were too busy noticing Angelina." She shook her head. "That girl never did wear enough clothes to cover all those curves of hers. In no time at all, the boys had surrounded her, and the girls were all trying to figure out how to *be* her."

Sucking in a breath, Alex's heart actually ached at the picture Miss Nettie described. "And Rebecca?"

"Poor little thing. When Angelina realized what was going on, she tried to direct attention to her daughter, but that only made things worse. I don't know how she's going to find someone in a huge city like New York to give her the attention she needs." Sighing dramatically, she rose. "Well, Miss Francine, we should go."

Alex stood as Miss Francine did, warily watching her produce items from her bag—a bottle each of Tylenol, cough syrup and vitamin C. She lined them up on the edge of his desk. "You take these until you get to the doctor."

"Yes, ma'am. Do you need help with your bag?"

"Oh, no." She hitched the massive purse on her shoulder and waddled toward the door.

Shrugging, Alex walked behind her, considering all he'd heard. He'd been going about his seduction all wrong. He hadn't made Rebecca the center of attention, either. He'd focused on himself, trying to make her come to him. Women usually came to him.

Rebecca was different in that respect and many others. He lost control when he touched her. His practiced, smooth seduction became clumsy groping. Fancy words dried in his throat when he saw her. Their relationship had carried him to an uncertain place. A place he wasn't sure he was entirely comfortable with.

But lavishing attention? Now *that* he was comfortable with; that was an area in which he considered himself an expert.

As he opened his office door, Miss Nettie wiggled her fingers in a wave. Her depressed expression had vanished— since she was obviously confident she'd dropped the right hint to the right person. "Good day, Mr. Carlisle."

"Thank you, ladies." *For everything.*

As they walked through the door, he could have sworn

he heard Miss Nettie mutter, "If I was just thirty years younger…"

Alex smiled. Now if only he could work the same magic on Rebecca.

CROUCHED ON the dining room floor, Rebecca leaned around the exterminator's shoulder. "See anything?"

Tom the Bug Man, as he liked to call himself, shook his head and continued to crawl along the baseboards.

Tom seemed an efficient, somewhat serious guy, so Rebecca figured he had everything under control, but fear had crawled its way inside the pit of her stomach and refused to budge. She hung on a precipice, dreading the moment he announced her house was doomed to become sawdust.

So she hovered.

From his perch atop the dining room table, Moose hovered as well, but with an entirely different attitude. He'd pranced around all morning, eyeing the exterminator as if he were prime tuna fish. And if the cat didn't possess a Persian's inborn, ticked-off expression, she would swear she'd caught the animal actually grinning.

With her knees aching, Rebecca stood, then paced alongside the table. "So?"

"Be patient, Miss Parsons. My work is extremely delicate," Tom said.

And extremely slow, Rebecca wanted to say.

The man had been telling her to be patient for the last three hours, as he crawled around the foundation, crawled around the basement, then finally crawled around the baseboards.

She figured she should be taking notes, since she'd probably be crawling to Alex when she begged him not to back out of the sales contract.

Moose sidled over to her, butting his head against her arm, purring like a maniac.

"At least somebody is happy," she muttered, stroking the top of his head.

"Hellooo," a familiar voice called from the kitchen door.

"In here, Linda," Rebecca called back.

Her neighbor strolled into the dining room. "I saw the bug man's truck out front. Good heavens, I hope nothing is wrong. Nothing is, is it?"

"Nothing a couple hundred-thousand dollars couldn't fix," Rebecca said, then frowned. Linda was practically dancing on the tips of her toes. Had everybody taken a happy pill when she wasn't looking? "What's with you?"

"With me?"

Rebecca waved her hand at her friend. "You're awfully happy today."

Linda planted her hands on her hips. "Whatever do you mean? I've just had a really nice morning, the sun is shining. You know, you're awfully crabby lately. Happiness isn't a criminal activity, you know."

"Says who?"

"So what's this?" Linda asked, waving her hand at Tom and obviously deciding to ignore her surly attitude. "Is it time for your inspection already? Gosh where does the time go? It seems like only yesterday—"

"I found some termites."

Linda's jaw dropped. "You *what?*"

Rebecca relayed the events of the night before; all the while Linda nodded and clucked in sympathy. "That's terrible. I came over to invite Alex to the block party but I guess with all these problems the sale has fallen through. It will take you forever to get everything fixed and put it back on the market. Maybe you should just forget this whole idea of moving.''

Guilt weighed on her conscience. ''Alex hasn't backed out—yet. He doesn't know about the termites.''

''How could he not? He's staying here, isn't he?''

Rebecca's gaze darted away from Linda's probing one. ''Well…yes. I—I lied.''

Linda frowned. ''I don't think that's such a great idea, Rebecca. What if he finds out? Is that illegal? Maybe you should just forget this whole idea of moving. How are you going to hide the exterminator? What if—''

Rebecca sliced her hand through the air to cut Linda off. ''I've got everything under control.''

Looking doubtful, Linda crossed her arms over her chest and tapped her foot.

Her friend's disapproval only added to the burden of guilt she couldn't shed no matter how hard she tried to justify her actions. Rebecca had no intention of selling Alex a house infested with termites. She would fix everything— or, more likely, pay Tom every penny she had to do so. She couldn't slip this by Alex even if she wanted to. The inspector for the sale was no doubt competent and thorough, and the only way around him was some illegal activity like bribery….

How can you bribe anybody when you're nearly out of money? her conscience reminded her.

She had no intention of bribing anyone—even if she could afford to.

Finally the exterminator rose to his feet. He pulled off his baseball cap, then scratched his head. ''Well, frankly, Ms. Parsons, I've never seen anything like it.''

Rebecca's heart plummeted. How much money could she

get for a hundred-year-old pile of wood and glass and purple carpet?

"If I didn't know better, I'd think someone captured a few termites and let them loose in here."

Rebecca's gaze darted from an astonished Linda to Tom. "What?"

Tom ticked off points on his fingers. "There's no sign of any invasion indoors or out, no damage, and you found fewer than ten termites. This incident is not an act of nature."

Rebecca warred internally with these results. No damage? No more termites? Could she really be so lucky? And yet the bugs had somehow found their way to the dining room.

And somebody had turned off the water.

How could she have made an odd enemy who turned off water and planted termites? And for what reason?

Biting her lip and trying to remind herself all this trouble had made her paranoid, she again wondered about Alex. Termites would certainly drive the price of the house down. Could he have planted them? They were the only ones in the house that night—again, just like with the water.

But they were always the only people in the house, and deep in her heart she couldn't picture Alex in the act of sabotage. He was sneaky, but he wasn't *that* sneaky.

Her mind logically insisted the evidence pointed to him, but her heart disagreed. And, to her surprise, she was listening. For the first time in her life, she was going to lead with her heart, not her brain. Maybe Mama had been right about *some* things.

"Well, that's certainly good news. No damage," Linda said as they walked into the kitchen with Tom.

Rebecca didn't want to scare her neighbor, but she

wasn't sure Dwayne and his deputies would ever get around to questioning anybody, and if there was a kooky prankster on the loose, Linda and Jake should know. "Yeah. You haven't seen anyone weird lurking about, have you?"

Linda's eyes widened. "Lurking?"

"You know, a stranger in the neighborhood."

"Nobody but your buyer." Linda smiled, but Rebecca could tell it was forced. "You don't really think somebody planted termites in your dining room, do you? Who would do such a ridiculous thing?"

"I'm not sure. But something else odd happened the other day. I even called the sheriff."

"Dwayne?" Linda asked with equal parts derision and concern.

Rebecca relayed the events surrounding the water shut off incident, leaving out only the tempting sight of Alex Carlisle in nothing but a towel. Selfishly, she didn't want to share the image forever emblazoned on her brain.

As soon as she'd finished the tale, Linda headed to the back door. "I need to go home. Jake should know about this right away."

While Rebecca felt more guilt for causing her friend to worry, Tom handed her the bill. She flinched and reached for her checkbook. Even with a "no invasion" verdict, Tom obviously hadn't wasted his time for free.

THE DISASTERS CONTINUED all through the next week—creaking floorboards, light fixtures shorting out, chipping paint and more. While Alex worked at his office during the day, repair people came and went like a revolving door, and the balance in Rebecca's checkbook fell to frightening lows. In fact, the only thing keeping her afloat financially were Alex's rent checks. The irony of the situation magnified her guilt, but, seeing no other option, she continued the charade.

As for her and Alex's personal relationship, he'd honored the "no touching" rule, giving her attention in ways beyond physical chemistry. He helped her pack, he laughed at anything she said that was even remotely amusing, he complimented her, he bought groceries, he planted flowers in the backyard, he cooked, he cleaned, he *wore clothes*.

He was wonderful. But he was slowly driving her insane.

The attraction she had dealt with, but this…this being…*nice*. Well, she had no idea what to do with him. That wasn't precisely true. She knew what she wanted to do, she just wasn't sure how to go about doing it—thanks to her stupid rule. At the same time, she was also wary of lifting the "no touching" rule. She already liked him. Now she was very much afraid she was falling for him.

To add to her mixed-up feelings, as she removed personal knickknacks and boxed her and Mama's possessions she found a weight settling over her heart. Mama loved this house so much, and Rebecca worried that she was tarnishing the memory of her mother by leaving. Instead of rolling her eyes as she packed the bordello bedroom, she smiled, then cried. She had a great job and an exciting future waiting for her in New York. Why was she doubting her decision now? Why did she feel as though she was running, not just moving?

So when Linda invited them to her annual homage to Southern tradition—the Georgia versus Florida college football game party—Rebecca was grateful for the distraction.

They arrived at her front door with tailgating-type snacks wearing red shirts and black pants. Alex—who looked beyond luscious—had questioned the required attire, but Rebecca simply gestured to the other guests, who were similarly dressed in the official colors of the University of Georgia.

As usual, Rebecca and Linda quickly grew tired of the screaming and constant armchair-quarterbacking of the party guests, so they convened in the kitchen.

Miss Nettie joined them briefly during a time-out and brightened Rebecca's day by assuring her Alex's credentials were impeccable, and that she and the Ladies' Investment Circle anticipated a prosperous future with their new consultant. This recommendation confirmed what Pam, her real estate agent, had already told her. Alex's down payment equaled nearly seventy-five percent of the house's purchase price. His rent checks had also all cleared without a hitch. Obviously, he had money.

Then what had that conversation been about with the lady named Alice?

As she puzzled through this question, Alex strolled into the room, with Pam clinging to his arm like kudzu.

While Rebecca had previously admired Pam's teasing personality, impeccable makeup and designer clothes, today Rebecca wanted to rip out the woman's frosted blond hair by the roots. Only Alex's somewhat panicked expression kept Rebecca in her seat. He was *hers,* by heaven, and if that woman stroked her nails down his forearm just one more time…

Hers? She tugged at her own hair. He didn't belong to her. What in the world was she thinking?

He all but dove for the chair next to Rebecca. "Hi," he said, his gaze hungry and focused on her.

Rebecca swallowed hard. He'd been banking that desire lately. Having his longing directed at her so obviously in front of Linda and Pam made her flush with both discomfort and pleasure.

"How's the packing going?" Pam asked.

Rebecca noted Linda and Alex both frowned. "Fine," she said. "Nearly done."

"It's just not going to be the same around here once you're gone," Pam said, her gaze going to Alex. She walked over to stand behind his chair, laying her hands possessively on his shoulders. "What will we do, Alex?"

Alex didn't even glance up at Pam. He angled his body toward Rebecca, causing Pam's touch to slide away. "I have no idea."

Would he be sad to see her go? She wasn't thrilled by the prospect of leaving him. As she searched his gaze for veiled meanings behind his words, she considered something important in his manner—he was uncomfortable with Pam's attention. If there was any place Alex was completely at home, it was around women—any age, any type, anytime. But he was certainly sending "hands off" signals to Pam.

"Hey, Carlisle, where's that beer?" Jake hollered from the other room.

Regret crossing his features, Alex rose. "Be right back." He retrieved several beer bottles from the fridge, Pam graciously helping him. When he returned moments later though, he was alone. Wondering how he'd accomplished that feat, Rebecca wanted to hug him. *No touching.*

Damn her practical nature, anyway. And damn her rules.

Linda's eyes twinkled. "So how's the game going?"

Alex sat next to Rebecca, laying his arm across the back of her chair. Close to touching, but not quite there. She ground her teeth. What was wrong with the man anyway? Two weeks ago, he thought she was irresistible. He couldn't keep his hands off her. Now he respected her. The cad.

"I'm not sure," he said. "They're winning, but everybody's mad."

"They're probably not winning by enough," Linda said. "Has Jake made you declare your undying dedication to the Bulldogs?"

"Bulldogs?" Alex asked, his deep voice rumbling through Rebecca's senses like a caress. He glanced at her, and her heart flipped over in her chest.

"That's our mascot," Linda said. "A bulldog."

"Right," Alex said, still staring at Rebecca.

Rebecca wet her lips. Her hands trembled, and desire pooled deep in her belly. She wanted him. She needed him.

He seemed to be under the same spell. He angled his head, leaning forward.

Woof, woof, woof. The obnoxiously loud sound of people barking like dogs flowed from the TV room into the kitchen.

Alex jerked back, and Rebecca laughed. "What the hell is that?"

"Touchdown," Rebecca and Linda said together.

LESS THAN A WEEK later, and three days before the farewell block party, as she packed Mama's shot glass collection in the foyer, Rebecca decided drastic measures were called for.

Her practicality had to be reined in. With a mother like Angelina Parsons, she had to have some outrageous, rebel genes in her somewhere. She just had to tap into them. Consequences be damned—other than buying a box of condoms—she was going to throw herself at Alex Carlisle.

Hunger for him had driven her over the edge. She was

determined not to let her heart get tangled up in their relationship, but she cared little about what she was risking emotionally. Weeks ago, she'd decided she needed excitement and a sense of belonging. And she knew without a doubt she would find both in Alex's arms. Maybe just temporarily, and maybe she'd be a blip in his love life, but no one had ever made her feel the way he did—special, sexy…beautiful.

She just had to let him know she was available. She had to make him forget about respecting her *former* wishes, and jump her bod instead.

As she was trying to figure out how to accomplish all that, Alex flung open the front door. "Sea-Com stock just split," he announced, throwing his arms wide. He was clutching a bouquet of bright pink roses in one fist and a bottle of champagne in the other.

Though Rebecca knew little about the stock market, she was fairly certain that meant the stockholders had just doubled their shares of a stock on the rise. By the rapturous expression on Alex's face, he was either one of those stockholders, or he'd just had the greatest sex of his life.

From the label on the pricey champagne, she was betting on the money.

He set the champagne on the foyer table, handed her the bouquet then captured her waist. "I'm a rich man, Becca."

Rebecca's pulse zipped through her veins. Maybe she wouldn't have to remind him to forget about the "no touching" rule after all. "I thought you were already rich."

Coaxing her into a smooth waltz, he grinned. "Ah, but if Sea-Com rises just a few more points…well, I can buy that small Caribbean island I've had my eye on."

Not entirely sure if he was serious, she eyed him closely—the sparkling green eyes, the satisfied curve of his lips and, while she was at it, the tailored fit of his white shirt and khakis. The man did possess the most engrossing way of filling out his clothes. The image of him wearing a towel and a grin filled her mind. While she waltzed with him in the grand hall of her house, the memory grabbed her, heating her face and loosening her muscles.

"Just how much of that champagne did you have before you got here?" she teased. Teasing was flirting, right?

He danced her down the hall and into the kitchen. "None yet. I wanted to share my success with you."

She fluttered her lashes. "Why, Alex, how sweet." Smiling, she brought the roses to her face, inhaling the sweet fragrance. "Mmm," she said, then lowered the flowers and licked her lips.

His gaze followed the movement. His pupils dilated, raw need slashed across his face. Then, sighing and looking more frustrated than she'd ever seen him, he dropped his arms from around her and stepped back. "Sorry. I forgot about the rules for a second."

Damn! This seduction business might be harder than she thought. Alex made it all look so easy.

"How about I take you out to dinner?" he suggested, taking the roses from her and crossing to the cabinets.

"Out where?" There weren't a lot of choices in Junction Gap that didn't involve rib bibs, and she had more at-home activities on her mind. Then she remembered a new place near the county line she'd heard about. The owner had renovated his house into a romantic and intimate restaurant. Or so Miss Nettie had said when she and Miss Francine had dropped by yesterday to deliver Miss Francine's moving present—ten cases of vitamins.

"The Rib House?" Alex suggested at the same time she said, "The Victorian."

The only way The Rib House was going to help her was if they could eat wearing their rib bibs and nothing else. *Think bold. Think sexy.* What would Mama have done?

She walked—swaying her hips—to the bar, then leaned her forearms against the tiled surface. As she'd hoped, he was watching her closely. He even pulled a bowl from under the counter, rather than a vase. Too bad she had on a paint-stained gray sweatshirt. He couldn't look down her blouse with that on.

"We should celebrate your stock success." She smiled. "Besides, ribs don't go with champagne."

"Right." Never taking his gaze off her, he stuck the roses, one by one, in the bowl. Half of them flopped out. "If that's where you want to go…"

"That's what I *want*," she said, her voice breathy.

Somehow those few words finally clicked with him. A slow, sexy, tempting grin spread across his face. He strode toward her, stopping on the other side of the bar, leaning on his forearms like her. Their faces were mere inches apart. She could smell his spicy cologne, feel his breath on her skin, see the flecks of gold in his eyes.

Power swelled in her. This was working. Was she finally going to hold all that heat and energy simmering inside Alex?

"Are you flirting with me, Miss Parsons?"

"Yep."

He laughed, then stroked one finger down her cheek. "And the 'no touching' rule?"

"Was the most practical, safest, *dumbest* idea I ever had."

"No, it wasn't." When her eyes widened, he continued. "It gave us a chance to become friends."

"I guess it did."

The intense longing in his eyes just now, though, was way more than friendly. "If I kiss you now, I won't stop."

Part of her wanted to jump over the bar and attack him, but she hadn't even raided her mother's closet yet. "What about dinner?"

"Right." With what seemed like a great deal of effort he merely brushed his lips across her cheek, then straightened. "If we're going to The Victorian, we need to change. Don't I need a tie?" He enveloped her hand in his, leading her from the room. "We'll spiff ourselves up, then meet down here in about an hour."

Rebecca started to nod, then stopped herself. "Wait a second. How do *you* know you need a tie?"

"Oh, probably because Miss Nettie called me yesterday to tell me."

Rebecca laughed. Maybe her neighbors weren't quite as nutty as she thought.

9

"HOLY HELL." Alex stared up the stairs, nearly dropping the chilled champagne bottle tucked under his arm.

Rebecca smiled as she continued her descent. She wore a slinky black dress that to describe as low-cut would be an insult to the designer. The halterlike top plunged halfway to her navel, so just the barest edges of her breasts peeked from the front and the sides. Stopping just above her knees, the skirt showcased her spectacular legs and the four-inch stiletto black-and-rhinestone shoes on her feet.

He was absolutely certain he couldn't compliment her, however—he'd swallowed his tongue.

She reached the bottom step, her gaze raking him from head to toe. "You look very nice."

Be cool, Carlisle. Where was one of his smooth lines? Where was his blasé attitude?

He wanted Rebecca with each beat of his heart, longed for her every minute of the day. And now that he might actually get what he wanted, he was afraid it wouldn't be enough. Would sex with her ease the hunger? Or would their lovemaking only increase his torment?

He managed to walk toward her. "I—thank you." Instincts finally kicking in, he managed to clutch her hand and lead her in a slow twirl. "You look…amazing." She'd gone from uncertain flirt to bold temptress in less than an hour.

"It was Mama's."

He barely contained the impulse to raise his eyebrows. She was embracing her mother's style?

The doorbell rang before he could stammer about her beauty some more.

"That should be the limo driver."

Her eyes widened. "Where in the world did you find a limo in Junction Gap?"

"Believe it or not, there is one, though it's rented mostly for funerals."

"Of course."

He opened the door, then, keeping one arm firmly around Rebecca's waist, followed the limo driver to the long, black car parked in the driveway.

"Isn't he one of Dwayne's deputies?" she whispered in his ear as the driver opened the door.

"Yeah." Alex angled his body to prevent the driver from staring any harder down Rebecca's dress as she slid into the car. "He's moonlighting," he said, giving the driver a hard look. If he wanted a tip, he'd better keep his eyes on the road.

In moments they were on their way. Alex stored the champagne in the minifridge to enjoy after dinner. During the drive to the restaurant he managed to find his charm and make small talk. He kept the conversation light and fun, not wanting to dwell on the depressing fact that Rebecca was leaving. Moving away forever in less than a week. And now, more than ever, he knew he couldn't let her go.

"HOW'S YOUR SALMON?" he asked, grasping for a cheerful tone as he watched candlelight dance across Rebecca's face and bare shoulders.

She forked up the last bite. "Wonderful."

As she finished her dinner, Alex poured the last of the wine bottle's contents into her glass. "Miss Nettie will be proud of her matchmaking efforts."

"Won't she? At least temporarily."

Alex fought against the frown trying to break through. "It'll be interesting to see what she tries to manipulate me into next."

Sipping her wine, Rebecca raised her eyebrows. "You felt manipulated into taking me out?"

"No, of course not." God, he was making a mess of this. Why couldn't he find a rhythm tonight? "I wanted you from the beginning, remember?"

"I remember," she said quietly. "Why do you suppose we were so attracted to each other right off?"

He shrugged. "Chemistry." But his attraction to Rebecca really wasn't that simple. Or easy. His feelings were a jumbled mess, constantly bombarded both by memories— stalking a would-be prowler, dancing in the dark—and sensations such as her smile, the sound of her voice, laughter in her eyes.

"Yes, there's that, but my life is at a big turning point. This is the worst time possible for me to get involved." She smiled a bit wistfully. "Then, of course, there's my list of reasons."

"Right." Alex scowled, despite his effort not to. "All that practical versus impulsive stuff."

She stared at him. "We're completely wrong for each other."

He stared back. "Of course we are."

"The last few weeks have been great, though." She reached across the table and squeezed his hand. "Thank you so much for all you've done to help me."

That sounded suspiciously like the beginning of good-bye.

"The next few days are going to be crazy, and I wanted to make sure I told you that before I go."

"Thanks."

"Are you okay? You're frowning." Before the words were even out of her mouth, something that suspiciously felt like her stocking-clad foot slid beneath his pant leg.

Not anymore.

Her foot slid higher, edging toward his thigh. He sucked in his breath, glancing around. No one was paying any attention to them, and with the long, white tablecloth covering their legs they had complete privacy.

"Is this part of the thank-you?"

Her blue eyes glittered. "If you like."

He hardened instantly.

His heart pounded as she inched closer to his crotch. Clutching the table in anticipation, he focused on her face, her glossy lips—painted fire engine red, which should have been a big sign that she intended to take this bold temptress thing all the way.

When her toes finally curled against his erection, he flinched, pleasure shooting through his body like an arrow. He banged his knee against the underside of the table. The silverware jumped, the candlesticks teetered and several diners glared in their direction.

Rebecca brought her hand to her mouth to stifle a laugh.

But she didn't move her foot.

Alex could feel the tips of his ears turn red, something he was positive hadn't occurred since he was five.

"Should we try again?" the coquettish nymph who'd invaded his conservative landlady's body asked.

He managed a nod.

She rubbed the ball of her foot up, then down slowly, curling her toes every few seconds. "So, what did you think of the football game the other day?"

Talk? The woman wanted to talk? "It was—" she slid down again "—long."

"I agree. And don't those guys hit *hard?*" She rested her foot over the length of him, then pressed.

Bowing his head, he fought for control. He couldn't believe how completely her simple touch was affecting him. He grabbed his wineglass, then gulped the remainder of the contents. Then the slow rubbing started again.

"Of course, it's difficult to score unless it's hard," she continued.

His hand jerked and knocked his glass over, causing it to fall into the candlestick and tip it over. On the way down, the candle bumped her glass, spilling wine all over the tablecloth. Thankfully, Rebecca still possessed her reflexes, and she tossed water over her flaming napkin just as three waiters and the wine steward descended on their table.

By the time they'd managed to assure everyone they were fine and the waiter had relit the candles, Rebecca had moved her foot. Sweating, Alex wasn't sure if he was grateful or disappointed.

"Let's go," she said, holding out her hand.

Tossing money on the table to cover the bill and tip, he stood, then pulled her to her feet. He decided he liked her taking the lead. He liked the bold creature she'd become— if only for one night. She was mysterious and confident in ways he hadn't seen so far. The fact that she was unveiling another layer of herself to him only made him fall further under her spell.

Buttoning his coat as they exited the restaurant, he guided her toward the valet stand. Just before they entered the limo, Alex pressed several bills into the deputy's palm. "Take your time getting us home," he said as he ducked inside.

Once they were rolling, Alex retrieved the champagne from the minifridge, resisting the urge to rest the bottle between his legs. The familiar hiss of bubbles as he poured reminded him of the state of his body—sizzling. He refused to even consider the implications of the cork-popping.

As he handed Rebecca her glass, their gazes caught. The desire he thought he'd shoved into idle mode surged into overdrive. Damn, she was beautiful.

He tipped his glass against hers, the crystal pinging like an exclamation point.

She sipped, then eyed him cagily over the rim of her glass. "About this deputy limo driver... Just how did you find out he'd be interested in moonlighting?"

He slid his finger along the curve of one of her slender thighs. "While our efficient Junction Gap police department has been watching our house, I've been watching them. We all have to be on the lookout for mysterious intruders bent on water deprivation, don't we?"

"*Our* house?"

Alex sipped his champagne. "What?"

"You said '*our* house.'" She angled her head. "You mean my house. In a few days, I guess it'll be your house. But our house was never—"

He laid his fingers over her lips, more than a little disturbed by his mistake, but trying to be casual about it. "Just a slip of the tongue."

As she crossed her thighs, she gave him an even better view of her silky-looking legs. "Mmm. Sounds fun."

Setting aside his glass, he leaned forward, inhaling her exotic perfume, his mouth only a breath away from hers.

His heart thumped like mad. The blood rushed from his head to his groin. Not wanting to waste another second before possessing that delectable mouth, he cupped her face in his palms, then brushed his lips against hers. Again and again.

Slowly, he reminded himself. Don't overwhelm her.

She grabbed his tie, yanking him closer.

He crushed his mouth against hers, driving his tongue deep inside the warm, sweet depths of her mouth. When she answered with her own confident caresses, his brain buzzed, and he lost all sense of time and place. He only knew her satin skin and the ripe taste of her mouth.

The contact of just their lips could only satisfy him so long, though. He wanted her lush body beneath him. He wanted to stroke every inch of her from head to toe, then start again at the top. Jerking her against him, her champagne glass flew from her hand and thumped on the carpeted floor. Alex barely noticed. Half lying on top of her, he eased her into the corner of the limo's black leather seat, her head falling back on the armrest, exposing the long length of her throat.

Unable to resist that invitation, he left her lips to trail kisses along her jaw, beneath her ear, then down her neck. Her half-reclining position exposed even more of her breasts. No bra to fool with. The thin scrap of material covering her was easy to shove aside. With a hungry smile, he gazed his fill, noting her nipples were the color of pale raspberries.

He trailed his tongue over the crest, while rubbing his thumb across the distended point. Her nipple puckered tighter, begging for him to take her in his mouth. Slowly at first, he slid his tongue across the tip. Licking, lapping, caressing with deliberate, lazy movements. She moaned again, and soon the stroking wasn't nearly enough. He bit lightly with his teeth, then suckled the whole nipple in his mouth.

She screamed.

Surprised, and not entirely sure if she'd cried out in pain or pleasure, he raised his head. "Rebecca?"

Panting, she blinked. "I can't believe I just did that."

"Did what exactly?"

She flushed to the roots of her hair.

"You mean you, uh...climaxed?"

Biting her lower lip, she nodded briskly.

"Oh...well, oh." He found a ridiculous, purely male smile creeping across his lips. "I don't suppose you ever...before..."

This time a brisk shake of her head. "Not with just touching my breasts."

His smile bloomed full.

"Uh, sir?" the deputy's voice came through the intercom.

Extending his arm across Rebecca's prone body, Alex pressed the speaker button. "Yes?"

The deputy cleared his throat. "Is everything okay back there? I thought I heard a scream."

Rebecca's blush deepened.

Alex sank his teeth lightly into her bottom lip. She moaned. "No screaming back here," he said into the intercom. "But I think we're through sightseeing. Could you take us to the house?"

"Yes, sir."

Alex gazed down at Rebecca. "To be continued...."

She grinned.

He lifted his weight from her, hiding a wince when his aching lower body brushed her thigh, then helped her right her clothes. She slid her hand through his hair, no doubt righting the strands that always managed to stand up after being with her. He caught her hand as she picked up the fallen champagne glass. "You take my breath away."

She clenched her hand around the stem of the glass and met his gaze.

She'd shared an extremely intimate moment with him. He thought it was time he met her at least halfway, especially since it was long past time someone told her how special she was. "It's never been like this before for me." He took the glass from her and set it in the holder, then held both her hands in his. "I don't just mean sexually. I want you more than I've ever wanted anyone, but I also feel closer to you than anyone. I like being with you." He turned over her hands and kissed each palm in turn. "You make me happy."

The shock in her blue eyes made him realize just how completely he'd fulfilled the role of easygoing playboy. He cupped her face, punctuating each word he said with a kiss on her cheek. "Spend the night with me…make love with me."

She grabbed his tie. "It's about damn time, Mr. Carlisle!"

REBECCA STOOD at Alex's side as he unlocked the front door to the house.

Was it still her house? His? Something in between?

And what the hell difference did it make? She was about to take a very big step with a man she'd only known a few weeks. A man who wanted her, who said she made him happy.

The house, with all its problems and complications, seemed simple by comparison.

He pushed open the door and gestured for her to enter ahead of him. "I'll be right back. I need to speak with the deputy for a few minutes."

"Sure." Her stomach clenched in anticipation, she walked into the house, flipping the switch for the chandelier as she reached the foyer. She glanced up the long staircase, wondering if she should go up or wait for Alex. With her lack of experience in the romantic liaison department, she wasn't quite sure how to begin.

Awkwardness threatened to overwhelm her. *Especially* after that scene in the limo. Mortifying would be a conservative description of how she'd felt, having an orgasm when Alex had merely touched her breasts. She'd always been sensitive in that area, but the magic of his mouth had sent her over the edge before she could restrain herself. But then she supposed great sex wasn't supposed to be about restraint. Before tonight, she'd considered lovemaking awkward and not entirely fulfilling.

But Alex… His touch was like shooting a live wire directly into her bloodstream. His lips electrified her, the hungry look in his eyes melted every muscle in her body. He didn't seem at all embarrassed by what they'd shared, and she desperately wanted to escape her cautious nature. She could be seductive, mysterious…exotic couldn't she? Damn right, she could!

Racing up the stairs, she threw open her bedroom door and rushed into the bathroom. Moose was perched on the counter, looking at himself in the mirror. At her abrupt entrance, he twitched his tail in irritation.

She paused to scratch the top of his head. "Sorry, buddy. You're not invited."

His golden eyes narrowed as she flung open drawers, looking for the lighter.

"Aha!" She snatched the device from a drawer half-filled with cotton balls and Q-tips. She really had to get the bathroom items packed this week.

Scooping the candles from the lip of the tub, she darted into the bedroom and started placing them on every available surface—the nightstands, the dresser, a stack of boxes pushed into one corner. While her heart raced, she hopped from candle to candle, lighting each one until the room glowed and flickered with romantic ambiance.

"Rebecca?" Alex called from downstairs.

"Up here," she shouted back, her heart racing full tilt.

She had to take several deep breaths when she heard the tread of his footsteps on the stairs. Quickly, she dabbed her best perfume behind her ears and in the valley between her breasts, then yanked her hair from its confining pins, letting the tangled mass spill across her shoulders.

Wouldn't Mama be proud?

A few weeks ago that thought would have brought a wince, or, worse, a retort filled with judgment. Today, largely thanks to Alex, she smiled.

"Where are you?" he called from down the hall.

"In my room," she said, fluffing her hair as she approached the doorway.

When he saw her, he halted, his gaze absorbing her appearance as if seeing her for the first time. A smile spread across his lips. "What are you up to?"

She crooked her finger at him. "Come and see."

His eyes glowing, he walked toward her with the innate grace she'd grown so used to the last few weeks. No other man in the world moved with such seductive ease. How would she ever get over him when she left?

Oh, boy. Get over him?

He stopped inches away from her, and she tossed her

worries and revelations aside, realizing she'd forgotten something important. "Hold on," she said, running back to the bathroom. She shook her finger at Moose, who still hadn't moved from his lofty perch. "Behave," she warned, and slammed the door. She didn't need her spoiled cat deciding Alex was occupying "his" spot on the bed.

She spun around and bumped into Alex's muscled chest.

He gripped her shoulders to steady her. "All this—" he waved his hand to encompass the softly lit room "—for me?"

She smiled. "For us."

His gaze raked over her again, and her body burned at each pulse point, almost as if he'd caressed her with his hand. "You do look good in candlelight, Miss Parsons."

"So do you, Mr. Carlisle," she said huskily.

He pulled her into his arms, and she laid her head against his chest, inhaling his spicy cologne. "Thanks."

"For what?" she mumbled against the open neck of his shirt, realizing belatedly he must have removed his tie downstairs.

"For making this special."

She looked up, past the tanned column of his throat, past his strong jaw, past his black hair just grazing his collar. Finally, she met his gaze. "My pleasure."

"Our pleasure," he corrected gently.

Then he laid his mouth over hers, and the ground fell away. She forgot her anxiety, the atmosphere, the future, the past. Only his warm, persuasive lips possessed her thoughts and senses.

The heat of his touch shimmered through her body all the way down to her toes. His tongue brushed hers, stroking, inviting, and she angled her head to deepen the contact. She slid her hands up his chest, sinking her fingers into his hair. The silky strands caressed her skin. The center of her womanhood went damp.

Before he'd arrived she'd never wanted a man like this—so much that nothing in the world mattered more than his hands on her body, the pleasure of inhaling his scent.

He grew more aggressive with his kisses, his tongue dancing with hers in an intimate imitation of the joining to come. He clutched her waist. "If I don't see your body soon, I'm going to lose it."

She didn't answer verbally; she just began yanking open the buttons of his shirt. His chest, his skin... She had to touch him, had to press her lips against his heartbeat to prove this moment was really happening.

He unfastened the zipper on her dress, but the straps caught on her raised arms. She lifted her hands from his chest long enough to let the dress slither down her body.

"Oh, Becca."

Rebecca glanced down at herself—braless, see-through black lace bikini panties, thigh-high stockings, velvet and rhinestone pumps. Her skin was flushed, her body blossoming under Alex's admiring gaze. "Yeah, well...I prepared, just in case."

His hands glided over her shoulders, to her waist, his fingers dipping into the tops of her thigh-highs. Almost worshipful, he rained kisses over her neck and shoulders, all the while caressing her flushed skin. "Reach in my back pocket," he said in her ear, then tugged the lobe between his teeth.

Rebecca's head dropped back, the intense pull of his teeth drawing her body tight as a bow, her naked breasts rubbing against his starched shirt. The same bubbling passion she'd felt in the limo rolled through her once more. How long before he brought her to climax again?

"My pocket," he reminded her, his breath whispering along her jawline.

The thought of feeling up Alex's backside had interesting possibilities, but she asked anyway, "What for?"

He grabbed her hand and placed it on his hip. "You'll see. Just do it."

Careful to keep her head angled so he could continue working his seductive magic on her throat, she fumbled into his pocket, working her way around his wallet, and his taut buttocks. His backside distracted her briefly, and she paused to run her fingernails along the slope.

He sucked in a breath and clenched his muscles. "We really need what's in that pocket. Otherwise, I'd just forget it and drag you to the floor."

Having a pretty good idea Alex had done some preparing himself, she wasn't surprised to close her hand around a circular foil packet. She grabbed the corner and pulled out the condoms. Holding the long series of packets—there had to be at least six—up in front of his face, she commented, "You're obviously feeling quite spry these days."

He wrapped his hand around her wrist, dragging it around to the front of his pants. The male hardness she found there pulsed at her touch. "You inspire me."

She tossed the packets on the bed. "We'll get to them all—eventually."

His lips crushed hers. He kissed her with all the restless, impatient passion she, too, felt shimmering through her blood. She felt as though they'd held back forever.

"You're wearing too many clothes," he commented.

"So are you."

She pushed his white dress shirt off his shoulders and down his arms. Before she had so much as blinked, she found herself back on the bed, panties gone, and Alex's tightly drawn face looming over her. He was completely naked.

She didn't have the opportunity to even regret missing the full effect of his fabulous body. His hardness nudged her between her legs, and her body answered by softening, liquefying and opening for her lover. She marveled at the change in her body. She, who was the least touchy-feely person she knew, could hardly contain the need for Alex's intimate touch.

"I'm losing control here, Becca," he said, his green eyes intense to the point of almost pain.

Skimming her hand through his hair, she drew a deep breath, tried—and failed—to calm her racing heart. "I want you so much."

He reached out with one arm, obviously fumbling for the packets she'd discarded. Once he'd found them, she got her eyeful of his physique as he rolled onto his side to put on the protection.

Her heart fluttered. *Oh, my.*

But she was beyond the ability to fully appreciate anything except the intense pleasure she knew he was about to give her.

Perspiration pooled on her brow. Her body throbbed, her muscles tensed in anticipation of their joining, straining for the volcano burst she'd experienced earlier.

He lifted her thighs and wrapped them around his hips. His hand drifted down to the juncture of her thighs, but she grabbed his wrist. If he touched her she'd explode. "I want you inside me first," she said, her breath already hitching in her throat. How could he do this so easily to her? Reduce her to panting?

Bracing his hands on either side of her, he surged forward, bringing his lips down on hers the moment their bodies joined.

Stars burst behind her eyelids. Her body pulsed, her senses rolled as the climax rushed through her. She clutched him to her, marveling at the intense pleasure, longing for the brush of his naked chest against hers with each rock of his hips.

Even as she glided down from one precipice, the tight fit of his body and the pressure against her womanly center drove her up again.

She gripped his waist with one hand, the comforter with the other, trying to anchor herself in the real world, though everything she'd known had fallen away. The pressure of Alex filling her was incredible, yet not foreign, as if she'd waited a lifetime for the kind of completeness he offered.

He rubbed his head between her neck and shoulder. "Don't leave me, Becca," he whispered against her skin. "I need you."

She didn't even have time to tense before he increased the pace exponentially. Another climax burst upon her just as he thrust against her, his own completion taking over his movements.

Glorying in his rapid heartbeat as he collapsed on top of her, she refused to think of the future they didn't have, or regret that she hadn't given in to her feelings sooner—she was too busy frowning at Moose, who'd obviously managed to shove open the bathroom door. He stared at her, confused, as if to say, "You two are at it *again?*"

Rebecca kissed the top of Alex's head and vowed to close the door firmly at her first opportunity.

10

FOR LACK OF a better gavel, Linda used the heel of her shoe on the old packing crate. "Let's get this going. It's taken me nearly two weeks to get all of you together. It's time we accomplish something."

Several of her neighbors, including her husband, grumbled at her authoritative tone, but she ignored them. *Somebody* had to take charge of this disastrous situation.

"Everything was fine until Rebecca called the sheriff," Miss Nettie put in grumpily, probably put out because Linda had forced everyone up before seven on a brisk Thursday morning. But the block party was only two days away, the closing scheduled for Monday. This meeting couldn't be put off any longer.

"I agree," Linda said. "We obviously didn't anticipate that turn in the plan." She didn't want Rebecca thinking she was being stalked by some strange intruder. She glanced at her husband. "But we have that all taken care of, don't we, Jake?"

"Yes, dear," Jake mumbled. He lifted one finger to make a point. "But I still don't understand why we don't just tell Rebecca we don't want her to move. All this sneakin' around just isn't right."

Linda sighed. They'd been through this many times. "We *tried* telling her. The stubborn girl just won't listen to anything sensible, so driving away Alex Carlisle is our only chance. She'll never find another buyer willing and rich enough to take on that old house.''

"I like Mr. Carlisle," Miss Nettie said, her innocent blue eyes turning steely. "I think we ought to go with my plan and get the two of them together. He could convince her to stay."

"It seems you've already gone ahead with that plan," Miss Francine said. "You told Mr. Carlisle all about that fancy new restaurant and wouldn't it be a nice place for him and Rebecca to have dinner."

Linda actually felt light-headed. "You did *what?*"

Miss Francine rolled her eyes. "Oh, yeah. She did." She shook her finger at her cousin. "You're also the one with the big plan to plant termites in her dining room. I told you that would never work. You probably gave Rebecca some terminal disease. Do you have any idea how unsanitary bugs are?"

As the cousins squabbled and Jake looked pained, Linda slammed her shoe down on the crate again. "That's another thing. We have to leave the breakdowns to Jake. He's the only one who knows how household things work and that termite fiasco wasn't part of the original plan." She turned to her husband. "We tried the garbage disposal, the electricity and the water. What else is there?"

Shifting in his seat, her husband looked toward the nearest exit, namely their basement door. "I don't think—"

"And what about the roof? Nobody even touched that," Miss Nettie said.

Miss Francine nodded. "Yeah. That just fell in our laps. What do you think about…"

Linda let their voices drift into the background. They

simply had to find something to make the sale of Rebecca's house fall through. She liked Alex Carlisle as much as anybody, but he had to find his own house. The one he wanted was occupied, and Linda wasn't about to let her best friend go without a fight.

ALEX STRETCHED his arms, smiling when he encountered the womanly curve of Rebecca's hip. Without even opening his eyes, he could envision her softly ripe body, her blue eyes clouded with passion, the gentle urge of her hips against his. And after only one night branding her as his, he had no intention of letting go.

In fact, he intended to grab hold with both hands. Literally.

He rolled to his side, clutching her waist and pulling her back against his chest. After brushing her long hair aside, he trailed light kisses along the curve of her neck and shoulder. With one hand he stroked her breasts in teasing, circular motions, careful to keep from touching her nipple, which had already budded tight, straining for his touch.

Her beauty and openness astounded him. Waking her like this was a pleasure he wanted to repeat again. And again. For as long as…well, for a very long time.

She moaned as he trailed his finger down her body to stroke the soft, wet place between her legs. Her skin flushed with arousal, and she lifted her arms above her head in a stretch. The movement hardened his aching maleness further. He groaned, pushing himself against her hip, the pressure only succeeding in shooting his blood pressure and need for her even higher.

"Alex," she whispered, turning her head toward his, so he could capture her mouth in a long, deep kiss.

"Good morning," he murmured against her lips.

"It's certainly looking that way," she said, then smiled and blinked her eyes open.

The emotion and delight in the deep blue depths of her eyes hit him like a punch to the gut. Happiness flooded his veins, and his hunger nearly overwhelmed him. He pressed his mouth against hers, trying to show her how much he needed her. Her tongue met his in a tangle of warmth and passion.

Unable to control the rising tide much longer, he pushed her to her back, then glided his body over hers. The dampness between her legs caressed his hardness, and he broke their kiss to inhale a much-needed breath.

Staring up at him, she arched her back and pressed her hips against his. "Please, Alex."

He needed no further invitation, and after locating a condom, he slipped inside her body, squeezing his eyes shut as the exquisite tightness closed around him. His body throbbed and screamed for him to move, but he held himself still for a few moments to savor the sheer thrill of touching her so intimately.

She drew her arms around his neck, threading her fingers through his hair, then used him as leverage to pull herself up and kiss him. Her lips moved over his in a sweet, needy exploration, and he lost the last threads of control, rocking his hips fiercely against hers.

Within minutes of the pulse-pounding friction, she tore her mouth from his, arching her neck back. A low moan rose from her throat, and he felt her body rise to the peak. She pulsed around him like the rapid beat of his heart, and drove him to completion.

He collapsed on top of her, his head on her chest. She

twined locks of his hair around her fingers as the ceiling fan stirred the air, cooling their naked bodies. Her heart thudded beneath his ear almost as fast as his own.

How would he ever get enough of her? He'd never even remotely experienced the kind of closeness he felt with Rebecca. Somehow, he had to convince her to stay. They couldn't just say goodbye without even giving their relationship a chance. Maybe settling down, at least with Rebecca, wasn't such a scary idea after all.

"What's that pounding?" she asked suddenly.

"My heart about to jump out of my chest."

Rebecca tried to pull her body from beneath his. "No. It sounds like someone's at the door."

He rolled to his side, propping his head against his hand as he watched her slip into her fluffy pink robe. He'd much rather yank her back onto the bed than worry about the door. "They'll go away," he said, reaching for her.

But she belted her robe and rushed to the doorway, pausing to listen. "There is someone at the back door."

He glanced at the bedside clock. "At eight o'clock on a Thursday morning? What could possibly be that important?"

Her eyes widened briefly, then she waved her hand at him. "I'm sure it's nothing. I'll just go check it out."

"Okay." He stretched his arms above his head, then rolled lazily out of bed. "I'll meet you downstairs in a few minutes."

Yawning, he rose and headed to the bathroom. He really needed some coffee. Rebecca had kept him up half the night. Oh, but what a night, he thought with a grin, pushing open the bathroom door.

A furry beige streak charged him, its teeth nipping his ankle before it bolted across the room.

Startled from his half-sleepy state, he grabbed his stinging foot and leaned his back against the door.

Moose paused in the bedroom doorway long enough to hiss before racing down the hall.

Noticing the animal hadn't broken the skin, Alex shook his head and padded into the bathroom. If he and Rebecca were going to work out their relationship, he had to learn to communicate with her feline. That cat just simply didn't like him.

Back in his own room, he tossed on a pair of jeans and T-shirt, wondering just how he and Rebecca were going to work out anything from hundreds of miles apart. Even if he could convince her to stay, he wanted the house, and she didn't. In fact, he wanted it more every day. The antiques, history, even the quirky decorating scheme had grown on him, reminding him vividly of summers with his grandparents. Times when his life wasn't a series of big cities, hotels and apartments. Settled times.

He'd fallen for Junction Gap—its sights, sounds and people—in a big way. He wanted to see Miss Nettie and Miss Francine's portfolio grow, he wanted to add his own stamp of improvement and change to the house, he even looked forward to rolling his eyes and sighing if he ever needed Dwayne the Sheriff to solve a problem.

How could he show Rebecca she belonged here, in this town, with him? How could he break down all those we're-not-right-for-each-other reasons of hers?

He continued to puzzle over the problem as he descended the stairs and headed into the kitchen. The back door stood half-open, but Rebecca was nowhere in sight.

A fission of alarm curled up his spine. *An intruder is on the loose, and I let her answer the door by herself.* He charged through the opening, his eyes scanning the backyard until he located her standing beneath the big oak tree with Jake.

His breath whooshed out. He walked toward them, attempting to look casual while cursing his stupidity. If something had happened to her...

He shook his head, not even wanting to consider the thought.

"What's going on?" he asked, trying to inflect his voice with casual interest and hide the panic.

Rebecca pointed up the tree. "Moose escaped when I answered the door," she said with equal parts worry and exasperation.

Jake scratched his head. "I have no idea how we're going to get him down from there."

Rebecca nibbled at her bottom lip. "He's never even been out of the house. What could have upset him so much?"

Uh-oh. Alex cleared his throat. "I'm afraid I might have had something to do with that."

Rebecca turned to him. "How?"

"Well, I—" He glanced at Jake, then, feeling utterly ridiculous at examining a cat's motivations, he whispered in Rebecca's ear, "When I opened the bathroom door, he bit me, then darted from the room. Maybe he was upset about...us."

She flushed and glanced over at Jake, who appeared to be boring a hole through the tree limbs in an effort not to eavesdrop. "Maybe so," she said.

"What about some cat food to lure him down?" Jake said.

Appearing relieved to escape the awkward situation, Rebecca started toward the house. "Great idea. I'll get some."

Once she'd closed the back door, Jake turned to Alex. "I didn't mean to interrupt anything. I just came by to tell you I borrowed a shovel the other day."

Alex had no idea what that had to do with Moose's escape, but he said politely, "Oh?"

"Dwayne came by yesterday and explained about the boot print in the basement. Of course, I had to admit it was probably mine."

"Oh, I see." Though he didn't. If the print was Jake's, then who had turned off the water? "You didn't touch the water valve by chance, did you?"

Jake didn't say anything for a minute or so, rocking back on his heels. "Not that I recall." He cleared his throat and ducked his head. "I just needed the shovel. Didn't think it would cause so much fuss."

Something seemed off about this explanation, something Alex couldn't quite put his finger on. He had an odd feeling Jake knew more about the whole incident than he was letting on.

Before he could question the neighbor further, Rebecca joined them. She held a dish of fishy-smelling cat mush. "It's his favorite. If food can't bring Moose down, there's no hope." She laid the bowl at the base of the tree. "Come on, Moose, honey. I brought the tuna-and-chicken combo."

The leaves rustled, and Moose peaked his fluffy beige head around a branch. Then he hissed again and disappeared.

"He doesn't seem interested," Jake said unnecessarily.

"I've already told Alex, but you should know, too, Rebecca." He told her the same story about the shovel he'd told Alex.

"Oh, well." Her gaze darted from Jake to Alex. "I guess that takes care of everything."

"Not really." A muscle on the back of Alex's neck twitched. The same muscle that always quivered whenever a stock had topped out and was ready to fall. "We still don't know who turned off the water."

Jake hooked his thumbs through the belt loops of his jeans. "I wouldn't worry about that too much. Probably just some kids playing a prank. Rebecca always leaves that basement door unlocked."

Alex set his jaw. "Not anymore."

Jake nodded, still staring at the tree. "Right."

Again Alex had the odd sensation he should be reading something else into this conversation.

Apparently, Rebecca did, too. Facing them both, she planted one hand on her hip. "What's with you two?"

"Nothing." Jake stepped forward and tapped his index finger against the tip of her nose, much as a father would do to quiet a small child. "I just hate to see you go. Do you really have to leave us?"

To Alex's surprise, tears flooded Rebecca's eyes. "It's time for me to go. This was never my house as much as it was Mama's. I need to find a place where I fit in."

Jake smiled sadly. "That's where you're wrong. You belong here. With us." Then he walked away toward his own house.

Alex slid his hand into Rebecca's and pulled her close to his side. He wanted to fold her in his arms but wasn't sure how much space she needed. "Are you having second thoughts about leaving?'' he asked, trying not to hold his breath while he waited for her answer.

Impatiently, she swiped her hand across her face. ''No, of course not. I'll just miss Jake and Linda when I go.''

''And me?''

She looked up at him, and he almost wished he could call the question back. Did he really want the answer?

''Yes,'' she said, her eyes tearing again. ''I'll miss you very much.''

Not caring that the neighbors might see, he tilted his head and kissed her, then pulled her into his embrace, holding her tight against his chest.

A loud, irritated meow interrupted the moment.

Moose sat at the bottom of the tree, his big golden eyes fixed on them. *Don't you two ever stop?*

And Alex realized he'd learned quite a bit during the morning—Jake had something to hide, Rebecca had doubts about leaving and no force on earth was stronger than a fat cat's stomach.

''How DOES IT LOOK?'' Rebecca shouted up the long arm of the bucket truck to the roofer, who was back to inspect his work. She only had an hour before the house inspector showed up, and she needed to move this roofing business along.

''Fine. I think everything's going to hold.''

Rebecca let a deep breath escape from her lungs. ''Hallelujah.''

Much to her confusion, though, she wasn't clicking her heels together and anticipating her move. Dread would be a more apt description for her mood.

Dang Alex Carlisle anyway. He'd sailed into her life and changed everything.

With his confidence and understanding he'd flipped her heart over and changed her perspective. He'd helped her come to terms with the differences between her and this town, her and her mother, and her and him. He might be imaginative and flashy while she was practical and plodding. She sighed. But in the end, he was staying, and she was leaving. Leaving her house, her home. A home she loved.

She found herself sitting in the various window seats built into the turrets, staring into the world and wondering which part of it she should conquer first, as she used to do as a child. While she wasn't crazy about the pink couches, she could call them mauve with a smile. And the bordello room wasn't that embarrassing. It was a symbol of her mother at her flashy, tacky, outlandish best.

And the money required to hold everything together? Hang practicality. Somehow, expenses didn't seem to matter as much. The memories were priceless. She only wished Mama had lived to see the change she'd helped bring about.

Nearly everything she owned was packed into boxes, the sale was all but complete and she had commitments in New York. But the big city suddenly seemed lonely and far away, and she wasn't sure she was willing to trade rocking on the front porch with her husband for a job. Alex was the only man she wanted in her future, though, and she had no idea how he felt about her. He wanted her and her house, for now, but for how long?

She still worried about the lies she'd told. Could Alex ever forgive her if he knew the truth? Although they still didn't know who had turned off the water and planted the

termites, she just couldn't picture Alex being the one behind the crazy sabotage.

She also couldn't get Jake's words from yesterday out
of her mind. *You belong here. With us.*

The roofer stepped out of the lowered bucket. "I guess
that takes care of everything."

Rebecca turned at the sound of the back door opening.
To her horror, Alex was headed toward them.

He's home early. A lump lodged in her throat. Her stomach rolled sickly.

*Is there any chance of hiding a two-ton bucket truck in
the next three seconds?* she wondered somewhat hysterically.

He stopped next to her, placing a light kiss on her cheek.
"What's going on?"

"Just rechecking those leaks I plugged a couple of weeks
ago," the roofer said helpfully, and Rebecca could have
cheerfully strangled him. "I told Ms. Parsons I'd come
back after the next big rainstorm."

Alex's gaze shot from the roofer to Rebecca. "You
did?"

Panic nearly buckled her knees. She'd gone beyond lying
to her buyer. She'd deceived the man she loved.

And in that moment, when the revelation of her heart
slipped out, she realized it was true. She loved him.

But what had she done? She'd worried for so long about
Alex canceling the sales contract, and now all she could
picture was the hurt in his eyes when he discovered the
truth. She didn't care about the stupid contract. She wanted
his tenderness, his laughter…his love. And she wasn't going to get it.

Once she'd signed the bill, the roofer tipped his cap and walked away whistling.

"What leaks is he talking about, Rebecca?" Alex asked softly, wrapping his hand around her arm.

She forced herself to raise her chin. No scorn yet in his eyes, just uncertainty. The least she could do, for him and herself, was face her mistakes. He never would have stayed with her anyway, she told herself. Trading the freedom of a jet-setting lifestyle for her and a quirky house? It was laughable.

"The roof began leaking the day after you arrived," she said, boldly staring into his eyes. "The house is a disaster, Alex. Just since you got here the garbage disposal has broken, the electricity keeps shorting out, I found termites in the dining room, you know about the water and now, the roof."

Silent, he just stood there.

Her heart was shattering into a million pieces, she could barely draw a deep enough breath to speak, but she had to get this done. *When it's over, only when it's over, I'll fall apart.* "Say something. Didn't you hear me? I've been hiding the repairs from you."

He tightened his grip around her arm. "Why?"

"You're the buyer, remember?"

The first traces of anger crept into his eyes. "I thought I was much more than that."

He would never know how much he meant to her. She could finally give him the truth, but she couldn't risk giving him her heart, knowing he'd reject her. And she could hardly blame him. She'd ruined everything perfectly.

"I didn't tell you because I was going to fix everything before the closing. The house is sound. It's just old. It needs constant upkeep. And I—'' She paused and fought for control before she continued. ''And I can't afford to keep it anymore.''

He gripped both her arms, but held her away from him. His gaze roved her face as if he was searching for something he had no hope of finding. ''Can't afford the house?''

A sob threatened to bubble out, but she swallowed her tears. ''I'm broke, Alex. The last three weeks I've spent nearly every penny of the small savings I had left.''

''What about your grandmother's money?''

She laughed harshly. ''It's gone. It's been gone for a long time.''

He let go of her to rake his hand through his hair, turning away from her. ''If only you'd told me, I could have helped. Hell, I manage money for a living.''

''I already told you—I didn't have any money to invest.''

He spun back to face her. ''Oh, *that* was the truth?''

She flinched.

''You didn't fake anything else, did you?'' His eyes heated briefly, reminding her of the intimate moments they'd shared.

She still didn't reply.

''What about that water valve business?'' he asked.

''What about it?''

''Did you shut it off?''

Reminding herself he was entitled to his distrust, she clenched her jaw. ''No. In fact, I wondered if you did.''

His eyes widened in shock, then darkened like a threatening storm. ''Why in the world would I do that?''

''To lower the price. I overheard you joking with somebody named Alice about bankruptcy, and I—'' she shrugged, embarrassed to be saying the words aloud "—I wondered if you needed money as badly as I did."

He crossed his arms over his chest. "Alice is my secretary, and I was *joking*. I take plenty of stock risks, but not recklessly. Just when did you decide I didn't need the money?"

Just now, when you looked shocked and hurt and confused all at the same time, she wanted to say. "Well, the Sea-Com stock thing was a pretty big clue. And then..." As long as she was being honest, she might as well go all the way. "A few minutes ago, you—"

"A few *minutes* ago?" His hand clenched into fists at his side. Anger rolled off him in waves. "And how did our sleeping together fit in with my grand plan to steal your house out from under you? You thought I'd try to seduce it away from you?"

"I didn't really think—"

"No. You didn't really think at all, did you?"

She'd known he would be angry, but she hadn't expected to hear the awful hurt in his voice. Did her opinion really matter that much to him?

"Dammit, Rebecca. I can understand you keeping the repairs a secret in the beginning and even misunderstanding my conversation with Alice, but I thought we meant something to each other. I thought we were at least friends. How could you think I'd do something like that?"

One more blow to her heart, she realized. Not only would she never again feel the rising tide of their passion, she'd lost a friend.

A friend she'd suspected of sabotaging her house for his own interests? The whole idea seemed so ridiculous now. She should be laughing. But she wasn't.

So when was he going to walk away from her forever? She couldn't hold off her breakdown much longer. "I don't regret anything we shared, but maybe this is for the best. I'm leaving in a couple of days and—"

His face flushed with anger. "Oh, right. Imaginative versus plodding. Flashy versus practical." He paced beside her with short, angry strides then stopped suddenly, staring directly into her eyes. "I've got news for you, Rebecca Parsons. Your not plodding in the least. Remember that night at The Victorian? If that's not imaginative, I don't know what is."

She opened her mouth to argue that was one night and all because of him, but he rushed on.

"And practical? Ha! A practical seller would have painted over all those silly wall colors. Let me see…what color would have been practical?" He paused, tapping his chin, as if deep in thought. Then he snapped his fingers. "White! Or beige. Or brown. Anything but purple, turquoise and pumpkin.

"You used our differences to keep from admitting our attraction. The only thing you were practical about was not taking a chance on us, not taking a chance on trusting me with something more than just your body."

Rebecca leaned back, away from his anger and frustration. Was he right? Had she made excuses to keep him away?

"You're right about one thing, though," he said. "You're leaving, and I'm staying. I've decided to settle. Permanently. Here."

She couldn't stop a small gasp of surprise. "You're still buying the house?"

He rolled his shoulders back, sliding his hands into his

pockets. "Yes. That's what I came here for, isn't it?" He lifted one black eyebrow. "Under the circumstances, I think it would be better for me to stay at my office until the closing. I'll grab my stuff and get out of your way."

She raised her gaze to meet his. *It's almost over.* But her stubborn lower lip trembled before she could speak. She sank her teeth into the skin and linked her hands, so their trembling wouldn't reveal how much this was costing her. "I'll see you Monday, I guess."

He turned on his heel and headed toward the house, never once glancing over his shoulder.

As a tear rolled down her face, she realized that now it was finally over.

11

ALEX TOOK A SIP of coffee and stared out his office window, watching the first glimmers of dawn stretch across the sky. Saturday had arrived with hope and promise but he couldn't even summon a ghost of a smile. The light in his life had been snuffed out yesterday.

He'd blown it with Rebecca.

Before yesterday he'd thought buying a house was permanent. He'd told Rebecca that the day he'd met her. *A historical house represents permanence and stability, right?* Wrong. Just look at Rebecca's frustration in holding the house together the last few weeks. A house was a roof and walls, easily torn down or restored.

Relationships were permanent, if you were willing to work at them, willing to give people your time, your attention…your heart. He'd taken the easy route. The safe route. Him, Mr. Risk Taker. Buying a house was a convenient way to convince Nana Carlisle and himself he was settling down. The house meant nothing—not without Rebecca to share it.

But since he'd met her, he'd spent practically every moment scheming to get her into bed. He'd hedged the issue of settling down. He'd never promised her anything beyond a few nights of passion. Yet he'd expected her to trust him about the house repairs, expected her to trust him with more than her body.

Right, Carlisle. Lighting candles and pretending the electricity was out was a great first step to establishing a trusting, long-term relationship.

After performing as the jet-setting playboy so thoroughly, how did he expect her to know how hard he'd fallen for her, the house and Junction Gap? Ever since the day of the football party, when he'd rebuffed Pam's advances by telling her "I'm interested in Rebecca," he'd known he meant *only* Rebecca. He hadn't wanted to face that revelation then, and he'd fumbled around, trying to express his feelings ever since.

But not anymore. He loved her. If he didn't have her, he didn't have anything. She belonged with him…forever.

"Alex Carlisle, I'm ashamed of you!"

Alex whirled, juggling his mug to keep from dropping it on the floor.

Miss Nettie, blue eyes hard as steel, pale face flushed, black patent purse swinging, stormed into his office. She shook her finger in his face. "Since you're smart as a whip you ought to have some idea what I'm talking about."

Alex backed up. That purse looked lethal. "I, uh—"

Miss Nettie marched forward. "Don't give me that, young man. Rebecca is just—" She halted, angling her head. "You look terrible."

Shoving his hand through his hair, Alex sighed. "Thanks."

"Your hair's a mess, your eyes are bloodshot and your clothes are wrinkled. I've never seen you like this. What's wrong?"

Alex sank into his desk chair, not even realizing he rudely hadn't offered Miss Nettie a seat. His manners and charm were shot. How was he going to get Rebecca back? He had to find a way. The usual flowers and chocolates

sounded stupid and empty. He was sincerely afraid even
diamonds couldn't fix this mess.

Miss Nettie leaned over the desk. "Alex?"

"I'm in love," he said, propping his chin in his hands
and wondering if he really looked as miserable as he felt.

"Well, now." Miss Nettie smiled slyly. "I'm sure everything can be worked out. You just go back there and—"

"She doesn't want me," he moaned.

Miss Nettie's eyes widened. "Has any woman ever not
wanted you before?"

"No."

She patted his hand. "Poor Alex. Everything comes so
easily to you. You may have to actually work for this one."

"Hey—" Alex raised his head "—I've spent the last
three weeks showering her with attention."

"How about showering her with your words? Your feelings?"

"Well, I—"

"Humph."

"There hasn't been time," Alex said, desperate for Miss
Nettie to understand his position. "We argued yesterday.
The house is falling apart, and she thought I sabotaged it
to drive down the price. Someone shut off a water valve
and then she discovered termites." They hadn't really gotten into the bugs too much yesterday, but he assumed Rebecca had suspected him of that, as well.

Miss Nettie cleared her throat and looked away. "Oh, I
see. Well, as to that…"

Alex frowned. Miss Nettie knew something about the
prankster incidents?

"I, uh…" Her pale face flushed a deep red. "I think I
can clear that up."

"You can?"

"The thing is…I did it. At least the termite part."

Incredulous, Alex stared at her bowed head. "You planted termites in Rebecca's house?"

She raised her chin, her eyes turning sure and proud. "Yes, I did. We didn't want Rebecca to move, so we sabotaged her house, hoping to drive away any buyers."

Just which part of that wild statement should he jump on first? *"We?"*

"Her neighbors. Mainly me, Miss Francine, Jake and Linda. It was Linda's idea. Jake caused the disasters, and I—well, I already told you about that part."

Alex banged his fist on the desk. "I *knew* Jake was hiding something." But in the last two days so much had happened, he'd pushed aside his concerns about Jake and his lame borrowed shovel story.

He stared at Miss Nettie for a few seconds, then burst into laughter. It really was a quite clever plan, though he doubted Rebecca would feel the same way. She'd obviously been under a great deal of stress the last few weeks worrying about the repairs. "I could have done without Jake turning off the water. We called the sheriff."

"We know. We're sorry about that."

Smiling, he rounded the desk. "How sorry?" He grabbed Miss Nettie's hand, leading her to the door. Her confession had given him an idea, one he hoped would show Rebecca how much he loved her and keep them both right where they belonged.

And if she wanted her new life in New York more than she wanted him and the house? He'd buy her the damn Empire State Building, but she wasn't getting rid of him. He'd follow her, pester her, chase her as long as he had to.

"Where are we going?"

"To see a lady about a house."

"WELL, MOOSE, only two more days and we're out."

From his perch on the kitchen table the cat blinked, then raised his chin and turned his back to her.

Rebecca sank into a chair at the table. Moose's bad attitude was nothing new. And she could hardly blame him.

She'd screwed up. In a big way.

Alex had shown her she was her own person, beautiful and unique in her own way. He'd shown her how to love, accept...belong. Too late, it seemed.

"Rebecca Anne Parsons, you're not giving up, are you?"

Swearing she could hear her mother's voice clear as a bell, Rebecca jumped. What *was* she doing? The house had passed the inspection, and she couldn't care less. She was leaving friends and neighbors who, while certainly odd, were hers nonetheless. And she was trying to escape memories and comparisons to her mother that no longer bothered her.

She rose to her feet with new resolve. If she'd changed her mind, then she'd simply changed her mind. *There isn't a law against that!* As she paced the length of her kitchen with Moose eyeing her suspiciously, she ran through her options. She'd ask Alex to back out of the contract. She'd unpack. She'd quit her job in New York. She'd ask Alex to move in with her. She paused to consider that idea. Risky. Definitely risky.

Yesterday, he'd said he wanted to settle here, but he hadn't said anything about wanting her. But then again...hadn't he always looked at her as if she was the only woman in the universe? He'd told her he was crazy about her. He'd said she made him happy.

Deep down she knew those weren't calculated moves to get her into bed, or just lines from his playboy repertoire.

She bit her lip, considering. He'd meant them. In fact, she was betting her future on it.

Her mind and heart racing, she snatched the phone from its cradle and dialed Manhattan. When her new boss's voice mail picked up, she remembered it was Saturday morning. The doorbell rang as she was leaving a message for a return call.

She dropped the receiver in its cradle and strode down the hall, her thoughts distracted by the numerous arrangements she needed to make before her new dream could become reality.

When she opened the door, though, all rational thought vanished.

Alex, Linda, Jake, Dwayne, Miss Nettie, Miss Francine and most of her neighborhood stood on her porch. Shovels, rakes, drills, metal toolboxes and hammers filled their arms. Even Jake's tractor sat in the driveway. An assortment of smiles of resignation, enthusiasm and, if she wasn't mistaken, guilt, were plastered across their faces.

"Good morning, Rebecca."

She jerked her gaze to Alex. A mixture of hope and fear filled his green eyes...his *bloodshot* green eyes. As her gaze traveled lower, she noted his rumpled clothes, the nervous way he shifted his stance.

She grabbed his hands. "What's going on?"

"Well, uh—" He cast a glance over his shoulder. "Maybe Linda should explain."

Rebecca pushed back the door with her backside. "Yeah. Sure. You look terrible."

Alex glanced at Miss Nettie as she filed past him into the house. "So I've been told."

"Are you okay?"

He kissed her forehead softly, then pulled back, staring at her with an odd longing and fear in his eyes. "No."

What the hell was going on? She had never seen Alex like this.

Before she could question him, Miss Nettie had hustled everyone into the parlor. She even assigned seats.

Her arms crossed over her chest, Linda stood at one end of the room. "Can I do this now?"

Miss Nettie took her sweet time looking around the room, smiling with approval when Alex sat on the arm of Rebecca's chair. Then the whole production came to a halt briefly, as Miss Francine insisted on taking Alex's temperature. Miss Nettie tapped her foot during the procedure, and when Miss Francine pronounced him healthy, her cousin shoved Linda forward. "Go ahead—quick."

"The thing is…" Linda began, her face flushing bright red.

Rebecca really wished she could pay better attention to her friend's obviously important speech. But Alex had slid his hand into hers. His strong pulse beat against her wrist, his thumb stroking her palm. He'd worried her by his appearance, but she clutched his hand, anticipating the moment she could get him alone and explain her plan.

"We don't want you to leave," Linda said succinctly— for once. "You've been our neighbor for so many years…."

But Rebecca found her attention drifting. Alex was so close, and he smelled so delicious. She wanted to wrap her arms around his neck, press her lips to his and convince him how much she'd loved him.

"…sabotaged the house."

"What?" Jolted from her romantic musings, Rebecca gaped at Linda. "What did you just say?"

"We sabotaged your house. I'm so sorry." Linda crossed the room to kneel at Rebecca's feet. "It's all my fault but you just wouldn't listen to reason even though any fool can see you belong here."

Rebecca knew her desire for Alex had slowed her thought process, but were her ears also playing tricks on her?

"*You* turned off the water and planted the termites?"

"I turned off the water," Jake broke in. "Oh, and dismantled the garbage disposal and tripped the electricity a few times. But Linda made me do it."

"And I planted the termites," Miss Nettie said.

Dwayne puffed out his chest. "Told you I could solve the case."

Rebecca shook her head. When had she dropped into this alternate universe?

Linda snapped her fingers in front of her face. "Are you still with us?"

"Sort of." Mentally, she ticked off the house disasters. "And the roof?"

"*That* was a sign from heaven," Miss Nettie put in, raising her finger importantly.

No one dared argue.

Overwhelming emotions crowded her throat. She met the gaze of each of her beloved neighbors and could hardly contain the deep well of gratitude. They all wanted her. Enough to scheme to keep her here. The sense of belonging she craved was suddenly there. In her heart.

Tears flooded her eyes. "You want me that much?"

They smiled and nodded.

Alex squeezed her hand, and she glanced at him. Apprehension stared back at her. "What about me?" he asked quietly. "Do you want me?"

Did she— She gaped at him. Was he actually worried she didn't? Was he a mess over *her?* The thought caused a warm glow to spread through her stomach, and made the scary declaration on her lips not so scary after all.

Standing, she tugged Alex up beside her. "Uh, we'll be right back," she said, sparing only a brief glance for the room full of people.

By the time they reached the kitchen, however, the worry on Alex's face had been replaced by a fierce determination. He wrapped one arm around her waist, drawing her to his chest. "You're not getting rid of me."

Before she could tell him she had no intention of letting him go anywhere, his lips connected with hers. He seemed to pour all of himself into the kiss—frustration, longing, persistence. She held on as desire slid sweetly through her veins. To think she'd actually considered moving away from the excitement and belonging she had every time Alex touched her.

When he finally raised his head, they were both breathing hard. His eyes glittered with hunger. His hair stood on end.

"I love you," she blurted out.

"I love you," he said at the same time.

"You do?" she returned, her heart rate spiking.

He grinned, then hugged her tightly against his body. "Thank God. There was a moment or two there…"

Happiness bubbled through her. She dropped her head back to meet his gaze. "You were nervous?"

"Well, just a brief moment." As he stroked her cheek, his hand shook. A vulnerability he'd managed to hide until now filled his eyes. "A very scary, very long moment. Say it again."

"I love you." She brushed her lips across his, and he

sighed into her mouth, as if she'd released a tight coil of tension. "I'm so sorry I didn't trust you about the house."

"I'm sorry for not showing you I was the kind of man you could trust."

Her eyes watered again. "But you were. You are. I'm the one who kept everything from you."

"I had my own moments, remember—the electricity during the storm. And I was selfish, too busy trying to get you into bed without even thinking how it would affect you."

She traced her finger along his jaw. "It *affected* me just fine."

He grinned, the same mischievous smile he'd given her that first day when he'd arrived at her door. It was no wonder she'd fallen for him so quickly. "Well, I've always been pretty skilled in that area."

"I'm quitting my job in New York."

"You are?"

Staring at each other, they laughed. "I belong here," she said. "I've already left a message with my boss. You were right. I'm not plodding and practical—at least not about everything. I'm part of Junction Gap and The House. I want to stay here—with you."

"I love you." He picked her up, then swung in a circle. "And I love this house, but I only want to settle here with you. I was planning to chase you to New York—"

She raised her eyebrows. "You were going to chase me?"

"Absolutely."

Setting her on her feet, his gaze lingered on her face. He leaned toward her, so their foreheads touched. "No one ever tempted me to settle down, because there's only one you. Rebecca Parsons. Mine."

"Mmm." She licked her lips. "I like the sound of that."

His gaze dropped to her mouth. "I'll second that *mmm,* but we have company. Everybody is here to work on the house."

In all the excitement, Rebecca realized she'd forgotten about the tools. "But everything is fixed—for once."

"What about the multicolored walls, the polka-dotted carpet, the bordello bedroom? Don't you want to get rid of all that stuff?"

"I've decided I like things just the way they are."

He stroked his hand across her cheek. "What about hanging Mama's portrait over the fireplace in the parlor?"

She laughed. "I'm not quite sure I'm ready for that." Though as she slid her hand into the silky hair at his nape, she realized with Alex by her side, she'd be ready for anything. "I made peace with her memory. I'm not embarrassed. I'm proud."

"She would be proud of you, too," Alex said as he trailed kisses down her neck.

Rebecca knew that to be true. Mama had always loved and accepted people just as they are. She would have told Rebecca from the moment Alex walked into her life that he was a man to hang on to. Maybe Mama had been the smart one....

"The only glitch in my plans is that I may have to work in New York for a while until they find my replacement."

Alex tugged on her earlobe. "Okay, but you have to be back in three weeks for the wedding."

"Whose wedding?"

"Ours."

She pulled back, planting her palm against his chest. "That was certainly a romantic proposal."

Obviously unrepentant, he grinned. "Miss Nettie already has everything planned. What could I do?"

She scowled.

"I know." Grabbing her hand, he tugged her down the hall.

She'd only been partially teasing. Marrying Alex was exactly what she wanted; she'd just been surprised by his abrupt proposal. Knowing his flare for romance, she'd envisioned dinner for two, candlelight, wine and whispered words of love.

They halted at the entrance to the living room, where half her neighborhood seemed to be waiting with bated breath.

Maybe dinner for twenty.

To her surprise, pleasure and slight embarrassment, Alex dragged her to the center of the room and dropped to one knee. His eyes twinkled with amusement, but she could also sense the serious intent behind his gesture.

His hand gripped hers tightly, and she was grateful, as her whole body had begun to tremble.

"Rebecca Parsons, before these curious—and somewhat nosey witnesses, I'm declaring my love for you. I'd be honored if you would marry me."

She took a quick moment to scan the moved expressions on her neighbors' faces, the various boxes scattered around the room, then returned her gaze to the man before her. Her heart kicked hard at her ribs. "I love you, Alex Carlisle. And I'll marry you on one condition."

He angled his head. "And that is…?"

She smiled. "That we never have to move."

Alex rose to his feet and wrapped his arms around her. As cheers rose through the house, a movement in the corner of her eye distracted Rebecca.

A lone, furry figure sat at the top of the stairs, staring

down at the proceedings with the nonchalant boredom only a Persian could achieve.

"You hear that, Moose?" she called to him. "We're not moving. This house is our home—permanently."

Then Rebecca closed her eyes and leaned into Alex's kiss.

FROM THE TOP of the stairs, Moose gazed at the man and woman kissing.

Not moving, huh?

Well, it's about time they came to their senses. He twitched his tail across the old wooden floor, watching the couple who were so wrapped up in each other they wouldn't notice if the chandelier crashed down on their heads.

Silly humans. He pranced down the hall toward the bedroom, deciding he'd remind them later this house was *his*.

But he'd really miss the bubble wrap.

MONTANA
Bred

From the bestselling series

MONTANA MAVERICKS

Wed in Whitehorn

Two more tales that capture living and loving
beneath the Big Sky.

JUST PRETENDING by Myrna Mackenzie

FBI Agent David Hannon's plans for a quiet vacation
were overturned by a murder investigation—and by
officer Gretchen Neal!

STORMING WHITEHORN by Christine Scott

Native American Storm Hunter's return to Whitehorn
sent tremors through the town—and shock waves of
desire through Jasmine Kincaid Monroe....

Silhouette®

Where love comes alive™

If you enjoyed what you just read,
then we've got an offer you can't resist!

Take 2 bestselling love stories FREE!

Plus get a FREE surprise gift!

Clip this page and mail it to Harlequin Reader Service®

IN U.S.A.	IN CANADA
3010 Walden Ave.	P.O. Box 609
P.O. Box 1867	Fort Erie, Ontario
Buffalo, N.Y. 14240-1867	L2A 5X3

YES! Please send me 2 free Harlequin Duets™ novels and my free surprise gift. After receiving them, if I don't wish to receive anymore, I can return the shipping statement marked cancel. If I don't cancel, I will receive 2 brand-new novels every month, before they're available in stores! In the U.S.A., bill me at the bargain price of $5.14 plus 50¢ shipping & handling per book and applicable sales tax, if any*. In Canada, bill me at the bargain price of $6.14 plus 50¢ shipping & handling per book and applicable taxes**. That's the complete price—what a great deal! I understand that accepting the 2 free books and gift places me under no obligation ever to buy any books. I can always return a shipment and cancel at any time. Even if I never buy another book from Harlequin, the 2 free books and gift are mine to keep forever.

111 HEN DC7P
311 HEN DC7Q

Name	(PLEASE PRINT)	
Address	Apt.#	
City	State/Prov.	Zip/Postal Code

* Terms and prices subject to change without notice. Sales tax applicable in N.Y.
** Canadian residents will be charged applicable provincial taxes and GST.
All orders subject to approval. Offer limited to one per household and not valid to current Harlequin Duets™ subscribers.
® and ™ are registered trademarks of Harlequin Enterprises Limited.

DUETS01

Who was she really?

Where Memories Lie

GAYLE WILSON

AMANDA STEVENS

Two full-length novels of enticing, romantic suspense—by two favorite authors.

They don't remember their names or lives, but the two heroines in these two fascinating novels do know one thing: they are women of passion. Can love help bring back the memories they've lost?

Look for WHERE MEMORIES LIE in July 2002— wherever books are sold.